Lady of Desire

Lady of Desire

Gaelen Foley

PIATKUS

Copyright © 2003 by Gaelen Foley

First published in Great Britain in 2006 by
Piatkus Books Ltd of
5 Windmill Street, London W1T 2JA
email: info@piatkus.co.uk

This edition published 2006

First published in the United States in 2003 by
The Random House Publishing Group

The moral right of the author has been asserted

A catalogue record for this book is available from the British Library

ISBN 0 7499 0770 3

Set in Times by
Action Publishing Technology Ltd, Gloucester

Printed and bound in Great Britain by
William Clowes Ltd, Beccles, Suffolk

To Mom and Dad 'G'—
Thanks for all of your enthusiasm and
support these many years
and for raising such a wonderful son . . .
Love also to Grandma and Grandpa,
who know how to smile under any circumstances.
Your lifetime of love together is an inspiration.
Love always,
Gaelen

ACKNOWLEDGMENTS

I wish to thank the much-admired Regency author Emily Hendrickson; trusty on-site correspondent, Sally Roberts; widely regarded Regency scholar, Nancy Mayer; friend of writers and canines, Gail Simmons of Galema Pointers; and new author Mary Blayney, for their generous help on various points of research that came up during the writing of this book. Several heads are definitely better than one! Thank you, ladies, for so graciously sharing your expertise.

Georgiana's Brood: THE KNIGHT MISCELLANY

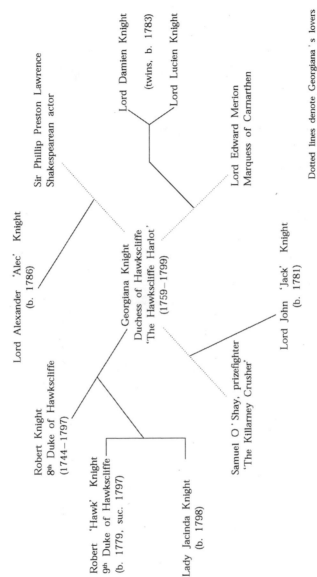

The robbed that smiles steals something from
the thief.

—Shakespeare

Chapter One

London, 1816

The hackney coach rumbled under the arched stone passage and rolled to a halt in the torchlit innyard, but even before the driver could throw the brake, let alone descend to assist his solitary passenger, the door swung open and she jumped out – a tempestuous, tousle-headed eighteen-year-old with the fire of rebellion in her dark eyes.

Sans maid, sans chaperon, Lady Jacinda Knight thrust the carriage door shut behind her with a satis-fying slam. She turned, shrugged her leather satchel higher onto her shoulder, and passed a simmering glance over the galleried coaching inn with its double tier of white-painted balustrades as a pair of postboys dashed out to assist her.

'My luggage, please,' she ordered, heedless of them gawking at her slender figure wrapped in a ruby velvet redingote with rich sable fur at collar and cuffs. She paid the coachman, then marched across the cobbled yard, her guinea-gold corkscrew curls bouncing with her every deter-mined stride.

At the threshold of the busy inn, she paused, warily scan-ning the motley assortment of bickering, rumpled travelers. A child squalled on his mother's hip; plain, rustic-looking folk dozed on chairs and benches waiting for their stage-coaches to depart. A drunkard was making a nuisance of himself in one corner, while a beggar boy had crept in to

1

escape the damp chill and huddled near the crackling hearth.

Lifting her chin a trifle self-consciously, she proceeded into the long room among what her countless wellborn beaux would have called 'the Great Unwashed.' She felt their stares following her, some rude, some merely curious. She noticed a man squinting at her feet as she passed and realized that beneath the long hem of her coat, her gold satin dancing slippers were visible.

She gave him a scowl that suggested he mind his own business and yanked the fur-trimmed hem over her toes. Doing her best to keep her feet tucked out of sight, she strode to the high wooden counter, where the booking agent sat ignoring the lobby's chaos, safely hidden behind a crinkled copy of the London *Times*. Above him hung a chalkboard scrawled with a timetable of arrivals and departures, fares and destinations.

Jacinda tugged briskly at her gloves and hoped she looked like she knew what she was doing. 'Yes, excuse me, I require passage to Dover.'

'Stage leaves at two,' he grunted without lowering his paper.

Her eyes widened at such rude, poor service. 'You misapprehend me, sir. I wish to hire a post chaise.'

This got his attention, for only the wealthy could afford to hire the yellow-painted private carriages. He peered over his paper, then heaved up out of his chair and slouched over to attend her just as the two post-boys came laboring in under her hastily packed traveling trunks. The booking agent plucked his quill pen out of the inkpot and wiped his nose with ink-stained fingers. 'Destination?'

'Dover,' she repeated crisply. 'How soon can the chaise be made ready?'

He glanced over his shoulder at the dusty wall-clock, then shrugged. 'Twenty minutes.'

'I shall want four horses and two postilions.'

'It'll cost ye extra.'

2

'It does not signify.' Absently pulling her small leather money purse out of her satchel, she hurried to tip the post-boys.

The booking agent's eyes glazed over as he stared at her purse, plump with gold guineas and bright silver crowns and shillings. His quill pen hovered over the blank waybill, his whole demeanor improving at once. 'Ahem, my lady's name?'

'Smith,' she lied evenly. 'Miss. Jane. Smith.'

He glanced around for her chaperon, footman, or maid, of which, for once in her life, praise heaven, she had none. He raised his scraggly eyebrows. 'Will Miss Smith be traveling alone, then?'

She lifted her chin a notch. 'Quite so.'

His dubious look alarmed her. Holding his gaze like a seasoned gamester, Jacinda slid a few coins across his desk. Pursing his mouth, he pocketed them with no further questions, and she breathed a sigh of relief. Then the booking agent entered her alias in his logbook and copied it onto the waybill. This done, he pointed with his quill pen to her two traveling trunks piled behind her. 'That all your baggage, Miss, er, Smith?'

She nodded, laying her gloved hand oh-so-casually over the gilt-tooled coat of arms emblazoned near the clasp. Hiding her family crest from his view, she waited until he bent his head again to continue filling out the waybill, for if he saw it, she knew that no bribe would be sufficient to dissuade him from sending back to Almack's for her tribe of formidable elder brothers, who would come rushing to drag her home in a trice. Aiding and abetting her escape, after all, was akin to crossing all five of the Knight brothers, a blunder no man in the realm dared make; but Jacinda refused to be thwarted. She was going to Dover and thence to Calais, and no one was going to stop her.

Soon the booking agent had collected her payment and had sent the lads out to ready the chaise. While they bore her trunks away to be loaded into the boot, she paced restlessly in the lobby, nearly jumping out of her skin each time the tinny horn blew, announcing another stagecoach's arrival or departure.

Since she had a bit of a wait, she sat down on the bench by the wall beneath the candle-branch. Loosening the ribbons of her bonnet, she reached into her satchel and pulled out her beloved, well-worn copy of Lord Byron's *The Corsair* to read a bit while she waited. She tried to lose herself in the romance of the dashing outlaw, but she could not concentrate with the excitement of her adventure racing through her veins.

Nervously, she checked her travel documents one more time, securely tucked between the pages of the book, while memories of her Continental tour danced through her head. Two years ago, her straitlaced eldest brother and main guardian, Robert, the duke of Hawkscliffe, had been assigned to the British delegation at the Congress of Vienna. He had taken his wife, Bel; Jacinda; and her companion, Lizzie, with him on the trip to enjoy the lavish festivities celebrating the end of the war. With Napoleon locked away at last, it had been safe again to tour the Continent. Robert had led them on a roundabout course to the Austrian capital, visiting some of the most important and beautiful cities of Europe along the way – and at each one, a whole new crop of charming young gentlemen to flirt with, she thought in wicked pleasure. What fun it had been – though blind Cupid, devil take him, had continually missed her heart with his golden arrows. Of all the places she had seen, Paris, the city her mother had loved, had been holy ground to Jacinda.

Soon, she thought dreamily, she would be in Paris again, among her mother's glamorous friends of the decimated French aristocracy. At last, she would be free. By heaven, she would not stay here and be forced to marry Lord Griffith, no matter how perfect he was or how advantageous the match, for their families' lands adjoined each other in the northern wilds of Cumberland; no matter, even, that he was the *only* man her brothers unanimously trusted to become her husband, their friend from boyhood days and on through Eton and Oxford.

A handsome, sophisticated man of nearly forty, Ian Prescott, the marquess of Griffith, was possessed of a cool, steady temperament that was just the thing, her brothers had decided, to balance her 'youthful passions' and 'headstrong ways.' For his part, Ian was tranquilly prepared to marry her whenever she was deemed ready and willing, but Jacinda refused to be given in holy matrimony to one who was not her love, not her soul mate, but a man she thought of as an extra brother – yet another skilled, patient guardian who would gently tell her what to do, make all her decisions for her, try to buy her obedience with expensive baubles, and treat her like a pretty little fool.

Tonight at Almack's, in the hopes that it was the one place she would not dare make a scene, Robert had told her that after her recent bit of mischief at Ascot, the much-anticipated match between their two powerful families must no longer be delayed. The negotiations for her marriage settlement were almost finished, he had said, and tomorrow they would set the wedding date. She had been nothing less than shocked.

The problem with her brothers was that they were a hundred times too protective and could not take a joke where she was concerned. It had been nothing but harmless fun, that day at the horse races, she thought innocently.

Informed of her fate, however, she had instantly realized drastic action was in order. There was no reasoning with Robert when he got that holier-than-thou look in his eyes. His wrathful gaze and rumbling tone had reminded her afresh that he was not merely the starchy, lovable eldest brother whom she had cheerfully tormented throughout her childhood; he was also one of the most powerful men in England, an imperious, august personage whom even the prince regent found intimidating. So, she had slipped out of Almack's; run all the way home;

5

hastily packed her things; and whistled for the first hackney that came rolling down St. James's Street around the corner from her home, the imposing Knight House on Green Park.

'Spare a penny, m'um?'

Startled out of her thoughts by a small, timid voice, she looked up from her traveling documents and instantly suffered a pang of compassion.

Before her stood the bedraggled street urchin who, earlier, had been crouching by the hearth fire. The child stared at her imploringly, his small, grimy hand held out in hopeful expectation. He looked about nine years old. His puppy-dog eyes were huge and brown, his little face smudged with dirt. His filthy clothes, little more than rags, hung off of his bony frame like a scarecrow's. His grimy feet were bare. Her heart clenched.

Poor, miserable pup.

'Please, m'um?' The pitiful thing shivered and sent a furtive glance over his shoulder at the booking agent, as though afraid of being noticed and thrown off the premises.

'Of course, my dear,' she murmured tenderly, opening her satchel at once. She pulled out her embarrassingly fat change purse and picked out three shiny gold guineas – then a fourth. It was as much as she could spare with the long and costly journey to France ahead of her.

The boy stared, wide-eyed, at the small fortune of gleaming coins, but made no move to take it, as though he didn't dare.

Her gaze softened at his mistrust. Clearly, the child had known little of kindness. Loosely holding her money purse in her left hand, she held out her right, offering him the coins. 'Go on, take it,' she coaxed gently, 'it's all right—'

Suddenly his grubby hand shot out and snatched her money purse. He bolted off across the lobby in an instant, her coin purse clutched tightly to his chest. Her jaw dropped. For a second, she could only stand there in shock, left holding nothing but the four gold coins she

6

had meant to give to him. Sheer outrage exploded through her veins.

'*Stop, thief!*'

Nobody paid her the slightest attention, and it was altogether possible that this shocked her even more than the theft.

Her eyes narrowed to blazing slashes. 'Right!' she muttered under her breath. Slinging her satchel over her shoulder lest it be stolen, too, she dashed out after the little pilferer herself. A moment later, she burst out into the clammy April night and saw the boy pounding across the sprawling innyard.

'You, sirrah! Stop this instant!'

She heard a trail of triumphant laughter as the scamp flashed out of sight around the corner of the inn-yard's enclosing wall. He was as quick as a cat, apparently accustomed to fleeing for his life. She picked up her skirts and raced after him over the dewy cobbles, but she might as well have been barefoot, for her dancing slippers were instantly soaked and torn.

Her untied bonnet fell off and went tumbling down her back. She left it where it lay and flung around the high brick wall. There was a fortune in that purse. Without it, her plans were a shambles.

She saw him racing up Drury Lane. 'Come back here, you little savage!' Dodging an arriving stagecoach, she kept her gaze fixed on the child, pouring on all the speed she could rally, her satchel bumping against her side.

Insolent as brass, the pickpocket glanced over his shoulder and saw her gaining on him. Taking evasive action, he ducked into a dingy side street, but Jacinda would not be shaken, heedlessly following him deeper and deeper into a maze of dark lanes and cramped, twisting alleyways, for it was a matter of pride now. She would not be gulled and robbed blind by a mere street arab. Not after the night she was having.

Giving chase with the same stubborn determination that

7

had earned her a reputation as a sportswoman of superior skill at riding to the hounds, she ignored each pounding jolt to her knees and hollered after him again like a fishmonger's wife, her breath beginning to strain against her light stays. 'Don't you know you could be hanged for this, you little heathen?'

He ignored her, weaving nimbly through a series of narrow, twisting passageways into the seedy back alleys toward Covent Garden Market. Here piles of litter crawling with rats lined the cramped brick walls, but Jacinda barely noticed them, all her focus trained on her wily quarry.

Malnourished as he was, the boy soon began to tire. Urged on by imminent victory, Jacinda poured on a fresh burst of speed, her fingertips grazing him. He glanced wildly over his shoulder. Surging forward, she caught him suddenly, seizing the back of his filthy coat collar.

He let out a cry of protest as she flung him around to face her. He fought like a fish on a line, but she held his coat tightly in her grasp.

'Hand it over!' she ordered, panting heavily. Dangling from his coat collar, the little boy spun around and kicked her in the shin.

She seized his ear, her brow knitted in fury.

'Ow!'

'You are a very bad little boy. Didn't I already give you more money than you could earn in months?'

'I don't care! Let go!' He held onto the purse with both grubby hands while she tried with her free hand to pry it loose.

As they struggled, more of her hair worked free of the artful arrangement her maid had taken such pains to create before the ball. 'Give it back, you little savage! I am going to France, and I need my *blunt*—'

'Aargh!' He let out a cry of kittenish fury as the change purse tore open, exploding in a rain of bright coins.

They flew up into the air like gold and silver fireworks

8

by the glint of the full moon, then clattered down in a hail around them, plunking unceremoniously into the thin, greasy layer of grime that coated the brick-laid alley. The child threw himself to the ground and began hastily collecting what he could.

'Leave it alone! That is my property!'

'Finders keep – ' the boy started, but abruptly froze and looked up.

Jacinda stopped, too, puzzled by his sudden stillness. 'What is it?'

'Shh!' He cocked his head, as though listening for some far-off noise. She could see the whites of his eyes, wide and staring in the darkness. His gaze scanned the impenetrable blackness behind her, his fist clutching the coins he had managed to collect. He reminded her for all the world of some little prey animal, his preternatural senses alerted to the imperceptible sound of some fierce predator's approach.

Though the full moon still gleamed brightly overhead and cast a strip of moonlight down the alley's middle, deep in the shadows along the walls, the blackness was almost palpable.

'I say—'

'Someone's coming!'

Suspecting another trick, she listened a second longer, then lost patience. 'I don't hear anything – ' But even as the words left her lips, a wild, barbaric howl like a war cry floated to them from over the maze of dark alleys. She drew in her breath. 'Good God! What was that?'

'*Jackals*,' he breathed, then leaped to his feet and fled into the night.

She stared after him in astonishment. 'Sirrah! Come back here this instant!'

He did not, of course. As silent as an alley cat, the boy had disappeared.

'Well!' Indignantly resting her hands on her waist, Jacinda glared for a second in the direction he had gone, then quickly set to work, eager to escape the lightless passage. She crouched down and began gathering up her scattered funds. Passing an uneasy glance over her surroundings, she plucked gold and silver pieces from the sooty slime, tossing both into her leather satchel. She grimaced at the repugnant job and was cursing herself for naively letting all those people in the lobby see her money, when suddenly, she heard swift, heavy footfalls pounding down the alley toward her.

She jerked her head up and stared into the darkness, the blood draining from her face. She heard hard boot heels striking the cobblestones, rough male shouts. Barbaric curses echoed off the maze of brick all around her.

'Blazes,' she whispered, shooting to her feet. The realization flooded her mind a bit belatedly that larger, more dangerous creatures prowled these back alleys than wily little pickpockets.

The voices were coming closer, bounding everywhere off the cramped walls, confusing her. She whirled around, not knowing which way to flee.

Clutching her satchel tightly, she backed toward the brick wall behind her, trying to melt into the gloom, but when she saw several man-shaped shadows charging toward her, she abandoned dignity and dove into the junk pile by the wall. Scrambling into the heap of rubble, she wedged herself into a small foxhole beneath a faded wooden placard for Trotter's Oriental Tooth Powder, propped at a steep angle against an old broken barrel. On all fours, she turned around to face the alley, her heart in her throat. Nearby, atop a moldering half boot and a coil of rusty chain, lay an abandoned spool of thick paperboard that had once inhabited the center of a bolt of fabric. Gingerly, she pulled the spool upright and leaned it against the placard's edge, the better to conceal herself. The sound of her frightened panting filled the cramped, close space, but she could still see into the alley through the crack between the placard and the spool.

10

How her arch rival, Daphne Taylor, would have laughed to see her in such a state! she thought, then held her breath as half a dozen men tore past, moonlight flashing on the knife each carried in his hand. A gunshot ripped down the alley and whizzed overhead. Ducking, she bit back a cry of alarm. More shots followed, then more footsteps sweeping down the alley toward her at a full run.

Through the small crack between the placard and the spool, she saw four big male silhouettes materializing from out of the fog, spanning the alleyway. Her eyes widened in the darkness as they came closer and she glimpsed the brutal weapons they carried – more knives, lengths of lead pipe as well, and horrible wooden clubs with nails sticking out of the ends. She dared not breathe for fear of being noticed, heard.

No wonder the boy had fled. A *gang*, she realized as gooseflesh shivered down her arms. Remembered tales and dark legends of what the London criminal gangs sometimes did to their victims filled her with terror. God help her if they found her, she thought. Desperately, she wished she were holding her favorite fowling musket in her hands, primed and loaded.

'Get into position, ye bastards; they're right behind us!' ordered a tall, wiry man with lank brown hair. She could hear the intense agitation in his voice.

'Did you kill 'im, O'Dell? I saw ye cut him!'

'Don't know. Got him good, though, I can tell you. Shite!' he muttered as their pursuers flung into the alley and charged at the first group.

Before her eyes, the chase turned into a brawl. The two gangs attacked each other with a furor, screaming incoherently at each other as they fought.

They might as well have been speaking another language, for she could not comprehend a word of their coarse Cockney jargon and the criminal tongue known as the 'flash language.' The shadows veiled the worst of the battle from her sight – all she could make out was fast, ferocious move-

11

ment, a great swinging and slashing – but the sounds alone were awful enough.

To her dismay, rather than moving on, three more thugs rushed into the alley from the opposite direction, coming to the aid of their six embattled comrades. Now the four pursuers found themselves, in turn, sorely outnumbered. She could hear their cursing and ragged breathing as the others surrounded them on all sides.

Then, without warning, a hideous roar burst directly overhead like a thunderclap.

She looked upward with a gasp just as a tall, sinewy shadow leaped up with tigerlike agility onto the pile of moldy bricks adjacent to her hiding place. She caught a flash of wild green eyes in the darkness.

'*O'Dell*!'

Jacinda stared at the newly arrived man. The fight in the alleyway paused, the others exhaling ragged oaths. Moonlight haloed his tawny mane, limned his broad shoulders in silver, and glinted off the dagger he clutched in his hand like a shard from a lightning bolt.

The wiry brown-haired man who apparently answered to that name cursed and wiped the sweat off his brow. 'Still not dead, you son of a bitch?'

The man in the shadows took a menacing step forward, edging into view with a cynical smirk. Jacinda's eyes slowly widened.

Why, it was Byron's corsair come to violent, throbbing life. The band of moonlight down the middle of the alley striped his black-clad body and slanted across his hard, chiseled face like war paint. He wore a short black coat over a loose shirt of natural linen that hung open halfway down his chest. Black trousers hugged his compact hips and long legs. As his hand curled into a fist at his side, she saw the gaudy gleam of thick gold rings on his fingers.

Jacinda stared at him, holding her breath. In a glance, she knew instinctually that, in this brick-and-mortar jungle, he was king.

Then the gang leader charged. The sharp blow of his boot heel resounded overhead as he sprang off the tooth powder placard, cracking it under his muscled weight, and leaped off the junk pile, landing in the midst of the fight. With a fist reinforced by his chunky metal rings, he dealt O'Dell a punch in the jaw that sent the man flying across the alley as though he'd been struck by a cannonball.

And then all hell broke loose.

Eagerly pressing her eye to the crack between the placard and the spool, Jacinda watched the gang leader wreak havoc on his opponents with dark thrill pounding in her veins. Once he had thrown the first punch, his men reengaged their enemies with renewed gusto. They were still outnumbered, but their leader's arrival had decidedly evened the odds. Back and forth across the alley the battle raged.

'How many times have I told you,' the gang leader growled as he threw one of his enemies to the ground, 'you stay off my turf or you die.' He kicked the prone man in the stomach, then swooped down and, she feared, made good on the threat.

She blanched.

Crashing blows, curses, and guttural male grunts of exertion filled the alley, then the gang leader appeared again in the strip of moonlight, nimbly twisting out of the way as O'Dell swung at his lean middle with a spiked club. She drew in her breath silently. It was a terrible weapon, though crude. The makeshift mace, with its bristle of long nails, was designed to tear flesh off bone, but its intended victim danced out of range by a hair's breadth as the club whistled through the air again and again. Wielding it menacingly, O'Dell advanced.

Jacinda cringed against the barrel as the fight moved closer. With another two steps, they were so near that she could practically feel the heat of their bodies. She hunkered down in her hiding place, but when O'Dell struck again with a bellow, the gang leader dove aside. The great club plummeted through the air, crashing into the top of the barrel mere inches over her head, showering her in a rain of dust and splinters.

How she kept from screaming or coughing in the sudden cloud of debris, she did not know. The placard, thank God, remained in place, keeping her hidden, but a meaty thud sounded from somewhere nearby, and the next thing she knew, the gang leader came crashing down on his back amid the garbage pile. She stifled a gasp, still clutching the snapped placard desperately over her head as she saw that his dagger had flown out of his hand amid the trash. It lay within her reach, gleaming in the moonlight.

O'Dell wrestled the spiked mace free from the barrel's wood; the gang leader, still on his back, scrabbled for his knife. With the alley ringing with shouts and the gang leader totally absorbed in his reckless fight, he did not notice her, though a mere two feet separated them. Jacinda's heart pounded. Everything in her shouted for her to nudge his knife toward his hand so he could defend himself, but what if they saw her?

O'Dell's eyes gleamed evilly in the darkness. He raised the club over his head to deal the death blow. Jacinda could not help herself. She stuck out her gold-slippered toe and furtively nudged the dagger toward him, but his searching hand found the coil of rusty chain instead. His fingers wrapped around it. With a growl, he yanked the chain upward like a whip, clomping O'Dell in the face. The man let out a scream and dropped the club, clapping his hand to his injured eye. Temporarily blinded, unable to fight, he chose to retreat.

The gang leader grabbed his dagger and leaped to his feet. His fury quickly broke the others' resistance. They turned and ran.

'After them!' he bellowed at his men.

Peering out the crack, Jacinda saw O'Dell's thugs fleeing. The rest gave chase, leaving the alley all but deserted. The gang leader started to run after them, too, as though he had not slaked his bloodlust yet.

14

'Blade, wait! Riley's hurt!'

The news slowed but did not stop him. He cast a torn, angry glance over his shoulder at the man who had called to him. 'Take care of him! Get him back to Bainbridge Street! I've got to finish O'Dell.'

In the shadows, Jacinda could make out the shape of one man lying on the ground. Two others crouched on either side of him.

'He's hurt bad, man.'

'Billy,' a weak voice pleaded.

Still in shock after all she had seen, his name did not register in her mind. Looking exasperated and thoroughly torn, the gang leader stalked back to his friends, glaring over his shoulder and muttering curses at his fleeing enemies. 'Bloody goddamn cowards . . .'

Jacinda blinked at his language.

'Billy,' the wounded man gasped again.

'Ah, Riley, you stupid mick, what have you gone and done now?' he asked gruffly, lowering himself to one knee beside the man.

'I'm done for, Billy!'

'I'll not hear such dramatics. Shut up and take a drink, for God's sake.' He raised a flask to the man's lips. 'Takes more than a bloody Jackal to kill an Irishman, isn't that what you always say?'

'Jaysus!' the man gasped out.

'Easy, lad.' He gripped the Irishman's bloodied hand. 'Come on, Riley. Come on.' Taut desperation edged his voice.

Ensconced in her hiding place, Jacinda stared helplessly from the shadows. Surely this poor wretch was not going to die right in front of her.

'You get O'Dell, man. Swear ta me,' the wounded man said, hoarse and trembling.

'By God, Riley, I'll get him if it's the last thing I do. You have my word.'

The other two seconded his vow, but none of them could

15

prevent the inevitable. A moment later, their friend was dead.

The three survivors were perfectly silent.

Jacinda gazed at their young leader's hawklike profile, silvered by moonlight as he bowed his head.

In all the alley, there was not a sound. Even the breeze had stopped.

'Short, nasty ... and brutish,' the gang leader said with a bitterness in his low voice sharp enough to cut the very darkness. Rising to his feet, he shook his head with a weary shrug. 'Bury him,' he ordered, and walked away, passing dangerously close to her hiding place, but Jacinda stared after him in bewilderment. Had her ears deceived her, or had that ruffian just quoted the philosopher Hobbes?

Impossible, she thought. There was no way this crude, violent, Cockney prince could read. He must have heard the famous quotation somewhere and was merely parroting it.

'Pick him up. Let's go,' he ordered his men, all fight and muscle and hot impatience like a stallion.

Yes, do, please, she mentally agreed, unsettled to the core. She could barely wait for the gang to leave the alley so she could come out of this wretched garbage heap and find her way back to the coaching inn, but for now, she studied the marauding heathen in reluctant fascination. *Who is he?*

There was something so familiar about him, something that snagged at her memory. She felt as though she ought to know him, but how could she possibly? They were from different worlds. Perhaps she had merely read his story a hundred times, she mused wistfully, for surely he had stepped out of the pages of *The Corsair*. God knew he was a dangerous beast – bad, wild, cocky, and mean. He was tall and lean and whipcord tough, with a giant chip against the world sitting almost visibly on his shoulder, but something in his weary air plucked at her compassion.

His borrowed words haunted her. Better for him if he

were too ignorant to comprehend the wretchedness of his state, she mused, for surely the only thing worse than having to live like this would be possessing sufficient sensitivity to *feel* the full despair of such an existence. As though sensing her scrutiny, he half turned away, his narrow, hungry face closed and brooding. His wide shoulders slumped a little as he waited for his men, his hands loosely planted on his lean waist.

When he paused to examine his left side beneath his coat for a moment, she realized that he had been injured – rather seriously, if the dark stain on his white shirt was any indication. He let his black leather coat fall over the wound again, hiding it, merely wiped the sweat off his brow and turned away as the other two joined him, carrying their fallen friend.

He nodded to them to go first. 'I'll watch your back.'

They went ahead as instructed. He pulled out his knife again with a soft, deadly hiss of metal and glanced over his shoulder, making sure that none of the Jackals were lurking nearby – a dreadful thought, in light of her predicament. She realized uneasily that she would have to move quickly to escape the alley before O'Dell's gang came back to retrieve their dead.

Good-bye, you heathen, she thought, rather mystified as she watched the gang leader head back down the alley, moving at more of a swagger than an ordinary walk. She thought again of the little pickpocket who had led her into this dark maze, and wondered if that was how the gang leader had started out. It was difficult to believe there were people living this way right under the very noses of the opulent ton, overlapping worlds virtually oblivious to each other's existence. Still, she was not sorry to see them go.

Somberly watching them carrying Riley's limp body away, she exhaled slowly, relieved to be almost in the clear. Her post chaise was no doubt ready by now and waiting to bear her away to the Channel.

In that moment – without warning – disaster struck.

Something small and sleek with claws and a naked tail went scampering over her foot. Her reflexive kick and small girlish shriek of revulsion were as swift and emphatic as they were involuntary. Her awkward movement jarred the placard, which sagged down over her shoulder and knocked over the fabric spool, sending it rolling before she could grab it. The rat vanished, but she was too late to call back her muffled cry.

She sat frozen, too late, watching, aghast, as the pasteboard cylinder went rolling right up to the toes of the gang leader's scuffed black boots.

Instantaneous yells of rage filled the alley. In a second, his men had abandoned the corpse and surrounded the garbage pile. Jacinda looked around wildly in terror, pushing back farther into her covert as her heart beat frantically.

'Come out! Come out of there, you Jackal son of a bitch!'

'We got one hidin' in here, Blade! Probably wounded.'

'Well, let's finish him, then.' She knew his voice at once, cool and low and deadly. 'Leave him to me.'

'Be careful, man . . .'

Oh, no, she thought in perfect horror, paralyzed with fright as a hard, callused hand adorned with thick gold rings grasped the edge of the half-broken placard and ripped it away. He threw it aside with a pirate roar, gripping his dagger in his other hand. As he swooped toward her, bent on bloody murder, Jacinda jolted backward.

'No!'

He stopped midmotion with a startled grunt. '*Huh?*'

She swallowed hard, then sat stock-still, not daring even to breathe as his big knife hovered inches before her face. Slowly, defiantly, she lifted her stricken gaze from the weapon's deadly blade and looked into the gang leader's fierce green eyes.

Chapter Two

Perhaps he had taken one too many blows to the head. Blade squeezed his eyes shut for fear they were playing tricks on him, but when he flicked them open again, she was still there – a beautiful blonde hunkered down in a little hidey-hole between the moldering brick pile and a broken barrel, her arms wrapped around her bent knees. He stared at her in wary astonishment.

'Well, well, what 'ave we 'ere?' Shaking off his daze, he slowly lowered himself to a crouched position before her. His men crowded in on either side of him.

'Wot the devil?'

'It's a lass!'

'Aye, a right little beauty, ain't ye, darlin'?' Blade murmured, not taking his eyes off her. Sheathing his knife, he offered his hand to help her up.

She made no move to take it.

'Come out, little stray. No one's gonna hurt you. Let us 'ave a proper look at you.'

She swept him with a nervous look of haughty disdain.

Stung, he withdrew his offered hand. 'What's the matter? You too good to talk to us?'

'Careful, mate,' Flaherty warned, 'she could be with O'Dell.'

He snorted. 'That bastard couldn't get near the likes of 'er in a hundred years.' Letting his stare roam greedily over

19

her, he felt like some rogue buccaneer who had just discovered someone else's buried treasure – and he was not above stealing it. Indeed, he was not.

Her hair was a golden wealth of bright, spiraling tresses. A few short, unruly curls fell over her smooth forehead, escaped from the small, star-shaped pins that had tried to keep them tamed. Beneath her prettily curved brows, her dark eyes blazed with defiance. There was a sweet roundness to the shape of her face, an elfin delicacy to her features – high cheekbones, a pert little point of a chin. The ruby hue of her lips was enhanced by the deep red coat that molded the curves of her slender body. He knit his brows as he studied her. No one around here wore a coat like that.

'Do you *mind*?' she clipped out suddenly with a fine, cultured accent like frosted glass.

His gaze flicked up from her chest to her blazing eyes. 'So, you can talk.'

'Obviously.'

'Too bad,' he drawled. 'I thought I just found the perfect woman.'

She narrowed her eyes at his chauvinistic jest, all bristling long lashes.

His lips twisted sardonically. Glancing at his rejected hand, he winced with chagrin and wiped the dirt and blood off of it onto his black drill trousers, then, quite fearlessly, he thought, offered it again. 'On your feet, princess.'

'Thank you, but I shall remain where I am.'

'In the garbage heap?'

'Yes. Good evening,' she added in a haughty attempt to dismiss him, as though he were some errand boy.

His men exchanged an uneasy glance at her foolhardy disrespect, but Blade stroked his jaw for a second and decided to forgive her, well aware that she was probably scared out of her wits behind her show of bravado. 'You don't look very comfortable in there.'

'I am perfectly comfortable – not that it's any of your affair!'

'Oh, but it is, love,' he said silkily.

'How's that?'

'You're on my turf.'

The silence after his quiet statement was deafening.

'I see,' she said in a small, tight, angry voice, no doubt realizing that she was trapped, but trying none-theless to stall for time. 'So, this is your alley, then. Your garbage heap.'

'That's right,' he answered, matching her sarcastic tone.

'You must be so proud.'

His men brayed with laughter, but Blade's eyes narrowed to angry slits. *That does it.* He reached into her hiding place with both hands and seized her, dragging her out by her waist, kicking and screaming.

'Damn it, girl, be still!' he yelled as she swiped at his face with her nails.

His men laughed uproariously at the row. The minute Blade set her on her feet, she clubbed him with her satchel and tore free, running only a step or two down the alley before Flaherty, ever helpful, grabbed her by her arm. Without the slightest hesitation, the little blonde spun and smashed him a facer.

Blade laughed aloud in astonishment. Flaherty cursed in surprise, losing his grip on her arm, but Sarge stepped into her path before she could flee, blocking her escape.

Blade swooped up behind her with one large stride and wrapped his arms around her waist with a brash laugh, holding her fast from behind.

'Get your filthy hands off me, you swine!'

'Not a chance, love. You're comin' with us. You've seen things tonight you 'ad no business seein'. I can't have you goin' to Bow Street to make a report.'

'I have no intention of doing any such thing!'

'So you say. Why should I believe you? I don't know you. Maybe you've got some trick up your sleeve. The thief-takers consider me big game, y'see. Sendin' Billy Blade to the hangman could make a man's career—'

21

'Billy Blade?' she gasped, freezing in his arms. Her gaze flew to his face with what he could have sworn was recognition.

Flaherty raised his eyebrows and grinned at him. 'Looks like your fame goes before you, mate.'

Without warning, the girl tried again to escape, driving her elbow into his stomach and stomping on his foot with her heel. Swinging her satchel over her shoulder, she nearly clocked him in the face, but he turned his head and took the blow on his ear.

Blade couldn't stop laughing, rather flattered that she had heard of his misdeeds. She had probably read about him in the papers. In all, her assault had little effect on him, like an attack from some incensed fairy queen, but it forced him to shift his hold on her, and the second his grip loosened, she tore free of his arms and started running.

Flaherty, still rubbing his cheek where she had punched him, spitefully stuck out his foot in the darkness and tripped her. The blonde fell, sailing earthward, and landed hard on her hands and knees. She looked up through her tangled mop of gold curls, wild fear in her fiery dark eyes.

Blade sent Flaherty a look of blistering disapproval for tripping her, but a pang of guilt stabbed him as well for having made sport of the little hell-cat. In truth, her fight had earned a measure of his admiration.

He went to the girl, intending only to help her up. It did not occur to him that, as he approached, he must have appeared to loom threateningly over her. When her glance flicked to the dagger sheathed at his side, her big brown eyes filled with an angry rush of tears that rendered him instantly powerless.

'Go on, do it!' she wrenched out, the icy hauteur cracking to show an innocent girlish misery beneath. 'I'd probably be better off!'

He stared at her for a second, taken aback by the note of genuine despair in her wail, then realized abruptly that the little simpleton actually thought he was going to kill her.

22

Lord, what were they writing about him in the serials these days? He didn't kill helpless women.

His men were still laughing.

'Shut up,' he growled at them. He scowled, insulted, yet vaguely ashamed of their jovial crudity. And his own.

'I don't care anymore what happens to me,' she went on. 'Make it a clean blow; that's all I ask.'

'Oh, leave off the dramatics, you daft chit. Get up.' He grasped her by the scruff of her coat's fur-lined collar and hoisted her none too gently to her feet.

She huffed in regal affront at being thus manhandled, but recovered her dignity quickly enough. Once righted, she glared at him over her shoulder as he thrust her ahead of him at arm's length. Loath to be clubbed in the head again, he relieved her of her satchel and tossed it to Sarge.

'Give that back!'

He ignored her frantic efforts to grab it and turned to the scarred ex-army sergeant. 'Carry it for her, but if you take tuppence from that purse, you'll answer to me.'

Sarge grunted in acquiescence; then he and Flaherty went back to heave Riley's body up off the cold ground once more.

Blade wrapped his hand in a possessive grip around the girl's slender arm above her elbow and gave her a flat look that dared her to protest. 'Now *walk*.'

Oh, yes, she remembered him now. Jacinda trembled a bit as Blade marched her down the alley, his sculpted face grim, his hard-eyed glance forever scanning the shadows. Occasionally, he looked over his shoulder.

Taken captive by the outlaw gang, she subsided into tight-lipped docility, but her head reeled with recognition. She struggled to recall the particulars of that bright, snowy afternoon when the outlaw captain, Billy Blade, had come to Knight House looking for her middle brothers, the twins, Lucien and Damien.

The details were sketchy in her mind, for it had

happened nearly a year and a half ago, when her war-hero brother, Damien, had brought his then-ward, now his wife, Miranda, to spend Christmas with the family. Someone had been trying to hurt Miranda, and the twins had combined their efforts to protect her. Jacinda had crossed paths fleetingly with Blade in the entrance hall of Knight House. How could she ever forget? She had been on her way out, bundled up for a brisk constitutional in the park when he had sauntered past her, startling her and the butler alike. He had trailed a leisurely stare over her and had slid her a scoundrelly smile that had caused her brother, Damien, to growl at him in warning, '*Blade.*' That was how she had learned his name.

She had never seen anything like him before, with his black leather trousers and his long, dirty-blond hair. She still recalled the insolent swagger of his walk, his garish purple waistcoat that she had glimpsed beneath his black velvet coat, and the red carnation he had worn in the boutonniere. She had been half appalled, half mesmerized, then had run to the window to watch him leave. She knew he was every bit as bad as he looked, for the twins had been angry at him for daring to come to the house.

Since the twins would tell her nothing about the rough, bold, mysterious, young cutthroat, Jacinda and her best friend, Lizzie, had come to the half-joking conclusion that 'Billy Blade' had been one of Lucien's informers about the goings-on in London's criminal underworld, and had come to bring the twins information about the villain who was after Miranda. Since the war's end, her spy-brother, Lord Lucien Knight, a diplomat and former operative for the Foreign Office, had occasionally lent his intelligence-gathering skills to Bow Street to help them solve crimes. Lucien was wont to consort with all manner of shady characters to obtain information. Now Jacinda could not help but think that her and Lizzie's wild guess about Blade had been right; thus, she found herself in a dangerous quandary.

She had seen the lustful way Blade had looked at her in the alley. The man was a violent criminal. If he began making advances on her when they reached whatever place he was taking her to, her only sure means of warding him off would be to tell him that she was Lucien and Damien's sister. But if she did that, he would probably take her straight back to her brothers. Not only would her one chance at freedom be foiled, she would also be in huge trouble for trying to run away, only giving Robert all the more reason to force her to marry Lord Griffith.

Extremely uneasy over her dilemma, she ordered herself to remain calm, stay alert, and keep her mouth shut until she saw how this was going to unfold. She decided only to reveal her true identity as a last resort.

Suddenly, more male voices floated to them from the darkness, approaching from the intersecting alley. Fearing another milling match with O'Dell, she instinctively moved nearer to her tall, brawny captor.

'Ho, Nate!' Blade called down the alley.

A tall, lean fellow with curly black hair and an amiable grin led his band of weary thugs out of the shadows. There were about a dozen others with him. The men greeted each other, expressed their gruff regrets about Riley's demise, and discussed the particulars of the battle in their incomprehensible Cockney jargon as the whole group continued walking in a northwesterly direction. Jacinda had no choice but to go with them, though she had no idea where they were bound.

Blade's men eyed her curiously, but he offered them no explanation, and it seemed they didn't dare question him. Draping his arm around her shoulders, he sent the message loud and clear that she was under his protection. Jacinda deemed it best, this once, not to argue.

At length, they came out to a deserted crossroads where the man called Nate waved to a hackney that had been waiting in the shadows. Apparently one of their own, the driver had been stationed there to bear away the wounded.

Riley's corpse was hefted into the coach; then the more seriously injured men climbed aboard. When the ragtag carriage had gone, the rest of the men broke up into twos and threes – to avoid attracting attention, Blade explained – taking different routes back to their gang headquarters in Bainbridge Street.

Nate joined Blade and her as they walked through the streets. 'Whew!' the lanky Yorkshireman exclaimed, fanning his hand before his nose. 'What the hell stinks?'

From the corner of her eye, Jacinda noticed Blade shoot him a discreet look as though to hush him; then it dawned on her that the unpleasant smell she had noticed in the air was coming from *her*! Her fine velvet redingote had absorbed the infernal odor of the garbage heap. The humiliation of it was the crowning blow of this night. She could almost hear her nemesis, Daphne Taylor, cackling with glee.

'I'm afraid, sir, that the unpleasantness you are referring to is emanating from my coat,' she forced out stiffly, trying to hide her misery and the fact that her pride was in shreds.

Nate blanched, looking genuinely embarrassed. 'Oh, gracious, miss, I didn't realize. Beg your pardon!'

Blade laughed softly at her discomfiture, his green eyes dancing. 'There, there, darlin,' you still look as pretty as a rose, even if you don't exactly smell like one. You can have my coat, if you want. It's a bit bloody, but you're welcome – ' He started pulling it off.

'Not necessary, thank you.' Scowling, she shoved off his loose half embrace.

They laughed at her.

'Plucky little thing,' Nate said with a chuckle to his friend. 'Where'd you find her?'

While Blade explained what had transpired, Jacinda glanced this way and that, noticing that their surroundings were becoming increasingly grim. The dirty streets narrowed, crooking past rows of ramshackle shops and lodging houses of dubious character. Every corner flapped with the remnants of old faded posters, deteriorating like ancient burial shrouds. The few people they saw either fled from the sight of Blade or bowed to him with a reverence she doubted they would have shown to the regent. Meanwhile, Blade concluded his story of finding her in the junk heap. She noticed he treated the good-natured Yorkshireman more like an equal than he had the others.

'She was there all the time,' he finished, sending her a mystified glance.

'Well, hang me,' Nate said. 'She got a name?'

'Deuced if I know. You ask her, Nate. She doesn't like me.'

She gave Blade a flat look in answer to his taunting bid for a denial from her on that point. She did not deign to indulge him.

'Aye, I'll do the introductions,' Nate agreed, turning to her. With an air of fun, he gave her a small bow. 'Nathaniel Hawkins at your service, ma'am, and who might I have the pleasure of addressin'?'

'Smith,' she lied coolly, using the same alias she had given the booking agent. 'I am Jane Smith.'

Blade's stare homed in on her – sharp, piercing, alarmingly intelligent. 'Bullocks,' he said softly.

'You accuse me of lying?' she cried. Good God, how did he *know*?

'Children, children – now, would that be a missus or miss, Jane Smith?'

'Miss.'

'Well, then,' Nate went on cheerfully. 'Miss Smith, allow me to present my good friend, Billy Blade, the elected captain of the Fire Hawks of St. Giles.'

'And you accuse *me* of using a false name,' she scoffed, looking past Nate's grinning face at her captor. 'Billy Blade, indeed.'

'Perhaps you wouldn't mind telling us what exactly you were doing in that garbage heap, Miss *Smith*,' the brute said.

27

'For your information, I was robbed. I was at the Bull's Head Inn waiting for a coach ...' She told them the whole story of how the beggar boy had snatched her money-purse.

'What did this boy look like?' Nate asked, exchanging a dire look with his captain.

'Brown eyes, thin, about nine years old.'

'Eddie,' Blade muttered, shaking his head. 'I'll give him a wiggin' for this.'

'You know that child?' she exclaimed.

'Eddie the Knuckler,' Nate said with a low laugh. 'He's an orphan.'

'Knuckler?'

Blade merely humphed, looking quite perturbed by her story.

'That's a rookery term for a pickpocket,' Nate told her with a cheery wink.

Just then, a male voice called down from somewhere above them in the darkness. 'Who goes there?'

Jacinda looked up, startled.

'Stand down, Mikey; it's us,' Nate called back, cupping his hands around his mouth.

Spotting men with rifles posted on the roofs of the surrounding buildings, Jacinda glanced at Blade in alarm.

'They're just sentries,' he murmured.

'Blade! Nate!' the man called excitedly from the roof. 'Did you get O'Dell?'

'No,' Blade yelled back in disgust.

'Next time,' Nate assured him as they walked on, entering the heart of Blade's rookery stronghold.

Jacinda turned to him. 'You really are at war, aren't you?'

He nodded grimly.

'But why?'

'Blade hates bullies of every stripe,' Nate said.

'The Jackals have come onto my turf,' Blade murmured, keeping his implacable stare fixed down the dark street. 'They've set fires, broken into shops, demanded protection

28

money from the shopkeepers. They've beaten civilians in the streets and harmed some of our women. I have promised to drive them out of London.'

'Promised whom?' she asked, rather humbled by the steely resolution carved into his profile.

'Them.' As they turned the corner, he nodded toward a crowd of perhaps forty people milling about in the street in front of a gin shop.

Some sort of rustic celebration appeared in progress, people standing around a blazing tar barrel, others cutting a reel to a rollicking tune on accordion accompanied by the shrill, fluid piping of a piccolo and the rousing beat of a bodhran. Bursts of laughter reached them over the music. She could smell a kettle of fish cooking. It was no doubt a rowdy, disreputable gathering, but it looked a hundred times gayer than Almack's. As they went a little closer and the gang's headquarters came more clearly into view, Jacinda paused, staring at it. *What a strange place.*

By the gleam of colored fairy lights hung here and there, the outlaws' hideaway seemed patched together with bits and scraps like a boys' tree house. It leaned at an odd angle against the dark sky and rang with merriment and activity on this moonlit night. Under a smoking pepper-pot chimney and a crenellated roof, it was of brick, with three stories and a curious assortment of oddly placed windows: round, square, and rectangular. It had a mousetrap of elaborate gutters and winding rainspouts that emptied into big barrels here and there, while a small wooden windlass secured with ropes and pulleys hung down the front of the building. As she watched, a man on the roof used the contraption to hoist up a load of something from a plump woman in a mob cap on the ground.

'Might as well face 'em and get it over with,' Blade muttered. 'Come on.'

Falling under the mysterious enchantment of the place, Jacinda followed him.

'It's Blade!' someone yelled as they neared the festivities. 'Blade! Nate!'

Instantly, they were surrounded. People greeted Blade all around her, reaching out to touch him as though he were a good-luck talisman. They patted him on the back and eagerly shook his hand as he passed, as though he were their bold young king back from slaying the dragon; yet she detected a current of nervous anxiety beneath their joviality. She held onto his arm, rather leery of the gaudy, chaotic mob hemming them in.

'Blade!' a man yelled. 'Did you get O'Dell? Is he dead?'

The crowd fell silent, awaiting his answer. Jacinda looked at her captor.

It seemed to cost him a great deal, but he squared his shoulders and lifted his chin. 'No. Not tonight. He ran, like a coward. Like he always does. He's still out there.'

A long moment passed as they absorbed the sobering news.

'Enough long faces!' Nate yelled at them in sudden, startling anger. He pointed at his captain. 'When has this man ever broken his word to you? Blade said he'll get him, and that means he will! Now, strike up the music! You're safe enough here, as you well know.'

The piper obliged, dispersing some of the tension with a nimble melody. The drummer joined in, and the accordion player gave his box a brave squeeze. The crowd seemed to exhale, and the party gradually resumed.

'Come on, Jane Smith,' Blade muttered drily to her, leading the way.

As they moved through the crowd, the people quickly returned to slapping his back and hailing him, urging him on with renewed vigor.

'You'll get him, Blade! You'll get him!'

He ignored them, scowling. As he pulled her along by her wrist, he stopped Nate. 'Tell the others not to get too drunk,' he ordered in a low tone.

'Aye,' Nate answered, then turned to join in the festivities, accepting a mug of ale and a hearty kiss from a buxom wench.

Blade got her satchel back from the man called Sarge and handed it to her, then led her around to the back of the building, whereupon she discovered that the gin shop fronted a large countinghouse set over a narrow back alley. A pair of lanterns above the wide barn door revealed business being carried out with a well-oiled hum of efficiency. Half a dozen sturdy bruisers were loading wooden crates onto a wagon, while a little man stood high up on the wagon's bed with a small writing board and pencil in hand. He appeared to be a clerk of some sort, charged with keeping count of the inventory. He waved excitedly to Blade while the grizzled driver in a long greatcoat greeted him, musket resting casually over his shoulder.

'Blade.'

'Evenin', Al. I trust you have everything in order.' He stopped to shake the older fellow's hand.

'Under way in no time, sir.'

'Watch yourselves out there tonight. Roads are crawling with highwaymen.'

The man laughed at his jest. Blade grinned and slapped him on the back, then shepherded her toward the few cement steps alongside the loading dock leading up to the door. It all looked like a legitimate business, but she regarded him dubiously.

'What are those men loading onto that wagon?'

'Used goods,' he said vaguely.

Just then, an eager, high-pitched voice filled the alleyway. 'Blade! Blade!'

He looked over as a small boy came darting out of the doorway past the men carrying the crates.

'That's the boy who robbed me!' Jacinda exclaimed.

'Hang back a moment,' he murmured, setting her behind him in the darkness. 'I want to hear what the little blighter has to say for himself.'

''Hoy, Blade! Did ye get O'Dell?' The boy rushed over

31

to him, fairly vibrating with puppyish excitement. 'Did you give 'em a belting? I'll bet you tapped his claret, all right! Blade, Blade, hey, Blade, I gotta show you somethin'! Look what I done!' With a flourish, Eddie the Knuckler lifted his cupped hands and presented the gang leader with an impressive stash of gleaming coins.

Her coins. Jacinda narrowed her eyes.

'Someone's been industrious tonight,' Blade drawled. 'Where'd you get it, Eddie?'

'Lobby o' the Bull's Head.' The boy beamed up at him, clearly worshipful and trying desperately to impress his hero. 'You shoulda seen me, Blade! My flat never knew what hit him! I was gone before he could say Jack Sprat! Actually, there was two – I mean three of them. They was big, too! Big as you, almost.'

'Really,' he said lightly. 'Eddie, I have brought someone to meet you. This is Miss, ahem, Smith.' He reached behind him, gently took her wrist, and pulled her into view.

Eddie's eyes widened. Jacinda gave the child an arch look.

'Shite,' the boy uttered, spinning around to flee, but Blade grabbed him by the scruff of the neck, halting his exit.

'A word with you, sir. Miss Smith, this way.'

'Aw, Blade, leave off! I was only jokin'!'

Complaining all the way, Eddie trudged ahead of them on Blade's orders, going up the steps to the door. Blade showed her into a broad workroom with a large table in the center, a battered secretaire in the corner, and a squat black coal stove on the wall to her right, which sat unlit. A few dusty shelves cluttered the dingy plaster walls, while a burrow of small filing boxes angled into the corner. He nodded toward the benches around the table.

'If you'll make yourself comfortable for a moment, I will see about your property.'

'You're going to return it to me?' she asked in surprise.

'Let's not get ahead of ourselves.' He sent her a provoking half smile and shepherded Eddie into the small adjoining office. Leaving the door open a foot or two, he turned to the child. 'Damn it, Eddie, are you trying to get strung up before your tenth bloody birthday?'

She half listened to him lecturing the little pickpocket, looking very stern, his hands braced on his waist. His stance drew back his short, black jacket a bit, revealing the bloodstain on his white shirt beneath, like the red carnation he had worn that day at Knight House. His indifference to his own wound disturbed her.

She forced herself to look away, then noticed that each time the unkempt-looking thieves came back from the loading dock to carry out another crate, they wrinkled their noses in distaste when they passed her. She blanched with embarrassment to remember the stink that clung to her redingote. Undoing the belt and buttons, she shrugged out of the offending garment almost violently – and immediately regretted it. At once, all around her, the outlaws froze.

They stopped and stared at her, some with the crates still in their arms. Jacinda glanced down nervously at herself, still dressed for Almack's in a white silk ball gown with gold-thread embroidery, finery the likes of which they had probably never seen. As their coarse stares ran all over, she tried to tug her shoulder-baring décolleté up higher, but the thieves were already exchanging evil grins and putting their boxes down. One or two leered openly at her bosom, but most of them seemed to have homed in on her throat. Realization dawned, and she paled, slowly lifting her hand to the ornate diamond necklace she had totally forgotten she was wearing.

It probably cost as much as the building. She gulped and began backing away as they started toward her, closing in like hungry wolves.

'Ah, Blade?' she ventured, still edging away from them, but Eddie was whining loudly at him. 'Blade?' she called a bit more forcefully, but when the heavy table at her back blocked her retreat, she knew she was trapped. '*Blade*!'

She looked over in alarm at the half-opened door. He had stopped midsentence in his lecture to Eddie and for a heartbeat just stared at her, his stunned gaze sweeping over her.

If the sight of her had dazed him in that dark alley, at this moment, in the light, the sheer extravagance of her beauty positively clobbered him. His mind went blank; his voice strangled in his throat. She was a *goddess*. He could not scrape two thoughts together, wonder-struck by her flashing dark eyes, milky skin, and the golden fire of her hair cascading over her white shoulders. His stare ran over her sweet, lithe arms and stopped at her cleavage. Then he was in agony.

The gold-trimmed neckline of her ball gown was cut low and square, and put the peachlike ripeness of her round, lovely breasts on wonderful display. His mouth watered as he stared at their upper curves, and the first thought that finally formed in his mind was that her nipples were almost visible. It was enough to drive a man mad.

'Blade!'

The effect, he saw, was not lost on his men, either. Not a moment too soon, he came crashing back to his senses.

Letting out an explosive oath, he threw the door wide open and stalked into the workroom. 'Get the hell away from her! Out of my way! Back to work!' he bellowed, shoving his way between them to reach her.

He grasped her arm and thrust her behind him. Clinging to him, she peered out from behind him as he blocked them from her with his body.

'I said get back to work,' he ordered in a warning growl, but they held their ground, a restless, uneasy mob.

'Fine bit o' sparkle, Blade. You plan on keepin' that for yourself?'

'No one touches her.'

'Why don't *you* keep the girl and give *us* the diamonds?'

'Aye, and nap us her fancy dress, too, eh? Could fetch a fine price at the pawn shop. Why don't you strip it off 'er for us?'

Behind him, the blonde let out an appalled gasp.

'We promise not to look!' another said.

They guffawed, but a murderous quiet came into Blade's voice.

'I'm gonna tell you buggers one more time. If you're goin' to act like animals instead of men, you might as well go join the bloody Jackals, 'cause I got no use for you here. Now, I want that wagon loaded. We got a shipment due tomorrow mornin'. Unless you want to make somethin' of it?'

A few of them grumbled, but slowly they backed down, turning away with surly looks. As they slouched back to their task, Blade turned to the girl with an exasperated glower. Giving her scarcely a second to grab her satchel off the table, he grasped her hand and pulled her out of the room toward the narrow, dingy stairwell.

'Where are you taking me?' she exclaimed, tripping along after him on her long skirts.

'Be quiet,' he growled. 'Come with me before they bloody mutiny.'

He marched up the steps, his implacable grip wrapped around her hand. She picked up her skirts with her free hand and hastened to keep up with him.

'I cannot believe they threatened to take my gown!'

'Can't you?' he retorted. At the top of the stairs, he stalked down the cramped corridor, pulling her after him, then threw open a door on the right.

At once, a breathless feminine voice greeted them, tinged with a torrid accent. 'Billy!'

He stopped at the threshold. 'Damn it, Carlotta, what the hell are you doing here? Get out.'

'Billy!'

'Out!' he ordered.

His fair captive waited in the hallway, rather wide-eyed,

35

as his unceremonious command was met with a stream of hotheaded foreign curses. A moment later, his latest conquest flounced out of the room, hastily tying her cottage-style bodice. Carlotta was an exotic-looking, olive-skinned Gypsy girl with long black hair.

When she saw the blonde, she whirled to him, her tanned face flushing with rage. 'Who is this? You bought yourself some high-priced harlot?'

'I beg your pardon!' the blonde exclaimed in haughty indignation.

Carlotta turned on her. 'He is mine, you little—'

In the nick of time, Blade caught Carlotta's hand as she raised it to strike the unsuspecting girl. 'Do *once* try to act like a lady, would you?'

Wide-eyed, Miss 'Smith' gazed at the Gypsy girl, looking astonished and quite fascinated by the notion of fisticuffs between women. Blade took the wild creature in hand and sent her on her way. Carlotta's vulgar, hotheaded curses trailed after her as she stormed off down the hallway. Turning to his guest with a long-suffering look, he could not have been more acutely aware of the contrast between the two women. Carlotta fairly steamed with exotic allure, but her foul language and crude manners embarrassed him as he stood before this high-bred demoi-selle of luxurious elegance, refinement, and grace. As she looked around in wonder at his rough-and-tumble world, he stole the chance to study her. Her beauty was at once wild and delicate. As dainty as sculpted porcelain, her face expressed a frank, lively mind and a mercurial nature as full of caprice as the English weather – clouds, sun, clouds, sun, all in one day. The sort of woman who would play the game on her terms or not at all, he thought. But as he watched her, what he was most keenly aware of was her innocence. Though her dark, sultry, almond-shaped eyes hinted at an untapped wantonness, he could feel the youth-ful freshness of her spirit when he stood close to her, a tangible force as golden as her hair. It simultaneously made

36

him want to run like the devil and to bare his soul.

Aye, this was a woman, he realized down deep in his bones, who could make a man crawl through hell on his hands and knees. *Bloody dangerous.* Without further ado, he swung the door open and nodded toward his chamber. 'After you, Miss Smith.'

'But ...' She turned to him, her voice trailing off in dismay at the prospect of going into his room alone with him.

A wicked smile crept over his lips. 'Don't disappoint me, my dear,' he murmured, his eyes agleam with a very personal sort of challenge. 'Surely you're not going to start acting sensibly now?'

Chapter Three

Jacinda stiffened at Blade's silken taunting, but could hardly take offense at his mild accusation, for he had heard the whole story from the boy's own lips and thus knew she had been duped by a mere street urchin. Lifting her chin with what remained of her pride, she gave him a severe look that warned him – probably in vain – not to try anything improper, then bravely strode ahead of him into his private sanctuary. He watched her pass with a look of amusement.

A swift glance around revealed walls washed in the same drab hue as the hallway, and a wood-planked floor painted dark brown. There was a threadbare braided cottage rug thrown down before the brick hearth, where charcoal embers gleamed beneath the small iron kettle. Against the wall, his low cot had been turned into a makeshift tent-bed, draped with long swathes of fabric that she realized on closer inspection were fine cashmere scarves, undoubtedly stolen. They appeared of finest quality, with swirling designs of red, orange, and gold. She smiled to herself, remembering the gaudy purple waistcoat and red carnation he had been wearing the day he had come to Knight House. Other than a taste for loud colors, he appeared to live very simply. Tidiness, however, was not among his virtues, she observed as a mouse went scampering along the seam of the wall and vanished into its hole. The furniture was dusty and looked decidedly battered by the light of the candles burning in colored glass jars here and there around the room. There was a wardrobe, an abused-looking secretaire with a simple wooden chair, and a chest of drawers – upon which sat a glorious Canaletto in a gilded frame.

Her eyes widened in disbelief as she stared at the master-piece: the gondolas on the Grand Canal, the Venetian palaces in rich tones of red and gold. Good Lord, she recognized the painting from Lady Sudeby's drawing room! She turned to her host in astonishment as the full reality of his occupation sank in. Used goods, indeed!

Oblivious to her racing thoughts, Blade followed her into his room, locked the door, then turned and leaned against it, folding his arms slowly across his chest.

Still reeling at the audacity of his theft, she pointed in bewilderment. 'That painting—?'

A ghost of something that might have been guilt flickered in his untrusting eyes. He had fascinating eyes – pale, sea-green irises rimmed by a dark band of cool, deep chalcedony. 'Beautiful, isn't it?'

'How did you get that?' she demanded.

'How do you think?'

She stared at him, resting her hands on her waist. She barely knew what to make of the creature. 'It seems a dangerous way to make a living.'

His roguish smile made her knees go weak. 'Aye, but if I die tomorrow, I'll go knowin' I had a hell of a lot of fun while I was here.'

'You're mad.'

He laughed softly. His light-tricked gaze caressed her. 'I had to have it, at least for a little while. You see, I enjoy beautiful things.' He stared at her, then leaned his head back on the door and gazed wistfully at the painting. When he spoke again, for a moment, it seemed his rough Cockney accent had gone missing. 'I'll sell it soon enough, I suppose, but this one . . . bewitched me. Sometimes I lie on my bed staring at it until I fall asleep. Then I dream I'm there – in Venice – the blue sky, the sun on my face, the lapping of the waves.' He sent her a half smile full of wry self-mockery. 'But artists lie. No place could be that beautiful.'

'But it is.' She looked from it to him. 'I have been there.'

He stared at her, suddenly on his guard.

'You don't believe me?'

He didn't answer.

'You should go.' She offered him a cautiously teasing smile. 'You might find the influence of so much beauty elevating to your moral sense.'

He snorted. 'Got no time for holidays. There's Cullen O'Dell to contend with.'

'You'll get him,' she said softly, then paused. 'Are you badly hurt?'

He shrugged. 'I'll live.'

They stared at each other uncertainly. Magic quivered like a plucked lute string in the silence between them for that moment. The room seemed smaller, the candlelight more richly golden as it played over his wary face, sculpting its sleek planes and sharp contours. When he spoke again his tone was low, urgent.

'Who are you? I must know.'

'I might ask the same of you.'

'I asked first.'

'I've already told you—'

'No. No 'Jane Smith' wears diamonds like that. I have seen you before.'

Careful, she warned herself, uneasily lifting her hand again to her diamond necklace. He might be illiterate, but he was sharp – clever enough to know quality when he saw it. She ventured a half-truth. 'You seem familiar to me, as well, but I cannot think where or how we possibly could have met.'

He eyed her as though weighing each one of her words.

'Eddie says you were hiring a post chaise to Dover, that you meant to cross the Channel.'

'That is true.'

'Why?'

'If it's all the same to you, monsieur, I prefer to keep my own counsel.'

He tilted his head slightly, a speculative gleam in his eyes. 'I have a theory. Care to hear it?'

She did not answer, but that did not stop him.

'I say you're eloping. To Paris.'

'*What*?'

'I hear it's all the rage these days among you fine young ladies.'

'Don't be absurd! I am doing nothing of the kind.'

'No? It's the only explanation that makes sense. I don't know who you are, but you're no common sort. Aye, I'm not such an ignorant brute that I don't know this much – respectable young misses don't set foot outside the house without their servants to protect them. Back at the coaching inn, where was your chaperon, footman, maid?'

She stood there awkwardly, no ready answer springing to mind. 'I can only conclude that either you are not respectable, which is absurd – your manner is too fine – or your family hasn't sanctioned your choice of paramours.'

'How shockingly narrow-minded of you, Mr. Blade,' she replied with a toss of her chin. 'Do you really think that all a lady's actions can only revolve around love?'

'Don't know. You're the only lady I've ever talked to.' He gave her a reckless, haphazard grin that made her heart flutter.

She gazed at him, quite at a loss. 'Well, I assure you, you are the first gang leader I have ever talked to.'

'Good! Then we will forgive each other if we make mistakes,' he said with sudden, sardonic cheer, sauntering into the room. Pulling a slim metal case out of his breast pocket, he took out a cheroot. As he bent over the candle and lit it, she did not have the heart to tell him that a gentleman did not smoke in front of a lady.

He straightened up again and turned to her, looking irresistibly dangerous with the thin cheroot dangling from his lips. 'So, where's the lucky bridegroom, eh, Miss Smith? Are you to meet him at the coast, or were you waiting for him at the Bull's Head?' He paused, let out a stream of smoke, and added prosaically, 'Was he late?'

'Blade, please. Just let me go. I have no intention of reporting you to Bow Street. Can't you just take my word for it and return me to the coaching inn? I will be on my way, and we need never think of each other again.'

'I am not sure that is possible.' His smoldering gaze inched down her body, as shocking and tangible as touch. 'Your fiancé must be quite a man to have turned your head.'

Rattled and blushing at his leisurely appraisal, she blurted out a protest, too fevered to think first. 'Did it ever occur to you that my going to Paris might be to *avoid* a betrothal rather than to fulfill one – blast you!' she cried as he lifted his eyebrow with a knowing smirk. Abominable man. She snapped her jaw shut and scowled, for the beast had just tricked her into admitting her destination.

'I see. In other words – ' He sauntered toward her with an intense stare. ' – you're running away from home.'

'So what if I am? I don't see how that's any affair of yours.' She pointed impatiently at his waist. 'You know, you're bleeding.'

'You'll never survive. You'll never make it to France in one piece.'

'Oh, yes, I will.'

'You were duped by a nine-year-old pickpocket, then chased him into the rookery like a damned fool. Did you even pay attention to where he was leading you? You never chase a thief who robs you. That's the way most of the murders in this city happen. Look at you.' The cheroot between his fingers, he swept a gesture from her feet to her head, scowling crossly. 'You're dressed like a princess, walking around with enough gold in your purse to get you killed thrice over, never mind the diamonds. That boy could have gutted you like a fish if he had wanted to, and – good God, woman! – do you know what would've happened to you if it had been O'Dell who had found you instead of me?'

'Go on, rail away.' She folded her arms over her chest and studied the wall. 'You're bound to pass out soon enough from loss of blood.'

He narrowed his eyes at her, then bent his head and moved his black leather coat aside to examine his wound. His long, tangled blond hair fell forward, veiling his face.

No wonder Lucien liked him, she thought. The brute was as domineering as any of her brothers. She winced at the sight of his bloodied shirt. 'I think you had better send for the surgeon.'

'I'll tend it myself,' he grumbled, clamping the cheroot between his teeth as he shrugged off his jacket. He nodded toward the hearth. 'There's hot water in that pot on the fire. Pour it into the washbasin over on the chest of drawers – if the task isn't too far beneath you.'

'I suppose, this once, I can make an exception,' she said sweetly, cursing his arrogance under her breath.

Grateful for any topic to divert him from his interrogation, Jacinda did as he bid her with a handy cooperation that would have shocked her beleaguered governess, Miss Hood. She collected the empty basin on the chest of drawers and stole a closer glance at the Canaletto. The painting was bizarrely out of place in this thieves' den, but it was truly exquisite. She turned around with the washbowl in her hands just as Blade lifted his thin white shirt off over his head.

She stopped in her tracks, nearly dropping the bowl. Firelight played across the broad, muscled splendor of his chest, powerful shoulders, and ironlike abdomen. His untamed beauty was somehow terrible to behold, smeared with the blood from the wound on his side, his lean waist still girded with an array of weapons in holsters and sheaths. Dropping his bloodstained shirt carelessly on the floor, he blotted his face with the knotted blue neckerchief loosely tied around his neck and went to the old, curve-topped trunk at the foot of his bed.

He undid the leather straps and opened it, but when he turned away, her jaw dropped at the heathenish tattoos that adorned his back and massive arms.

'Do you even speak French?' he asked without turning to her.

For a moment, she could not find her wits to reply. 'O-of course,' she stammered, gazing at his fascinating body. Most of her education had been conducted in the French tongue, but at the moment, she could only recall that it was the traditional language of *amour*.

The smooth, bronzed satin of his skin had been etched with an array of swirling designs and colorful drawings that ranged from the fanciful to the humorous. Her marveling stare traveled over his painted warrior's body. Oh, how deliciously *horrid* he was, she thought, utterly mesmerized. A crossed sword and pistol wrapped in a laurel wreath adorned his right biceps; a fire-breathing dragon coiled around his left. A Union Jack rode his left shoulder, while a big-breasted mermaid posed prettily on a rock near his right hip, but the largest picture, spanning the center of his back, showed a dark phoenix rising from flames, its wings outspread.

The dragon on his left arm stretched sinuously as he reached into the trunk and pulled out a wooden medicine box. As he straightened up again, she belatedly remembered her task. Turning away, her cheeks crimson, she hurried to fill the washbasin with warm water from the kettle, but his low, rich, pirate laughter followed her.

'Want to pet my dragon, sweetheart?'

'You really are too crude for words,' she said hotly as he passed behind her with an easy stealth in his walk, like

44

a great, golden leopard covered in his fantastic markings.

Chuckling, he set the medicine box on the chest of drawers. 'You're the one who was staring.'

'No. I wasn't.' Doing her best to ignore him, she found a small towel on the mantel and folded it

to protect her hand from the heat. Gingerly reaching toward the fire, she was acutely aware of him coming up behind her. Her fingers curled around the handle.

'Liar.'

Her heart pounding foolishly at his whisper, she lifted the pot out with care, the steam rising in tendrils to moisten her chest and throat and cheeks in wet swirling warmth like a lover's breath upon her skin. Mere inches behind her, his overwhelming magnetism and the sudden wave of heat as she poured the water into the basin made her head faint. 'It's all right, you know. I don't mind if you look at me. I've been looking at you.' He reached over her arm, lingering dangerously near as he took the pot out of her trembling hold; her stomach flip-flopped when their hands touched.

'Keep your distance!' she ordered, dismayed when her voice came out breathlessly. 'That is – I will thank you to behave with a bit more decorum.'

'Decorum? Right.' He flicked a wary glance

over her. 'Look at milady, hard at work in her ball gown,' he taunted softly, his warm breath tickling her ear. 'You weren't made for doin' chores, princess. Allow me.'

To her vexation, she quivered even as he mocked her. Sending her a knowing little smile, he set the pot back on the fire and took the large bowl of water from her.

He went over to set it on the chest of drawers and put it down, then pulled the wooden chair over, twirled it about-face, and straddled it, draping his elbow across the top slat. 'Never seen tattoos on a man before?'

She had never seen a man's naked torso before, tattooed or otherwise, but it hardly seemed worth mentioning. 'Where did you get them?'

'Church Street.'

She blinked in surprise at his unexotic answer.

He smiled. 'An old sea dog retired from the Navy keeps a parlor there. Supports himself nicely in his old age, I daresay. He learned his art from the natives of Tahiti while serving aboard one of His Majesty's frigates.'

'Did it hurt much?'

'Don't recall,' he said with a lazy grin, scratching his scruffy jaw. 'I was stone drunk every time.'

With a snort of amused disdain, she looked away.

As he commenced tending his wound, she stood awkwardly a short distance away, trying to keep her gaze averted. She felt she really ought to help somehow – his injury looked dreadfully painful – but she barely dared glance at him, belatedly unnerved by the presence of a very large, virile, half-naked man in the room with her. What her brothers would have said of this, she did not wish to contemplate.

With so many people to answer to, she wondered in a sudden surge of rebellion what it was like to be Blade. He was a ruffian, to be sure; but he was as free as an eagle, and she was deuced certain that no one ever told him what to do. He would laugh in their faces.

Glancing at him, chagrined to find herself envious of the lovely brute, she let out a sudden exclamation. 'Blade! You're going to get water on the painting! For goodness's sake, it's a Canaletto—'

'I think I know what it is. Why else would I have bothered to steal it?'

'Then you shouldn't leave it where it can get covered in water spots!'

He watched her curiously as she marched past him to the chest of drawers and whisked the masterpiece out of harm's way. Carrying it over to his writing table where it would not suffer the indignity of stray splashes, she took her time fussing over placing it just so, relieved to have some small task to distract her from gawking at him.

Looking back on it, she couldn't believe that her best

friend and lady's companion, Lizzie Carlisle, hadn't thought that Billy Blade was handsome. She had called him 'A Nasty Man' and had been scandalized by Jacinda's interest.

She wanted to laugh at the thought. Only Mama would have understood, she thought with an inward sigh, stealing another wicked peek at him from across the dim chamber. What a gorgeous air of wildness and rebellion he had about him, with his dark gold mane flowing back from his forehead and those pagan tattoos adorning his finely honed body.

Still, though the vast gulf between Billy Blade and the fashionable dandies of her acquaintance was obvious, she could not escape the nagging intuition that the gang leader was not entirely what he seemed. Perhaps he was the product of some highborn rake's dalliance with a tavern wench, for he had a bold, strong, sensual face with a fineness to his features that whispered of loftier bloodlines than his seeming Cockney origins. The princely lines of his thick, tawny eyebrows winged over his wary yet thoughtful eyes. He had austere, knife-hilt cheekbones; a square, determined chin; and a generous mouth that would have tempted a paragon, let alone the daughter of the Hawkscliffe Harlot.

Yet his face also bore the marks of his rough life on the streets. His aquiline nose crooked slightly to the right, and above the outer corner of his left eyebrow was a scar in the shape of a scraggly star. As he began binding his lacerated side with a length of clean linen and an air of practiced efficiency, she dragged her stare away from him by sheer dint of will.

'You're awfully good at looking after yourself, aren't you?' she remarked in a tone of studied idleness, running her fingertip along the dusty top of the Canaletto's gilded frame.

'Have to be. No one else is goin' to do it.' He got up and threw out the blood-tinged water, refilling the washbowl with fresh, cool water from the drinking pitcher. He leaned down and began splashing his face.

She fell silent, guiltily counting the number of servants who saw to her needs every hour of every day. She had never known any other kind of life. She was the daughter of a duke, after all. 'Doesn't your Gypsy girl look after you, at least?'

He sent her a hard-eyed glance over the water bowl. 'I look after myself. Always have. Always will.'

She shrugged and looked away. 'Of course.' He reminded her, she decided, of the little boy who had robbed her – too proud to take her offered charity, but desperate enough to steal. While Blade continued splashing his face and neck, she took off her diamond necklace and hung it gently over the corner of the Canaletto's frame, then walked away so he would not notice what she had done.

Her body felt strangely lighter, freed of her diamond collar. She clasped her hands loosely behind her back and waited for him to finish freshening up. Though she tried very hard not to keep staring at him, those strange pictures on his smooth skin seemed to beckon to her, teasing her, arcing and writhing sinuously over his muscles with his least, careless movement.

She turned her head just enough to see that each tattoo seemed specifically designed to cover up the traces of older scars. She furrowed her brow.

Dripping with water, Blade straightened up from leaning over the washbowl. Firelight tracked the gleaming beads of water that trickled down his chest as he slowly pushed his long hair back with his hands. Damp from his hasty ablutions, its color had darkened to sandy brown. She felt a shiver of awareness low in her belly and seized a longer gaze at him than she ought.

As though reading her thoughts, he opened his eyes slowly and looked into hers from across the room, tiny water droplets glistening on his spiky lashes. As their stares connected, Jacinda's voice failed her. She swallowed hard, feeling flushed and feverish all of a sudden. She could not seem to look away.

Casting aside the hand towel, he sauntered toward her. 'Don't you think it's time you confessed?'

'To what?' she asked faintly.

'The truth. Who are you?'

'I've already told you—'

'You can't gull a lad from the rookery, love.'

'I'm not so sure you *are* from the rookery.' She lifted her chin to continue holding his gaze as he drifted closer.

'Hmm.' His murmur was husky, noncommittal. 'What if I threaten to kiss it out of you?'

She trembled at his words and hoped he had not seen it. 'I don't think your mistress would like that.'

'Ah, but the question is, would you?'

She held her breath, her heart pounding. His deep green eyes smoldered like emeralds on fire as he came to her with sure, unhurried strides – giving her time, perhaps, to run. Or scream. Or stop him.

She did neither.

Locked in the spell of her dark, sultry eyes, Blade could not look away. Once again, she defied his expectations. Instead of flying from him in scandalized dread like a genteel miss, she stayed where she was, an innocent temptress, waiting for him, her chest rising and falling in soft, rapid anticipation, her hands at her sides.

She dazzled him, like looking too long at the sun's glitter on the sea, an image half forgotten from his boyhood, and like the tides, she drew him to her with a power that enthralled him, overcoming his survivor's sense of caution and his will. Yet the closer he went, the more hopelessly lost he became, his heart pounding, his senses climbing toward some exalted bliss. She stood before him like a captive goddess, as ravishing and out of place in his rough chamber as the Canaletto. The firelight played over the exquisite gold embroidery of her white gown, which was made of such zephyr-fine silk that it seemed to float weight-lessly about her legs.

As his gaze descended, his breath caught in his throat, for her skirts turned translucent by the fire's glow, outlin-ing her slender legs. She was slim and modestly proportioned, all elegance and demure charm. He stared at her body with a hunger that went beyond the physical. He lusted for her – God, yes – but as his gaze swept back up over every inch of her to her lovely face, her eyes whis-pered to him of the gentling influence – the elevating companionship – he had so long been starved for.

Someone to inspire him, teach him, make him think. Someone to hold her ground no matter how loudly he roared. To understand when he talked about the deepest questions that plagued his soul.

He had no hope of finding that here. He was too differ-ent from everyone else in the rookery. Unlike Nate or even O'Dell, he was an outsider; even as a boy-thief like Eddie, he had quickly seen that his only means of being accepted and allowed to stay was to make himself indispensable. Now he was their leader, but he had never really been *one* of them. He would have given his life for his friends, but they could not comprehend the puzzles that obsessed him. He had his books to comfort him, as well, but they could not listen, care. This girl, whoever she was, embodied all the beauty and grace he craved in his dark, brutal world.

She ... *sparkled*, he thought dazedly. He stopped mere inches before her, and still she did not back away; nor did she tilt her head back to meet his gaze, but stared straight ahead at his bare chest. He could feel the warm, beguiling sweetness of her soft breath on his skin; he studied every intricate twist and whorl of her glorious golden curls.

His heart slammed. Moving with care so as not to scare her, he lifted his hands from his sides and slowly ran his palms down her arms, savoring the satiny perfection of her skin. He felt her quiver under his light touch, heard her breath catch. He caressed her again, gliding his hands back

50

up her lovely arms, past her puff sleeves and low neckline, until he came to the creamy expanse of her chest. He could feel the hectic beating of her pulse as he touched her, gently stroking her alabaster neck with his fingertips. Her long lashes drifted closed, and her shimmery rose lips parted with desire, her head tipping back ever so slightly.

My God, you are so bloody beautiful. His smoldering stare took in the sight of her rapt face, so innocent, so ripe for seduction. He gazed at her beautiful, waiting mouth, lowering his lips toward hers; but halfway there, he paused with a brief, anguished wince.

William Spencer Albright, he said harshly to himself, *you must* not.

The girl was vulnerable, traumatized. He could not take advantage of such an innocent creature. Good God, she was in the midst of running away from home. He knew from experience that what she needed right now was someone she could trust, not some rough stranger groping her. The thought of this naive beauty alone on the streets of London filled him with genuine alarm. She had no idea what she was getting into. Somehow he found the strength to divert his kiss to her smooth forehead, capturing her chin between his fingertips. He closed his eyes, determined to show her that he wasn't an utter barbarian. When he needed to, he could still act like a gentleman – but then she moved closer.

Nestling against him, she laid her cheek on his chest with a sigh as soft as the brush of a dove's wing, as contented as that of a weary traveler who had just come home.

Blade trembled with thwarted desire as she caressed his dragon tattoo, studying it with a fascinated stare. Unable to resist, he went exploring, as well, his deft, thief's fingers loosing the little star-shaped pins that held her wild, resplendent curls captive. He slid them out of her gleaming tresses. She did not seem to mind, closing her eyes in pleasure. One by one, he freed them, until her long hair tumbled around her delicate shoulders in shining cascades the color of sunlight.

He caught a pair of her long curls between his fingers and pulled them gently, unfurling them to their full length. Pulled straight, her hair reached all the way to her elbows. He was still marveling over her when her lashes swept open. She tilted her head back and smiled at him, slightly starry-eyed.

'Whatever are you doing?' she asked in a deliciously flirtatious purr.

He met her smoky gaze. He couldn't believe he was letting the chance to make love to this angel slip through his fingers.

He released her curls. 'Just ... playing,' he murmured in a husky voice. Her curls bounced back up toward her shoulders, perfectly re-forming in their natural spiral shape. He returned her smile, feeling drunken and tender. He took her small, delicate hands in his. 'You are,' he whispered, raising her knuckles to his lips, kissing each pretty hand in turn, 'the most luscious, outrageously lovely thing I have ever seen in my life. Including the Canaletto.'

She smiled again, gratitude shining in her magnificent eyes. Such eyes. Dark and sparkling like a starry night.

'However,' he continued, 'it occurs to me that I have been shockingly remiss in offering you my hospitality.'

'Oh? I hadn't noticed.'

He narrowed his eyes with a wry smile at her saucy answer. 'You're a bit of a hellion, aren't you?'

'Never. Just ask my governess.'

Though sorely tempted to kiss that vixenish smile on her lips, somehow he resisted. 'You're dangerous,' he muttered, leading her over to the secretaire. He pulled out the wooden chair, offering it to her.

She sat, her every movement graceful and ladylike, even the way she crossed her ankles and tucked her dainty feet under the chair. He just stared at her for a second, dazed to realize how she had let him touch her. He couldn't believe it.

She likes me. The shock of it sent a jolt of wild joy

through him that stole his breath and robbed him momentarily of his common sense. He, Blade, who stared down cutthroat thugs in the meanest streets of the city, who laughed at death and snapped his fingers in the hangman's face, found himself nervous and jumpy in the presence of a pretty girl. *How utterly stupid.* He felt like an ass.

He didn't care.

'Is something wrong?' she asked.

'Uh, no.' He jerked himself out of his daze, casting about for the proper care and feeding of a lady. 'Let's see. Perhaps you would like some, er, tea?'

She looked at him dubiously, possibly surprised that he had ever heard of the stuff. 'I'm sure that would be lovely, thank you.'

'Right.' His mission clear, he strode to the fireplace and promptly discovered he had used all the hot water to cleanse his wound. *Bloody hell.* He turned around again, chagrined.

She lifted her eyebrow at him quizzically.

'Perhaps ... wine?' he attempted.

She smiled, trying and failing to hide her amusement at his efforts. 'Even better.'

He marched over to the storage trunk at the foot of his veiled bed, opened the creaky lid, and pulled out his best bottle of claret. The sight of his clean shirts lying balled in one corner of the trunk reminded him of his state of undress. He yanked one out and shook out the wrinkles, then quickly pulled it on over his head. What she must make of him and his tattoos, he barely dared think – but that thought itself was alien, for it was a policy of his never to give a damn what any living soul thought of him.

I am out of my element, he reflected as he poured out two glasses of the purplish-red wine. If he were with Carlotta, they'd have already finished their primal coupling by now and would be sharing a cheroot. He brought the wine over to 'Miss Smith.' She accepted it with a nod. Taking a drink from his wineglass, Blade sauntered over to his bed a few feet across from her and sat down.

He watched her sample a few sips of his mediocre wine, then smiled as she politely lied to save his feelings. 'It's ... very good.'

She was the worst liar he had ever seen, but he was amused by her attempt to reassure him. He lounged back on his bed, leaning on his elbow. 'So, Miss Smith, if you refuse to reveal your true name, won't you at least tell me why you're running away?'

She looked into her glass, tension in the angle of her shoulders. 'I don't see why you should care.' She glanced at him from under her long lashes. 'You have troubles enough of your own with O'Dell.'

'True, but it so happens I have some experience with these things.' He paused. 'Generally, I've found that running away is a very bad idea.'

She looked at him in surprise. 'Did you run away from home, too?'

He nodded, looking around at his room with a sigh. 'Many years ago. Trust me; I don't recommend it.'

'What made you run away? That is – if you're willing to say.'

He eyed her in wary indecision. So, she wanted to swap war stories, did she? He shrugged. 'My old man had a penchant for blacking my eye,' he said in a broad, offhanded sort of way. 'After a particularly unpleasant bout of his discipline, I left. I was thirteen.'

'I'm so sorry,' she said softly, staring at him.

'I'm not,' he replied, and took a drink.

'You come from the West Country?'

'How did you know?'

She smiled. 'You roll your R's.'

'I was born in Cornwall. You?'

'Cumberland.'

'Ah, now we are getting somewhere. So, why are you running away, Cumberland?'

She stared at him, looking wary and perplexed, but he

could see the little wheels and cogs turning in her mind. She drew her slippered feet up onto the chair and wrapped her arms around her bent knees, regarding him with a lonely, mistrustful gaze.

'Ah, come, you can tell me. There's no harm in it,' he cajoled her with a half smile. 'Soon you'll be off to France and you'll never see me again. Say what you want; it won't leave this room.' He paused, studying her. 'Was someone cruel to you, frighten you?'

'Nothing like that.'

'What was that you mentioned about an unwanted betrothal?'

'Truly, it's of no consequence—'

'Oh-ho, what's this, Cumberland?' he teased her, passing an assessing glance over her face. 'Papa wants you to marry some decrepit old wigsby?'

She gave him a charmingly rueful smile, all tousled golden curls like some angel who had rolled off a cloud in her sleep, he thought, and had fallen to earth with a thud.

'Something like that,' she said in vague amusement.

'I see. Well, surely we can find a solution.' He snapped his fingers and gave her a grin. 'Shall I ruin you? That should solve your problem. The old wigsby won't want you if you're used goods, and I assure you, I'd be happy to oblige.'

'Hmm, an interesting suggestion.' She tapped her lip and pretended to consider it. 'Thank you for your generous offer, but on second thought, I'll pass.'

'Is there someone else that you prefer?' he asked a bit more intently.

'No.'

'Well, marry the old wigsby, then, and cuckold him. That'll show 'em – and you'll have his money when he's dead. What you need,' he said, 'is to learn how to think like a thief.'

'You are a devil,' she scolded him, laughing.

'I hope at least your old wigsby has a title.'

'Indeed, he does, but I would never cuckold the man I marry.'

'That's what they all say.'

'Not me.'

'Gracious, Miss Smith, are you a romantic?'

'It's a bit more complicated than that.'

'Talk nice and slow, then,' he drawled, 'so my poor Cockney brain can absorb it.'

She smiled wryly at his sarcasm and blew a curl off her forehead with her sudden sigh. 'I don't know why you care. Nobody ever listens to me.'

'I'll listen.'

She shrugged. 'Well, if you must know ...' Rising to her feet, she took a sip of her wine and paced over to the chest of drawers. 'I'm afraid I was rather naughty a fortnight ago at Ascot. Because of that, my eldest brother has arranged my marriage to a man he deems well suited to keep me in line.' She picked up her leather satchel from off the floor where she had left it and dusted it off.

'Naughty ... exactly how?' His glance flicked to her bag as she carried it back over to his secretaire. There was probably something in it that would tell him her name.

'All I did was make an innocent little wager on a horse race.' She jerked the mouth of her satchel open and rather violently began throwing her star-shaped hairpins into it.

'How much did you lose?'

'Oh, the wager wasn't for money. I had already spent my pin money for the week; so, you see, I wagered against a couple of my suitors for a kiss. It was all in fun – I was sure my horse would win anyway. He was the favorite. Unfortunately, he went a little lame in the final furlong and finished third.'

Blade's smile flattened. 'Exactly how many men did you end up kissing?'

'Exactly zero. My brother arrived on the scene with my governess before I did it. Can you believe Robert actually made me renege on my vowels? Honestly! The next thing I knew, he was drawing up my betrothal to—'

Blade lifted his eyebrows as she nearly blurted out the name. His curiosity was intense.

'A family friend,' she finished warily, then gave a heavy sigh. 'I meant no harm. But Robert says I must be ever so careful about such things or I will end up ostracized from Society like Mama.' She turned away and gazed broodingly into the fire, twining a lock of hair around her finger.

So, that was it, he thought, watching her for a long moment in silence. The harpies of the ton had sent her mother packing, leaving the daughter torn between filial loyalty and the quite understandable need not to be black-balled herself.

She turned to him with an air of distress. 'You mustn't think badly of her, Blade. Mama never *meant* for all the other ladies' husbands to fall in love with her. They just *did*, and they would woo her, and Mama, well – Mama was a "frail vessel," as Robert says.'

'Robert?'

'My eldest brother. Why is it that no one ever complains when a man takes a mistress, but let a lady take a lover, and she is called all sorts of names?' She paced across the room. 'It isn't fair! Nobody ever remembers Mama's genius, or the marvelous essays she wrote on the rights of women, or the rounds she drove about London making sure her gentlemen friends got out of bed and into the House of Lords to cast their votes on important matters of state – and no one ever even *mentions* the heroic death she died!'

Momentarily entranced by her gown floating weight-lessly about her neat, trim legs as she paced, Blade had to shake himself back to attention. 'How did she die?'

She sighed and stopped her agitated pacing, leaning her hips back against the chest of drawers. She rested her pampered hands on the edge of it. 'Mama loved France. She had gone to the Sorbonne and had countless school friends among the ladies of the Ancien Regime. When the Revolution came, she and one of her lovers, the marquess of Carnarthen, got involved in smuggling the aristocrats' children out of France to escape the guillotine, but she was eventually caught and executed for a spy.'

'My God,' he murmured. 'Is this true?'

'It is.' She returned to her chair, sighed heavily, and sat down again, looping the leather strap of her satchel over her shoulder. She rested her elbow on the table, laid her cheek in her hand, and gazed at him, restless and pensive, the very sketch of tempestuous youth. 'Do you see my plight? I want to be like her – I want to be something *more*, but how can I when I can't even move, pinned down under all Society's endless petty rules, plus the added millstone 'round my neck of being expected to atone somehow for my mother's sins?'

'Wagering your kisses on a horse race does not sound much like atonement to me. It sounds to me as if you're deliberately flouting Society.'

'Maybe I am, a bit – but can you blame me for resenting them? My mother was worth more than all those pompous hypocrites put together, but they banished her and now she's dead. I never even had a chance to know her.'

'Well,' he said drily after a moment, 'I hope you at least left your family a note.'

'Of course. I don't want them to worry.' She glanced at the dusty wall-dial timepiece, which read midnight. 'I doubt they have seen it yet. They're probably still at Almack's. Blade, are you going to show me back to the inn, or am I going to have to find my own way?'

He did not answer at once. 'Why don't you stay here for a while? Sleep on the matter before you go all the way to France. You can take my bed.'

She dropped her hand and gave him a startled look.

'I hate the thought of you out there alone. No one will harm you here, I give you my word – and who knows? I might find the influence of so much beauty ... elevating to my moral sense.'

58

Blushing with a little smile at his echo of her earlier words, she looked away, her long curls falling forward to veil her face. 'That's really very sweet, but my mind is made up. I am determined to reach the coast by dawn. Besides, all my things are still at the inn. My post chaise will be waiting.'

'Suit yourself, then.' He looked away, irrationally stung by her refusal, but still seeking some way to keep her a bit longer. 'May I ask you a question?'

'I suppose.'

'What exactly were these 'sins' your mother committed that were so awful?'

'Do you really want to know?'

'Aye, I'm asking.'

She stared at him for a second, then lowered her lashes. 'Mama had six children by four different men.' Lifting her gaze again, the defiance in her dark eyes warned him that his reaction to her revelation would determine everything between them.

If she was worried about him passing moral judgment, she would have done well to recall his occupation. Careful to keep his expression nonchalant, he lifted his eyebrows wryly before taking another sip of wine. 'Impressive.'

Relief skimmed her fine features at his smooth acceptance of her secret. 'She was beautiful and brilliant – and brave, as well. Most of the men were in love with her, and most of the women ... hated her.'

'I see.' He lowered his gaze, studying a small hole in the knee of his trousers. 'So, your dam made a scandal of herself ... and now all the ton expects you to prove a 'frail vessel,' as well?'

'Precisely. They're no doubt laying wagers on it even now. 'How long before that girl comes to ruin, and with whom?' Especially Daphne Taylor.'

'Who?'

'The plague of my existence. She's the daughter of Viscount Erhard – the *reigning beauty* of the Season,' she said in droll sarcasm, then waved it off impatiently. 'Oh, but let her talk. The ton will never have the satisfaction of seeing me fall into scandal. I may misbehave from time to time, but unlike my mother, I know to a very hair's breadth the limits of what I can get away with. I had better know,' she added cynically. 'I was still in the schoolroom when the whole ton began predicting that 'Georgiana's daughter' would prove a wanton.'

He would kill whoever said that about her, he thought with a rush of violence, but he checked it, holding her in his fascinated stare.

'Well,' he asked slowly, 'are you?'

She looked startled by his dangerous question, but for a long moment held his gaze expectantly with a look of innocent perplexity, as though she wondered if *he* might hold the answer. 'Truthfully? I'm ... not sure.'

A jolt of electric hunger ran through him.

She smiled candidly, blushing as relief flitted over her youthful face at having set her secret free.

He realized full well that she had just told him something even more important than her name, and though she was innocent, he knew an invitation in a woman's eyes when he saw it.

'Would you like to find out?' he murmured.

Her burning blush and shy silence could only be interpreted one way.

He got up quietly, set his wineglass aside, and crossed the few feet between with three slow strides, then lowered himself to his knees in front of her chair and rested his hands on her thighs, caressing her. God, she had no idea how attracted he was to her.

'Blade,' she murmured with a sweet, ingenuous gaze, sliding her arms around his neck in sensual welcome, 'do you promise not to think too badly of me even if I like it?'

A smile curved his lips. 'My lady,' he replied huskily, 'I have every intention of making sure you like it exceedingly.'

60

Then he claimed her mouth in a kiss.

Nothing in all her eighteen years could have prepared her for Billy Blade. His kiss sent an explosive thrill crashing through her body. Her heart raced with guilty pleasure. This, heaven help her, was exactly what she had wanted, needed him to do.

He urged her lips apart, hungrily plundering her mouth; she gave eagerly. He tasted of wine and smoke and male, his bare chest pressing against her like sun-warmed steel in the V where his shirt hung open in the front. She moaned softly against his lips and wrapped her hand around his nape beneath his dark gold mane, pulling him closer, drinking him in yet more deeply. She kissed him in sheer abandon, knowing she would never see him again – knowing that, with this reckless kiss, she fired her maiden salvo over the bow of convention and picked up her mother's battle flag for liberty.

After all, the duchess Georgiana's first illicit lover had been a rough, low bruiser, the champion prizefighter Sam O'Shea, the Killarney Crusher. Mama would have thoroughly approved of Billy Blade.

Jacinda eagerly slipped her hands inside his shirt and caressed his velveteen skin, marveling over the breadth of his shoulders and the sculpted iron of his arms while his hands gathered her hair, gently dragging her head back. His hot, wanton mouth left hers and moved down her neck. His hands, so clever and sure on her tingling skin, found the fashionably low-cut neckline of her gown and slipped it down over the curve of her shoulder. She writhed, helping him to free her breast. Fascinated, barely able to believe that she was doing this, she watched him kiss her nipple.

The initial reverence of his lips at her breast dissolved as the seconds passed, and turned into greedy suckling. The pleasure of it and his low sounds of relishing enjoyment overwhelmed her. She closed her eyes and rested her head on the hard, wooden chair back; a hot, silken vortex of

61

bliss stole over her senses, turning faster and faster as her desire for him took on a dangerous life of its own. She needed more.

'Billy,' she whispered faintly, petting his hair, his elegant cheekbones, running her hands down to the sweeping planes of his muscled shoulders. Her insistent touch summoned him.

Kissing his way back up her throat to her mouth, his eyes aflame, he nuzzled her mouth; then, not asking permission, he lifted her in his arms and carried her to his sensuously draped tent-bed. For a heartbeat, she protested, her voice hoarse and feeble, but then she was distracted by the voluptuous perfume of exotic spices wafting up from his mattress as he laid her down. Bracing himself on his hands above her, he eased his muscled body atop her. The white silk of her skirts enfolded the sturdy black cloth of his trousers as he coaxed her legs apart with a gentle nudge of his knee. Jacinda wrapped her arms and legs around him. Every point where their bodies met pulsated with fiery need. The mad, wild thrill of his kiss, the feel of his firm weight on top of her made her body burn, her heart race. Her hand trembled as she stroked his long, sandy hair.

He gently captured her hand and linked his fingers through hers. The intimacy of holding hands as he moved against her sent a wave of even deeper longing through her. She could feel his steely hardness chafing against her, stroking her pleasure center with every undulant caress of their bodies. She lifted her hips, arching in time with his slow, intoxicating rhythm. Her heart was racing; her skin was on fire. Blade was shaking. He tore his mouth away from her kiss.

'I have to be inside you.'

'No,' she panted, sweeping her eyes open in hazy alarm.

'I'll make you ready,' he soothed her. He moved onto his side next to her, sliding her gown up over her thigh.

'Blade,' she whispered in the frailest of protests.

'*Shh*.' As his lips hovered feather-light upon hers, he ran the lightest, most beguiling caress right up between her legs and with exquisite delicacy pressed into the heated wet core of her womanhood.

'Oh, God,' she moaned, squirming with delight. She kissed him like she would consume him as he stroked and pleasured her with his marvelous hands, his fingertip rubbing her wetness liberally over her pulsating center. He drove her mad with want. Her legs spread wider with a will of their own; her body arched in shameless hunger for the intoxication of his touch. She was on the edge of some blissful cataclysm when he abruptly stopped, reaching with trembling hands to unbutton his trousers. With a helpless whimper, she came up onto her elbows, reaching for him.

'Please—'

He glanced at her in surprise, but as he looked into her eyes, his expression softened incalculably. 'Oh, sweeting. It's all right.' He obeyed her shameful plea, pressing her back gently on the bed. With unbelievable tenderness, he kissed her eyelids and abandoned his own pleasure to fulfill hers.

The throaty endearments he breathed in her ear ruled her senses. When he told her to let go, she could do naught but obey. His strong, warm fingers finished the ravishment she craved, penetrating her with a depth that could only have satisfied a virgin like herself. In the throes of ecstasy, her fevered body convulsed. All the while, she felt him watching her with an intense, savoring stare, drinking in her surrender, until, at last, she collapsed on his mattress – spent, shocked, panting, and blissful.

It took several moments for her pounding heartbeat to slow to normal. She felt wanton, free, and joyously alive in his arms; she nearly laughed breathlessly as his kiss softened, nuzzling her mouth. His hand gently cupped her breast. Caught up in sensation, she was still floating on a pink cloud of euphoria, ignoring with a will the dark thunderhead of guilt she sensed in the near distance.

'Blade, I'm sorry – I didn't know. I couldn't—'

'Hush,' he whispered, kissing the tip of her nose then her cheek. 'Feel better?'

She could hear the smile in his voice.

'Better? It was *divine.*' With a velvety laugh, she gave a catlike stretch beneath him, holding him loosely. 'I never imagined such splendid sensations.'

'You don't say,' he replied in amusement.

'*Ahh,*' she sighed, snuggling deeper into the mattress with a mischievous smile, 'now I am ready for France.'

He laughed and kissed her forehead. 'Absurd, lovely creature,' he said, his voice low and husky. 'Relax and enjoy it.' He withdrew from her arms and rose, walking away from the bed. For a moment, she gazed dreamily at him. His broad back was to her, the dark outline of his phoenix tattoo visible through his thin white cotton shirt. Then she closed her eyes with another happy sigh and cast her forearm over her brow, savoring the lingering lights, tones, and glimmerings of her newfound heaven and stubbornly refusing to think one moment into the future.

In this state, she was blissfully unaware of Blade lifting her satchel by its strap and carrying it over to the chest of drawers, where he opened it and began riffling through her things.

'Where are you, my pretty fellow? Come back to me, Billy-boy,' she murmured after a moment, amused at the scratchy purr of her own voice. Growing impatient to kiss him again, she dragged her eyes open and gazed at him from across the room. For a moment, amid the delicious haze, what she saw did not quite sink in.

Then she noticed some of her belongings strewn out upon the chest of drawers, and her senses came crashing back.

She gasped, jolting upright in his bed. 'You *cad*!'

Chapter Four

'Not at all, Cumberland,' he replied smoothly. 'I'm only looking out for your best interests. What sort of man would I be, after all, taking liberties with a young lady when I don't even know her name?'

Jacinda scrambled out of his bed and marched after him in shocked fury. 'That was a despicable trick. Despicable!'

'You seemed to enjoy it.'

'I demand that you give me back my belongings this *instant*!'

'No.'

At the sharp note of warning in his voice, she stopped a few feet from him, incensed, her heart pounding with her frantic fear of discovery. She felt helpless to stop him, for he was far too physically powerful for her to overcome. 'I trusted you.'

'If you trusted me, you would have told me your name.'

'Don't do this, Blade. What does it matter who I am?'

'Let's just say I'm curious to know exactly how far above my touch you are.' He reached into her satchel again.

Jacinda pressed her hand to her forehead, realizing her fate hung upon his illiteracy. Her traveling documents were in that bag, and if he could read, he would indeed learn her name and almost certainly send her back to her brothers.

She folded her arms tightly across her waist while he

made a pile of the loose coins she had thrown into the bag from the grimy alley. Next, he tossed aside her hairbrush and combs and her extra pair of gloves. Reaching into the satchel again, he pulled out her neatly pressed handkerchief, shook it open, and studied her initials embroidered on the corner.

'J.M.K.,' he read aloud, eyeing her askance.

So, he knows his letters, she thought with a gulp. But that didn't mean he could form words. She met his taunting glance with a defiant mask of indifference.

'Hmm.' He regarded her skeptically, but made no comment. 'What's this?' He pulled out her book and thumbed through it like an amiable savage.

She strove for patience. 'That is *The Corsair* by Lord Byron. Please don't damage it—'

He merely snorted and started to cast it aside; then her traveling papers fell out from between the pages. 'What-ho?' he murmured to himself, picking them up.

His find snapped her into a renewed assault. 'Give it back this instant, you heathen!' She closed the distance between them with a few swift strides, reaching to snatch the papers out of his grasp, but he switched them to the other hand, laughing at her ire. 'Give it back right now, I say, or I shall go to Bow Street! I promise I will!'

'No, you won't,' he taunted. 'You'd cry for days if they hanged me.'

'Odious man!'

He held her off with one hand planted on her midriff. With the other, he shook her passport free of its neat folds and squinted to read it at arm's length by the light of the nearby candle. Dread trapped her words in her throat. She could only stare at his chiseled face, trying in vain to interpret his reaction as he examined her papers.

For a very long moment, he was silent. He dropped his hand from her waist and grasped the document in both hands, poring over it closer to the candle's flame.

He can't read; he can't read, she thought, willing it to

66

be so, but by the candle's glow, she saw his face turning pale.

'Oh, my God,' he said hollowly. 'You're Lady ... Jacinda Knight.'

She closed her eyes briefly. *Blast!*

'You treacherous ... *brat*!' he roared, spinning to face her with a shocked look. 'You might have warned me! You accuse *me* of a despicable trick? I never would have touched you if I had known who you are, *my lady*. If I had known you were Lucien's sister – good God, are you trying to get me killed?'

'I am *trying* to keep you out of it.' She snatched again for her papers, but he lifted them over her head, out of reach.

'Well, I'm in it now, aren't I? I don't believe this. You – of all people! Lord Lucien's maiden sister!' He stared at her incredulously, then walked over to the fireplace and braced his hand against the mantel, shaking his head as he stared into the flames. 'Jacinda Knight, running away from home! Are you daft, girl? You've got food on your table, a roof over your head. You've got a family that loves you and blood that's nearly as blue as the king's. You've had life handed to you on a silver platter. What more could you possibly want?'

'Liberty!' she cried. 'God, Blade, do you really think that creature comforts are all that matter in this life?'

'I think you've got *bats* flapping around in your belfry, that's what I bloody think.' He turned and glared at her, resting his hands on his lean waist. 'You have no idea how good you've got it. Have you noticed the state of the country, my lady? These are dangerous times. People starving. Poor harvests. Half a million men back from the war, and no jobs for 'em. Businesses, factories closin' all over the place. You may well need your famous brothers to protect you, because this whole city could rise up and erupt like Paris did in the Revolution. All it would take is just one spark for the whole powder keg to blow

– and your fine lords know it. Aye, every one of 'em, especially that snake, Sidmouth, in the Home Office. His Lordship's only got one answer to every problem – build another gallows.'

'So, what, then, Blade? You mean to overthrow the government?' she asked in a long-suffering tone, folding her arms across her chest.

'On the contrary, my lady, I am doing my best to keep order,' he bit back. 'Why do you think it's left to me to fight O'Dell? I'll tell you why – because the city officers won't even set foot in our neighborhood. I'm going to be frank with you, Lady Jacinda. O'Dell and a few of his gang raped a thirteen-year-old girl a block away from here last month – forgive me if I offend your sensibilities. Her father went to the authorities, but he's an Irish Catholic without tuppence to his name, so do you think they're going to lift a finger to give the girl justice? Of course they won't. That's why he came to me – it's just not worth it to them. But let Lady Sudeby lose a painting,' he yelled, flinging a gesture toward the Canaletto, 'and those buffoons will turn the city upside down trying to find it. We're fighting for our lives here, while your class can think of nothing but whether to furnish the new country house in the Chinese style or the Gothic!'

The room rang with his deep, impassioned shout.

She was silent for a moment, then shook her head. 'I know there is injustice, Blade, but if you would use your head for a moment instead of your fists, you could easily see that you are far richer than most people, with your dozens of loyal mates and this place. You don't understand because you're *free*. You don't have a hundred people breathing down your neck, watching your every move, waiting for you to make one mistake so they can throw you to the wolves.'

He was quiet for a second, studying her; then he shrugged. 'I am sorry, my lady. Maybe you're right – maybe we can't understand each other. But I do know one

68

thing. You've got far better chances of surviving in your world than you do in mine.'

With that, he bent and tossed her traveling papers into the fire.

Her eyes widened. With a stricken cry, she rushed toward the hearth, but he caught her about her waist and held her back, hushing her softly as she watched her freedom go up in flames.

There was no helping some people, Blade thought with a mental huff as he sat across from Her Ladyship a short while later in the dark, shabby interior of the hackney coach. Well, what did she expect?

Daughter of a bloody duke.

Once more she was bundled up in her soiled coat, the buttons primly latched, her hair somewhat tamed again by the star-shaped pins. All her belongings had been thrown back into her satchel, and every penny that Eddie had stolen had been returned to her. Blade's heart had nearly stopped when he had noticed that she wasn't wearing her diamond necklace, thinking that one of his men might have deftly snatched it while he had gone to whistle for Jimmy, the coachman, but she had coldly informed him that she had put it in her satchel.

Those were the last words she had spoken to him. Now she wouldn't even look at him. She sat across from him, staring out the window, looking withdrawn, betrayed, out of hope, and coldly angry. He knew he was doing the right thing, but just like a woman, she had decided to hate him for it. The mad chit had nearly dived headlong into the fire up there in his room trying to save her traveling papers. She would never make it to Dover in one piece, let alone France. At the moment, however, he was only glad she hadn't resorted to the ultimate weapon of tears.

Still, the defeated look in her eyes made his stomach hurt vaguely, and the impossibility of ever seeing her again made him want to put his fist through something, not to mention the fact that her brothers were probably going to castrate him when they found out how he had pawed her. He refused to regret for one second what he had done, but he was not looking forward to the coming collision. Lucien Knight could dissect a person with his steel trap of a mind, and his twin, Damien, the war hero, was nothing short of bloody terrifying. He had heard there were a few other brothers, but he had not met them, nor did he care to, under the circumstances.

Gazing at her from across the rocking coach's dark interior, he caught a brief glimpse of her profile as they passed through a shaft of moonlight streaming in between two tall buildings; then they were plunged in darkness and shadows again as the coach rattled on. The horses' clip-clopping hoofbeats and the heavy grinding of the wheels did little to ease the charged silence between them. It was beginning to stretch his nerves thin.

'Someday you'll thank me for this,' he informed her, unable to stand it anymore.

'It won't work. I'll only run away again.'

'I'll be sure to warn Lucien you said so.'

She turned to him, the dim glow from a streetlamp giving him the barest glimpse of her face. 'You have no right to do this to me. Why must you crush my will with your own?'

'Because I'm right, and you're wrong. I am doing this for your own good.'

'Oh, you men,' she whispered bitterly. 'You roll women under your wheels like great millstones grinding wheat. I shall never forgive you for this.'

'Well, it hardly matters, dear.' Insolently, he lit a cheroot to distract himself from the guilt. 'It's not as though we move in the same circles.'

'Hardly.' She fell silent for a moment. 'So, that is all, then. It's over. Now I shall have to marry Lord Griffith.'

'Is he so bad?'

She gave him a lost look that pricked at Blade's feeble conscience.

'If you don't want him, you must tell your family flat-out,' he said hotly.

'You don't understand. Robert won't listen—'

'Make him listen! Stand up for yourself, girl.'

'You don't know very much about dukes, do you?'

He could not help but smile slightly at her quelling tone. 'No, but I do know that your brothers would do anything for you, and that you can't just run away from your problems.'

'You did.'

'It's different with me.'

'Because you're a man?'

'Because I had no choice. My father would have eventually ended up killing me if I had stayed.'

She stared at him for a moment in the darkness, then looked away.

They were silent just long enough for Blade to begin regretting his admission. He shifted self-consciously in his seat, crossing his ankle over the opposite knee. His injured side hurt.

'What about my things? You know I cannot do without my pretty baubles and material comforts,' she said in cool, cutting irony. 'I left my traveling trunks at the inn.'

'Your brother can send for them.'

'How do you know Lucien, anyway?'

'It's of no consequence.'

'Ah, but, of course. It would no doubt tax my poor female brain too much to be told the truth. It's so good of you men to be always protecting me. Fortunately, I'm able to figure things out for myself. Lucien pays you for information about the criminal world, no?' In the darkness, he could just make out the sparks of derision in her eyes; then she turned away and stared out the window again. 'I daresay you will do anything for a few pieces of silver. How much do you think you'll get for ruining my life?'

Already uneasy with his confession about his father's violence, he went on the defensive, losing patience. 'I am

71

not ruining your life, you daft chit. I am saving your neck.'

'You are not. I know why you're doing this. Because you're afraid of my brothers—'

'I'm not afraid of anyone,' he warned.

'They don't have to know,' she said tautly. 'You can still let me go.'

'Sorry, can't do that.'

'Sorry? You will be. If I tell my brothers what you did to me—'

'You mean what you begged me to do to you?'

'You're life won't be worth a farthing.'

'Go ahead and tell them.' He sat back and gave her a flat look. 'They'll put you in a bloody convent.'

She narrowed her eyes at him. 'Do you ever stop swearing?'

He smiled and blew smoke gently at her from his cheroot. She waved it away with an indignant cough and opened the window by its strap, then looked askance at him with a crafty gleam coming into her eyes. He watched her warily as she got up, crossed the small space of the coach, and slid into the seat beside him. He went very still as she laid her hand on his leg, but his pulse quickened at her touch.

'Billy,' she cajoled prettily, walking her gloved fingers up his thigh, 'you'll let me go if I pleasure you, as you did me, won't you?'

He lifted his eyebrow. 'You really *do* want to go to France.'

'Show me how.' With a wild, vixenish smile, she took him off guard with a warm caress all the way up to his still-aching cock. He flinched with need, but somehow found the strength to pluck her hand off his groin.

'You little hussy,' he said pleasantly.

'Come, you need it,' she whispered.

'There's always Carlotta.'

'Ugh!' Cursing him under her breath in French, she flounced back to her seat with a huff, folded her arms across her chest, and glared at him.

72

He grinned, his cheroot clamped between his teeth. There was another embattled silence as the coach carried them into Lucien's elegant neighborhood. In moments they would reach his handsomely appointed townhouse in Upper Brooke Street.

'Well,' she said, 'you learned my real name. I think it's only fair you tell me yours.'

He looked at her without comment.

'No one is really called 'Billy Blade.' What is your real name? Is it William?'

He didn't answer.

'Will. William. Willy.'

'Do you ever shut up?'

'Yes, William,' she taunted. Baby sister of her clan, she had obviously perfected her skills for annoying a male on her army of elder brothers.

He grumbled about her under his breath, then looked away as the hackney coach turned into Upper Brooke Street. In moments, he would hand her over and would probably never see her again. He glanced over and found her studying him. They stared at each other as the coach rolled to a halt in front of her brother's house.

'Blade, please,' she whispered.

'Don't,' he muttered brusquely, weakened by the frantic distress in her big, dark eyes. At once, he shoved open the door and jumped out of the carriage. 'Mind 'er, Jimmy. Don't let her run off,' he ordered the driver as he shut the carriage door behind him. He braced himself to face her brother as he strode toward the entrance.

All sophisticated understatement, much like its owner, Lord Lucien Knight's town house had a flat front with small wrought-iron balconies off the upper windows. Brass lanterns burned on either side of the elaborately carved door. In an upper window, where light beamed through the shade, he could see the slim silhouette of Lucien's young wife brushing her long hair. Reaching the front door, he knocked loudly, then waited. He could feel Jacinda watching him from the coach. An elderly butler answered the door. He asked for Lord Lucien.

'Tell him it's Blade.'

The thin old fellow gave him a guarded look and closed the door in his face. Again, he waited and smoked in restless silence, hooking his thumb idly in the waistband of his trousers. A few minutes later, the door opened again, and a tall, black-haired man stood in the doorway.

'Blade?' Lord Lucien Knight stepped out of his house, pulling the door closed silently behind him. Though his cravat hung untied around his neck, he was dressed in formal black and white, as though he had just come back from the same ball his sister had fled.

Blade suddenly wondered if anyone had even realized yet that Jacinda was missing. Maybe she had guessed correctly when she had said that her note might not yet have been found.

'What's afoot?' Lucien asked, his silvery eyes glowing keenly in the moonlight.

'I found something of yours. Thought you might like to have it back.'

Lucien regarded him curiously. Blade nodded toward the coach, then told him everything that had happened. Well – not quite everything. He wasn't suicidal.

'Good God! Is she hurt?'

'Only her pride,' Blade muttered, but Lucien was already striding toward the carriage.

'Jas?' He hauled open the carriage door as Blade came sauntering up behind him. 'Sweeting, are you all right?'

'Yes, Lucien, I am perfectly well,' she drawled in a bored, long-suffering voice from inside the coach.

Reassured by her insolent tone, anger flooded Lucien's aquiline face. 'Perdition, girl, have you lost your mind? Get into the house this instant! You have some explaining to do!'

Glowering, the young beauty emerged from the shadows

inside the vehicle, thrust her satchel into Lucien's hands, then hopped out of the coach with an air of bristling defiance.

'And no temper tantrums,' her brother warned. 'If you wake the baby, I'll throttle you.'

Without a word, Jacinda took her bag back from him and turned to Blade, regarding him in silence for one final, excruciating moment with a look of bitter regret. She needed no words to express her disgust; her slight shaking of her head said it all. Shrugging her satchel up higher onto her shoulder, she walked into the house and closed the door behind her without looking back.

'What a piece of work!' Lucien exploded when she had shut the door, but Blade could only stand there feeling like an utter Judas.

'Ah, I had a feeling something like this was coming, but I didn't think she'd really do it. I don't know what we'll do with her. The sooner she's safely married off, the better – it is her second Season.'

Blade hesitated, knowing it was none of his business – nor did he really care – but he had to say something to try to help her. 'Whoever it is you want her to marry,' he blurted out, 'she really hates the notion.'

'She told you that?'

He nodded. 'Who is the chap, and what's wrong with him?' he asked cautiously.

'Wrong with him? Nothing. He's the marquess of Griffith – only one of the ton's most brilliant catches. He grew up with us in the North Country. She's known him all her life. His wife died two years ago in childbirth, and we all think it's time he rejoined the land of the living. They'd be good for each other.'

Blade stared at him in confusion. 'He's not an old wigsby?'

Lucien laughed. 'Is that what she told you?'

Blade swiftly reviewed their conversation and shook his head as he realized. 'It's what she let me assume.'

Lucien gave him a wan smile. 'She's devious like that.' He sighed. 'Who can fathom the mind of a woman? And that one's as mad as her mother.'

Blade looked away uneasily, beginning to wonder all at once if he had done the wrong thing by bringing her back. She had confided in him; he had told her he would listen. But had he?

With a sigh, Lucien turned to him and extended his hand. 'Thank you for bringing her back safely, Blade.' He shook his hand firmly. 'God knows, anything might have happened to her out there. I owe you, truly. If there is anything I can do, you have but to name it.'

'It was nothing,' he said gruffly, remembering her icy taunting about his getting a reward for this. He turned to leave, his mood gone surly, then stopped himself halfway across the pavement. He rolled his eyes in self-disgust and turned around again.

'Lucien.'

'Yes?' The man paused, reaching for the doorknob.

He braced himself. 'I kissed her, all right?'

Lucien's eyes narrowed. '*What*?'

'I didn't know she was your sister! She refused to tell me her name until after I had already done it.'

The ex-spy held him in a grim stare. 'Why are you telling me this?'

'Why the hell do you think? Because you'd find

out anyway. And ... because I want you to know, it wasn't her fault. It was all my doing.'

He waited for a charge, a punch, possibly a bullet.

'Your fault?' Lucien echoed, sizing him up.

'Entirely.'

Both men knew it was a lie, the best kind – a chivalrous one.

'Well, I should say,' Lucien sputtered, 'you're damned right it was your fault!'

'That's right, and I apologize.' Blade regarded him with a stare as deliberately obtuse as that of an ox.

Lucien studied him for a long moment in his piercing way. 'Do not attempt to see her again, Rackford – at least, not until you are prepared to return to the life you left. She is the daughter of a duke.'

'I have no intention of it,' he answered coldly, 'and the name is Blade.'

'As you prefer. If that is all, I will bid you good night.'

Blade tossed him an insolent nod.

'One more thing,' Lucien added, pausing in the doorway. 'I was sorry to hear about your brother.'

Blade just looked at him. The man knew too damned much about everyone and everything.

With a cordial nod, Lucien went back inside and shut the door firmly behind him. Blade heard a series of locks sharply sliding home as he walked away, and he took insult even though he knew none was intended. He looked over his shoulder in scorn. *Don't worry, Lord Lucien. If I wanted to break into your house, I could do it in a trice.*

Bloody aristocrats. His mood gone foul, he jumped up onto the driver's bench and sat with Jimmy for the ride back to the rookery. He didn't need to be driven around Town like a bloody prince.

As the coach wove through the dark, deserted streets, he looked down broodingly at his rough, callused hands resting loosely on his lap. They shook with anger and shame at the reminder of just how far he had fallen in life and with the cold, slightly nauseating uneasiness of a schoolboy who has just pinned the wings of a butterfly that he had thoughtlessly netted in a sunny meadow.

The last thing he had wanted was to hurt her.

Waiting for her brother in the darkened front parlor, Jacinda paced in restless agitation until she heard the front door close as Lucien came in. She rushed to the sofa and quickly sat down, smoothing her skirts. She lifted her chin and squared her shoulders, braced for battle. The diplomatic Lucien was her most broad-minded, lenient brother, but – still. This time she knew she was in for it.

He strode in a moment later and propped his fists on his waist, shaking his head at her. 'You are in the suds, my girl.'

She clenched her jaw and looked away.

'Are you completely mad?'

'I have my reasons.'

'We will be most interested to hear them all, I assure you. Is there anything you wish to say for yourself before I take you over to Knight House to speak with the others?'

She groaned at the thought of a full-fledged family meeting. 'Lucien, please—'

'I am not covering for you on this,' he said flatly. 'It was a blasted foolish thing to do. I don't know what possessed a cutthroat like Blade to show mercy, but thank God he did.'

She snorted and folded her arms across her chest.

Lucien sauntered closer. 'Did he harm you, insult you in any way?'

'His arrogance is most insulting, yes.'

'You know what I mean,' he chided. 'He admitted kissing you. If he did any more than that, one of us is going to have call him out.'

The blood drained from her face as she looked swiftly at him. 'No! Good God, do not speak of dueling! He didn't do anything like that. Lucien, it was my fault!'

'Your fault?'

'Entirely.' She gave an earnest nod as her cheeks turned red. 'I rather . . . fancied him at first.'

He lifted his eyebrow.

'Well, I hate him now, of course. I meant to go to France, and that insolent peasant brute had to interfere!'

Lucien stroked his chin with a bemused expression.

'What did he want as his reward for bringing me back?' she asked in wary cynicism.

'Nothing. Perhaps your kiss was payment enough,' he added with a sardonic shrug.

'Are you going to tell Robert and the others that I kissed him? Please, don't, Lucien, I beg you. This has all been humiliating enough.'

He considered for a moment, then gave a philosophical sigh. 'You appear unharmed by your adventure, and God knows you're already in hot-enough water without adding that bit of fuel to the fire. Besides, it wouldn't do to have Damien or Alec rushing off to put a bullet in him. The blackguard has his uses.'

'Who is he, really?' She asked, leaning toward her brother confidentially.

'Why,' Lucien said with an opaque smile, 'the leader of the Fire Hawks, of course. Come along, my dear. It is time to pay the piper.'

Eddie the Knuckler kept the hours of an alley cat. When most children his age were still safely tucked in their beds and dreaming, he was ambling along through the predawn darkness toward Covent Garden Market to see what he could get from the vendors who would soon be setting up their stalls for the day's business. The highborn rakes who came staggering out of the whorehouses off the piazza early each morning, sick with too much drink from the night before also made excellent targets for a lad ambitious to pinch a fine silk handkerchief or a gold watch.

As Eddie approached the junction of two narrow city streets not far from St. Giles's Church, his thoughts turning industriously upon the coming morning's adventures, he was suddenly seized by the shoulder and felt a large hand clamp down over his mouth, so big it nearly wrapped from ear to ear. He was yanked around the corner like a rag doll, where somebody slammed his back against the brick wall of the alley.

'Got him, O'Dell! Here's the little whoreson.'

Looking up in terror, scarcely able to breathe past the giant hand over his mouth, Eddie found himself surrounded by several top members of the Jackals' gang. These were

79

the men, he realized, who had done unspeakable things to Mary Murphy, who was only a few years older than he.

Tyburn Tim was the one holding him, but Bloody Fred was there, fresh out of Bedlam and looking half rabid; Flash, striking a dandyish pose against the wall; and Baumer, who had a laugh like an earthquake and loomed half as big as a house. Eddie's heart hammered against his ribs as the Jackals parted to admit their leader, the wiry, brown-haired Cullen O'Dell.

O'Dell prowled out of the deeper shadows of the alley past his henchmen. An ordinary child would have screamed outright, but hardy young Eddie managed to restrain himself to a large gulp when he saw what had become of O'Dell's face.

The leader of the Jackals had long acted like a monster; now he looked like one, as well. The left side of O'Dell's face looked normal, but the right was a swollen, shapeless, purple mass. His right eyelid was a horrifying bulge like a big, quivery blob of grape jam. A series of welts in a diagonal line bruised his cheek. Eddie thought the bruises resembled chain links.

'Well, if it isn't Blade's little mascot.' As O'Dell bent down slowly to Eddie's height, his good eye, crazed and blue, swept the boy's face with feverish intensity. 'Top o' the mornin', little man. You're not gonna scream like a girl, are you?'

When Eddie shook his head in fright, O'Dell flipped a nod at Tyburn Tim, who eased his hand off Eddie's mouth. The boy gasped for breath, his chest heaving.

'Now, then, Master Eddie. You know who we are, don't ye?'

'Aye, sir. The Jackals.'

'That's right. And pretty soon, all you see around you is goin' to be our turf. Why do you want to cast your lot with a pack of poltroons like the Fire Hawks, Eddie? A plucky little knuckler like you can do better. We think you should join wid' us.'

Eddie held very still. O'Dell's tone was sly and silky, but the hard, wild glitter in his blue eye scared him.

'Aye, now you're listening, ain't ye?' O'Dell reached into his pocket, pulled out a shilling, and held it up in front of Eddie's face. 'I'm gonna give this to you, little Master Eddie.' He dropped the coin in Eddie's coat pocket. 'There's plenty more where that came from if you do what I ask.'

'And if I don't?' he asked defiantly, trying to be as brave as Blade. O'Dell laughed gruffly and turned to his mates. 'I told you he had pluck.'

Eddie looked at him warily.

O'Dell turned back to him with a cold, indulgent smile. 'If you don't, I'll have Bloody Fred here skin you alive and make your hide into my wallet.'

Eddie gasped, jolting back against the wall at the horrible threat. When he looked up at the ex-Bedlamite, Fred held up his knife and breathed on it with a smile, polishing the blade with his dirty sleeve. For a second, he felt he might puke. There was no doubt in his mind that Bloody Fred would happily flay him and make him into a wallet.

Rookery lore claimed that Bloody Fred had once murdered and eaten one of his former landlords.

'What do you want with me?' Eddie cried, turning to O'Dell.

O'Dell smiled, edged closer, and dropped his voice. 'I want you to become my spy, Eddie. I want to know where and when Blade means to carry out his next housebreakin'.'

'Why?' Eddie breathed, wide-eyed.

'Don't ask foolish questions, laddie. And don't even think about double-crossin' me, because I'll find out and let Fred have at you. You'll do as I ask, or you'll wish you was never born.' With that, O'Dell let him go.

Eddie slipped free and ran away as fast as his pumping legs could carry him.

Chapter Five

Reclining on his tent-bed under the draped veils, a cheroot dangling from his lips, Blade stared sullenly across the room at the spot where the Canaletto had sat. Earlier today he had pawned the painting to buy more guns for his war against the Jackals. It was no mean trick moving a one-of-a-kind work of art through the black market, but his acquaintances in the art specialty were reliable and discreet. Now the aura of glamor that had visited his drab cell had fled, leaving it as it had always been, mean and hard and bare. The walls were cracked, the ceiling stained, and every damned time it rained, the roof leaked.

With an exhalation of smoke, he rested his elbow on his bent knee and lifted his hand to gaze at the diamond necklace wrapped around his fist like a tiny, glittering lifeline. What a devil that girl was, leaving it here for him to find.

His stare was faraway as he brooded on what to make of the gift. What did it mean? His male pride bristled; his survivor's wariness warned of a thousand dangers; hope danced painfully like flickering flames torturing his implacable will. By God, he was no charity boy. His pride would not countenance her pity. For all he knew, she had left the necklace as a trap, setting him up with the outrageous donation only to accuse him of stealing it. It would be a neat means of revenge for returning her to her family and to the unwanted marriage that awaited her.

But maybe, just maybe, came his vulnerable heart's small whisper, she had left it because she had seen something good in him. Something worth saving. The possibility that this was a gift freely given simply because she had thought him worthy shook him. And as he stared into the glittering facets of the diamond, brilliant in the dusty daylight slanting through the window into his room, his mind drifted back to a day long ago, the day he had learned, for once and for all, that he was worth nothing, to memories he rarely dared revisit of Cornwall and the sun's bright glitter on the wide blue sea ...

'*Biiill-yyy!*'

'Look at that one, Billy!'

'I'm looking!'

Laughter. Boyish voices.

The low-sinking sun glinted gold off the brass folding telescope as Billy Albright braced his foot on the gunwale and steadied his aim against the skiff's pitching, the salt wind riffling through his flaxen hair. One suspender fell over his shoulder, and the breeze billowed through his loose white shirt as he stared through his father's borrowed telescope at the bewhiskered gray Atlantic seals posturing and barking at each other from their various perches upon the greenish black rocks. Before the days of King Arthur, the giant of Portreath had hurled the boulders there to help him catch his supper in the form of unsuspecting ships. *Already told them that one.* Every inch of this corner of Cornwall had an old legend or strange tale attached to it. Billy racked his brain for another with which to regale his two schoolmates, who had come home from Eton with him for the spring holiday.

All three boys were thirteen years old. Reg Bentinck, dark-eyed and slightly anemic, was fishing excitedly off the port bow, while freckled Justin Church, with his shock of carrot-red hair, minded the oars and tossed up bits of bread now and then to the screeching gulls that tirelessly flapped apace with them. Billy was anxious that his guests should not grow bored. He had never had friends to stay with him before – he was not sure he could say he'd ever been allowed to have friends before – but now that he was a proud Etonian, his whole life was different.

Many of the new boys had been wretched with home-sickness during Michaelmas Half, but not him. For him, school was just the thing. Outside the reach of his father's dark shadow, he had begun to thrive. In the span of one short term, the masters at Eton had already begun to fortify his bravado with true confidence. He had been astonished to find that, contrary to his father's frequent assertions, he was actually rather intelligent.

At home he was treated with all the welcome of a rabid stray dog, but at school, he was shocked to find himself well liked, even popular, thanks to his skill at fives, his willingness to impress the other boys with reckless feats of daring, his occasional cheekiness to the teachers, and the word *lord* in front of his name. Lord William Spencer Albright, to be exact, second son of the marquess of Truro and St. Austell.

It was the last factor that had gained him his friends' company for the spring holiday. Reg and Justin were of the landed gentry and the lower nobility; their parents had practically tossed them headlong into the coach upon hearing that their offspring had been invited by the younger son of a marquess to spend the break at His Lordship's castle in Cornwall. Amid many hurrahs, the three boys had been on their way. Of course, if Reg and Justin's parents *really* knew his father, he mused with a cynicism beyond his years, they would think differently. In any case, all that concerned him now was making it through the break and getting back to school without incident.

His young face hardened as he slowly lowered the tele-scope from his eye. He would never admit to it aloud, but the truth was, he had brought Reg and Justin home with him not merely for their jolly company, but out of the rather desperate hope that their presence would help to

84

mitigate his father's inevitable black spells.

Thank God the old blighter was not expected back until the day after tomorrow, he thought. Snapping his father's telescope shut with a vengeful snick, he turned to his companions, pink-cheeked with sun and wind, a sparkle of mischief in his eyes.

'Want to see some smugglers' caves?'

'Real smugglers?' Justin cried, turning to him, the wind running riot through his carroty hair.

Billy nodded with cool bravado. 'Coast is crawlin' with 'em.'

'Aye, Captain!' Justin yelled, but Reg paled and clung to the gunwale with a white-knuckled grip as the little boat rode the blue waves past the towering, folded cliffs.

'It sounds a bit ... dangerous.'

'It is.' Billy flashed him a fearless grin, handed the telescope back to Reg, and slid down jauntily at the oars. Justin took his place at the bow to catch the sea spray on his face, while Billy rowed hard against the seething sea.

He was a strong boy, taller than the others. Everyone said he was going to be big like Papa, for he was already as broad across as his seventeen-year-old brother, Percy.

Beneath the stark, stone ruins of an ancient fort high upon the sun-baked pinnacles, he rowed past the round-mouthed cave where a fortune in black-market goods was rumored to be stored. All the girls around here were in love with the romantic dashing smugglers. With a cock-sure look, he asked his friends if they wanted to go and have a look inside the caves, but was secretly relieved when both shook their heads in fright. They were glad enough not to have spotted the French fleet and Boney come to carry out his long-standing threat to invade England.

At length, Billy rowed them back to the short stretch of beach from which they had set sail that morning. While sunset smoldered in the west behind them, he and Justin hopped out of the boat, barefooted, their trousers rolled up around their shins, and dragged the skiff back up onto the golden sands. Their bellies rumbling, they climbed up onto the dramatic vantage point of the promontory to have their picnic of Cornish pasty and West Country cheese washed down with a jug of delicious scrumpy.

They sat in contented silence for a while, watching sunset light the ocean, a spreading stain of liquid gold. The sky glowed fierce fiery orange and pink streaked with purple, while restful blue stole down softly from the east, lighting the little stars one by one. Billy felt lulled by the rhythmic thunder of the waves buffeting the rocks below like a mother's heartbeat.

Slowly the sea deepened to indigo and the sky to black, and the lighthouse on the small rocky islet a league offshore sent its beam sweeping out over the water and the rocks where the seals snuggled down for the night. The boys remembered then that Cook had promised them clotted cream with black treacle when they returned. They climbed to their feet; gathered up their play pirate swords and fishing rods, their catch of bream and monkfish in the bucket, their finds of seashells and interesting rocks, bits of serpentine and feldspar wrapped securely in a polka-dotted neckerchief; and trudged homeward through the twilight.

Billy slipped the telescope into the deep pocket of his coat just as he walked through an odd chilly patch. The misty coolness grazed his cheeks like a ghost wafting past. The sensation raised the hackles on his nape, but then, as the boys stepped up onto the crest of the ridge, the towers of Torcarrow came into sight, then the rest of the sprawling pile. Torcarrow consisted of a fourteenth-century fortified manor house appended to an ancient towered keep over-looking the sea, for the warrior lords of Truro and St. Austell had guarded Cornwall against French invaders for nearly three hundred years.

But as Billy gazed down the sloping green toward his home, he felt his blood run cold.

Father's carriage was there.

At once, his heart began to pound. He had not expected Truro the Terrible back for another few days, but there, by the light of the flambeaux burning around the courtyard of the east entrance, he beheld the marquess's coach crouched like a beast ready to spring.

Billy swallowed hard and did his best to mask his fear from his friends. He suddenly lost his appetite for Cook's sweet treat and could think of nothing but returning his father's telescope to its glass case in the study before it was missed. Unfortunately, the dusty oak-paneled study was the first place the marquess usually went upon returning home, to see to any matters of business or correspondence that might have arisen during his absence. Drunk or sober, Lord Truro enjoyed the duties that enhanced his sense of power and control over all matters pertaining to his holdings and possessions, among which he counted the members of his family.

It took the lads another twenty minutes before the meandering drive brought them into the shadow of Torcarrow. Billy led Reg and Justin around to the kitchens to deliver their fish and to tell Cook they were ready for their dessert. Anxious to return the telescope before his sire reached his study, he excused himself and told his friends he'd be right back, but he paused, glancing at Mrs. Landry, their dear old Cook.

'Cooky, where's Mother?'

'Why, Master William,' the stout old woman said, giving him a subtle warning look, 'Her Ladyship has just retired to her rooms for a rest. A bit of the headache, I'm afraid.'

Billy absorbed the news grimly. Mother had a sort of internal barometer that always measured Truro's brewing storms. Whenever she felt one coming on, she wisely retreated to the safety of her chamber and did not come out until the headache had passed. She never asked Billy about his bruises.

With the telescope hidden in his loose coat pocket, banging guiltily against his side with every step, he prowled stealthily through the corridors, past the big, mahogany staircase. He saw the servants huddling here and there, trying to keep out of the master's way. A familiar, eerie quiet had come over the house, but well before his father's study came into view, he heard the marquess yelling at a footman. The dressing-down sounded even more stringent than usual.

'Bloody hell,' Billy whispered to himself as he heard his father accusing the footman of stealing his telescope and threatening to turn him over to the sheriff.

'Father, perhaps they were only cleaning it!' Billy heard his elder brother, Percy, say inside the library.

A superior seventeen-year-old down from Oxford, Percy, the heir, was, aside from Mother, the only one in the household who never took a beating. It was just as well, for he was a thin, poetic sort of lad who caught a sniffle in every cold breeze. One round against Father would probably have killed him. Billy, however, was another story. Billy could take a punch.

As he walked toward the study, his palms went cold and began to sweat, but somehow he summoned his courage. Even before he stepped into the room and saw his old man, drunk and disheveled in his rumpled velvet coat, slamming the bewildered footman against the wall, he knew that when he confessed to the deed, it was going to be a bad one.

Best to go out boldly, he thought, unaware that Reg and Justin had followed him and were about to see everything that was to happen.

He squared his shoulders and strode into the library, pulling the telescope out of his pocket. 'Sir.' He held it up. 'I have your telescope. No one stole it. It's right here.' He stopped, holding up the spyglass as his father turned around, his chest heaving, his face red from his tirade. 'I borrowed it.'

Truro's bleary eyes narrowed at Billy. He dropped the liveried footman unceremoniously. The young man-servant scrambled away. 'Well,' said the marquess. 'Borrowed it, did you, now?'

88

Billy held his ground. The redness of Truro's eyes due to drink made his green irises look all the more wild and bright. With his lank brown hair streaked with gray and his scruff-darkened jaw badly in need of a shave, the marquess looked more pirate than Billy could ever hope to be, but as his father bent near, breathing liquor fumes in his face, all Billy could think of was the giant of Portreath.

'Father,' Percy said in a warning tone as the marquess stalked slowly toward his younger son.

Billy held his father's stare with the insolence of one who had long since learned it was no good groveling.

'Father,' Percy begged in despair, 'please! Leave him alone—'

The first blow sent Billy flying into the nearest bank of bookshelves. He banged his lip on a wooden shelf and fell, a rain of books tumbling down upon him. His father strode through the pile of dusty, unread tomes and picked him up by his arm, lifting him just high enough to get a good angle for a second punch and a third. From the corner of his eye, Billy saw his blood fleck the open pages of *Le Morte d'Arthur*, but there was no escape from the hail of his father's punches and kicks. Truro even picked up a hefty dictionary and slammed him in the head with it.

'How many times have I warned you not to touch my things? You little thief! Thought you could sneak it back without my knowing, did you? You think you're clever?'

Billy was aware of his own voice spluttering out a frantic denial and a cascade of apologies that did him no good whatsoever. He let out a sharp cry of pain as his father grasped a handful of his hair and jerked his head back.

That was when he realized that this time his old man was going to kill him.

'Father!' Percy shrieked, rushing toward them, only to be sent sprawling when Truro swiped him away with a stinging backhand.

'*Never* touch my things. It's that school that's teaching you to put on airs, ain't it, William? Well, maybe you just need to stay here with me where I can teach you some manners!'

Bleeding from the nose and the corner of his mouth, feeling his left eye already swelling shut, Billy lifted his head and looked into his father's face in silent, pleading pain. The marquess slammed his head down on the strewn books and kicked him in the stomach. Over the next few minutes, several eternities ran together, and Billy felt awareness slipping away from him. His ears were ringing almost too loudly to hear someone crying.

'*Stop*!' a high-pitched voice screamed.

Miraculously, the command worked, but when Billy rallied himself to look over at the doorway, he saw Justin and Reg standing there, pale and terror-stricken – and his humiliation was complete. His pride crumbled, his terrible secret revealed. In an instant, his whole life was ruined. His new friends were bound to tell the other boys at school what they had seen; then everyone would know that he was worth nothing, unwanted. The haven he had found at Eton vanished into the mist like the lost kingdom of Lyonesse, which according to legend, had sunk into the sea off the Cornwall coast centuries ago. His father straightened up slowly and regarded the intruders for such a long, hazy moment that Billy half feared he would attack them, too.

'L-lord Truro?' Justin stammered in appalled amazement.

The marquess cleared his throat, tugged at his coat, and smoothed his long, wild hair. 'Gentlemen, my son is guilty of a serious infraction of the rules of this household. I'm afraid you will have to return to your families at once. The holiday is over.'

'Billy?' Reg whispered. 'Are you all right?'

He could not bring himself to look at him or at Justin. Tears stung the backs of his eyelids, but he refused to let them fall.

'Do not be alarmed, boys. William is quite hardy. Moore, ready the coach. The young masters will be leaving tonight.'

'Tonight, Father?' Percy cried. 'It's dangerous on the roads at this hour—'

'Accompany them yourself if you don't like it,' Truro bit back.

'I will!' Percy answered in affront. He turned to the younger boys. 'Justin, Reg, I will go in the coach with you to make sure you arrive safely.'

'See you at school, Billy,' Reg offered timidly.

Please don't tell anyone, he wanted to beg them, but his pride forbade him to ask any favors from any person. Not when he had been told no from the day he was born.

Truro ordered everyone out of the study, leaving Billy half buried under a heap of books, teetering dizzily on the verge of unconsciousness. When Reg and Justin had gone to collect their belongings, the marquess warned the servants not to interfere, but to leave him to his punishment of solitude.

The marquess passed a hostile glance over the destruction he had wrought. 'I want this room cleaned up before you retire,' he growled at Billy, then closed the door behind him, plunging the room into cool, silken darkness.

For a long while, Billy didn't move. He closed his eyes, awash in misery as pain throbbed through his body. Unable to hold them back anymore, silent tears rolled down his cheeks more for the loss of his brief happiness at school. He wondered in despair if anyone was ever going to love him. But then, as he lay there, crushed in body and spirit, a maelstrom of unholy rage began churning in him, gathering force. It drove him up onto his hands and knees in the darkness. He looked down blindly at the books he had been ordered to put away and saw the flecks of his blood that speckled a few of the pages. He reached down slowly and began picking the books up, but as he lifted one, the fury burst from him. With a cry of pent-up rage, he grasped a handful of the pages and tore them out.

He shredded the book, and another, throwing the leather bindings across the room, a creature gone wild. He no longer cared. He felt his body shaking but was outside himself somehow; the pain ceased to matter. He had come to the end of what his pride and his spirit could endure; his revenge felt glorious.

He seized his father's telescope and used it to smash the glass case, bending the instrument in the process. His chest heaving, he looked wildly at his father's desk and stalked over to it, sweeping its contents onto the floor. He picked up the ink bottle and hurled it, splattering blue-black stains across his father's naval portrait from his youth. With the image of young Lord Truro irrevocably destroyed, the anger left him suddenly.

Billy stood staring in the moonlit room at the ruined painting, his father's hated face blacked out by the misshapen ink stain. A tide of pure terror rose within him as he returned slowly to his senses and looked around in belated disbelief at what he had done.

His father's study was destroyed. The business letters, ledger books, and accounting statements were strewn about the room, torn, crumpled, chaotic.

What have I done? He'll kill me now for certain. I have to get out of here ...

I have to get out of here. As the past and all its pain receded behind the gray veil of time, Blade found himself staring once more at the resplendent diamond necklace.

His hand closed around the jewel-encrusted chain, and he drew a jagged breath, overwhelmed by his sudden, anguished need to see her again – the beautiful giver of this unexpected gift. Had she truly seen something good in him? The mere question filled him with anguished vulnerability, and he, who had never needed anyone, found his very soul crying out for the soft touch of a girl he barely knew. A girl who had every reason to despise him. He cast about desperately for any excuse to see her again.

Of course, he thought suddenly. He had to give her back the necklace.

He did not know what he intended to do beyond giving

her back her diamonds, but at the very least, he had to make sure she was all right.

His hand trembled slightly as he reached over and crushed out the smoldering butt of his cheroot in the nearby ashtray. Lifting on the shoulder holster of his pistol over his head, he buckled on the belt that held his knife's sheath, then pulled on his black leather coat and glanced at the timepiece on the wall. Five o'clock.

Even a low thug like him knew there was only one place where the rich and fashionable of London could be found at this hour: Hyde Park.

Blade left his room and stalked down the corridor, ready to face whatever kind of trouble he might run into beyond the borders of his rookery stronghold. After all, the naive, polished debutante had had the courage to come into his dark, lawless world.

Now it was time for him to invade hers.

The next day had come and, with it, the inevitable family meeting. Last night when Lucien had brought her back to Knight House, everyone had already retired, so her doom had been saved for today. It was without question the most mortifying experience of her life.

'What were you *thinking*?'

'How could you, Jacinda?'

While the alarmed servants eavesdropped outside the library door, Jacinda sat on a hard wooden chair in the middle of the whirlwind, sullen and ashamed to the core, not knowing what to say for herself while her irate brothers blamed themselves, each other, her governess, the impetuous nature of womankind, their mother's blood in her veins, and most of all, Jacinda herself. Their wives, Bel and Alice, had angrily come to her defense, which had only resulted in numerous marital quarrels.

Jacinda was only glad that Damien and Miranda were still closeted at their Berkshire estate following the birth two months ago of their twin baby sons; otherwise she

93

would have had to contend with her most formidable brother, the army colonel, as well as Lucien and Robert.

'Robert, she shouldn't have to marry anyone she doesn't want to marry,' Bel was saying as diplomatically as possible. 'She should be allowed to choose for herself, as we did.'

Jacinda had hoped for moral support from the rakish Lord Alec, her favorite brother, the youngest of the five, and the closest to her in age and in temperament, but no one had seen him.

'All I want to do is protect the girl!' Robert nearly shouted. 'If she isn't married soon, she's going to end up headlong in a scandal. Is that what you want to see happen?'

'Please! Please, everyone – ' poor Lizzie kept saying, though no one listened to her, either. Poor Lizzie, Jacinda's best friend and companion, was guilt-stricken, trying to explain that it was all *her* fault somehow for not minding Jacinda better, while Miss Hood, her duenna, repeatedly announced her resignation.

'You may send the balance of what I am owed to this address,' Miss Hood was saying, thrusting a scrap of paper at Robert's graceful duchess. 'Never in all my days have I encountered such a naughty, headstrong girl—'

'Miss Hood, please,' Bel implored her. 'You cannot walk out until we have at least had a chance to interview other governesses—'

Lucien tried to moderate, but his diplomatic skills, so useful with foreign dignitaries, were useless on his own family. He tried in vain to calm the others, but could only fold his arms over his chest and scowl at Jacinda reproachfully. He kept his word, however, not revealing to the others that she had let Blade kiss her.

Why that rookery scoundrel had confessed, she did not know. He must have believed her idle threat of telling her brothers about their dalliance.

'For exactly how long, young lady, have you been planning this escape?' Robert demanded. A tall, black-haired man in his late thirties with strong features and penetrating brown eyes, the duke braced his hands on the polished surface of his large, baronial desk and leaned toward her with a thunderous stare. 'Or was there any plan to begin with? Was this merely one of your hen-witted whims?'

Jacinda lowered her chin, twisting her hands in her lap.

'Did it even occur to you that we would be frantic with worry?'

And on it went. Every time she tried to answer one of the questions they fired at her, she was never permitted a moment to speak. Such was the fate of being the youngest of a loud, boisterous family, and the only female of the brood. Then the bewildered nursery maid brought in little Morley, Robert's two-year-old son. The tiny heir to the dukedom was wailing loudly, upset by all the shouting. Bel took her screaming toddler from the nurse and left Alice to argue with the indignant governess.

Jacinda closed her eyes, her head pounding. And just when she was sure that the ordeal could not get any worse, Lord Griffith arrived to sort out the final details of their marriage settlement. When the amiable marquess learned that his prospective bride had tried to run away from home rather than take him as her husband, it was the first time Jacinda could remember ever seeing his agreeable face darken with anger.

Ian's eyebrows drew together as he turned to her with an almost lionlike affront coming into his regal posture. 'I see,' he said with a deepening look of insulted displeasure.

Jacinda wanted the earth to swallow her. Her cheeks reddening, she began stammering a stream of cringing apologies that were quickly drowned out as Lucien and Robert, both talking at once, tried to explain away their sister's perfidy. Then Alice and Bel rejoined the fray, coming to her defense. Meanwhile, Ian looked askance at her suspiciously, as though he had half expected something like this all along. The baby began howling again, and Jacinda's head started pounding with all the yelling.

95

Make them listen, girl, Blade had said. *Stand up for yourself.* She was failing – she could feel the last vestiges of her freedom slipping away. Even the cool-headed Lucien was getting angry now. She saw she would be kept under guard for the rest of her life if she didn't do something fast.

Unable to take another second of it, she shot to her feet. '*Stop it!*' she cried, her face flushed with anger. 'Please!'

They all fell silent, taken aback by her outburst. Even the baby subsided into small, weary snuffles, worn out with crying.

Trembling, she looked around at her beloved, maddening family. 'Please don't fight anymore because of me. I know you're all just trying to protect me, but I can't bear it. I realize now that I was wrong a-and stupid and I'm sorry for all the trouble I've caused.'

Her governess let out a prim huff.

Jacinda lowered her chin but glanced at her with a chastened look. 'Miss Hood, please do not resign. I apologize for what I've done and I will try to be better in the future.' Tears of remorse and humiliation rushed into her eyes, but she did not spare herself, turning next to the handsome marquess. 'Lord Griffith, you deserve an explanation, as well as an apology. You must not think I don't adore you. You are the best of men – you are honorable and kind and good. It's just that I – I cannot marry you when you are still in love with Catherine—'

'Jacinda!' Robert exclaimed, aghast at her mention of the man's dead wife.

'It's all right. Let her talk,' Ian murmured, holding up his hand.

Jacinda swallowed hard. 'I will say it now so all of you will understand, and if you think ill of me for it, at least I will have said the truth plainly. If I were to marry you, Ian, knowing you did not really love me, not that way, I fear – oh, forgive me for what I am about to say, but so loyal a friend deserves the truth. I know myself just well enough not to trust myself completely. You would be distant, I'd

96

feel neglected, and I would be weak. I am my mother's daughter, after all. That is why I must decline your generous offer. You were so hurt by Catherine's death. Not for the world would I add to your pain,' she finished.

The room was perfectly silent after her shocking revelation.

Standing there feeling naked and exposed, she waited desperately for someone to react.

'She's right, Robert.' Staring at the floor, Ian lifted his head and looked at the duke. 'I care for Lady Jacinda like a sister, and if she believes the only way she can rise above her mother's example is by marrying for love, then you had better let her wait until she finds it.'

'Ah, damnation,' Robert muttered, dropping into his leather chair with a sigh of defeat.

Jacinda closed her eyes and lowered her head in silent relief, wondering if she would regret this one day, all the same, for Ian really was a kind, wise man and would have taken very good care of her.

Robert asked to speak privately to Ian, then, and ordered everyone else out of the library. Even Jacinda was dismissed for the time being. 'We will finish this later,' the duke grumbled sternly.

The dire look in his dark eyes promised her that whether Ian was angry or not, there would be consequences to pay for her reckless actions of the previous night.

She could not really blame Robert, who was surely at his wits' end with her. She walked out into the marble corridor in a state of misery. When she noticed the caring but reproachful frowns from her sisters-in-law, she murmured more useless apologies, then fled. Hurrying off down the marble corridor, she even brushed off Lizzie's attempt to express her solidarity.

'Jas! Where are you going?'

When she looked back, her friend had rushed out into the hallway. Lizzie was a fair-complected young woman of twenty, with thoughtful, grayish blue eyes and smooth, light brown hair in a loose topknot. 'Is there anything I can do?'

'Please – I just need to be alone right now. Tell Robert I've gone for a ride in Hyde Park, would you? I'll be back soon. Tell him not to worry,' she added, unable to keep the note of bitter chagrin from her voice. 'I'll take a groom with me to watch my every move.'

Not waiting for an answer, she rushed to her luxurious apartments on the fourth floor and ordered the servants to saddle up her white gelding while she changed into her riding habit.

Only when she was cantering her horse swiftly over the rolling green of the park did she feel as though she could breathe again. She had this remote region of Hyde Park nearly to herself, though the park would soon be crowded with the fashionable hour drawing near. The only person she saw at present whom she knew was something of an idol to her: Lady Campion, a fast, glamorous, ultrafashionable *femme de trente ans* cut after Mama's own cloth.

Eva Campion's family had forced her at Jacinda's age to marry 'an old wigsby,' as Blade had put it, but her decrepit husband had died a few years later, making Lady Campion a widow by her early twenties. The woman had done whatever she liked, with whomever she liked with impunity ever since. She had done her duty, and now she was free; she had played the game by Society's rules and had won.

When Jacinda glimpsed her near the Ring, the gorgeous baroness was being driven in a gleaming yellow phaeton by a handsome, mustachioed officer of the Dragoons.

Jacinda sighed with vague envy, then put Lady Campion and her newest lover out of her mind, urging her leggy Thoroughbred on even faster over the turf. The groom in Hawkscliffe livery rode after her, hard-pressed to keep up on his hack. She let her cares drift off behind her like the gauzy bright pink scarf tied around the crown of her riding hat. It rippled gracefully behind her in the breeze, and the long cloth skirts of her riding habit billowed along her gelding's flank as she rode expertly in the sidesaddle. And yet, circling the Ring, well within the confines of the park, she could not help but feel like one of the wild jungle animals in the dismal menagerie in Exeter Street, ceaselessly padding along the perimeter of their cement-and-metal cages, looking for some way out.

As Hyde Park began filling up with the Quality, she came across a group of her male friends and admirers; the fastidious leading dandy, Acer Loring; his boon companion, George Winthrop; and an assortment of other fashionable young fribbles astride their prime bits of blood. With their droll sarcasm, high spirits, and practical jokes, Acer and his set took it upon themselves to flatter and tease Jacinda back into her usual good humor.

In no hurry to return to Knight House to learn her sentence, she allowed them to coax her into racing down Rotten Row. George Winthrop sulked because she beat him in spite of the disadvantage of her sidesaddle. Riled up from the race, her high-stepping gelding danced fretfully as the group of young men gathered around her on the green, well out of the way of the park's elegant traffic on the enclosed lane. Acer, winner of the race, reined in his splendid chestnut hunter beside her. A tall, handsome, brown-haired young man, he wore an exquisitely cut bottle-green coat and fawn breeches, with black riding boots polished to a dazzling sheen.

'Don't look now, my lady,' he drawled, smirking as he cast a supercilious glance toward the railing, where spectators often came to gawk at the rich and famous, 'but I believe one of those dull fashion journalists from *La Belle Assemblée* is making notes on your riding costume.'

'Perhaps I should take a promenade past her so she can better admire me,' she said wryly.

'I don't advise it, unless you want every shopkeeper's wife in London wearing it next week.'

'Where is she?'

'Yoo-hoo! Lady Jacinda! Oh, Your Ladyship! Over here!'

Acer made a graceful, ironic gesture in the direction from which the high-pitched voice had come. Then he frowned. 'Good God, what is that barbaric thing beside her?'

Jacinda turned around and saw a woman in a large straw bonnet waving frantically at her, but the amused smile on her lips died as her gaze homed in on the 'barbaric thing.'

'Winthrop, look at that long-haired fellow,' Acer said in amusement. 'I say, is he coming this way?'

'I hope not,' George quipped. 'He looks like a deuced murderer.'

They laughed, but Jacinda stared, frozen, her heart in her throat. *God's teeth, what is he doing here?*

Chapter Six

Jacinda couldn't take her eyes off him. Bracing one hand on the railing, Billy Blade vaulted lightly over it and into the mad traffic of the lane, his rookery-honed reflexes barely fast enough to save his neck as he crossed Rotten Row on foot, amid the dust cloud of zooming chariots and thundering hoofs. Several people cursed at him, but he ignored them, advancing with an alarming air of determination.

'Ten quid says he gets crushed before he gets to the other side,' Acer said.

'Done,' George answered.

Jacinda watched in mingled astonishment and dread until Blade had safely reached the other side of the lane. He ducked under the railing and walked out onto the peaceful green, brushing the dust off his jacket.

'Well, hell, there goes our wager.'

'Pay up, Loring. By Jove, I daresay the ruffian is coming straight for us.'

'I – I'm sure you're wrong,' she interjected, suddenly realizing that disaster was coming if she didn't retreat at once.

'Don't be alarmed, my lady. We will protect you,' Acer said drolly.

Wide-eyed, Jacinda looked from the leading dandy to the leader of the gang. It was not her protection but Blade's that concerned her. Her hot-tempered, aristocratic male friends would all but spit on him if he dared approach her, and the violent row that was bound to result would end not only in bloodshed, she realized, but would also summon one of the policemen who patrolled the park. Blade was outnumbered and outclassed. He could not possibly win. She had to think of something or he would end up arrested, and with his long list of crimes, hanged. Her heart pounding, she racked her brain for some way either to head him off or distract her suitors.

'What the deuce does he want?'

'No doubt he'll either beg for a shilling or murder us.'

'What an interesting ensemble,' Acer observed, his haughty gaze raking over Blade's dusty black jacket; tough, tan-colored drill trousers; and scuffed boots. In place of a cravat, he wore the faded blue neckerchief, loosely knotted. 'I wonder if he'll tell us who his tailor is. Captain Blue Beard, perhaps?'

'Oh, be quiet, Acer,' Jacinda retorted sharply. 'He is obviously poor. Let's go. I'm bored.'

'Where do you want to go?'

'I hardly care! This day is monstrous dull.'

The dandies agreed but loitered, and still Blade advanced, as though he thoroughly believed himself the equal of any of the highborn young men surrounding her. He was almost upon them, his fearless stare fixed on her. In seconds, he might call out her name, and that would mean catastrophe for them both.

What was the blackguard thinking? Surely he ought to know better! He was a fool to try to talk to her here. Then she saw something sparkly wrapped around his hand and realized it was her diamond necklace. So, he had discovered her gift, she thought, realizing that nothing was going to deter him. She looked at him, at a loss. He left her no choice. She stared through him coolly, as though she did not know him – indeed, as if he did not exist – then looked away, dealing him a rapierlike snub.

102

The cut direct stopped him in his tracks.

Her chest constricted at the hurt surprise she saw in his face, but she refused to feel guilt. It was the least he deserved for the way he had trampled her will last night; but from the corner of her eye, she saw the astonishing speed with which his expression of wounded bewilderment turned into cold disgust.

A little piece of her heart died in that moment. She could not bear to look at him. Though he came no closer, she saw it was already too late. Acer was staring at him through narrowed eyes, as though Blade were the first fox of the hunting season.

'That scoundrel is armed,' he murmured slowly. 'And I don't like the way he is looking at you.'

'Come, Acer. I'm bored,' she repeated nervously, but Acer ignored her.

Without warning, he clucked to his horse, starting toward Blade.

'Acer!' she said furiously.

'What is it?' He turned to her in the saddle.

'You are supposed to be paying attention to me! Am I not your best asset for making Daphne jealous?'

He scowled.

Her forced, merry laugh rang somewhat hollowly. 'Race you to the Long Water!' Switching her gelding's flank lightly with her riding crop, she set off at a blazing gallop.

Blade stared after her with a firestorm of humiliated fury erupting from his heart, searing its way through every vein and artery. His pulse pounded out a primal drumbeat as he watched her riding her fine white horse off across the park with expert grace, a ruthlessly beautiful huntress in dove-gray skirts, the bright pink scarf tied around her hat blowing in the wind. The dandyish fops with whom she was holding court followed her with high-spirited cheer. All but one.

His gaze locked with that of the arrogant man in the bottle-green coat.

103

Blade wanted to kill him.

After having been obsessed with the girl for the past sixteen hours, he had been taken aback to find her surrounded by suitors, but had managed to keep his temper in check. He had seen her warning look clearly signaling him back, but still he had approached. He had not known if she had been trying to discourage him because she was ashamed of him or if she had been merely trying to protect him from what she feared would be a thrashing at the hands of her pretty gentlemen. As either possibility was intolerable to his pride, he had ignored her warning. After all, he had real business with her, in the matter of returning her diamonds. But now she had made her feelings crystal clear so that even a clod like him could understand.

Oh, he had gotten the message, all right. The lady was done with him. Her icy slight had brought him back rudely to his senses, a cutting reminder of the impossibility of any further association between them. God, what a fool he was. She had been nothing but a rich girl looking for a thrill. He felt used. And to think, he had held himself back like a tender lovelorn swain when he ought to have taken his pleasure of her – and her brothers be damned. He wasn't afraid of them.

He wanted to hit something very, very hard.

Perhaps the pampered, polished dandy somehow sensed the murderous anger behind his stare, for he reeled his chestnut horse around after taking only a few steps forward. Sending Blade one last scornful glance over his shoulder, the dandy rode off after Jacinda. Blade was left wondering if he had created a monster in the girl. Now that he had taught her how pleasurable such dalliance could be, would she sample those other men, too? Well, she had warned him that her mother the duchess had been a thoroughgoing hussy. A man would have to be mad to love such a woman.

'You, there!'

Blade looked over with a dark, dangerous glance and saw

a policeman watching him from some distance away.

'Move along!'

Belatedly remembering self-preservation and the numerous bounties on his head, he pivoted and walked away with a black scowl on his face.

Within a few minutes, he had hailed a dilapidated hackney and was speeding back to St. Giles. Yet another place where he did not belong, he thought bitterly. He rested his elbow on the window ledge, bringing his knuckles up against the grim line of his mouth. He closed his eyes briefly in roiling anger and persistent shame of himself, of the low, crude ruffian he had become. Had chosen to become.

Forget her.

It would be easy. To hell with her and her sweet, wanton body, her fine friends and her brilliant marriage. He didn't need her. He didn't need anyone.

If things were different, he could've had her. He could've made her crawl for him, but he had chosen his path fifteen years ago. There was no going back. He refused to – not for her, not for anyone.

His old man did not deserve to get off the hook that easily. With his elder brother Percy dead now and no other heirs to be found, the extinction of his line was, Blade thought, a most fitting punishment for Truro the Terrible.

Aye, like the poet said, better to reign in hell than serve in heaven. He was Blade of the Fire Hawks now. In for a penny, in for a pound. As the shabby, creaking coach plodded back into the shadowed, winding streets of the rookery, he thought of the humble folk who had become his new family. They depended on him and counted on his protection in this rough place.

He looked out the window at the ragged children playing in the gutter as the hackney rolled by, and with a silent vow, rededicated himself with twice his former effort to his life of crime.

*

Having barely staved off disaster in the park, Jacinda rode through the tall, black, wrought-iron gates of Knight House, still shaken by the hurt, angry look in Blade's eyes when she had cut him. *But he gave me no choice!* She dismounted lightly on legs that shook beneath her and left her horse with the groom.

Striding up to the white porticoed entrance of Knight House, she braced herself to hear her sentence from Robert, but now the more pressing matter in her heart was to confide in Lizzie about Blade. With uncanny timing, the butler, Mr. Walsh, opened the door for her as she swept into the house.

'Good day, Mr. Walsh. Is Lord Griffith still here?' she whispered.

'No, my lady,' he answered discreetly.

'Thank goodness. Where is Miss Carlisle, please?'

'In the drawing room.'

'Thank you.' She looped the long train of her riding skirts over her forearm and hurried up the curved marble staircase, drawing off her gloves.

Dear, wise, motherly Lizzie was a tower of strength and always had an ear to listen, a shoulder to cry on. Lizzie would know what was to be done.

Having been raised together from the nursery, she was Jacinda's most trusted friend and had long been like a second sister to the family. Lizzie's father had served as Robert's trusted estate manager at Hawkscliffe Hall, just as his father had, and his father before him. Mr. Carlisle had died, however, when Lizzie was only four years old, whereupon the small orphan had become the ward of the duke. It was decided that she should become the companion to the then three-year-old Lady Jacinda, and especially welcome playmate for the lonely little aristocratic girl, also an orphan, who had only her caretakers and, of course, her much older brothers to amuse her. As Jacinda neared the top of the staircase, she heard a commotion from upstairs.

At first she thought that the argument over her 'stunt' of

the previous evening was still going on. Amazed and angered at the thought, she ran the rest of the way up the curving marble staircase, only to find, to her relief, that her misadventure was not the cause of the ruckus.

It was Alec.

Lord Alec Knight, the youngest of the formidable five, was a golden-haired Adonis and a rake who could charm his way out of anything, especially when it came to the fair sex. Women adored Alec. They couldn't seem to help themselves. She had seen little girls of five ask him to marry them when they grew up and titled dowagers of advanced age discreetly pinch his bottom when he walked past the whist table.

Everyone, especially Lizzie, was fussing around him in distress as he sat, princelike, in the middle of the room with his stockinged foot propped up on a footstool. One of the better local surgeons was poking cautiously at the limb.

'Ow! Damn your eyes, you impudent fellow,' Alec said haughtily. 'I told you, the dammed thing hurts!'

'Alec, darling! What's happened? Are you all right?' With a worried frown, Jacinda rushed to his side. She was relieved to note that marital harmony had been restored among the two pairs of spouses; little Morley sat smiling in his nurse's arms; and Miss Hood was knitting in a chair by the wall, looking sour as ever, but mollified.

'Hullo, Jas.' Alec gave her a sheepish smile, then winced with pain and scowled at the surgeon. 'My good man, I am warning you . . .'

The surgeon looked up at Robert, who was standing nearby, his arms folded wearily over his chest. 'Your Grace, the ankle is broken.'

'That's what I've been trying to tell you,' Alec retorted.

'Fix it,' Robert ordered.

'Yes, Your Grace.'

'Oh, Alec, you chuckle-head! What have you done to yourself?' Jacinda leaned down and gave him a doting kiss on his cheek. 'What mischief have you been up to?'

107

'Nothing as bad as yours, I warrant,' he muttered, sliding her a knowing look askance. 'Another stupid wager, I'm afraid.' He shifted uncomfortably in his armchair.

'You'll have to tell me all about it—'

'I think not,' Robert interrupted. 'Don't go giving her any ideas. Mr. Walsh, see to it that Lord Alec has everything that he needs from his rooms at the Albany, please.'

'Very good, Your Grace,' the butler said with a bow.

'Capital idea!' Alec chased off his grimace of pain, brightening at the suggestion of a recuperation at home where the loyal family servants and his womenfolk could look after him. No doubt their care would be much more solicitous than that of the busy staff at the fashionable hotel in nearby Curzon Street where he had his bachelor lodgings.

Lizzie was hovering nearby looking distraught over his injury when Alec captured her hand, pressed a kiss to it in his carelessly flirtatious way, then held it to his heart. 'Bits, be an angel and fetch me some wine?'

'Of course, dearest,' Lizzie murmured, smiling fondly at him when he called her by his favorite pet name for her.

'Oh, Alec, ask one of the servants to do it,' Jacinda protested.

'It tastes better when Bitsy gets it,' he said, flashing Lizzie one of his dazzling grins.

'It's all right – I don't mind – it'll only take a moment.' Blushing profusely, Lizzie extricated her hand from Alec's light but possessive hold and hurried off to do his bidding.

Jacinda folded her arms across her chest, suddenly disliking the idea of Alec and Lizzie under the same roof together, but she said nothing. Lizzie had been in love with the scoundrel since she was nine years old, though she claimed to have long since outgrown her infatuation. Jacinda hoped so, for as much as she loved her rakish brother, everyone knew that Alec collected ladies' hearts the way Lord Petersham collected snuffboxes. As much as she would have loved for Lizzie to become her true sister through marriage, she knew that Alec would only smash Lizzie's gentle heart into smithereens.

'Jacinda, I would speak with you privately,' Robert ordered.

'Of course,' she murmured, then followed him out into the hallway.

He closed the door and turned to her. 'Bel has persuaded Miss Hood not to resign – though I am tempted to dismiss her for failing to detect and prevent your foolish attempt to leave us. In the meanwhile, I have settled matters with Lord Griffith. The wedding's off.'

'Is he angry at me?'

'No.'

'Are you, Robert?'

He just sighed and shook his head at her.

'I'm sorry. I truly am.'

'I know.' He gathered her into a fatherly embrace. 'It's just that you worry me so, little one. The way you enslave your admirers ... How can I help but fear disaster? It's like the time I came out into the hallway and saw Morley teetering atop the staircase. I never moved so fast in my life—'

'I am not a two-year-old.'

'Forgive me if a part of me wishes you still were. It was a good deal easier keeping track of you then. In any case, to answer your question, no, I'm not angry at you, but I am terribly concerned.' He grasped her shoulders gently and held her at arm's length, staring soberly into her eyes. 'I am sending you down to the country—'

'Robert, but the Season's just started!'

'Ah, ah, you've brought it on yourself,' he chided. 'You will spend the rest of April at Hawkscliffe Hall, where you will use the peace and quiet of the country to contemplate the error of your ways.'

She groaned.

'You may return to Town for the Devonshire ball on the night of Princess Charlotte's wedding. I know how much

109

you have been looking forward to that.'

'May I bring Lizzie with me, at least?' she asked in despondency as he shepherded her back into the drawing room.

'Yes, if she wishes to go.'

But when Jacinda asked her friend a few minutes later to accompany her to the country, Alec interrupted before Lizzie could reply. 'Oh, no, you don't. I need Lizzie here to take care of me.'

Jacinda scoffed at him, taking her friend by the arm. 'Alec, I am sure Lizzie has got better things to do than play nursemaid to you.'

'No, she hasn't,' Alec said jauntily. 'Do you, Bits?'

Lizzie turned to her in dismay, as though the suggestion of coddling Alec for the next few weeks sounded perfectly acceptable to her.

'Lizzie!' Jacinda cried, seeing her friend's hesitation. 'I shall perish of boredom up there by myself!'

'Nonsense. You'll have Miss Hood,' Alec said slyly. 'It is a punishment, after all, Jas, not a holiday. Besides, don't you think you're being a wee bit selfish? Why must Bits miss out on the Season when it was your own stupid stunt?'

'Lizzie doesn't care about the Season and as for my 'stupid stunt,' at least I didn't break my ankle on some addlepated wager. You just want her here to fetch and carry for you, as if she were a spaniel—'

'You little diva! You only want her to follow you around like your own personal audience—'

'Please, stop it, both of you!' Lizzie exclaimed, looking from one to the other. 'I do not wish to go to the country right now. I really should stay here to help Alec—'

'You're choosing him over me?' Jacinda demanded.

'Don't you remember how dreadful my hay fever is in spring? The last thing I want is to go traipsing through the fields after you and your hunting dogs, sneezing my head off.'

'You tell her, lass!' Alec said, gloating in his chair behind her.

'Besides,' Lizzie added, a rare tinge of anger pinking her cheeks. 'He is right. It is your punishment. I don't see why I should go just to make it pleasant for you. After all, you didn't trouble yourself about leaving *me* behind when you set out for France. Besides, Lord Alec needs me.' She laid her hand on his shoulder. 'Her Grace and the servants cannot look after him all by themselves.'

Alec's hand closed gently atop Lizzie's.

Jacinda stared at them, taken aback, then murmured, 'As you wish.' But she gazed into her friend's eyes, communicating a silent warning to be careful with him.

'Come, my lady,' Miss Hood said, rising from her chair. She draped her knitting basket primly over her forearm and crossed the room to her. 'We must pack your things for the country. We'll leave bright and early.'

Sure enough, the traveling chariot and the entourage of servants accompanying her to Hawkscliffe Hall were ready to go by seven the next morning. Lizzie still did not change her mind, but was all the more firmly determined, it seemed, to seize this one chance to spend time alone with her dream man. Jacinda bid her family good-bye.

The journey from London to the Cumberland wilds around Hawkscliffe Hall, her family's ancestral castle, was a four-day affair, but this time, it felt twice as long, confined inside the close quarters of the traveling chariot with her affronted governess. Miss Hood was so terse, sharp, and out of charity with her errant charge that Jacinda's maid, Ann, finally took to riding on the roof seat for long spells to escape the tension inside the coach. As their trek progressed through the second day, however, Jacinda slowly became aware of just how much meeting Billy Blade had changed her.

She had made the journey up the Great North Road from London countless times, but only on this occasion was she truly struck by the suffering and hardship she saw throughout the realm. It was just as he had described it. They passed the lifeless, half-burned hulls of cotton mills, still

111

and silent; heroes of Waterloo begging, crippled and drunken, in the towns. When they stopped for the night in York, she heard a fiery peasant rabble-rouser shouting to a crowd in the square about the destruction of their livelihoods by the new machines that were putting people out of work. She wanted to stay to listen to him, but Miss Hood fetched her briskly into the hotel.

And during the nights, she discovered that it was not only a greater awareness of the world that Blade had awakened in her. She lay in her hotel bed burning with the unwanted memory of his mouth on hers, his hands on her breasts. When she closed her eyes, she could still see in vivid detail the fascinating tattoos on his skin, and in her dreams, she traced each one with her lips and fingertips.

Oh, she must try harder to ponder the error of her ways! she thought, struggling against her desire for that bold, ill-mannered rogue. For away from Robert's scrutiny, she could admit that she truly did not know what would become of her. Blade had proved to her beyond any doubt that her mother's disastrous wantonness flowed in her veins. She was a very frail vessel, indeed, eager for a man's caresses.

Or maybe it was only Billy Blade who had that effect on her. Somehow, that possibility was worse.

As another night passed in empty wanting, she thought in despair of the difference in their stations and the impossibility of ever possessing him. Even if he were a prince, and eligible, she argued with herself, he had already proved himself every ounce as domineering as her brothers, and that was exactly what she did not want. The thought helped to bring her back to her senses, along with remembering the coldness that had come into his eyes when she had dealt him the cut direct at Hyde Park.

Forget him.

Whatever thread of connection had existed between them that night in his room, in his bed, she had severed it that day in the park, and that, she supposed, was for the best.

*

A week later, Blade was finishing a cheroot and sharpening his knife for his night's work. His decision that day coming back from Hyde Park had spawned a crime spree throughout the luxurious neighborhoods of Mayfair and St. James's. Hearing someone coming down the hallway, he glanced warily at his closed chamber door, then quickly hid Jacinda's diamond necklace in his boot.

He had not yet pawned her jewels, nor did he dare hide them around here, sharing the house, as he did, with a large band of accomplished thieves. Though he told himself he might keep them just to shove them down her lovely throat someday, the sorry truth was he did not want to give them up because they were his one remaining connection to Lady Jacinda. Who could say? Maybe they would bring him good luck.

A knock sounded just then.

'Aye,' he called.

The door opened, and Nate popped his curly head in. 'Almost time to go.'

'Jimmy got the carriage ready?'

'Nearly.' Nate sauntered in and closed the door behind him. He rubbed his hands together as though to warm them, then cracked his knuckles.

His cheroot dangling from the corner of his lips, Blade slowly finished sharpening his favorite knife.

'Seen little Eddie today?' Nate asked, leaning in the window.

'No.'

'Nobody seems to have seen him around the past few days.'

'Maybe he fell down a sewer,' Blade drawled.

'You're not worried?'

'Little blighter's got nine lives. He's probably still cross at me for making him give back all the gold he stole from that rich girl. He'll be back.'

Nate shrugged and studied the wall for a moment.

'What's the matter?' Blade asked him.

Nate turned to him with a frown. He scratched his head. 'I'm thinkin' we should call off the job tonight.'

'What? Why?'

'I don't know. Somethin' don't feel right.'

Blade scoffed.

'I mean it, man,' Nate said. 'We've hit six houses in four nights. We're gettin' a bit reckless, don't you think? Maybe it's too much.'

'Aw, don't whine at me, Nate. If you need a night off, get Andrews or Mikey to stand in for you.'

'It's not that! I can pull my weight as well as any man.'

'What, then?'

'I don't know.' Nate shook his head. 'There's somethin' in the air. Can't put my finger on it.'

Blade snorted and climbed to his feet, flicking his spent cheroot into the fireplace.

'Doesn't it strike you that O'Dell has been too bloody quiet lately?' Nate pursued.

'No wonder. He can't see. I damned near knocked his eye out last time we met.' Blade efficiently loaded his pistols, then pulled on his black leather coat and gave Nate a clap on the shoulder, steering him affectionately toward the door by the scruff of his neck. 'Go tell the ladies it's time for the dance.'

'You're a proper bastard,' he muttered, pausing as he went out, 'but they'd follow you through hell, and so would I.'

Blade's raffish smile sobered. 'I know it. Thanks, Nate.'

'Just bring us back alive, eh?'

'I always do,' he retorted as Nate went off down the hallway to fetch the others.

A short while later on a cobbled side street off of stately Portman Square, five black-clad figures slid out of the passing hackney and glided through the darkness at a stealthy run, leaping up to scale the garden wall, dropping down lightly upon the spongy grass of the garden.

With practiced efficiency they advanced toward the back

114

entrance of the vast, empty, opulent town house, one pair darting ahead, then positioning themselves to provide cover for the next two, who passed them as they glided in even closer. Reaching the flagged veranda, they bounded silently over the stone balustrade. The weather, foggy and wet, made for sloppy work, but the sound of the rain muffled any slight noise they made.

Blade and Nate went for the door, Nate giving him cover as Blade drew the 'dabbs' from inside his coat, crouched down, and began the delicate business of picking the door's three locks, his hands steady. Meanwhile, Sarge and Flaherty crept to the windows with Andrews, the most promising of the younger lads. The three peered inside. Seeing no one within, they signaled Blade, who had just sprung the last lock.

His heart pounded with the thrill of the game, but his breathing was even and relaxed behind the blue neckerchief tied around the lower half of his face. He pushed up to his feet, laid one hand on the door, and gently turned the knob. The others waited, poised to enter, as he inched the door open. He listened for sounds of life within but heard nothing.

His information, as always, was accurate. Young Miss Daphne Taylor had been staying with her cousins until now, he had learned. Her parents, the Viscount and Viscountess Erhard, had been delayed by their younger children, who had been taken with the flu, but they were due to arrive in Town in a fortnight. The servants were to begin preparing the house for their return this week, but for now the grand house stood empty.

He threw a taut nod to his men and slipped inside. Hardened professionals all, they knew their exit route in advance; each man knew the precise moment that Jimmy would drive past the other way in the hackney in which he had dropped them off. They even had a fair idea of the layout of the house, having done this countless times before. They expected to be in and out in twenty minutes.

115

There was no need to take undue chances by lingering. Once over the threshold, they stole through the house by the same sly method.

Blade had told them in advance that his goal was the vault, but as they searched the house, the other four made a thorough sweep of each room they came to, taking whatever of value they could find, tossing it into their sacks – silver candlesticks, fancy snuffboxes, objects d'art from the mantelpieces. Single-minded in his focus on the vault, Blade waited for them in the hallway. Watching them, however, he found himself eyeing the holland-draped furniture that sat, ghostlike, in each darkened room.

God, he thought, *it's as still as a tomb.*

The hairs on his nape prickled slightly in man's most ancient warning signal of danger, but he could see no source of threat. He glanced behind him and ahead down the hallway, suddenly beginning to dislike this crack intensely. He couldn't say what was wrong. But it was too easy.

'Come on, you buggers,' he muttered.

They followed him upstairs. Blade moved quietly out of habit, but the others were growing overconfident, unmindful of the steps that creaked beneath their weight as they mounted to the second floor, then the third. They moved in a tight V down the hallway, searching for the master's chamber, where the vault would most likely be situated.

They found His Lordship's quarters at last in the west corner of the main block. The door to the suite opened to a large sitting room. Moonlight glimmered along the sleek lines of the Sheraton highboy and illuminated a Chinese vase displayed on a pedestal near the window. Sarge and Flaherty immediately began searching the sitting room while Andrews stole ahead of Blade into the adjoining bedchamber. Following him, Blade paused in the doorway, gazing at the enormous four-poster draped in gold cloth. The kingly mattress was set so high off the ground that one had to climb the four polished wooden steps to lie on it. He

116

shook his head in disgust, thinking of the children in his neighborhood who had to sleep on the pavement near open sewers. At least tonight's work would keep a few more of them alive a while longer, he thought just as Nate called to him in a taut whisper from the sitting room.

'Found it!'

Blade was stalking through the sitting room and crouching down by their side in a moment. Before him sat the safe, poorly concealed within His Lordship's writing table. The safe was a no-nonsense affair, a simple, drab iron box about three feet square. Blade ran his hand over the key-lock with a wily smile. All thoughts of his earlier uneasiness forgotten in the thrill of imminent victory, he finessed the lock with the dabbs, then held his breath with anticipation as he pulled the small door open. He reached one hand inside the smaller inner shell and felt cool metal.

There was a small chain. Something round. 'What the hell?'

'Is it empty?' Nate whispered urgently.

'No, there's something ...' His hand closed around the strange object, catching something else, too, something rough, like ... rope.

Andrews was at the window looking out for Jimmy and the carriage, but Sarge and Flaherty came over to him and Nate and bent over his shoulder, waiting eagerly to see their take. Blade pulled it out, and his eyes flared with horror.

'What the devil?' Nate said.

'Run,' Blade breathed, but all four men could only stand frozen for that split second, staring at what had been placed for them there in the safe – a pair of manacles and a length of rope tied in a noose.

'*Run!*' Blade roared, leaping to his feet and whirling around to face the enemy even as the holland-draped furniture came to life.

Twenty Bow Street thief-takers threw off their shapeless cloth coverings and rushed them.

117

Chapter Seven

The sweep of the sun-splashed fells and folded valleys wrapped around her in an endless vista, with the blue foothills of the Pennines in the distance. A steady wind, invigorating but not cold, drove the high-piled clouds across the cerulean sky. It riffled through the gorse and tufted heather on the moors and molded the twilled woollen skirts of her dun-colored sporting costume around her legs as Jacinda waited, her fowling musket braced against her shoulder, while her Brittany spaniel flushed the pair of red grouse feeding on the tender shoots of new heather.

The plump, mottle-plumed birds flapped into the air; the silky-coated spaniel immediately dropped to its haunches, crouched and waiting for the order to retrieve. Jacinda's gaze narrowed as she trailed the swift, veering game birds with her gun. The first birds into the air were the older, stronger ones; since grouse turned sterile after one breeding season, these could be conservatively culled without damage to the breeding population.

Boom!

Her shot released a puff of drifting smoke and echoed down the valley. The larger bird fell. She nodded to the gamekeeper, who gave the order to the dog. The expert spaniel moved at a springy glide through the shrubs and grasses, the sun glancing off its long, liver-and-white coat. The younger dog, however, a flashy tri-colored pointer, was still an apprentice at her trade and dodged about with exuberant energy, barking with excitement over the kill and altogether irritating her more experienced bracemate, who took its duties as seriously as any upper servant. The spaniel carried the grouse back gently in its jaws to the gamekeeper. Mr. McCullough accepted the grouse with a chuckle and placed it in the bag, then glanced up at her, squinting against the sun. 'A fine bird, my lady.'

Jacinda smiled and glanced into the leather pouch at her quarry, nodding in answer to the gamekeeper's compliment, then handed off her musket to his boy, whose duty it was to reload for her.

Except for the loneliness of being without Lizzie, she had always found it very easy to settle back into the leisurely rhythm of country life.

''Twas an admirable shot, my lady,' said a prim voice behind her.

With one leather-gauntleted hand, she shaded her eyes from the sun and turned to her governess. 'Why, thank you, Miss Hood.'

The woman was only now just beginning to warm up to her again.

The hunting party continued on, walking upwind across the open moor in a broad line. The dogs scouted the terrain ahead of the gun, their keen noses sniffing out the quarry amid the aromatic wild thyme and yellow cinquefoil. Behind Jacinda, servants in the dark green Hawkscliffe livery rounded out her entourage, three footmen following with their picnic hampers and a large parasol, and a pair of grooms leading the ladies' saddle horses. As they neared the boundary of her family's property where the low stone wall followed the sinuous curve of the ridge, the gamekeeper nodded to her. The Brittany had pointed another grouse.

Jacinda accepted her reloaded musket from the boy and

cocked it, then lifted the gun to her shoulder, awaiting the bird's rush from cover. The spaniel pounced, scaring the pair of startled fowl skyward. She trailed the larger bird on its crazy, zigzag path.

Boom!

She missed. The bird swooped in a miraculous escape toward the trees. It flew over the wall; then Jacinda's eyes widened as the daft pointer tore off after it through the field, ears flapping. Before anyone could stop it, the dog had scrambled over the stile and disappeared into the trees, trailing a barking echo.

'Blast,' she murmured.

'Get the dog, boy,' McCullough ordered the lad, who bobbed a nod and ran after the animal.

'Is that Lord Griffith's estate?' Miss Hood asked with a speculative lift of her eyebrows.

'No, ma'am,' McCullough answered. 'Lord Griffith's holdings border His Grace's lands to the northwest. We are looking southeast. Those woods are part of the park of Warflete Manor, the home of the earl of Drummond.'

'The politician, Lord Drummond?' Miss Hood asked in surprise.

Jacinda nodded. 'The same. I imagine he's quite elderly now. I haven't seen him since I was a wee thing.' She petted her impeccably behaved spaniel's head. 'Robert says he is a curmudgeon. Of course, Robert says all Tory politicians are curmudgeons. I believe Lord Drummond is a special adviser to the Home Office.'

McCullough grinned. 'Did you hear the old gent has built a golfing course on his estate?'

'Has he?' Jacinda asked with interest. The Scottish sport was becoming all the rage.

Suddenly, crazed barking erupted from inside the distant woods. Jacinda drew in her breath as a human voice joined in, shouting furiously at the dog. She heard the boy's high-pitched voice, as well. She and McCullough exchanged a startled look.

120

'I'll see to this,' McCullough declared, already running toward Lord Drummond's property.

'Wait for me!'

'My lady!' Miss Hood cried in exasperation.

'What if Lord Drummond thinks the boy was poaching?' she called back, then ran after the gamekeeper, still carrying her gun. At the wall, she hitched up her skirts about her ankles and nimbly scaled the wooden stile. She jumped down and raced on, a minute or so behind Mr. McCullough.

At the edge of the woods, she found a deer path between two tall, brushy stands of yellow-flowered Scotch broom and plunged into the dappled woods. She followed the sound of the pointer's eager barking over the soft soughing of the wind through the trees. Hornbeam, ash, and oak swayed gently, with an occasional black mulberry posted here and there, ancient and imposing. The sounds were getting louder. She could hear several dogs barking ahead, a man's blustery tirade, the boy shouting, and Mr. McCullough trying to take control of the situation.

Waving off an insect, she burst into the clearing just in time to see the pointer chase around in a circle with two large collies, then take a flying leap into the pond, going after the ducks floating along the banks. The ducks flapped away with a frenzy of panicked quacking while the dog splashed this way and that trying to catch one.

The furious owner of the collies stood on the banks, fishing pole in hand. He was a rugged-looking, weathered old sportsman in jack boots and country tweeds. He shouted futilely at her dog, who had churned the pond into a whirlpool and had undoubtedly scared away all the fish.

Dodging the boy's attempts to catch her, the pointer bounded up merrily onto the banks again to make the fisherman's acquaintance, splattering his wire-rim spectacles and drenching him in muddy water as she gleefully shook her short coat.

'I said *sit*, you ridiculous creature!' the old man roared.

121

The overgrown pup dropped at once to her haunches and cowered before him, the soul of obedience.

Jacinda winced, needing no formal introduction to know that the imposing figure they had so rudely disturbed was none other than the earl himself. The authoritarian tone of his voice made that instantly clear, but if there had been any doubt, it was removed by the pale, black-clad physician who approached the old man gingerly.

'My lord, pray, sit you down. Such temper is not good for your heart.'

'Oh, flap off, you damned old crow,' the earl muttered, but he rubbed his chest vaguely.

The pointer let out a contrite whine and offered the earl her paw.

'Get this idiotic animal out of here before I shoot it. You, sir, are trespassing!' the fire-breathing earl declared, turning to glower at McCullough as he hurried to collect the dog. 'What are you doing on my property? Poaching, eh? Helping yourself to a bit of my game? Didn't expect to find me at home, I warrant!'

'Beg your pardon, my lord. Her Ladyship's hunting party was coming across the moors when the dog bounded off. We sincerely apologize for the mishap—'

'Ladyship, what? Hawkscliffe's duchess?' he asked in a scathing tone. 'She's too refined for shooting, God knows, damned gentry upstart.'

'No, sir, but I enjoy it,' Jacinda spoke up, suppressing a bemused smile as she marched toward him.

The curmudgeonly old fellow squinted at her, polishing his spectacles with a handkerchief. 'What are you doing with that gun?' he demanded.

'Grousing, my lord. I hope I did not give you a start. Take the dog away,' she instructed the boy, who slipped a collar over the pointer's head.

'Well, as long as you are not some Radical assassin come to shoot me over the Corn Laws,' Lord Drummond grumbled, then put his small, round spectacles back on. 'Good

God!' he said abruptly. 'You are the very image of Georgiana!'

'That is because I am her daughter,' she answered wryly, offering him her hand.

With an automatic air, the earl clasped her gloved fingers lightly and bowed over her hand, then squinted at her again in searching amazement. 'Little Lady Jacinda?'

'Yes, my lord. Is aught amiss?'

'You are all – ' He waved his handkerchief, gesturing vaguely. ' – grown.'

'Indeed, sir. I made my debut last Season.'

'Why aren't you in Town?' he clipped out, stuffing his handkerchief back into his breast pocket. He lifted his square chin, inspecting her like a general his troops. 'It is the start of the Season, is it not? Shouldn't you be husband-hunting with the rest of the silly young chits?'

She was taken aback by his bluntness, but on second thought, decided she found it refreshing after all the smooth hypocrisy of the ton. 'I'm afraid I have been sent down to the country for misbehavior,' she replied matter-of-factly.

Slowly and, much to her surprise, the gruff old man began chuckling. 'Well, you would be, wouldn't you? You are Georgiana's daughter, after all.'

She scanned his face in sudden, deepening interest. 'You knew my mother, sir?'

'From a safe distance,' he said, with a wicked twinkle in his steel-gray eyes. 'I had the privilege of her friendship, yes. Your mother had the heart of a lioness.'

Jacinda drew in her breath, barely able to contain her delight. Someone who had known firsthand the glamorous stranger who had been her mother! 'Won't you come and join us for our picnic, my lord? My governess and I have not had much agreeable Society since we left London.'

'I am never agreeable, ask anyone, but – as a pretty young lady is bound to be better company than Dr. Cross – I accept. Gladly.' His shrewd gray eyes twinkled behind his spectacles as he offered her his arm.

Jacinda smiled brightly at him and took it.

Bruised and still, Blade sat in a condemned hole in the bowels of Newgate Prison, on a bench hewn into the stone. His head was in his hands, his elbows resting on his bent knees. A musty smell rose from disease-ridden straw scattered across the floor, and he could hear rats scurrying about in the corner. There was a narrow, barred window too high to see out of; through it came a gray, glassy light. The walls sweated, and from some far-off place he could hear the echo of a prisoner shouting under a brutal flogging.

They were going to hang him. And Nate. And the others.

It was over. All, all ... over.

His men had been thrown into a mass cell to await their fates among their fellow criminals, but as their leader, Blade had been confined in this solitary dungeon. This, he supposed, was intended to break his spirit. He had not been in Newgate since he was fifteen. Back then, he had been caught stealing an old gentleman's silk handkerchief. A few tears of feigned contrition had earned him the judge's pity and thirty days in the 'Start.' After that, he had walked out scot-free to put his new skills into practice, for a month in a mass cell had quite rounded out his education in the criminal arts.

Now the 'beaks' wanted information, details about the goings-on in London's criminal underworld. Indeed, they had offered to commute his death sentence to a life of hard labor in New South Wales. In exchange, he only had to give them the names of the men behind certain rackets they were investigating, and the locations of where a few other choice criminals whom they had long hunted could be found. Blade had refused the deal, offering his complete cooperation instead for the release of his friends, but the magistrates had sneered at him; so he had kept his mouth shut and had taken a beating for his insolence.

He didn't even want to think about what was happening right now at the Fire Hawks' headquarters in Bainbridge Street, for he had no doubt that O'Dell was in the process of trying to seize control. He hoped to God that Carlotta had gotten the other women out of there.

Leaning his head back against the wall with a shallow sigh, he stared at the cobwebbed corner. *They've got me by the balls.*

Just then, a clank of metal resounded down the dark stone corridor. He looked over sharply. *God, what now?* He slid off the bench and crossed the cell, wondering if the court had finally appointed some quixotic solicitor to plead his defense.

'Ten minutes,' the guard above gruffly ordered his visitor.

But instead, a high-pitched voice cried into the darkness, 'Blade! Blade!' Light footfalls echoed down to him as a small figure scampered down the thick stone stairs.

His eyes widened incredulously. 'Eddie?'

'Blade!' The boy jumped off the lowest step and started to run toward him, but stopped abruptly. His pale face went somber and he slowed, staring at his idol in a cage.

Blade bristled defensively at being seen like this. 'What the hell are you doing here? This is no place for you. How did you get them to let you in?'

'I told them you're my father. I – I wish you were.'

Blade winced at the orphan's pitiful words.

The boy's gaze traveled over the bars of his cell. 'They're not really gonna hang you and Nate and Sarge and the others, are they, Blade?'

His harsh stare softened, and he leaned against the bars with a sigh. 'Oh, Eddie.' He shook his head. 'I'm afraid it doesn't look very good.'

'But – they can't!' His face was stricken. Still he hung back. 'You never get caught! This wasn't supposed to happen!'

Blade furrowed his brow. 'What do you mean, Eddie?'

125

The boy said nothing, staring dazedly at him.

'Eddie? Did you have something to do with this?'

The little boy's eyes filled with tears; then he broke down. Blade crouched down and gazed somberly at him through the bars.

'O'Dell forced me to spy on you. He said if I didn't help him, he'd make me into a wallet! Oh, Blade, they can't hang you!' he choked out, his rascally bravado fled. 'It's all my fault!'

'No, it's not,' he said sternly, though it was all he could do to hide his shock and anger at O'Dell's ruthless treachery. 'You're just a pup, Eddie. I know how O'Dell is. He threatened you. You had no choice. It's not your fault, lad.'

The boy looked at him bleakly, then hugged Blade through the bars.

He tried to comfort the distraught urchin as best he could, but his mind churned. 'There, child,' he said gruffly, rumpling Eddie's hair affectionately before rising to his feet. 'Dry your tears. Your old Blade's still got one last trick up his sleeve.'

Lucien Knight still owed him a favor.

He sent Eddie to fetch his sole government connection, pacing endlessly in his cage, but when Lord Lucien arrived and heard how Blade and his gang had been caught red-handed, his usually cool expression turned grim.

'I will do what I can to help you, Rackford, but I don't have that kind of influence.'

'Know anyone who does?' he bit out impatiently.

Lucien paused. 'No, but you do.'

'Bloody hell,' he whispered, turning away as though the man had struck him. He dragged his hand through his thick, tangled mane and leaned back against the clammy wall to stare at the ceiling, arms folded over his chest.

Knots formed in his stomach at the mere thought of facing his old tormentor again, but he had had a feeling all along that he would have to. Indecision ticked in his veins.

Nate's life and the others' hung in the balance. What did

126

the tattoos on his skin signify if not loyalty to his brothers, his gang? God in heaven, he would have rather swung from the noose than go crawling back to his old man begging for help.

'*Just bring us back alive,*' Nate had said.

'*I always do,*' he had boasted.

Closing his eyes, he let a shallow sigh escape him. This was a humiliation almost beyond bearing, but he saw he had no other choice. He didn't know whether or not it was even going to work. His father might well have the last laugh by leaving him here to rot.

'Well?' Lucien probed, studying him intently.

Unable to find his voice, he merely gave the man a taut nod of consent.

Holding his smart black top hat in his hands, Lucien gave its brim a jaunty flick. 'A wise choice,' he said. 'I'll be back soon. Don't go anywhere.'

Blade scowled at the man's wry jest.

Lucien sent him a bolstering, rather self-assured smile, then pivoted, walked smoothly to the stone steps, and jogged up them, leaving to fetch the one man Blade never wanted to see again – the one man he hated even more than O'Dell. The marquess of Truro and St. Austell.

His father.

Jacinda's mind was whirring a hundred miles an hour as she sat on the picnic blanket beneath the umbrella with her governess and Lord Drummond. The old statesman was relating a story about her mother's madcap antics at a masque ball. She listened in rapt amazement as the earl described the headdress Mama had worn, her tall, white wig adorned with countless tiny birdcages, each one occupied by a live bird. Jacinda laughed incredulously, and even Miss Hood succumbed to an indecorous chortle as he described how, at the stroke of midnight, the duchess had opened all the birdcages.

'Canaries, little parakeets, buntings, cardinals, a bluebird. All the guests were ducking as the whole flock of 'em went swooping back and forth across the ballroom trying to find a way out. I believe a pair of cardinals used the punch bowl for a birdbath. Lady Ilcester, our hostess, wanted to throttle her – and that was even before one of the creatures left its droppings on her shoulder. What a row!' he exclaimed, his shoulders shaking with gusty laughter. 'Lady Ilcester flew into hysterics and gave your mother such a scolding, but Georgiana simply turned to her, cool as you please, and said, "But my dear Amelia, don't you know it signifies good luck?"'

Even the footmen waiting on them could be heard trying to suppress a chuckle.

'Oh, my dear Lord Drummond, tell us another!' she begged him, wiping away a tear of laughter.

He searched his memory and indulged her.

Jacinda had already decided she liked her neighbor very well. She had quickly sensed his ruthless side behind the silvery flashing of his hawklike eyes – he was not someone she ever wanted to cross – but since she had no intention of ever doing so, and because she was used to the company of powerful men, she felt as relaxed and natural around him as she did around her brothers. He was blunt, stoic, and opinionated – a man who said exactly what he thought and damn your eyes if you didn't like it. He also happened to be a widower. Miss Hood had asked if Lady Drummond had come to the country with him and had learned that the countess had died nearly a decade ago.

The revelation had started the wicked little wheels and cogs turning in Jacinda's brain. While she listened, smiling, her speculative gaze roamed over her neighbor. He had surely been a strapping, handsome fellow in his youth. Lord Drummond was almost seventy, and though still quite robust, he was in the country on his doctor's orders to relax, for his heart was not good.

'Ah, here comes the torturer,' he said glumly, glancing over as Dr. Cross marched toward them. 'He is most assiduous, devil take him. He may just cure me, if I don't kill 'im first. I suppose he is going to mortify me in front of a young lady by telling me it is time for my nap. Alas, he is right.'

'We all need our beauty sleep, my lord,' Jacinda teased him, and he smiled, rising to his feet.

'Thank you for allowing me to join your picnic.'

'I am glad you did. As a matter of fact, I'm inviting some of the local gentry to dine at Hawkscliffe Hall next Wednesday evening. Reverend and Mrs. Picket will be there. I would be delighted if you'd join us.'

'That sounds very agreeable.'

'Consider it an invitation, then. Shall we say seven o'clock?'

'Why, you are very elegant, keeping Town hours in the country.'

She laughed at his teasing.

'Thank you, my lady. I will be there,' Lord Drummond assured her.

'Excellent! And do please feel free to try your fishing pole at any of our streams or ponds. My brother keeps them well stocked. It's the least I can do for my silly dog scaring off all your fish today.'

'You seem quite the sportswoman. Perhaps you'd care to try your hand at golf? I've built a course at Warflete, you know.'

'So our gamekeeper tells me,' she exclaimed.

''Tis a noble sport. If you and Miss Hood would like to call on me tomorrow, I will give you a lesson in the game.'

'I'm sure I'd like that very much,' Jacinda said warmly, giving him her hand.

'I can tell you golf is better medicine than that apothecary's dreaded digitalis tea.' He bowed over her hand, nodded to Miss Hood, then trudged toward his physician. 'I'm coming,' he growled at the man, grouchily taking the beaker of odd-colored tea the man handed him. He winced and drank it.

129

As the two men set off toward Warflete Manor, the women exchanged an amused glance.

'I daresay His Grace was right,' Miss Hood whispered. 'The earl is a bit of a curmudgeon.'

'I think he's charming,' Jacinda declared, but when Miss Hood raised her eyebrow, her teacup and saucer poised in her hand, she gave her governess an innocent smile. 'In a curmudgeonly sort of way, of course.'

Two hours had passed, but now the sound of footsteps and voices in the stone corridor above brought Blade's chin up sharply. He slid off the bench and went warily to the rusty metal bars, peering through them as the iron-reinforced door heaved open at the top of thick stone stairs. The gnomelike jail keeper thrust a torch into the dank space.

'This way, my lord. Careful on the stairs.' Lucien walked in after the short, ugly jailer, then stood aside with a polite gesture.

Blade swallowed hard, his fingers wrapping around the bars.

Under the lintel ducked a tall, lean man in a top hat and a fine black cloak, a walking stick in his hand. Sauntering down the stairs, the marquess took in the cavelike dungeon with an arrogant glance. As the man swept off his hat, Blade drew in his breath, his heart pounding, old angers rumbling stormily within him.

Truro turned to the keeper and dismissed him, then drifted nearer with an air of calculated caution. 'Lord Lucien, would you excuse us, please?'

Lucien glanced at Blade in question.

He nodded, but the ex-spy shot him a silent warning to hold his temper at the way Truro was looking him over, as though he were a horse on the bloody auction block.

'If you need me,' Lucien said, 'I shall be in the corridor.' Quietly, he withdrew.

There was a long, tense silence after he had gone. The two men studied each other in bristling hostility.

130

'Well, well,' Truro drawled coldly after a moment, ambling closer. 'What have we here?'

Blade's hands tightened around the bars of his cell, but he kept his mouth shut.

Truro was still a tall, broad-shouldered man, but he looked rather gaunt and ill. Perhaps he couldn't eat anymore, only drink, he thought bitterly. His aquiline face was more deeply lined, harder than Blade remembered, his brown wavy hair and goatee beard gone nearly all gray.

Beneath his open cloak, his red woollen waistcoat brought out the dissipated ruddiness of his skin, but his bloodshot green eyes, the color of tainted copper, still held that piratelike intensity that once upon a time had made a young boy quake in his shoes.

Blade met the marquess's gaze in defiance and thought he detected a flicker of pain in the depths of the bleary eyes. The man's mouth curled in a mocking, world-weary smile that stuck like a splinter in Blade's heart.

He looked away. The silence was excruciating. For a moment, Truro lowered his head, thoughtfully fingering the lion-headed walking stick that he probably didn't remember having used as a club on his younger son after three bottles of brandy on any given evening, but when he looked up again, his gaze homed in on the small, undeniable scar on Blade's forehead in the shape of a rough star.

Whatever doubts he may have had about the identity of the man in the cage, the sight of the scar that he had made on his son's face clearly laid them to rest. Perhaps it was more shame than hauteur that made the marquess drop his gaze, inclining his head in a cursory nod. 'So. You are alive.'

'Yes, for the moment, so it would seem,' he answered tautly.

'Lord Lucien says they will hang you.'

'Quite.'

His father's marveling gaze ran over him, taking in the tough, sinewy lines of the man he had become. A flicker of something passed behind his eyes – not pride, certainly, but perhaps the recognition that if he ever hit him again, he was going to be hit back very, very hard.

'Try to contain your euphoria, Father,' he drawled, staring dully at him, but his heart was pounding.

The marquess stared at the lion-carved head of his walking stick. 'Your brother is dead. Tuberculosis.'

'I know.'

Truro shot him a look of surprise, then frowned warily, brooding upon the revelation that his younger son had been alive all this time, aware that he had become the heir to a rich marquisate, yet had made no claim on his heritage. A muscle clenched in the marquess's jaw. 'What, then?' he asked acidly. 'Am I to kill the fatted calf for you?'

Blade bit back a sharp retort and looked away, leaning his shoulder into the bars as he slid his thumbs loosely into his trouser pockets. 'Hardly. I know you take no more joy in this than I do. I had not intended to do this, you see. Ever. I wanted to make you suffer the only way I could.'

'By standing back and allowing our line to be obliterated.'

'Precisely.'

'But now ... why, it seems you've got yourself into a spot of trouble, haven't you?'

Blade checked his temper at his father's taunting, superior tone and prayed God to help him bear the scourge to his pride. The whoreson was gloating. 'I don't give a damn for your money or your title,' he said hotly. 'The only reason I called you here was for the sake of my friends. They've been more family to me than you ever were.'

'What exactly do you want, William?'

He reined in his temper by sheer dint of will, his nostrils flaring as he drew a deep, steadying breath. 'Use your power and influence and whatever sort of bribery it takes to get my men freed and, in exchange, I will come back and do ... whatever you say.'

His father stared at him, unperturbed. 'It seems to me you are in no position to be making demands.'

'Refuse me, then, and walk away. I am not afraid to die.'

Lord Truro began laughing slowly at his fiery bravado. He turned and paced on the other side of the bars. Blade watched him keenly, his heart pounding. He willed himself to be still.

'By God, if I take you back, you will toe the line.' His father pivoted to face him. It was only then that Blade read the profound emotion in the depths of his eyes, noticed the slight trembling in his voice and hands. 'You will sever all ties with these ruffians. You will leave this criminal life without looking back, do you understand me?'

'Yes.'

'Moreover, I will expect you to marry – promptly! Aye, at once. An appropriate girl, of good family. I will not have you flout me on this. Our bloodlines have been imperiled for too long. You will wed and begin breeding immediately. I don't know how I shall ever present you to Society. I shall have to think of something, some story to tell them about where you've been, but in the meantime – look at you. You look half wild.'

Blade smiled rather cynically at him.

They stared at each other.

'Damn you,' his father uttered after a long moment. 'If Percy were alive, I'd leave you here to rot, by God, I would.'

'Yes, Father, I do not doubt it.'

'Do you have any idea what you've put your mother through?'

Leaning against the bars, Blade just looked at him.

'I will see what can be done.' With a huff, the marquess marched back up the stairs to consult with Lord Lucien.

Blade closed his eyes and only allowed himself to exhale after he had gone, but the one burning thought that emerged from the chaos like a fiery star was the fact that if this worked – if his father indeed took him back, acknowledged him as his heir – he would enter Jacinda Knight's lofty circles, as eligible a bachelor as any haughty Society debutante could want, no more to grovel at her feet, but to make her his own – provided, of course, that Lord Lucien didn't object.

Pacing in his cell, rubbing the back of his neck in irritation, he waited as patiently as possible for his father to return so he might hear his fate. When the massive door scraped and creaked open again, he strode to the bars of his cell and saw that Truro and Lucien had returned with Sir Anthony Weldon, the magistrate.

A shrewd former attorney, Sir Anthony was a short, middle-aged, pugnacious-looking man with piercing eyes and russet-colored side-whiskers. He clasped his hands behind his back and studied Blade as he neared his cell.

'Ah, the illustrious Billy Blade, scourge of the West End, hero of the rookery. At last we meet.'

Blade looked at him uncertainly, but his father would have none of it.

'Sir Anthony, allow me to present my son, William Albright, the earl of Rackford,' the marquess clarified, using the courtesy title that had once been Percy's but that now belonged to him.

'Hmm,' the magistrate said in a noncommittal tone.

'I have explained the situation to Sir Anthony, Lord Rackford,' Lucien broke in smoothly. 'I have told him of the vital help you have provided in the past to me and to my family.'

'All the same,' Sir Anthony said, 'I cannot simply open the cages and set your associates free—'

'Then we have nothing to discuss,' Blade said.

'Let me finish, if you please,' the magistrate curtly rebuked him. 'There are three points on which I must have your full cooperation before I will agree to hand you over to His Lordship's custody.'

He met Lucien's encouraging gaze, then gave Sir Anthony a taut nod. 'Go on.'

'First, if you are indeed to become the earl of Rackford, Lord Truro and I both agree that Billy Blade must die.'

'Sir?'

'You must cut all ties with your past associates, and to aid you in doing so, we will let it be said that 'Blade' was hanged privately to avoid any rioting of the mob. Secondly, I will be lenient to your fellows. I will send them to hard labor in New South Wales, but under no circumstances will I set them free.'

'Hard labor?' he cried angrily. He was to go live in a mansion with servants and fine clothes, while his friends worked the fields and quarries of Australia?

'Take it or leave it, young man. The lot of you were caught red-handed. They work or they hang. I am a reasonable man, but I cannot be bought.'

Nostrils flaring, Blade checked his temper and swallowed hard. 'Yes, sir. Your third point?' he growled.

'Information,' he said, edging closer to Blade's cell with an intense look in his eyes. 'You could be most useful to us. Names, locations, details about various individuals we have been hunting, criminal rings we have long sought to break.'

Bloody dangerous, he thought, regarding him warily. If any of his past criminal associates learned that 'Blade' was actually alive and informing on them, his father would have to find another heir, after all, for he wouldn't live long.

'With your inside knowledge of the underworld's workings, Bow Street can make great strides in cleaning up this city.'

Blade flicked his tongue nervously over his lips, his heart pounding, but maybe, he thought, a change of sides was in order. He thought again of those ragged children playing in the gutter. The knowledge had long nagged at him, that the moral decay of the rookery was as much to blame for their condition as the harsh laws handed down by Parliament. With his help, maybe things could change. Perhaps Bow Street could actually do something to tame the lawless

135

streets that provided the perfect environment in which monsters like O'Dell could thrive. He considered for a heartbeat, then gave a stiff nod.

'Very well. I will do it.'

Lucien's silvery eyes flickered with sly approval; Truro nodded slowly.

'Mind you, we will be watching you,' the magistrate warned.

He lifted his chin in guarded insolence. 'Anything else?'

'Only that you look like a savage, Lord Rackford,' Sir Anthony wryly replied. 'I suggest you cut your hair.'

Chapter Eight

Rackford. William Spencer Albright, Earl of Rackford.
Will Rackford.

Three weeks later, Rackford stared at himself at close range in the mirror, taking one final moment as he buttoned his mother-of-pearl cuff links, to ensure that his new name was adequately drummed into his head. Alas, Billy Blade was no more – privately hanged in the courtyard of Newgate, dying young and unlamented, to the surprise of none.

In the looking glass, he thought himself barely recognizable in formal black evening clothes, his hair cropped short. It looked darker, with all its sun-streaked lengths cut off. His face was closely shaved, his hands impeccably groomed, though his old calluses showed no signs of going away. He had sat through the manicure as best he could, but had quickly lost patience with his valet's attempts to lighten his complexion to a gentlemanly pallor with an assortment of potions and lotions. Beneath his chin, his starched cravat chafed like a collar one might put on a particularly nasty dog to keep it tame. He flicked a glance downward over his clothes – fine white linen shirt, smooth black trousers held up by suspenders that made a Y in the back, well-shined black shoes.

Ah, well. Inside, he was the same man. But if he looked more civilized on the outside, the truth was he felt even less so, surrounded by people he dared not trust, in a world where he was uncertain of the rules.

His loyal mates had all been transported to hard labor in Australia. What was happening now in the rookery, he barely wanted to imagine, but he intended to find out very soon. O'Dell no doubt thought that he had won, but it was far from over.

A slight movement behind him swiftly drew his gaze, but it was only his valet, Filbert, a slight-framed, balding, efficient little man who stood at a respectful distance, patiently holding up his white silk waistcoat. Behind him in the reflection lay his opulent apartments in his father's redbrick mansion on the square at Lincoln's Inn Fields.

The walls had gilded pier glasses and panels of damascened French silk, the ceiling a painted medallion. The two symmetrical windows were hung with heavy blue velvet curtains with gold tassels. Lovely, but a cage, nonetheless.

'Your vest, my lord?' Filbert prodded.

Rackford slipped his arms through the armholes and let the little man put the elegant waistcoat on him and button it. He had finally begun to understand that he was not to lift a finger in anything unless it was absolutely necessary. He played along without comment because he strongly suspected that Filbert was his father's spy. He dared trust no one in this new life of his, not even his mother, who still wept every time she looked at him.

He had spent two of the past three weeks with his irritating parents at his father's secondary estate in Surrey. There he had been fitted up for a new wardrobe, put through a refresher course on basic manners, interviewed almost daily by Sir Anthony and his pair of Bow Street investigators, and advised on what traits he was to look for in a wife – the acquiring of which, he gathered, was not unlike buying a milch cow at market.

Still, in spite of the myriad dangers he had to watch out for here, it was good to be in London again. He had hated the country. Too bloody quiet. Back in Town again, his first forays into Society had gone smoothly, though there had been a dangerous few minutes the first time he had been formally introduced to Acer Loring. Fortunately, the dandy had not recognized him as the wild man he had mocked in Hyde Park.

Beyond the meeting with the leading dandy, the buzz of curiosity he had aroused in the ton merely amused him. Indeed, he thought as he allowed his valet to put his black tailcoat on him, he was perfectly poised at this moment to ensnare Jacinda Knight.

She had been absent from Town since his arrival, but he had heard she was expected at the Devonshire ball this evening. He could not wait to see her face when she laid eyes on him. In the mirror, a faint smile of perverse anticipation twisted his lips as he pulled on his pristine white gloves. Ah, tonight he would have some fun. Entice her, torment her, shake her up a bit. Toy with her pretty head as she had toyed with his.

Not only did he owe her for her arrogant cut that day in Hyde Park, but looked at a certain way, his loss of freedom was her fault. It was she who had angered him so deeply with her blatant scorn. She had provoked him into redoubling his efforts at crime, which, in turn, had led to his arrest. He was under his father's thumb again, and it was all because of that maddening chit. If he had not been out of his head over her, he would have listened to Nate; he would have realized something was wrong instead of dragging his men into that disastrous robbery. Even the chosen victim that night had been the result of his talk with her. He had specifically targeted the Taylors because, as Jacinda had confided in him, their eldest daughter had routinely been cruel to her.

Well, this was what it had got him, he thought. Nevertheless, he wanted her, and he intended to have her. His reasons were practical, in addition to simple lust. He needed to get control of her to ensure she kept silent about his past. When they were man and wife, her interests would be one and the same with his own, thus she would be bound to secrecy. Finally, he needed her savvy in negotiating his way through the ton. He knew he was out of his element; he needed an able and trustworthy guide in this strange world.

She would resist him, of course. She was no doubt still angry at him for returning her to her family, but then, he also knew her weakness – the wanton nature that burned in her veins. She might think him a rough, low brute, but her desire for him had been very plain the night he had given her her first taste of pleasure, and he was not above using it against her.

'Look all right, Filbert?' He smoothed his coat, then regarded himself critically in the glass.

'Very smart, indeed, sir.'

Rackford eyed his valet warily, then pivoted and strode toward the door. On his way out of his chamber, he plucked a carnation from the daily bouquet of fresh flowers that his mother ordered for nearly every room in the house. He snapped off the long stem and tucked the crimson bloom in his boutonniere.

It was not to be borne! Some of her best flirting was going completely unnoticed.

If Lord Drummond were a normal suitor, he would have been on his knees by now begging for her hand in marriage, Jacinda thought with a huff, but for such an astute and worldly-wise politician, the possibility that she might be in earnest with all her lavish attentions and sugary compliments seemed beyond his comprehension. Instead, he treated her like an amusing child.

Grandchild.

'Watch the fireworks, pet,' he chided when she begged him to dance with her. 'I am too old for dancing.'

She sulked; she pouted; then she tried beguiling him with a graceful attitude, leaning over the balustrade to pull a sprig of the cherry blossom tree closer, drinking in its sweet perfume. Out of the corner of her eye, she saw that he just went on talking with his aged cronies and a few foreign dignitaries, there on the lamplit veranda overlooking the lavish gardens of Devonshire House. He paid her no mind whatsoever. Clenching her jaw, she folded her high-gloved arms across her chest and watched the blasted fireworks.

At half-past nine, the palace and Tower guns erupted with a roaring salute. Church bells began ringing in every direction, drowning out the pretty Haydn minuet that the orchestra was playing in the ballroom. All England was rejoicing tonight over the royal wedding of her fat, jolly, beloved Princess Charlotte to the handsome, bookish Prince Leopold of Saxe-Coburg. By all accounts, their union was a love match.

The thought tugged at her romantic's heart and brought a soft sigh to her lips, but her mind was made up. The idea of her eventual freedom had taken hold, and she was determined to see it through.

In the past weeks, up in the North Country and now back in London, an unlikely friendship had developed between the gruff veteran statesman and the sparkling young debutante. The earl's physician, Dr. Cross, had privately informed her that she was the only person who had made Lord Drummond laugh in the past two decades. Indeed, she thought, her plan was going along swimmingly, if only he would realize her attentions were in earnest.

And yet, listening to the joyous din, a mercurial wave of loneliness washed through her. She lifted her gaze above the gaudy fireworks to the cool white moon – again, full. It was hard to believe it had been one whole month since her adventure in the rookery. Wistfully, she looked out over the expansive gardens of Devonshire House as the last glimmer of light faded in the west. Of all the London mansions she frequented in the social rounds, this one had the best view – gorgeous, sculpted gardens as far as the eye could see. The Devonshire gardens bordered those of Lansdowne House, and beyond them lay the garden in the center of Berkeley Square.

Night enhanced the luscious perfumes wafting from the burgeoning lilacs, the cherry trees dripping with snowy blooms, pearly white in the darkness, and the jasmine climbing up the side of the house. The neat walkways below were lined with demure lilies of the valley and rose-bushes showing off their first fruits, red and lush.

As she stood at the balustrade, the night breeze rippling gently through the skirts of her high-waisted ball gown in a delicate almond-blossom shade, she heard giggling and pattering footsteps, and turned as a few trusted members of Daphne's clique came tripping out over the threshold of the open French doors. The girls hurried across the veranda toward her, all bouncing side-curls and fluttering fans.

'Jacinda! There you are! You must come at once, this *instant*!' Helena commanded with a breathless laugh, rushing over to her in a whoosh of pink taffeta.

Amelia followed, in jonquil-yellow India muslin with flounces around the hem. 'She's out here, Daphne!'

'Yes, I'm right here,' Jacinda answered brightly, turning to them. 'What is it?'

The most curious thing had happened once the news had gotten out that she would not be marrying Lord Griffith: Daphne Taylor had gone on a campaign to become her bosom friend.

Inwardly, Jacinda was having none of it – she was no fool. The reigning beauty's sudden sugary sweetness merely revealed that Daphne had wanted Ian for herself all along. Still, no matter how Daphne tried to butter her up, Jacinda had no intention of playing matchmaker. That was no way to repay a loyal family friend.

'Oh, there you are!' Daphne exclaimed, striding out to them. 'We were wondering where you had gotten off to.' The tall, willowy redhead was clad in a pale green gown of gossamer satin with large pink roses embroidered around the hem and short puff sleeves. 'Dear me, you're not feeling poorly, are you?' she asked solicitously, coming over to her.

'No, I just needed a bit of air,' Jacinda said with a practiced Society smile.

'Good, then come back inside! You are missing the party. Besides – ' Daphne gave her a coy smile. 'Guess who's here? Lord Griffith! He's just arrived escorting your sister-in-law, Lady Lucien. Mightn't we go greet them?' With a giggle, Daphne grasped her arm, not waiting for an answer.

'Where are you going, my dear?' Lord Drummond asked in amusement, watching the giggling girls tug her back toward the French doors.

'I hardly know,' she called.

'We'll bring her back shortly, my lord!' Helena assured him.

Abandoning her wineglass on the balustrade, she allowed her new 'friends' to shepherd her merrily back inside, Daphne steering her through the crowded ballroom with Helena and Amelia flitting after them a step behind. After the soothing darkness of the garden, she blinked against the bright lights of the pendulous chandeliers that hung down from the ornately plastered ceiling; each one bore two dozen white candles whose illumination was flung back from the great, gilt-framed mirrors on the surrounding walls.

The ball was already a splendid crush, for the duke of Devonshire's hospitality was always of the highest caliber. The girls had to take a roundabout course to reach the spot where Lord Griffith stood chatting with Alice and Robert and Bel. Passing through the salon where refreshments and whist tables had been set up, they found Alec sitting at one of the green baize card tables, his crutches leaning against his chair. He was gambling against three old dragon-lady dowagers for the genteel sum of a shilling a point, unabashedly charming them and taking their money. Since

143

he was also a favorite of the young ladies they had to stop to greet him. He sent Jacinda a sly grin, pooh-poohing the girls' inquiries about his poor broken ankle.

You are shameless, she told her favorite brother with a pointed glance.

Lizzie was hovering about him like a mother hen. Her pretty figure was clad in a sedate gown of sea-green satin trimmed with ivory lace, but lovely as her ensemble was, somehow she always managed to blend into the background. She preferred it. At the moment, Lizzie, who rarely even had a temper to lose, looked like she wanted to pick up one of Alec's crutches and swing it at the girls who were ogling him. Seeing Jacinda, she detached herself from his side with a look of exasperation and bustled around the card table to her, leaving Alec flirting with the girls.

Jacinda smiled as her hapless friend joined her. Lizzie offered her a sip of her lemonade without a word, but she declined; then both girls glanced at Alec.

'What a scoundrel he is,' Jacinda remarked in amusement.

'I know,' Lizzie sighed, 'but one can never stay cross at him.' She shook her head with a worried frown. 'I hope he gets the night's play out of his system before the gentlemen come in to gamble for higher stakes, but I am afraid he is only warming up.'

'I'm sure he can't be that great a fool? For heaven's sake, Robert warned him no more high-stakes gambling or he'll be cut off, didn't he?'

Lizzie eyed her nervously.

'What is it?' Jacinda prompted.

She lowered her voice in distress. 'Robert *has* cut him off, Jas – partially. It happened while you were in the country. Alec confided it to me a few nights ago. Robert has said he will not give him any more spending money until Alec demonstrates that he can stop gambling for a month. Alec lost quite brutally again at Brook's, I'm afraid. They had a mighty row. I don't blame Robert at all.

Someone must do something with the poor scoundrel, but ... oh, I don't know. I cannot bear to see him unhappy.'

'Dearest, Alec is going to do what Alec is going to do,' she said gently. 'It's not your responsibility to save him.'

'I know. I just don't want to see him get into any trouble,' Lizzie said softly, gazing at the rogue in dismay.

'Nor I, you.'

'Nor I, you, Miss Runaway,' Lizzie retorted, then scowled at the other girls. 'Would you please get these flighty, jingle-brained henwits out of here?'

Chuckling, Jacinda nodded. Lizzie hurried back to Alec's side while she and the other girls moved on through the salon, going into the other side of the ballroom. They squeezed their way through the thickening crowd of aristocratic guests until they reached the spot where her family was gathered.

Instantly going onto their best behavior, Daphne and the others curtseyed to Their Graces of Hawkscliffe and Alice, complimenting both ladies lavishly on their gowns before eagerly crowding in around Lord Griffith. Ian appeared rather taken aback by the vivacious attentions of a trio of fast young debutantes. Robert glanced at his friend in amusement, while Bel and Alice each gave Jacinda a kiss on her cheek.

Lucien's wife, Alice, was a petite fey creature with vivid blue eyes and strawberry-blond hair. She was clad in a pale peach satin gown that beautifully flattered her creamy complexion. Bel, the present duchess of Hawkscliffe, considered one of the most ravishing women in Society, wore a gown of soft rose silk with long sleeves of transparent aerophane crepe. She was a cool, graceful, serene goddess with wheat-colored hair and cornflower-blue eyes, a perfect foil to Robert's black-haired, dark-eyed intensity as he stood beside her in black superfine magnificence.

'Are you enjoying yourself, Jacinda?' Alice asked her.

'Very much. But where is your silly husband tonight?'

'Pastoral woes in Somerset, I fear,' Alice said with a smile.

'Oh, dear,' Jacinda said. She had not yet seen Revell Court, but she knew that Lucien had inherited the sprawling Jacobean manor from his real father in a state of considerable disrepair. 'It's your first productive harvest there, isn't it?'

'It should be, but the land agent Lucien hired seems incapable of conducting the harvest in an orderly fashion. Not enough laborers ... the tenants are complaining. I don't know what all has gone awry. He did not want to go, but I told him if the man bungles the job, it will put the whole crop at risk. So he's gone to try to sort it out before the hay-making begins.'

'Well, I am sure he will have it all in hand quickly.'

'Are you?' Alice asked with a laugh. 'I wish I shared your confidence, my dear. Lucien is hardly the farming type. If not for the children, I would have gone to manage it myself, but,' she added loftily, 'I suppose he has to learn sometime.'

Jacinda laughed at her droll tone and agreed.

'Fortunately, Ian was kind enough to escort me tonight in my husband's absence,' Alice went on, turning fondly to regard the marquess, who looked a little disconcerted by the flirtatious attentions of Daphne and her clique.

'Oh, he is always the best of men,' Bel agreed sympathetically, dropping Jacinda an unmistakable hint.

'And you know ...' Alice cast her a wicked look askance. 'He has such nicely turned calves. Don't you think?'

'No padding either, I daresay,' Bel agreed.

'Oh, you are a pair of stubborn creatures!' Jacinda scolded them in a whisper while they laughed at her. 'I am not marrying him.' She shook her head at Alice. 'You used to be so prim and proper, ma'am. What happened to you?'

'Your brother,' Alice declared.

'I'll drink to that,' Bel seconded her with a wink.

146

Laughing, they sipped their wine and regarded Lord Griffith, awash in smitten girls half his age. The tall, brown-haired marquess cast Alice and Bel a look that clearly said, *Help*!

The ladies merely smiled at him, enjoying his discomfiture.

'We really have to get that poor fellow married off, don't you think?' Alice remarked. 'If not to Lady Jacinda, then to someone.'

'I know of at least one volunteer,' Jacinda murmured dubiously.

Alice wrinkled her nose and glanced discreetly at Daphne. 'Oh, no. Never.'

'I think not,' Bel agreed. Twirling a lock of her wheat-blond hair around her finger, she idly looked away. 'I wonder, Alice, perhaps Lady Jacinda will change her mind. She does, you know. A lot.'

'True.'

'Humph.' Scowling at their teasing, Jacinda firmly changed the subject, asking Alice about little Harry and Pippa. Alice was reporting her one-year-old daughter's latest brush with the sniffles when their host unexpectedly joined their group.

'Your Grace,' the women said with pleasure as he greeted them with a gallant bow.

If there was one bachelor in all the ton even more hotly pursued than Lord Griffith, it was the twenty-six-year-old duke of Devonshire. His title was ancient, his pockets deep, and he was not only a fine host and a man of information, but tolerably attractive, to boot. As the young duke shook hands with Lord Griffith, the fluttering girls hardly knew who to fawn upon. Jacinda sincerely hoped someone nearby had smelling salts, for she feared Amelia was going to need them.

'Devonshire, good to see you,' Robert said, stepping forward to shake his hand in turn. 'Thank you for the invitation.'

'My pleasure. I hope you are enjoying yourselves,' their host greeted them.

'Very much. It is a lovely ball,' Bel said warmly.

'It will be, when you ladies have graced us with your dancing.'

Her kinswomen laughed at his charming riposte.

'I was wondering if you all have yet had the pleasure of meeting the newcomer in our midst.' The duke glanced over his shoulder, beckoning genially to someone she could not see over the crush of the crowd, then turned back to them. 'Allow me to present William Albright, the earl of Rackford.'

Jacinda waited for him to step into view. She recognized the name, for Amelia and Helena had been all abuzz over the mystery man who had appeared in Society during her sojourn in the country. It seemed Lord Rackford was the long-lost son of the marquess of Truro and St. Austell; he was rich, handsome, and eminently eligible. He was a bit odd, in a dangerous sort of way, the girls had told her, giggling with excitement. He reminded them, they said, of a caged tiger. His family had thought him dead since his disappearance as a young lad, but now that he had turned up in London alive and well, the stubborn creature refused to say a word about where he had been or what he had been doing all this time.

In the face of his silence, a few theories had naturally begun to circulate among the ton – that he had adopted a false name and had gone off to sea, or to fight in the war against Napoleon, or that he had been adventuring in the frontier provinces of India. Any of these possibilities explained his rough manners, the girls said, but wasn't it horrid of him to torment Society this way with curiosity?

Jacinda privately thought it was his way of saying it was nobody's business, but the only thing that could be said for certain of Lord Rackford was that he had the women in a swoon and the haughtier sets of dandies sulking with jeal-

148

ousy. She was not sure she cared to meet the fellow, for he sounded like pure trouble.

Then he stepped out of the crowd toward her group, and Jacinda's world stopped. *It couldn't be.*

Her stomach flip-flopped like the first time she had taken a six-foot fence on her Thoroughbred hunter. The ballroom spun around her in a colorful blur, and she could not seem to draw a breath.

Lord Rackford? It was Billy Blade.

Either it was he, or her mind was playing dire tricks on her. In a state of utter shock, she watched him meeting each member of her family and felt as if the slightest puff of wind could have knocked her flat. She knew him in an instant, though he was barely recognizable with his sandy hair sleekly cropped and slicked back, showing off the gorgeous bone structure of his chiseled face.

From the starched perfection of his neckcloth to his polished black dress shoes, he looked like the perfect gentleman, but the unbidden image that bloomed in her mind was of his bronzed skin adorned with pagan tattoos. When her stunned gaze drifted to the red carnation in his boutonniere – just like the one he had worn on that day long ago at Knight House – the sight of it snapped her out of her daze.

Good God, I've lured a criminal into the ton!

Her light stays suddenly felt too tight. Heart pounding, she glanced around frantically, wondering if anyone had those smelling salts after all.

As she tried in a panic to think what to do, Blade shook hands with Lord Griffith, sizing him up with a shrewd glance. Jacinda was seized with the urge to run before the introductions came round to her, but suddenly, it was too late.

'And this,' said the duke of Devonshire, directing his attention to her, 'is the lovely Lady Jacinda Knight.'

Tall and powerfully built, beautiful and virile as a demigod, the elegant stranger turned, looked slyly into her eyes, and gave her a polite bow. 'My lady.'

The intimate caress in those two simple words made her shudder. His appearance had changed, but the deep timbre of his voice was the same, aye, and his mesmerizing eyes – fierce and deep. Beneath his tawny lashes, they gleamed, pale, seagreen rimmed with chalcedony.

Her voice was gone, but a world of meaning passed between them as she held his gaze. What he was doing here, she did not want to imagine.

She could scarcely even hear above the crazed pounding of her heart. Though she had been presented at half a dozen of Europe's crown courts, at the moment, she had no idea how to react. It was all she could do not to faint when he touched her, gently lifting her hand to place a kiss on her knuckles.

His face betrayed nothing, but his bold, rebel's stare captured hers and flashed with mad, swashbuckling humor and a warning of the danger to them both if anyone realized they were already acquainted. He gave her fingers a firm, subtle squeeze. 'My lady, may I have the honor of a dance?'

In dazed, tumultuous alarm, a vague incoherency tumbled from her lips.

Audacious as ever, he took her stammering for a yes and grasped her wrist, tugging her away from her family with a cheerful farewell, as though he had no intention of ever returning her to them. She looked back at them in alarm but had little choice but to follow as he pulled her along by her hand.

He strode a step ahead of her through the crowd with the same vibrant aura of leadership that she remembered from the rookery. The next thing she knew, she was in his arms on the edge of the dance floor as the orchestra struck up a waltz.

'You can dance?' she cried, finding her tongue all of a sudden, though it was an absurd question, under the circumstances.

'Not really,' he said breezily, casting an alert glance around the ballroom, 'but you're worth me making a fool of myself.'

'Blade!'

'Rackford,' he warned softly. 'You're going to have to help me just a little, love. I believe your hand goes ... here.' He placed her left hand on his right shoulder, then smiled at her, a soft, possessive glow in his eyes. He offered her his left hand and waited for her to take it.

She stared at it, utterly at a loss, then lifted her stunned gaze to his face. When she spoke, at last, her voice sounded dazed. 'You cut your hair.'

He smiled wryly. 'Don't worry, Delilah, I haven't lost my strength.'

'What are you *doing* here?' she cried.

'Jacinda, my darling, I'll explain everything, but we are going to be trampled by waltzing debutantes if you don't do *something*. Quickly.'

'But I'm not allowed to dance the waltz,' she said in dismay. 'Robert will have a fit.'

'Let me deal with Robert,' he murmured with a knowing little smile. 'Take my hand.'

She looked at it, remembering the night in the alley and the moment that he had offered his hand to help her up from the junk heap like some renegade pirate. His rough, callused hand had been streaked with dirt and dried blood. Now it was sheathed in a spotless glove of white kid.

Slowly, tentatively, her heart beating swiftly, she laid her right hand in his left.

'That's better,' he whispered. 'My God, you are luminous.' He slid his right hand around her waist to take her in a slightly firmer hold.

Her soul-deep shudder of response to his touch snapped her out of her daze. A rush of fury and mistrust gusted up from the depths of her confusion.

'What the devil are you doing here?' she whispered fiercely as the music started.

151

'Widening my horizons, you might say.' Deftly leading her in the dance, he gave her an enigmatic smile.

'So, it is as I feared,' she said tautly, her stomach in knots. 'You sold the diamonds I gave you for this. To masquerade your way into the ton so you can plan even bigger and better robberies. That's it, isn't it?'

'My clever lady, you have divined my scheme exactly. Damn me, have you seen the paintings Devonshire has in his gallery? I could make my fortune—'

'You're mad!' she cried in rising alarm. 'You mustn't! Blade, you must leave now and never come back! You'll be caught – hanged. Trust me, it will never work.'

'Why? You're not going to tell on me, are you? After all' – he held her a bit more tightly – 'there are things I could tell the ton about you, too. I have not forgotten how sweet you were in my arms,' he murmured, lowering his head and nearly brushing the tip of her nose with his own. She could smell the soapy clean warmth of his skin and the pleasing scent of his shaving lotion. 'We aren't through yet, you and I. There is much more of pleasure that I have to teach you.'

'Do not mention that night!' she forced out.

His wolfish smile widened with a gleam of white teeth. 'Why not? You had your fun. You still owe me, you know.'

'Blade—'

'Rackford,' he whispered.

'Whatever you want to call yourself, you will never get away with this! Really, it is too cruel of you to make Lord and Lady Truro believe you are their long-lost son—'

'Jacinda, my heart, I *am* their long-lost son. I was jesting.'

She searched his face in confusion. His expression was so perfectly open and earnest that it threw her. 'But – how?'

'By the usual way, I daresay.'

She huffed at his irreverent answer.

152

He laughed. 'On my honor, my outlaw days are over. I have thoroughly reformed. Remarkable what a man can do when he's faced with the noose,' he added sardonically.

'What noose?'

'The one they showed me when I got arrested and thrown into Newgate. I sure in blazes wouldn't be in this dull place, otherwise,' he muttered under his breath.

'*Arrested*?'

Grimly, he nodded. 'O'Dell set us up. He cornered little Eddie and terrified him into telling where we planned to strike next. O'Dell then simply told Bow Street where to lie in wait for us – a tidy way of getting rid of the Fire Hawks – but I assure you, the Jackals have not seen the last of me.'

Her mind reeling, Jacinda studied him as they turned about the dance floor in time with the music. She had a feeling she was merely being drawn in, but she couldn't resist hearing more of his cock-and-bull story. 'I hope O'Dell didn't harm the child,' she said warily.

'He shook him up a bit, but you know the Knuckler. He's none the worse for wear. I sent him to a boarding school in the country as his anonymous benefactor. Hopefully now he will make something of himself.'

'What happened to Nate and the others?' she asked skeptically.

'Transported to Australia. That's why I'm here. We were all to be hanged until I told them who I am.'

'Who you purport to be. It isn't going to work, you know, and I am certainly not going to help you in your madness, if that is what you're angling after. If anyone figures out your game, you're going to be in huge trouble—'

'Jacinda, I'm telling the truth! Try to understand,' he said more softly as he took in her bewildered gaze. 'This is why I couldn't tell you my real name that night in the rookery. I had kept it a secret all those years. None of my men ever knew of my high birth. They would never have accepted me. Don't you remember I told you that I had run away from home as a lad?'

'Yes, but ... you cannot be serious! That monster of a father you ran away from – with a penchant for blacking your eye – was the marquess of Truro and St. Austell?'

'The same.'

'I don't believe you!'

'It's true. Since my elder brother Percy's death last winter, I became the heir. I did not intend to claim my rights because the final destruction of our line seemed a fitting punishment for everything he did to me.'

'You're jesting,' she said in awe.

'I am not.' The murderous cold that came into his eyes sent a chill down her spine and seemed too genuine to be false, but she could only shake her head, rather dizzy with his claims and the endless circling of the dance. 'You still don't believe me,' he said after a moment in a flat voice.

'I don't know what to believe! As far as I know, you're a hardened criminal.' Remembering anew to lower her voice, she glanced around nervously, making sure no one had noticed the intensity of their discussion.

He stared sullenly over her head, scanning the crowd. 'If you really thought that, then why did you leave me your diamond necklace?'

She blushed in spite of herself. 'The better question is, why didn't you sell the blasted thing instead of turning again to robbery? If your people were really in need, all you had to do was hawk the necklace.'

He rolled his eyes. 'I couldn't.'

'Why not? None of your vile associates would buy it?'

'No. I don't take charity, Jacinda. I meant to give the necklace back to you. That's why I came to Hyde Park to see you. You do remember that day, I trust?' he added in an acid tone.

'Rather.' The reminder of how she had cut him quashed the foolish flutter of her heart and called to mind anew how he had thwarted her attempt to run away to her mother's friends in France. 'Well then, if you're telling the truth that this is real, and that you didn't pawn my necklace to fund your charade, then you may deuced well give it back to me at your earliest convenience.'

He pursed his lips and looked away with mule-like obstinacy. 'Can't.'

'Aha.'

'I had to ditch it at the Taylors' house. Jacinda, I'm telling the truth!' he protested as she scoffed. 'It's in a vase in the master bedroom. I was able to hide it there during the scuffle. Twenty Bow Street runners ambushed us in the middle of the job—'

'Do you mean to say that Daphne Taylor has my diamonds?'

He just looked at her.

'Blade!'

'Rackford. Jacinda, the Taylors' house was the one we were robbing when we got caught. I did it for your sake, after what you told me. Aren't you pleased?'

'This is absurd! To think, I almost believed you for a moment! My diamond necklace magically vanishes, you show up to claim the Truro marquisate, somehow the authorities let you simply walk scot-free out of Newgate, and you expect me to believe this is *not* some glorious, giant con?'

'It isn't a con. What exactly are you suggesting?'

'I'm suggesting that you somehow found out about the story of Lord Truro's missing son and decided to play the part for your own gain. That you sold my necklace to fund your charade—'

'That's a damned lie!' he whispered in outrage. 'Ask my father if you don't believe me. He knows who I am. He made this scar on my brow. Ask your brother Lucien! He figured out the truth a long time ago – and for your information, they did not let me go scot-free. I had to agree to give Bow Street detailed information against some of the worst criminals in London. Do you think I am happy about making enemies of these men?'

155

'So what? There's no risk to you,' she whispered back at him angrily. 'You just told me everyone in the rookery thinks Billy Blade is dead!'

'Aye, and I will be, if these men learn I've ratted on them. I am no liar. But even if this *were* a con, what would you care, anyway? You loathe these people, the same 'pompous hypocrites' who were cruel to your mother. As I recall, that was a large part of the reason you were running away in the first place.'

'An effort you foiled, as I recall!'

'So ... you still refuse to acknowledge that I did it for your own good?'

'It was not your decision to make. It was mine!'

He clenched his jaw, visibly trying to school his temper, then shook his head in resolute patience. 'Jacinda, Jacinda, my wayward little minx. Don't you see?' Holding her a bit closer, his warm breath stirred the curls by her ear. 'Now we can be together,' he murmured. 'After the scare of Percy's death, my father insists that I marry at once – to protect the imperiled family bloodlines, don't you know. I heard you got out of your match with Lord Griffith – and bravo to you for taking my advice. Lord, what a dull, bloodless thing that fellow is. He could never tame you. So, what do you say? You and I are the only two people here who see through all these pompous fools. Besides, if we join forces, we can both rest assured that our secrets will be safe.'

So, that's what he's after. She pulled back and looked up into his eyes, amazed and angrier with each passing second. 'Our secrets?'

'My past in the rookery. Your ... dangerous weakness, my little 'frail vessel.' ' He smiled roguishly.

Her jaw dropped. Obviously, his arrest and sojourn in prison had not made a dent in his arrogance. 'Are you seriously asking me to marry you? Just like that?'

He shrugged, all brash confidence. 'Aye, just like that.'

'Why?' she demanded. 'So you can keep a close watch

on me, make sure I don't expose you?' Her voice climbed with anger. 'So you can keep control of me, just like my brothers? Is that what you want?'

'Now, Jacinda, wait a minute—'

'No, *you* wait a minute, sir.' She shook her head at him. 'Things have changed around here. After you hauled me back to my family, for your information, I found someone else!'

Chapter Nine

She thought he was going to explode, the way his face darkened and his muscles tensed beneath her hand, resting lightly on his shoulder as they danced.

But he didn't miss a step. The perilous moment passed.

With a calculating gleam in his eyes, he forced a taut smile, then shrugged slightly. 'Well. Be that as it may, we both know it's me you really want.'

Her eyes widened at the sheer arrogance of the man. 'You are *unbelievable*!'

Laughing softly, he bent his head down to her ear as he whirled her lightly over the dance floor. 'Not at all, my lady. There are advantages in marrying me.' His warm breath sent shivers down her spine. 'You're worried about following in your mother's footsteps, but rest assured I'll keep you so satisfied you'll never even think about straying.'

'Ugh!' With an appalled gasp, she tore out of his arms at the edge of the dance floor and fled out the French doors to the veranda, furious and blushing profusely at his lascivious promise.

Her cheeks flamed at the wanton memory that his words had summoned, of that night in his room. How unspeakably horrid, how odious he was! She had to get away from him before someone noticed her wild reaction to the scoundrel. She had to regain her composure.

Rackford, or Blade, or whatever his name was – the beast came outside a few steps behind her. 'Jacinda!'

'Go away! You are not a gentleman!'

He laughed.

Trying in exasperation to escape him, she hurried down the shallow stone steps into the garden, but again, he followed her along the grassy allée and under the trellis of climbing roses, pursuing her with long, brisk strides.

'Jacinda! Blast you woman, don't put me off when I have just offered myself and my title to you on a silver platter. Forget your silly infatuation. We both know you belong with me.'

'I'd rather die!'

'Who's the lucky fellow?'

'None of your business!'

'If it's Acer Loring, I may have to shake you back to your senses.'

'It's not,' she retorted, hurrying ahead of him. 'Go away!'

'Who is it, then?'

'Nobody you know!' The path she had been following suddenly came to a dead end, and she found herself facing a little fountain in a neat, circular garden 'room' whose walls were tall, curved box hedges.

As she stood there, not knowing where to turn, her heart pounding, his strong arms closed around her waist from behind her. Before she could even gasp, he turned her around and claimed her mouth in heated urgency, wrapping his arms around her.

'Stop it!' she started to protest, but opening her mouth only invited his kiss more deeply. She moaned softly as his left arm tightened around her waist, his right hand sensuously, possessively cupping her nape.

Oh, she knew the taste of him, the warm, beguiling sweetness of his mouth. She knew his touch, his smell. *Billy* ... He gathered her closer in his arms, but she fought his dizzying potency and the urge to let her body melt against his. She willed herself to stop kissing him back. At her stubborn refusal to participate, she felt his lips curve against her mouth in a wicked half smile.

'Come, my lady.' His voice had turned husky. He ran his fingertips along the line of her jaw, tilting her head back, forcing her to look into his eyes, aglow with hungry need. 'Give me a proper greeting.'

Slowly lowering his head, he kissed her lips apart with masterful demand.

She did not have the strength to resist as he plundered her mouth. Unconsciously wrapping her arms around his neck, she clung to him.

Billy . . .

He slipped the red carnation out of his buttonhole and trailed its satin petals down her cheek as he kissed her, then tenderly tucked the flower behind her ear. The sweetness of the gesture made her ache with longing. She caressed his clean-shaved cheek, ran her fingers through his hair – but when she felt his hand cup her breast, she came back sharply to her senses. This was madness!

She tore herself away, panting harshly. He reached for her again. She shoved him away. 'No! I don't want this. I don't want *you*.'

His jaw clenched. His eyes glittered with thwarted lust and anger at her denial. 'Who is he?' he growled.

'Lord Drummond,' she flung out in defiance.

'Can't say I know the man. I can hardly wait to meet him. What do you think he'll say when I tell him about your little visit to Bainbridge Street? Or how you tried to seduce me in the carriage so that I would let you go on to France?'

'Don't you dare threaten me,' she whispered, murderously holding his gaze. 'Two can play at that game, *Blade*. If you breathe one word about that night to Lord Drummond – or to anyone else – I will tell the whole ton about your past with your filthy, thieving gang.'

He regarded her in simmering amusement. 'Well,

touché, my dear. Seems you learned a thing or two in the rookery.'

'You're the one who said I should learn to think like a thief. Just stay out of my way, and I will stay out of yours, agreed? You're the one who dragged me back to this life. If I am to be confined here, then I intend to make the most of it.'

He studied her shrewdly. 'Staying away from you is the one thing I cannot promise.' She started to turn away with a scowl but he stopped her, grasping her arm. 'I want you, Jacinda,' he warned softly. 'One way or the other, I will have you.'

'Try it, and my brothers will have your head. You're in my world now, and if you cross me, Lord *Rackford*, you're the one who will be sorry.' With that, she threw the red carnation on the ground and hurried back through the cool, dewy darkness of the garden, returning to the glittering ballroom before she was missed.

Cursing himself for making a thorough botch of it, Rackford was left standing there, staring after her, not quite sure how to proceed, but thoroughly vexed to find himself rejected yet again by the maddening chit. He watched her marching rather shakily up the moonlit path, her golden curls swinging, her gauzy skirts rippling around her legs. She ran up the few shallow steps to the veranda and disappeared inside.

He let out a long exhalation and started to drag his hand through his hair, then scowled at the reminder that they had made him cut it short.

Lord Drummond? he thought furiously. *Who the hell is he?*

Tugging at his starched silk cravat with a low growl, he stalked back into Devonshire's sprawling palace, stomping the carnation into the turf as he passed. At the threshold of the French doors, he paused warily, feeling out of place again and frustrated to the point of exasperation with his clumsy ignorance of this glittering world and all its subtle dangers.

Scanning the ballroom for his golden-haired quarry, his brooding gaze wandered back to the place where her family had been standing. Determined to have a look at this beau ideal of a man whom she deemed worthy of her hand, he moved warily through the crowd until he noticed his host talking with a knot of guests nearby. Devonshire would tell him who this Drummond fellow was. Reaching the young duke's side, he endured another round of introductions, bowing, shaking hands with the men, proclaiming himself enchanted to meet their diamond-dripping women. Everybody gave him that same speculative look and seemed compelled to mention their daughters or nieces, but privately, he had already chosen his bride whether she bloody well liked it or not.

As discreetly as possible, he pulled Devonshire aside after the guests' meaningless chatter and asked him the all-important question. When the duke told him what he wanted to know, nodding across the ballroom to where the Knight clan still stood, Rackford could scarcely believe his eyes.

'You're jesting,' he said, glancing again at his host.

Devonshire shook his head earnestly.

'That's ... the same Lord Drummond of the Home Office?' he pursued, just to be certain.

'Yes,' the duke told him, nodding.

The name had not occurred to him till he saw the man. It hadn't seemed possible. Now it appeared even less so. *What the hell is she up to?* Rackford narrowed his eyes.

The radiant young Jacinda, whom he had already come to think of as his, was clinging rather desperately to the arm of a man who was seventy if he was a day. A man who was known as one of the most infamous Tory oppressors of Lord Liverpool's government. She was openly flirting with the old tyrant. He saw it in her carefree laughter, her sweeping lashes, the pretty tilt of her head, the fluttering of her fan. He couldn't believe his eyes.

She's lost her mind, he thought. *That old wigsby – over me?*

Why, it would be easy stealing her from that doddering ancient. Sturdy and square-jawed, Lord Drummond was not a frail-looking elder, but his skin was lined and weathered, his hair the same dull gray of his tailcoat. His round spectacles glinted in the candlelight, as though he were even now dreaming up some clandestine court intrigue or some new way to trample the poor.

As Rackford's astonished gaze moved back to Jacinda, he remembered her that night in his room, speaking with such impassioned determination about her longing to be free; he remembered how he had teased her about marrying an old wigsby. Slowly, understanding dawned.

Why, you sly little baggage. You scheming, darling, errant little vixen. He stared across the ballroom at her in amazement. *You have found the keys to your cage, after all.*

It seemed the only husband who would not inconvenience the lady was a dead one.

He was stunned. He would have laughed outright at her daring ploy, except that it suddenly meant the old man was a more serious rival than he had first assumed. The threat was not Drummond himself, but what he could give Jacinda.

Freedom.

The very thing that he, Rackford, had taken away the night he had returned her to her family.

His slight, sarcastic smile faded as he sought to orient himself to this confounding new set of circumstances. As though feeling his stare, she looked over and peered furtively at him from over the edge of her fan, meeting his gaze through the crowd. For a heartbeat, he couldn't breathe as the fire of her dark, sultry eyes engulfed him.

Chiding her with a sardonic smile, he shook his head slightly at her. *It won't work. You want me too much.*

The stubborn curl that fell down the middle of her forehead jumped as she tossed her head in haughty disdain and looked away, but a blush crept up her cheeks. Then her aged suitor led her off to mingle among the foreign dignitaries who had begun pouring in from the royal wedding.

With growing anger and deepening doubt, Rackford watched the mismatched pair for as long as he could hold his temper in check – approximately nine seconds – then abruptly stormed out of the ball, not taking his leave of anyone.

He'd had enough of this damned civility.

It was time to go hunting Jackals.

Yanking the knot of his cravat free, he stalked out to the new, absurdly expensive curricle his father had bought him – in a pitiful effort, he suspected, to assuage his conscience for bashing his head in on any number of occasions.

The groom hung on for dear life as Rackford drove the curricle brashly through the streets. It was so much lighter and faster than the lumbering wagons he was used to that he nearly overturned the thing tearing around the corner of Piccadilly and St. James's Street. He heard the groom gulp aloud and realized he was on the verge of taking out his wrath on the poor stupid horses. He was not his father.

Reining in, he drove the rest of the way back to the grand, gloomy mansion in Lincoln's Inn Fields at a more reasonable pace, still brooding. God, she was a stubborn creature! Yet despite his will to the contrary, he could not remain indifferent to her. It was madness to want a woman like her. Even Lucien had called the girl devious. Perplexed and seething, he eased the horses to a halt in front of the tall brick house built eighty years ago by George Dance the Younger.

Vaulting out of the curricle, he left it to the groom. As the servant drove the flashy vehicle away, returning to the stables through the nearby narrow passage, Rackford walked up the front stairs, habitually glancing over his shoulder. Behind him, the garden square, once the scene of public executions, was dark and quiet, the other great houses sitting around it in aged respectability like dowagers reminiscing on their debutante days. The great houses still remained, but the neighborhood was past its prime. Even the handsome theater on nearby Portugal Street had slipped out of favor and was now being used as a china warehouse. The fashionable world had moved west to Mayfair; indeed, from the window in his apartments upstairs, he could almost see the border of his former turf.

If there was a reason why he had chosen his territory so close to his father's residence, he didn't want to think about it. The old bastard spent most of his time in Cornwall, anyway, getting foxed, and could hardly be bothered to attend the opening of Parliament each year. Rackford knew because he had, with a jaundiced eye, followed his family's activities from a distance.

He continued up the steps and was surprised when Gerald, the night butler, opened the door for him with a cordial bow. 'Lord Rackford.'

'Evening, Gerald. Is my father at home?'

'No, sir, His Lordship is at his club. Shall I send anything up for you?'

He waved off the offer. 'I'm fine.' He was still not used to having people do everything for him. Indeed, he could not seem to treat the servants like the efficient automatons they were hired to be. 'Thanks, old boy,' he said, giving the man a hearty clap on the shoulder as he strode past him.

'O-of course, my lord,' the startled servant replied as Rackford left the entrance hall, jogging up the wide mahogany staircase to his apartment.

He had just passed the landing at the first floor and was continuing up to the second when a weak, wan voice called after him.

'William.'

Recognizing those helpless tones at once, he checked the current of bitter, long-nursed resentment that instantly flowed through his body. He stopped on the staircase and wearily turned around as his mother glided out of the salon

165

below, as silently as some frail shadow.

At fifty, the thin, once-glamorous marchioness of Truro and St. Austell was a brittle, fading beauty with a haunted air. As a boy on the streets of London, he had sometimes felt a pang of homesickness recalling his mother's smell, or rather, the smell of her cosmetics: the black frankincense mixture with which she blackened her eyebrows and lashes, the henna with which she lightened her hair, the oil of talc that gave her her milky smooth complexion, and the rouge he had sometimes watched her put on with a slender camel-hair pencil. Powerless to stop her husband from beating her younger child, the marchioness had fled from the reality of her shattered family, finding her escape in taking exquisite care of her appearance.

Rackford did not think he could ever forgive her, but he dared not express his anger at her for fear that the fragile creature would collapse and crumble into a pile of dust.

He bowed to her. 'Good evening, madam.'

'You are home early.'

Home? he wondered in jaded weariness. *Is that where I am?*

She wafted out onto the landing, where the wall candles made gaunt shadows in the hollows under her high cheek-bones. 'Was the Devonshire ball not to your liking?'

He stared at her, biting his tongue. He wanted to tell her to leave him the hell alone, that it was too late now for her to try to befriend him, but instead he merely shrugged. 'I have a bit of the headache.' He could not keep the slight edge of irony from his tone, but she failed to catch it anyway.

Her eyebrows lifted with interest at his mention of a physical ailment, for illness was her second hobby. The almighty headache had been her favorite excuse for closeting herself in her rooms whenever she smelled a storm brewing, abandoning him when he had most needed an adult ally. Her nerves could not withstand all the yelling, she had often said, but now that he was an adult, Rackford

166

understood her reasoning. If she did not actually see what was going on, in her mind, it didn't exist.

'I will ring for a headache powder for you—'

'No, thank you, my lady. Some rest is all that I require.'

'Oh.' Her delicate shoulders sagged with disappointment at his refusal to let her mother him at this late date. 'As you wish, William.'

'Goodnight, madam.'

'Good ... night,' she answered faintly as he turned away and hurried up the rest of the stairs.

Shaking off the clinging sense of her neediness, he reached his opulent apartment on the second floor and quietly let himself in. Light-boxes glowed on the pair of claw-footed parquetry tables in the dim sitting room, low candlelight shining through the tiny pinpricks in the perforated tin housings.

Closing the door behind him, he crossed the room and rang the bellpull. Filbert, his valet, would be expecting the summons and would be reporting back to the marquess. Nothing must appear amiss.

The efficient little man promptly arrived to attend him, lighting the candles, then putting away each luxurious article of formal clothing that Rackford took off. When he stripped down to his long white drawers and wool stockings, Filbert held up his dressing gown of rich blue satin. Rackford slipped his arms into the sleeves and shrugged it on. With the voluminous robe draping loosely from his shoulders, he picked up one of the books on India that he was reading to keep the ton guessing about where he had been all these years and sauntered across the large chamber, the book in one hand, a candle in a pewter holder in the other.

Absently, he asked Filbert for a brandy, which the servant duly poured and brought to him. 'That will be all,' he said coolly.

'Very good, my lord.' Filbert bowed and retreated to the door, quietly slipping out.

Rackford cocked his head and listened keenly, waiting to

hear the servant's footsteps retreating down the corridor, but Filbert remained on the other side of the door for a moment, no doubt listening to him.

Fully aware he was being observed, Rackford merely sipped the brandy, riffled the pages of the book, and continued his slow pacing back and forth across the room. At last, the valet was satisfied that his master wasn't up to anything that might be of interest to his sire. The moment the servant's footsteps faded down the corridor, Rackford closed the book and set it swiftly on the table, going to lock the door. His robe billowed behind him as he strode through his bedchamber to his dressing room.

Emerging a couple minutes later in plain trousers and boots, a simple shirt and a loose black coat, he went stealthily to the parquetry table and pulled out the dagger he had hidden in one of its secret compartments. He paused only for a moment to push aside the heavy velvet curtain, scanning the street below to see if the Bow Street runners who were assigned to shadow him were on duty.

He saw in satisfaction that he must have lost them somewhere back at Devonshire House. His abrupt exit from the ball had had unanticipated benefits. They were probably still posted outside the duke's mansion. His eyes narrowed, his mouth a grim line, he looked out over the black city skyline in the direction of Bainbridge Street.

He let the curtain fall and blew out the candle.

A few moments later, he slipped out of the house by a side door, then scaled the garden wall and sprang down lightly on the other side.

His heart pounded with the fresh taste of freedom. For a man accustomed to doing whatever he liked and answering to no one, the past month had been sheer hell – under his father's thumb, spied on by Bow Street and his own valet, under the constant scrutiny of Society with its rapacious appetite for gossip.

Reasoning with himself that since he was going to kill Jackals, not fraternize with them, he was not technically breaking his word to Sir Anthony, he ducked into the gloom of the nearest alleyway and began making his way toward St. Giles.

About half an hour later, he crept into position on the rooftop where he had once stationed his sentries.

Badly outnumbered, he thought, counting fifteen of the Jackals loitering in the street and lounging on the front stoop of the gin shop that had been the Fire Hawks' former headquarters.

His sole advantage was the fact that his enemies all thought he was dead. He stared down into the street where the party had been on the night he'd brought Jacinda into the rookery. His muscles tightened with the realization that the Jackals had thoroughly settled into the new territory they had taken over.

He narrowed his eyes in bristling hostility as O'Dell came strutting around the building with a musket resting over his shoulder and a liquor bottle dangling from his other hand. He sounded drunk on his newfound power as he yelled abuses at his men. O'Dell still appeared to be gloating over the way he had handed the Fire Hawks over to Bow Street, thus ridding himself of his enemies and safeguarding his own position with the authorities in one fell swoop. The police wouldn't go after O'Dell after he had been so very helpful to them.

Then Rackford noticed the four large men flanking O'Dell. *Bodyguards*, he mused. Perhaps O'Dell was beginning to feel the constant dangers involved in being top dog in the rookery. Then his gaze traveled over the ransacked square, and his face darkened. *Look what they've done to this place*. The warehouse had been looted, and the poor quizzical building had taken a beating. Windows were broken, the windlass hung askew on tangled ropes, the door was torn off its hinges, and those sons of bitches were lounging around everywhere. The sight of it pained and infuriated him, an agonizing, guilty reminder of how he had failed his people, aye, while he now lived in luxury.

169

Well, tonight was his chance to strike back. He knew exactly what he wanted to accomplish. He longed to launch a full-out frontal assault, but with one man against dozens it would have been madness. His strategy was to turn the Jackals against each other until their group unity devolved into a war of every man for himself. Their gang would self-destruct from within, and when they went their separate ways, he could pick them off one by one.

His gaze flicked from where O'Dell was lording it over a few of his underlings to the old abandoned carriage manufacturer's adjacent to the gang headquarters. What O'Dell did not know was that the abandoned factory connected to the building through one of those thieves' trapdoors that existed throughout the rookeries of London.

As a boy, he had memorized the locations of as many of them as he could discover. He had quickly learned that, contrary to popular belief, thieves were anything but lazy. Over generations, the criminal classes of London had constructed a whole maze of claustrophobic tunnels between buildings, hidden ladders, holes knocked in brick walls just big enough for a man to fit through, then concealed with an advertising placard that swung on hinges for an easy escape. There were secret cellars and crawl spaces, false closet backs, hiding places under floors that gave out onto some back alley – all built and dedicated to the great game of giving thief-takers the slip.

Using this knowledge, he knew just how to get into his former headquarters and out again before any of the Jackals even realized he was there.

Unsheathing his knife with a whisper of metal, he melted into the shadows.

A few minutes later, he was moving stealthily through the hollow silence of the abandoned carriage factory. Only the faintest gleam of moonlight slanted in through the high, narrow windows, but he knew the way. The air was thick with dust. The Stygian gloom in the distant corners of the factory rustled with scampering rats.

Clamping his knife between his teeth, Rackford climbed the ladder to the old storage loft. At the top, he crept to the trapdoor and silently let himself into what was now the Jackals' stronghold.

His selection of his dupes was a mixture of strategy and chance. He had to pick rooms that were easy to get into, but he only acted when he found the rooms occupied by strong members of the Jackals.

The first one he stung was Flash, the 'good-looking one' of the gang, he thought drily. The black-haired, blue-eyed young man was singing a bawdy music hall song in front of the mirror, carefully combing and trimming his sideburns. Silently, Rackford reached down from the ceiling crawl space and lifted away the large, shiny fob watch lying on the chest of drawers. No doubt Flash had stolen it from some poor dupe in the streets. The young man paused midsong, inspecting his nostril hairs, then continued blithely with the next verse. Rackford vanished back into the crawl space, his heart pounding. It was bad of him, he knew, but to him, this was fun.

In another corner of the building, the second of the Jackals to be snared in his web was the infamous ogre Baumer. Rackford found the towering oaf, with his bulbous nose and tangle of dark hair, in flagrante delicto with a hefty whore built to withstand the siege. Like rutting giants, they took no notice of him stealthily slipping into the far end of the dimly lit room.

He tiptoed over to the pile of abandoned clothing, took Baumer's small leather money purse, and left Flash's pocket watch in its place. He looked over his shoulder quickly, realizing the giants' crude groans were intensifying. Unseen, he slipped out again, only wishing he could be a fly on the wall when Baumer reached for his coin purse in order to pay his companion.

Lastly, he came to the lonely upper room of the weirdest gang member, Bloody Fred. Even O'Dell was a little afraid of Fred, who had been in and out of Bedlam. The

171

corridor was empty, for the rest of the gang gave sweet little Freddie a wide berth.

When Rackford smelled opium smoke wafting out from under the crack of Fred's door, he knew he had to take a gamble. Big Baumer against Bloody Fred. It was perfect.

A moment later, he opened the door and calmly walked in.

The wiry little man with a shock of red hair and a goatee beard was sitting on the floor, staring at nothing. His Turkish water pipe was knocked over beside him. With what seemed a huge effort, Fred looked up slowly, barely able to keep his bloodshot eyes open.

'Hullo, Fred,' Rackford said in a low, amiable tone, careful not to make any sudden movements.

'Blade?' Vague surprise registered on Fred's pale, pointy face. 'Thought you were dead.'

'I am,' he replied. 'That's why I'm here.'

'A – a ghost?' The drugged man scrambled back against the bed. 'Stay back!'

'Don't be afraid, Freddie. I've come to give you a present,' he said soothingly.

'Me? W-why?'

'Because you and I have the same enemy.'

'W-what do you mean?'

'You'll find out soon enough. Here. Take this as a token of my goodwill.' He swung Baumer's money purse gently before the man's glazed eyes, then tossed it to him. It fell onto the floor with a soft clank between Fred and his pipe.

'For me? Thanks, Blade! Why you givin' me gold?' Fred turned and struggled to find it, muttering. 'Nobody ever gives me nothin'.'

'Trust me, you deserve it.'

'Crikey!' he breathed, staring at the rain of coins as he poured them out onto the floor between his sprawled legs.

While he was distracted, Rackford deftly swiped the man's little wooden box of first-rate Turkish opium.

Slowly, silently backing out of the room, he went and

deposited it in the largest room in the building – the one that used to be his and which now belonged to Cullen O'Dell.

Before long, Rackford was free of the place, elated with his success as he strode down the street. Soon the thefts would be discovered and the Jackals would be at each other's throats.

If Bloody Fred told the others he had seen Billy Blade's ghost, they would consider it naught but the hallucination of an addicted opium-eater.

Cocky and free for the moment, he felt like his old self again, but all of a sudden, he missed his mates terribly. Especially Nate. He shoved the pain away. He could not afford it. He had done his best for them. Still, the fact that he was totally alone, cut off from everyone he trusted, drained his fleeting sense of victory.

Hopping on the back of a passing dray cart, he stole a ride like he used to as a boy. Within twenty minutes, he was in front of his father's house. He vaulted over the garden wall again and crept back obediently into his silk-hung cage.

Chapter Ten

The next morning promptly after breakfast Jacinda went to the subscription library on the corner of St. James's and Pall Mall to make her own investigation of Lord Rackford by consulting the very oracle of the ton, *Debrett's Peerage*. All savvy young ladies knew to look up their suitors and other persons of interest in this esteemed volume in order to learn their lineage and background. She flipped through the delicate pages of the massive tome, a woman on a mission.

With Lucien still in the West Country, the almighty book seemed her best hope for finding independent confirmation of Blade's tale. Meanwhile, behind her, the other patrons moved quietly over the hardwood floors, taking their selections to the clerk's large circular desk. Miss Hood was reading an article in the latest issue of *La Belle Assemblée*, her bonnet neatly tied under her chin, her folded parasol hooked over her forearm. Lizzie had torn herself away from Alec's side long enough to accompany her, as well, never one to miss a chance to pop into a place where books were housed.

Lizzie was squinting through her reading spectacles, scanning the shelves for the latest volumes by the newfangled German philosophers. She emitted a little cry of delight that echoed through the quiet library when she seized upon the newest work of Goethe.

'Shh!' the library clerk hushed her.

'Sorry,' Lizzie said absently, blushing.

Jacinda shot her a look that brimmed with laughter. Lizzie held up the Goethe and pointed excitedly at it. Jacinda shook her head at her in amusement. A hopeless bluestocking, she thought, but smiled at her friend. Things were finally beginning to get back to normal between them now that she had confided in Lizzie.

Last night in the carriage on the way home from the Devonshire ball, Alec had teased Jacinda unceasingly about her waltz with Lord Rackford, which had apparently raised a few eyebrows, not to mention Robert's hackles.

Jacinda had thought she was in the clear when Bel had soothed the duke's displeasure, but later, when she had been getting ready for bed in her chambers, Lizzie had tiptoed in in her night rail and had started asking questions.

In the end, Jacinda had finally told her best friend everything. Well – almost everything. She had told her the whole story of how she had met Billy Blade in the rookery and had even admitted that she had let him kiss her, but already blushing crimson, she could not bring herself to tell Lizzie just how far she had let that tattooed heathen go. The girls had sat on her bed drinking chocolate and talking into the wee hours of the night.

Jacinda had felt much better after sharing the whole account with her best friend. She ought to have done it sooner, she knew, but Lizzie had taken her attempt to run away personally and had remained miffed at her, so that Jacinda hardly dared wonder how she would take the news of her visit to the rookery. Besides, Lizzie had judged Blade a 'nasty man' on sight that day long ago when he had come to Knight House to provide the twins with information. Lizzie was still as skeptical about him as she was, but since he had stopped Jacinda from running away and had brought her back safely to her family, Lizzie was willing to give him a chance. Above

175

all, Jacinda knew she could trust Lizzie to keep the secret of his past. Even if he was lying, she did not want to get him into trouble with the law.

Presently, she turned to the pages in *Debrett's* devoted to the Albright family. Her heart beat faster as she trailed her gloved fingertip down the narrow column of print.

Albright, Ld. William Spencer. b. 1788 Perranporth, Cornwall – 2nd son M. of Truro and St. Austell. edu. Eton. Missing, 1801. Presumed dead.

'Well?'

She looked over. Lizzie stood beside her with an expectant look. Jacinda tapped the paragraph in perplexity.

Lizzie peered down at it, then turned to her, taking off her reading spectacles. Lizzie glanced over her shoulder at Miss Hood, then looked at Jacinda again. 'Maybe he is telling the truth?'

Jacinda bit her lip in thought. Burning curiosity raced through her, but although she did not know what to believe, she had to admit that his entry into Society had brought an undeniable sense of thrill to the Season ahead.

Could his cock-and-bull tale be true? A dozen questions about his past spun through her mind. If he was really the son of a marquess, how had he fallen in with thieves? Had he truly never meant to claim his rightful place just to have revenge on his father?

'What are you going to do?' Lizzie asked as Jacinda shut the large book with a snap of resounding finality.

'Make him talk,' she declared, determination glowing in her eyes. 'I must know everything.'

'I daresay it's damn unsporting of a chap not to say where he's been the past decade and a half,' George Winthrop grumbled that evening, frowning over his port.

'Nonsense, George,' Acer Loring drawled, turned to give him a superior smile. 'If Rackford prefers to be mysterious, that is his prerogative. I daresay, by keeping mum, he has provided the ton with more entertainment than they've had since – well, at least since Byron's fall from grace last month.'

The dandies snickered among themselves.

'Though I must admit,' Acer went on, scratching his smooth cheek, 'it does leave one wondering if perhaps our new friend has something genuinely worth hiding. What say you, Rackford?'

The fashionable set of young bucks waited expectantly for his reply.

Rackford wanted to kill them. Somehow he managed to check his temper, however, knowing he was fortunate enough merely that none of them recognized him as the barbaric man they had mocked in Hyde Park. Smiling blandly, he refused to rise to the bait. And they were baiting him.

Make no mistake of it, he warned himself, growing more coldly furious by the second. Right there in Lady Sudeby's drawing room, he was besieged. Unlike Cullen O'Dell and his Jackals, the glib Acer Loring and his chums were experts in the sneak attack. New as he was to the polite world, he did not know how he was supposed to react, how to defend himself against these droll insinuations and taunting remarks. In the rookery, where respect was everything, he had killed men for less. When he had turned on one of the impudent young bucks with a sudden snarl, Acer had laughed at him for his inability to take a joke. That was when he realized that they were trying to lure him into an angry outburst in the hopes of seeing him make a fool of himself.

They dared not challenge him outright. They were afraid of him. He could smell it. Only their numbers gave them nerve. There was nothing to be done but to endure, waiting for the rest of the guests to arrive for Lady Sudeby's dinner party.

He had only come in the hopes of seeing Jacinda so he could try again with her after having botched things so badly last night. Now, however, he was in dread of seeing

177

her, knowing that these pampered bastards were going to humiliate him in front of her just like they had done that day in the park.

Acer went back to bragging about his racehorse. Rackford glanced again at the doorway. Only the possibility of seeing Jacinda kept him from storming out as he had last night. He had already been taken to task by a few of the women for abandoning the Devonshire ball so early.

Next, the dandies began reminiscing about their Oxford days, well aware that he had not been there with them. Already a bit bewildered by their flurry of Classical references and Latin maxims, he was lost when Acer and George exchanged a few lines in French, watching out of the corner of their eyes to see if he had understood. He just stood there, feeling like an oaf. The implication was clear: He was an ignorant brute.

Fair enough.

Then they turned to the amusing subject of who had made his clothes.

'Er, Stulz, I think,' he said haplessly.

'You think? You don't know?' George exclaimed, appalled.

Acer laughed idly, looking him over. 'Really, Rackford, a purple waistcoat? You should horsewhip your valet for allowing you to leave the house. Black or white for evening, man. Don't you know anything?'

'Oh.' He pretended to take it all in lazy good humor, but with Jacinda expected at any moment, his pride was half trampled. He dreaded seeing her, certain she was going to take one look at him and laugh; yet, glancing around the drawing room, he honestly thought he was dressed as well as any of the men. His father had his clothes made by Stultz, after all. Rackford's single-breasted coat and trousers were conservative black silk, his cravat flawless. His damned shoes had been shined with champagne. So what if a man liked a waistcoat with some color to it? Why did he have to look exactly like everybody else?

178

He wondered what they would have said about his tattoos.

'A gentleman only trusts Mr. Weston of Conduit Street to get the cut of his clothes right,' Acer was in the midst of informing him. 'Boots from Hoby's, hats from Lock's. Anything else is barbaric.'

'Well, perhaps I have a bit of the barbarian in me,' he warned with a dangerous smile, his patience wearing thin.

'Quite,' Acer agreed.

A chorus of 'ooh's' and 'aah's' arose from the others, who seemed to want a good milling match. Acer smirked, oblivious of how close he was to being put through the nearest wall.

At that moment, like his guardian angel, Lady Jacinda walked into the room.

His heart caught in his throat at her charming smile as she greeted their hostess. Her upswept golden curls were artfully disheveled, confined with a ribbon tied into a bow above her left eye. Her dinner gown was of pale tangerine silk with short puff sleeves trimmed with white lace. She wore a modest string of pearls around her neck and high white satin gloves. An India shawl of rich gold, amber, and purple swirls was drawn negligently through each arm, forming a flowing drapery along her slender figure.

Then she turned away to greet someone else, and Rackford drew in his breath at the low-cut back of her dress. He stared, riveted by the expanse of creamy skin, the supple sweep of her spine, and the delicate architecture of her shoulder blades. The soft gathers of her silk shawl brushed the back of her waist. Seized with visions of kissing every inch of her body, he did not remember to breathe until she moved on, gliding into the drawing room.

She greeted people here and there with a warmth and refinement that ran deeper than all her rebellious protests against the ways of the ton when she had turned up in the rookery that night, angry at the world.

As Rackford promptly recovered from the initial jolt of

179

want, somehow merely seeing her eased some of the tension from him, even though he knew she despised him. He stood a little taller, breathed a little easier, and watched her with a possessive glow coming into his eyes. She sparkled like the rarest of jewels and embodied the fineness that the aristocracy could produce at its best. Any man with sense, he supposed, would have resolved to forget her after her flat setdown the night before, but somehow, Lord help him, the challenge of her every rejection only made him want her more.

His heart beast faster as the party from Knight House made their way through the room. There was no sign of her ancient beau, Lord Drummond.

After what felt like an eternity, Jacinda casually strolled over to their group with another young lady by her side, but he soon realized in chagrin that she was ignoring him. Yes, he felt a distinct chill floating in his direction from her. Meanwhile, the idiotic dandies plied her with compliments. These Jacinda laughed off, calling them absurd and gaily abusing her admirers with her wit.

'Jas,' Acer drawled, 'what do you think of Rackford's waistcoat?'

The others laughed.

She passed a bored look over Rackford.

He scowled ferociously at the leading dandy, his heart pounding with restrained violence. He had known the moment of humiliation would come, but he had been too stupid to run while he'd had the chance.

Jacinda turned back to Acer with an indifferent shrug. 'What about it?'

'It's purple.'

'I see that,' she said.

'Purple's all exploded,' Acer said in contempt.

Jacinda studied Rackford for a long moment. He could barely bring himself to meet her gaze, wanting to wither of shame where he stood, but then something, maybe pity, flickered in the depths of her starry-night eyes. 'That's not

180

what Alec says,' she informed Acer in a quelling tone, nodding toward a blond young man on crutches.

The dandies let out a collective gasp.

'Lord Alec's wearing purple?' George Winthrop asked in alarm.

'Not at the moment, you dolt, but he was just telling us on the way over here about a purple marcella waistcoat he ordered last week. He'll be cross at you, Lord Rackford.' She favored him with a quick, aloof smile, though her eyes snapped sparks at him. 'My brother always likes to be the first to usher in the latest thing. He is quite the arbiter of fashion.'

He said nothing, holding her gaze. He knew she was lying through her teeth for him, had just come to his rescue when she could have delivered the coup de grace to his pride. He could do nothing but stare at her in utter adoration.

Giving him a saucy little look of private reproach, she turned away and started to move on with her friend. *Think fast.*

'Lady Jacinda,' he called, stopping her. 'Pray, have you seen Lady Sudeby's Canaletto?' He gestured toward the painting that hung above the fireplace.

Jacinda's golden eyebrows arched high. Her gaze followed his hand. Hanging above the mantel in all its splendor was the Italian master's luminous landscape.

'Why, it's beautiful,' her companion murmured, taking a step closer.

Jacinda turned back to him in question, barely hiding her bemusement. 'Goodness, I had heard that it was stolen.'

He shrugged, his eyes dancing. 'Lady Sudeby was telling us a short while ago that some anonymous benefactor managed to retrieve it, and returned it to her.'

'An anonymous benefactor?' she asked meaningfully.

'Indeed.'

'How very mysterious! I am so pleased it has been returned to its rightful owner.' She paused, casting him a wily look. 'Actually, Lord Rackford, I was not aware that you were acquainted with Lady Sudeby.'

'She is my aunt,' he said drily. 'My mother's twin sister.'

She blinked with astonishment, then quickly looked away, biting her lip to hold back her mirth at his revelation. She cleared her throat. 'Lord Rackford, allow me to present my dearest friend in all the world, Miss Elizabeth Carlisle.'

He bowed to her modestly pretty companion. 'Miss Carlisle, it is a pleasure.'

'How do you do, my lord,' the older, brown-haired girl murmured, curtseying.

Rackford felt himself closely inspected by Miss Carlisle's penetrating gaze as he bowed over her hand. Truly, he wanted the earth to swallow him at the moment, for he sensed that the best friend was making her own judgment on his worthiness or lack thereof for Her Ladyship. That could only mean Jacinda had told her friend heaven-knew-what about him, maybe even about his blundering proposal of the previous night.

Blasted women. They could never keep a thing to themselves, but this one, he realized, could make or break his cause with the queen bee.

Straightening up again, he glanced at Jacinda, rather miffed by his suspicions. He only hoped Miss Carlisle could hold her tongue about whatever she had been told.

Upon the announcement shortly thereafter that dinner was served, Jacinda saw fit to award him the privilege of taking her down to dine. In the luxuriously appointed dining room, the candelabras glowed, burnishing the gilding throughout the room and gleaming upon the fine silver and exquisite painted china. He walked his lady to her place and pulled out her chair for her, waiting as she daintily sat down. His gloved fingertips brushed the bare skin of her back. He saw the small shiver that ran down her spine at his light, accidental touch.

'You look ravishing,' he murmured loud enough for only her to hear as he pushed in her chair.

She slipped him a haughty look that warned he was not in the clear yet. Rather chastened, he nodded to her, then went in search of his seat. He soon found that his dotty aunt had surrounded him with young ladies whose mothers had never dared break Society's rules.

Jacinda sat on the opposite side of the table, two chairs down. Taking his seat, he blanched at the intimidating array of silverware before him, spread out like so many surgeon's tools. *Wonderful*, he thought in disgust.

Acer was sitting nearby and was watching him with interest, as though he already suspected that half of the odd-shaped spoons and tiny forks were completely foreign to him. Rackford dropped his gaze, placing his napkin on his lap.

When the first course was served, he realized by watching the others that the gentlemen were expected to carve the meat dish that happened to be set in front of them.

He eyed up the steaming chine of lamb before him, picked up the long, serrated carving knife, and gave Acer Loring a hard, meaningful look, needing not a single word to make his threat concisely plain.

Acer's smug hauteur wilted as he watched Rackford slice the eight pounds of steaming red meat; Billy hadn't earned the nickname 'Blade' for no reason. By the time he was through with the job, he trusted the dandy had gotten the message.

Done, he stuck the knife into the saddle of lamb with a flourish and offered the dish to the debutantes seated around him.

He noticed Jacinda giving him an exasperated look. He sent her a small shrug. She looked away, shaking her head.

When it came time to attack the meal, however, he floundered, as uncertain as the dupe of some shell-game trickster, his hand wavering above the selection of silverware. He swept a rather desperate glance over the other

183

guests until he saw Jacinda staring forcefully at him.

The person next to her asked her a question, and she rejoined the conversation with a smile, but he watched her hand as she slowly picked up the second fork from the left and twirled it playfully between her fingers.

He made his selection in relief. She glanced at him briefly a moment later, making sure he had not made another faux pas.

Somehow she got him through the three-hour meal, until at last, it was over. The ladies withdrew, while the men stayed at table for a short while longer, drinking port and sherry. He met her rakehelly brother, Lord Alec Knight, who was of an age with him, and liked the man at once.

At last, the sexes reconvened in the salon, where card tables were set up for a few respectable games of whist. The debutantes, however, seemed more interested in showing off their musical talents on the pianoforte, either playing the instrument for the crowd of guests or singing with its accompaniment. Rackford stood at the back of the room, leaning against the wall and sipping another glass of the thick, fortified wine. He was most interested in waiting for Jacinda's performance, but rather than going to the piano, she meandered slowly through the crowded drawing room.

He looked into her eyes as she casually sauntered toward him. Pure lightning leaped between them, but she demurely looked away and leaned against the wall beside him, sipping her wine. He pretended to enjoy the music, but all his senses were ferociously focused on her.

He could feel her acute awareness of him, as well. It was torture, not being able to touch her. 'Thanks for your help in there,' he said under his breath.

She waved her silk fan idly, avoiding his gaze. 'I know you think me a useless ornament, but sometimes my trivial expertise has its uses.'

'I never said you were useless.' He could think of any number of uses for her, all of which would have gotten him slapped. 'Dare I hope your kindness to me means you have decided to believe me?'

'No.'

'Then why did you help me?'

'I have decided to withhold judgment until Lucien comes home. That is all.'

'Fair enough.'

'Till then . . .' She sighed. Pretending to watch the next piano-playing debutante's performance, she slid him a wary, sideways glance. 'I haven't much time, and this is not to be interpreted as encouragement, but you, Lord Rackford, are a pitiful sight. You will never survive the ton on your own, but for reasons I do not wish to contemplate, I am disposed to help you. Call on me tomorrow at one. Do not be late.'

Taken aback, he had no time to react as she gave him a bolstering look, then drifted on through the crowd, chatting with people here and there.

He watched her with newfound hope wafting up from the core of him.

A pitiful sight? he wondered in amusement. How could anyone possibly interpret that as encouragement? But he hid his widening smile and sipped his sherry, too happy, suddenly, to care.

Chapter Eleven

At five minutes before one the next day, a splendid black town coach with the Albright coat of arms on the door rolled through the high wrought-iron gates of Knight House. Jacinda watched from an upper window just long enough to note that the driver and footmen were in tan livery with frothy white lace jabots and black tricornes. The four black horses were perfectly matched, their black harnesses shot through with smart crimson stitching. Her eyes shining with excitement, she dashed off to the drawing room to receive her caller.

She doubted he was familiar enough with Society's customs to realize he had been invited at a most informal hour reserved for visits with one's most intimate friends; social calls grew more ceremonious as the afternoon advanced. Lord knew she might well need the whole day to bring him up to scratch. Since the afternoon was sunny and pleasant, she had already decided that she and Lord Rackford should walk in Green Park, where they could talk privately. Knowing beforehand that he would be coming, she had sent Miss Hood out on a fool's errand. Lizzie would accompany them, a much more agreeable chaperon than the eagle-eyed governess.

Downstairs, she heard Mr. Walsh answer the door. She slipped into the drawing room, where Bel and Lizzie were sewing, and hurried to arrange herself in a graceful attitude on one of the sofas, neatly smoothing her skirts around her. Lizzie gave her a mirthful look, in on the secret, but Bel was intent on her work, carefully rethreading her needle. Robert, thankfully, was at White's – not that his presence would have deterred Billy Blade.

Jacinda's heart beat faster as she heard Rackford's sure, heavy footfalls following Mr. Walsh's dignified march up the curved marble staircase. In another moment, the butler gave a knock on the drawing room door and opened it at the duchess's summons.

Stepping into the room, Mr. Walsh stood to the side of the door and bowed to Bel, the lady of the house. 'Your Grace: the earl of Rackford.'

Jacinda felt her spirit leap as her caller appeared in the white-trimmed doorway of the drawing room.

In spite of herself, a surge of pleasure coursed through her veins.

Perhaps there was hope for him yet, she thought wryly as her approving gaze swept over him. He was dressed with leisurely elegance in a double-breasted spencer jacket of deep Spanish blue, a pristine white waistcoat, a handsome trone d'amour cravat, and drill trousers in a creamy biscuit shade.

He swept off his black top hat and strode in, greeting the ladies in order of precedence. In one hand, he held a silver-handled walking stick, in the other, a giant bouquet, which he presented to Jacinda with a bow.

'How thoughtful,' Bel exclaimed, while Lizzie watched them in delight.

Jacinda blushed brightly, inhaling the delicious mingling of perfumes from the profusion of tiger lilies, irises, tulips, and roses. While the others exchanged pleasantries, she summoned a servant to put the flowers in a vase. Soon, she had procured Bel's permission to walk in the park with Rackford, Lizzie accompanying them. With an air of complicity, her best friend became absorbed in her book and walked several paces behind them, too honorable to eavesdrop.

'Is it your intention to drive me mad, Lady Jacinda, or does it just come naturally?' Lord Rackford inquired in a naughty murmur, flicking an admiring glance over her carefully chosen promenade gown with its small, tight, decidedly low-cut pink bodice and long white skirts. Since her gown was short-sleeved, she wore long white gloves and a flowing transparent pink scarf draped artfully around her shoulders. Its billowing end reached for him and brushed against him teasingly.

'William,' she warned, boldly using his first name as she glanced at him from behind the brim of her round bonnet, which was trimmed with silk daffodils and tied with a pink ribbon.

He smiled in flirtatious contrition. 'Very well. I'll be good.'

God knew he made her heart beat faster, but she struggled to maintain at least an outward show of cool skepticism. They strolled slowly in step with each other down the wide, quiet, tree-lined path. Rackford measured out his paces with his walking stick while Jacinda languidly did the same with her upended parasol.

'Thank you for the flowers.'

'It is the least that I can do after you came to my rescue last night. I did not expect it, to say the least.'

'Well, it's very simple. As I am a lady, it is my duty to help those less fortunate than myself, and, forgive me, but it is very clear that, without my guidance, you will be eaten alive. Therefore, I have decided to help you, Lord Rackford. That is why I asked you here today.'

'Help me? How?'

'By civilizing you.'

'I see.' A dashing smile spread slowly over his handsome face. 'An intriguing proposition.'

'I believe it should prove an amusing project, yes.'

'Well, I am your eager pupil, my lady, clay in your hands. Mold me as you will,' he said in a lazy purr.

She eyed him skeptically, for every word from his lips

188

seemed laden with rakish innuendo – or maybe it was only her own errant imagination. Clearing her throat with a little, businesslike cough, she opted to ignore it. 'Before we begin, I must know everything.'

'What do you mean?'

'About your past.'

'You already know it.'

'Not all of it. You say you started out as the younger son of Lord Truro, and I saw for myself that you ended up as the leader of the Fire Hawks. What I want to know is what happened in between – how you got from point A to point B.'

He slid her a wary look askance. 'And all of this pertains to your civilizing me, how?'

'It doesn't,' she admitted with a sheepish grin. 'It is merely the payment I demand for my services.'

'Oh-ho, your 'services'? I wasn't aware I was going to be serviced, my lady.'

'Oh, come, Billy, you have to tell me! I shall expire of curiosity!'

'All right, all right, if you are so bent on hearing my sorry tale, but first, I have one small, harmless question for you.'

'What is it?' she asked guardedly.

He stopped and turned to her.

'Don't you think it's a trifle heartless the way you are using that old man?'

His smooth accusation startled her, but she knew he was referring to Lord Drummond. 'I am not using him.'

'Yes, you are.'

'No, I'm not!'

'Don't bother telling me you are in love with him. We both know what you're really after. Your freedom.'

She stared at him uneasily. 'You ... realize my intention?'

He nodded. 'It's risky, you know. What if he should perceive your true motives?'

She turned away sharply, scowling. 'It's not like that. There's no sentimental nonsense between us. Lord Drummond is no fool. It is merely a matter of companionship in his old age. Once, he was an admirer of my mother's; now, he is a lonely old man with no one to take care of him. I make him happy.'

'Does he make you happy?'

'I don't need a man to make me happy, Lord Rackford.'

'What of love?'

'Love?' She gave a short, wry laugh. 'Why, that seems to be the one luxury I cannot afford.'

'My, my,' he said softly with a regretful gaze, 'what has become of my little romantic?'

'Oh, please,' she retorted. 'You know the proverb, Billy. 'Better an old man's darling than a young man's slave'.' She quoted the saying with a gleam in her eye.

Rackford snorted. 'By all means, marry him, then, if that's what you want – a dry, dull old man who makes you feel nothing. But I don't understand why this notion of freedom is so blasted important to you.'

'I'll tell you why. Because I'm not going to love someone only to have them abandon me,' she bit out. Realizing she had spoken more vehemently than she had intended, she quickly fixed her stare down the shady lane again and walked on.

He raised his eyebrow and followed her. 'Abandon you?'

'Yes,' she replied in a prickly tone. She argued with herself to keep quiet, but could not hold back. 'I know what Society husbands are like, Lord Rackford. They're not much different than brothers, in fact. They give their wives a beautiful home, then keep them there as though it were a cage, all under the auspices of protecting them. Meanwhile, the men go striding off into the world – having adventures, doing interesting things, making a difference. For the wives, it's nothing but card parties and social calls and gossip over tea. No, thank you. I will not waste my whole

190

life pretending to be interested solely in the latest style of bonnet and the scandal of the month. I will chart my own course, go where the devil I please, and answer to no one – and if that means marrying an old man so I can be free all the sooner, so be it!' Her impassioned voice broke off abruptly; she realized she had nearly been shouting. Her chest heaved with the fierceness of her tirade; her cheeks were flushed. 'I'm sorry,' she forced out tautly as she turned away, mortified by her outburst, but Rackford gently grasped her arm.

'If you were mine,' he said quietly, firmly, looking into her eyes, 'I'd take you with me when I went 'striding off into the world.'

Her heart twisted painfully. 'Don't, Billy.' With a confused wince, she pulled away from his light hold. 'Don't look at me like that. Don't speak to me of marriage anymore, I pray you. I'll only hurt you. I've offered you my friendship; take it or leave it. If you can't accept that—'

'Easy, sweeting,' he soothed in a deep, soft voice, staring into her eyes. 'Don't be afraid of me. I will do . . . whatever you want.'

She gazed at him intensely, clinging to the steadiness he offered. He nodded in reassurance and took her hand. He started to walk on, but she stayed.

He turned back to her in question, gazed at her for a long moment, then moved closer. Lifting his gloved fingertip to her cheek, he brushed a blowing curl back from her face.

She shuddered and closed her eyes briefly, leaning her cheek against his knuckles. 'Billy?'

'Yes, Jacinda?'

When her eyes swept open, they stared at each other. Her wistful gaze sank to his lips.

She was unaware that she had been leaning toward him in breathless longing until a demure 'Ahem!' sounded from a few feet away.

Lizzie's tactful warning snapped them both out of the enchantment. Rackford dropped his hand to his side again.

Jacinda glanced over in embarrassment, but Lizzie had buried her nose firmly in her book once more.

Blushing, Jacinda fidgeted with her blowing pink scarf and cleared her throat. 'Forgive me; I can't imagine how we wandered onto the subject of me. You were going to tell me how you came to be involved in the gang.'

He glanced at their chaperon, then smiled wryly at Jacinda. 'Why don't we call Miss Carlisle over to listen, too? That will save you the trouble of having to repeat it all later.'

At his words, Jacinda's coral lips formed an O of guilty indignation, but to Rackford's amused satisfaction, she did not attempt to deny the charge. Flashing him a playful scowl, she called her friend over eagerly.

Truly, the two young girls entertained the hell out of him, he thought sardonically, regarding them in protective affection as they took their places on a bench in the shade and waited in kittenish solemnity for him to begin.

He glanced warily from one lovely creature to the other, touched by how sheltered they were. For that reason, he masked the true brutality of his boyhood experiences behind a casual manner, as though he were relating the plot of some amusing fiction he had read. Breezing over that final, savage beating from his father, he spoke of how he had walked from Cornwall to London, staying away from the main roads and traveling by night to evade the men his father had sent to find him.

He told them of that first night on his own – how he had curled up among the roots of an ancient oak, wrapped in his coat, and had lain, bruised and shivering in the chill of the spring night, looking up at the crescent moon between the whispering branches. The broad bands of blue and indigo clouds around the moon had made him ache for his beloved sea with the seals and the mermaids and all the old legends, but no matter how it broke his heart, he vowed that night never to set foot in Cornwall again.

192

Instead, he had set out for London to find his fortune.

The girls listened with intent, softhearted gazes as his tale unfolded.

For several days, he had pushed eastward, traveling off the main roads through the fields and byways, refilling his canteen in country wells. He had discovered the small bag of coins that Mrs. Landry, their cook, had slipped into his knapsack, probably half her life savings. Though he had preserved his rations as best he could, his belly was grumbling the day he arrived on the rural outskirts of London. He had been a sorry sight, the April rain drizzling down on him, his eye still black from his father's fist. He remembered his morbid fascination upon seeing the corpses of some criminals who had been gibbeted on the brow of a hill and left there as a dire warning to all who would contemplate evildoing. He had watched them swinging in their nooses, then turned his back on them and marched on toward London with determination, wondering what he should become.

He had considered enlisting in the army, but soon found out that he would have to show his birth certificate to the recruitment officer to prove that he was at least fifteen: He was only thirteen. He had applied at a fine stable as a groom, hoping to get work exercising the horses, but the jockeys there were grown men who only came up to his chin: He was too big. He had thought of taking up some respectable trade, only to learn that he would have to go before the magistrate and bind himself to a master craftsman for a term of seven years. For this, he was much too impatient.

Out of food, money, and ideas, he had stepped in out of the rain at a tavern where the kindly innkeeper had told him of the brickyard nearby where a boy could earn his bread and board along with a few shillings by working as an 'off-bearer.' Following the old man's directions, he had found the large, busy brickyard easily enough. His employment there, however, had only lasted one day.

The instant he saw the place and the overseers driving the boys, he had doubts, but since he had so few other options, in he went to learn how to make bricks. Noting his tall height and sturdy build, the overseer had quickly agreed to give him a chance.

The work of the off-bearers, he explained to Jacinda and Miss Carlisle, was simple, consisting mainly of carefully picking up the wet, newly formed bricks from the brickmaster and carrying them to the drying fields a fair distance away. Carrying, carrying, back and forth, like ants in a line. It was messy work and quite precarious for gangly pubescent boys. Though the boys had not been allowed to talk to each other during work, one had quickly drawn his attention: a skinny, curly-haired charity boy in a green workhouse uniform. The puny lad could not seem to carry a brick without dropping it. Each wet brick the master gave him was soon splattered on the ground, a mud pie.

The girls laughed, listening in absorption as he described his increasing difficulty in keeping his mouth shut as the big, potbellied overseer had bullied and berated the charity boy for his ineptitude.

'But when I saw him strike the boy, something inside of me . . . snapped.'

The girls sobered, and his expression turned grim. He shook his head and told them how he had hurled the muddy wet brick he had been carrying at the overseer.

'It hit him square in the back, knocking him off balance, leavin' a big muddy smear on his shirt.'

The overseer had whirled around in fury, standing two feet taller than him, but the man's black look had not stopped Billy Albright's charge. '*Leave him alone!*' he had screamed.

'I was so enraged, I could barely see straight.'

He told them of how the owner of the brickyard had come rushing out of his office and had broken up the row. The charity boy and he were brought into the office, reprimanded, and summarily dismissed.

194

'And that,' he said, 'is how I met Nate Hawkins.'

Jacinda's eyes widened with recognition at the name, for she had met Nate that night in Bainbridge Street.

'Nate complained bitterly against me for getting him sacked from his job,' Rackford said with a smile, 'but we fell in together quite naturally, since he was an orphan and had no one and would have rather died than go back to the workhouse. In the end, the old barkeep, Sam Burroughs, hired us on as potboys to help out around the pub. He housed us in a loft in the outbuilding where the chickens and goats slept, but we were happy, for we had an easy master and there was always plenty to eat.'

Then he went on to describe how, one rainy night, three men in black greatcoats had arrived at Sam Burroughs's alehouse.

Billy had been carrying a rack of clean beer mugs out from the back when he saw them. He had instantly recognized them as his father's servants. They were asking old Sam if he had seen a blond, green-eyed boy of thirteen summers. Billy had silently retreated into the back, left the rack of tankards on the floor, grabbed Nate by his shirt, and fled.

After that narrow escape, they had traipsed into the heart of the city, once again on the scrounge for food. Within a few days, he had managed to get them both hired onto a Thames fishing boat, where they were assigned all the most unpleasant tasks: tarring the decks, gutting the catch, bailing out the bilge.

'Nate hated it,' he told the girls. 'The captain was a decent man, but the crew were a rough lot. We were afraid of them and soon found we had good reason to be.'

After a fortnight of laboring like dogs, they had received their pay of two shillings each and were given permission to go ashore, but late that night, they ran afoul of the drunken first mate. The girls gasped as he described how the man, armed with a knife, had threatened them and demanded their pay.

195

'We had no choice but to give him our money. He said if we told anyone, he would gut us and feed our bodies to the fish.'

'How awful!' Jacinda exclaimed.

'We did not deem it wise to return to the boat,' he said drily. 'By the time dawn came, we were once more faced with the question of how we were going to survive. It so happened that we were sitting by the river pondering our fate when we noticed the usual parade of young mud larks wading out into the water at low tide.'

These, he explained, were the poorest of the poor, beggar children who searched the riverbed each day at low tide, trying to find dropped coins, bits of coal that may have fallen off the passing barges, or anything of value they might resell for a few pennies. That morning, not knowing what else to do, Billy and Nate had rolled up their trousers and tried their hands at mud-larking. It was not long, however, before a small Cockney bruiser had come marching through the fog toward them.

'What are you blighters doing 'ere?' he had demanded pugnaciously. 'I'm Cullen O'Dell, and this is my stretch of the river!'

From the first, Nate and Billy had been impressed by him. Cullen O'Dell was pure Cockney, born in earshot of the Bow bells. City-born and city-bred, he knew how to fend for himself. Though they had first encountered him mud-larking, he had made it clear that this low business was only a sideline for him. He had claimed that if a boy was smart, he could live like a king in the city. To their surprise, he had offered to help when they explained what had happened to them. He knew a good old gentleman, he said, who would give them food and a place to stay.

They had been skeptical, but without any other choices at hand, they had gone with him. The place where O'Dell had assured them they could find shelter had turned out to be a shabby, dilapidated flash house, and the old gentle-man's line of business had been training and dispatching

196

young thieves. As long as the children under his dubious care brought back wallets, watches, silk handkerchiefs, and such, he provided them with enough bread, milk, and weak broth to subsist on, and a kind of home.

'My goodness,' the girls breathed.

'That very day, Nate and I went with a group of boys to a hanging outside of Newgate. I remember it like it was last week. The crowd that had gathered was in the thousands. I had never seen a hanging before, but Nate and I had been instructed to forget about the show up on the gallows and watch O'Dell and the other boys instead.'

He described how the other boys had dodged about, neatly picking the crowd clean. He remembered how his heart had pounded in fear that one of them would get caught, but none did. They had even made it look fun. The irony of robbing the citizenry of London even as the trio of highwaymen were being led to the gallows seemed not to have struck the young thieves, but it had certainly not been lost on Nate and him.

Their work done, the boys had all walked back together to the flash house. The others had been chattering about how pleased the old gentleman was going to be with their success, but Billy had been silent, brooding on the high consequences to be paid if one were caught.

'I suddenly asked the boys why they should hand over all their profits to the old gentleman when it was they who took all the risk,' he said to his fair listeners. 'Needless to say, the question made them rather uneasy, but I showed them that the expenses he paid to feed and house them were only a fraction of the profits the children were bringing in.'

Unschooled and illiterate, quite innocent of even the most basic mathematics, the young thieves had had no idea of the value of the goods they stole; having been hungry and destitute from the day they were born, they did not realize that the food the old man served them was meager and foul.

'The boys were angry when I did the math for them.

197

When I showed them how much profit they were unwittingly handing over to the old man and gave them a few examples of what such sums could realistically buy, it was O'Dell who said we should not go back to the flash house, but should start our own gang. And that,' he said, 'is exactly what we did.'

'Gracious!' the young ladies exclaimed.

'You were in a gang with O'Dell?' Jacinda asked.

He nodded. 'He was the one with all the street smarts, while I had the education. Combined, these traits made us quite a menace. I would make up the various tricks and rackets to gull unsuspecting marks, and O'Dell would lead the other boys in carrying them out.'

'What kind of tricks?' Jacinda asked with a mischievous smile.

'Let's see.' He scratched his chin. 'My favorite one had us posing as a company of chimney sweeps. We would go into large homes on the pretense of cleaning the chimneys, while in fact we would be methodically casing the house for a future robbery – identifying routes of entry, where the valuables were kept, whether there was a dog. That sort of thing.'

The girls were laughing, scandalized.

'As long as our skills were balanced with O'Dell as the brawn and myself as the brains, things went smoothly. But one night, all of that changed.'

'What happened?' Jacinda asked.

He fell silent for a moment, choosing his words very carefully, for he did not wish to mar their innocence with any mention of the unnatural men that existed in the world who would use a child, even a boy, for their own gratification.

In truth, none of them had known how vulnerable they were. Fast asleep in their hideaway, an old burned-out warehouse by the river, none of the members of their little boy-gang heard Yellow Cane creep into their midst that night.

198

All the street children knew to stay away from the strange, predatory dandy known as Yellow Cane after the elegant yellow walking stick he always carried. He had a long, painted fingernail on his pinky from which he was always taking snuff. Billy had often seen him around the streets, in the gambling hells, and scouring the more peculiar brothels.

That night, something had made him awaken from a dead slumber. Through sleepy eyes, he had been horrified to see Yellow Cane holding a knife to O'Dell's throat, forcing the boy to keep silent and to come with him. He still remembered his shock at seeing tough O'Dell's face wet with tears of sheer terror.

Billy had jumped to his feet with a roar and, rather stupidly, had charged. It could have gotten O'Dell's throat slit, but instead, it had startled Yellow Cane, giving O'Dell the chance to shove the man's weapon hand away. Yellow Cane had tried to run, but Billy had barreled into him, diving for his knife. The fight was a blur, for his battle cry had awakened the rest of the boys. Everyone was screaming. O'Dell had picked up the infamous yellow walking stick and began clubbing the man with it. The next thing Billy knew, he had Yellow Cane's knife in his hand. When the dandy reached into his greatcoat pocket for his pistol, Billy had stabbed him in the neck.

'Lord Rackford?' Jacinda's gentle touch on his forearm startled him back to the present.

He looked at her abruptly, the dark shadows of the past clearing from his eyes.

'What happened?' she repeated softly.

He forced a slight smile. 'O'Dell was attacked one night, and I saved him.'

Her dark eyes flickered, as though she sensed he was not telling her the worst of it, but she did not press him.

'From that point on,' he continued, 'the others regarded me as their leader. O'Dell refused to forget the humiliation of having been rescued by me, since he was supposed to be the tough one. His shame turned to hatred of me. Eventually, he left us and formed a gang of his own and became corrupted, I suppose, by the hardship he had suffered all his life. The rest,' he murmured, 'you already know.'

The girls glanced at each other, then at him.

Jacinda caressed his shoulder, frowning with concern. 'I am sorry things have been so hard for you, Billy.'

'Me, too,' Miss Carlisle added softly.

'Well, my circumstances have decidedly improved,' he said with forced brightness. 'True, I am under my father's thumb once more, but Nate and the others are alive. That's what counts.' He gazed off wistfully into the distance for a moment, then tried to shrug off his persistent sense of guilt. 'I have hired a gentleman of business to find me some property in Australia. I intend to buy a plantation there so they can serve out their sentences in a place where at least they will be humanely treated. Unfortunately, I must remain anonymous as their benefactor. I am to have no contact with them ever again. They have all been told that 'Billy Blade' is dead.'

'How sad,' Jacinda murmured. 'They were like brothers to you.'

'At least I managed to keep them out of the hangman's noose. Still,' he said pensively, tilting his head back to study the wind-riffled branches above them, 'it doesn't seem enough. I get to sit here in the park with two pretty ladies while they're in chains aboard some prison hulk.'

'You did the best you could,' Lizzie said sympathetically.

'You saved their lives,' Jacinda agreed.

'Do you know what you could do, Lord Rackford?' Lizzie spoke up all of a sudden.

'What could I do?' he asked, turning fondly to the unassuming girl.

Lizzie stared into space, tapping her lip in thought.

'Gracious, Lizzie's got an idea,' Jacinda said in a tone of

excitement. 'Have I told you, Lord Rackford, that Miss Carlisle is a genius?'

'No, you hadn't mentioned it.'

'Once you have your plantation in order, you could send a schoolmaster to educate them,' Lizzie said. 'Artisans to teach them honest trades. That way, when they've served their sentences, they shall have the means to adopt a new way of life independent of crime.'

'Hmm. They wouldn't want to be bothered, I'm afraid. They're not boys anymore. The time for apprenticeships is ages past, and I'm not sure you can teach an old dog new tricks—'

'My dear Lord Rackford, when Lizzie has an idea, it usually works. I agree with her,' Jacinda said. 'Actually ... I can think of one motive that might be all that's needed to inspire your fellows to change their ways.'

'What might that be?'

'Wives,' she declared. 'Get them women.'

Rackford and Lizzie burst out laughing.

'Wives, Jacinda?' Lizzie exclaimed.

'Why not? Surely a man with a wife and children to look after is less inclined to risk his neck in daft criminal schemes,' she insisted over their laughter. 'Give them more to lose, and I wager that within a few years, you will have molded them into upstanding citizens.'

'You know, that might actually work,' Rackford murmured. It delighted him to think of Nate, Sarge, Flaherty, Andrews, and all the rest as married men with wee ones underfoot. He looked at Jacinda, who smoothed her skirts, looking altogether pleased with herself. 'I think you both are geniuses,' he said.

The girls exchanged a tickled look at his compliment.

Chapter Twelve

Theirs was a friendship entwined with lust.

In the weeks that followed, Jacinda poured her efforts into civilizing Rackford – but did not really want to see him tamed. Not when she basked in his thrillingly dangerous advances. He flirted openly with her whenever he could get away with it, and though she pretended a droll annoyance, it was deliciously heady flattery to find herself the one continual object of his smoldering attentions.

She chose not to take his rakish advances very seriously, but their private flirtation had added a zest of excitement to her life that had been decidedly missing before. Whenever they were left alone even for a moment, he was always touching her, however subtly – a caress on her cheek, a playful tug on her hair, a gallant kiss on her hand. Somehow she never found much reason to protest, though she sometimes made a show of anger at his bawdier compliments. It seemed important to keep him in line.

Fortunately, Lizzie's frequent presence helped diffuse the craving tension that sometimes made the very air between them crackle and hum. As for her governess, Rackford had charmed his way past Miss Hood with ease, but he was essentially a man's man, and even her brothers had taken a guarded liking to him, thanks to Lucien's vouching for his character.

Little did she know Rackford had already made his intentions known to her brothers and had procured Robert's permission to court her . . .

Rackford had had no choice, really. She was under twenty-one and could not marry without her guardian's consent, not to mention the fact that her formidable tribe of elder brothers could end his courtship before it had begun, if they saw fit. He did not want to make enemies of them. It was a great risk, but he knew that the only solution was to show his hand, prove himself, earn their respect, and thus seal his place among them from the start. In truth, he had so often willfully done wrong in his life, but this was important enough to him that he wanted to do everything right.

Boldly, he requested an audience with the duke of Hawkscliffe on a day when he had learned beforehand that Jacinda would be out shopping with her beautiful sisters-in-law and the lovable Miss Carlisle.

Perhaps Hawkscliffe had divined the purpose of his call, for when Rackford walked into the duke's study, he found four of the five Knight brothers already arrayed before him.

Only Lord Jack Knight, the second-born, was absent. Rackford later learned that Lord Jack was quite the black sheep – and could not be expected to appear anytime soon. None of the others even knew where he was.

Fortunately, however, Lucien and Alec were there and had already decided to accept him. Hawkscliffe watched his every move with skepticism in his dark eyes; then Rackford was reintroduced to the one who had worried him the most – Lucien's twin, Damien, the earl of Winterley. The silver-eyed, war-hardened colonel had brought his wife, Miranda, into Town to go shopping with her womenfolk. Winterley shook his hand, looking him over – indeed, taking his measure, as though he were a rather unsatisfactory new recruit of the regiment. As it turned out, however, the stone-faced warrior was prepared to give him a chance because of Billy Blade's help so long ago in saving the raven-haired beauty Miranda.

The grueling, two-hour interview made his many hours of questioning from Sir Anthony Weldon and his Bow Street runners look like child's play. He knew he was not the favorite – he knew he was no Lord Griffith – but he forced himself to be utterly honest with her kin.

He sat uncomfortably under their scrutiny, giving them a matter-of-fact account of his past – one considerably more thorough than the one he had given the girls in the park. Grimly, he confessed the true extent of his father's violence so they would understand he had been justified in running away. He told them next of how he had conducted things in St. Giles, providing for hundreds of people with his ill-gotten gains, uniting various gangs to stop the killing among the young men, and using the threat of his might to impose some sense of order on the rookery when it had been under his control.

He did not know if his accomplishments, such as they were, held any weight with her brothers, or for that matter, if they even believed him; but when Lucien told them that it was Billy who had found Jacinda and had brought her back safely the night she had tried to run away, they exchanged a few shrewd glances with each other.

Then Lucien told them of his secret aid to Bow Street, which had already helped to bring about a flurry of arrests. Counterfeiters, crooked money-lenders, illegal gaming hell operators, horse thieves, a band of murderous highwaymen, black-market dealers, one assassin-for-hire, an extortionist, and a pair of arsonists who would, for a price, help one burn down one's home in order to collect the fire insurance – all had gone to prison on the strength of his information.

Hearing all this, Hawkscliffe and Winterley regarded him with grudging respect in their eyes.

Lastly, Truro's solicitor had drawn up certified documents stating the sum of his fortune and the holdings that would one day be Rackford's. The papers had been prepared in advance of the wife search his father had ordered him to make. As Hawkscliffe skimmed the pages,

Alec sent Rackford a rather envious smirk.

'Now I know who to come to for a loan.'

'Alec,' the duke warned.

'I spoke in jest, Rob. For God's sake,' he said haughtily.

Drumming his fingers on the desk a moment longer, Hawkscliffe stared at Rackford's financial statement, then looked around the room: first at Lucien, who gave him a furtive nod; then at Damien, who shrugged slightly and sat back in his chair; then at Alec, who had begun boredly flipping a coin.

Hawkscliffe put the papers down and steepled his fingers, staring at Rackford for one moment longer. 'Very well,' he said with a curt nod. 'You may court her. But we will be watching you. One wrong move ...'

'I understand, Your Grace. Thank you. My lords, I am grateful for your time.'

They stood; he prepared to make his exit.

'Join us for a brandy, Rackford?' Hawkscliffe invited him as he sauntered around his desk.

'Gladly, Your Grace. Thank you.'

'Call me Hawkscliffe.'

He was still marveling over their decision to accept him when Alec heaved out of his chair onto his crutches. 'I cannot wait to tease the little henwit about this.'

'No!' Rackford exclaimed, turning to him a bit too vehemently as the others ambled toward the door. 'Beg your pardon. But—' He looked around at them rather haplessly. 'No one must mention this to Lady Jacinda. Not yet, anyway.'

'Why not?' Lucien asked with a curious glance.

'You know what a feisty, skittish creature she is. If you try to encourage her in my direction, it will only make her go the other way. She doesn't like ... being told what to do, I'm afraid.'

Each one looking taken aback, they burst out laughing at his words.

'Sirs?' he asked, furrowing his brow.

'You're a brave man, Rackford.' Damien clapped him on the back. 'God help you.'

With her brothers' nod of approval, then, he set out to win Jacinda's heart and her trust. As the Season progressed, he bided his time, willing to play the game by her rules for the time being. He danced attendance on her like the most obedient cavalier servente, fetching her glasses of champagne punch, opening windows when she was warm, bringing her wrap when she was cool, even sitting through endlessly dull rounds of whist and losing large sums of money just for the pleasure of sitting across from her.

She was softening him up, even toward his father. Rackford was on his way out of the house early one afternoon to pay his almost daily call upon his lady when he passed the morning room and noticed his father collapsed in an armchair in his dressing gown, his slippered feet propped up on an ottoman, cucumber slices over his eyes. On the little table beside him were a cup of strong coffee and a bottle of headache powder. The marquess was so still that Rackford found himself rather alarmed.

Moving warily toward the room, he paused in the doorway. 'Father?'

'Huh?' came Lord Truro's unceremonious grunt. Apparently dozing, he did not look over.

'Are you all right, sir?'

'Never better,' he said blandly.

Rackford smiled wryly in spite of himself. 'Hard night?'

'Must have been. Can't recall.'

Leaning in the doorway, he fought with himself for a moment, gathering his nerve. 'Father? I was thinking about going by Tatt's later this afternoon to buy a suitable riding horse—'

'Spend what you want, William. I told you you may.'

'Yes – I wondered if you might like to come with me.' He couldn't believe he was even offering, reaching out this way. 'You've always had an eye for horseflesh.'

For a long moment, the marquess didn't move.

Rackford swallowed hard, hanging on his answer like the little boy he once had been, dying for the approval of the terrifying, godlike man.

'Not today, Son. I'm ill as a dog.'

Rackford lowered his head at the rebuff, anger pulsing through him.

Truro slid the cucumber slices off his bloodshot eyes. 'Tomorrow, perhaps?'

But the only answer that greeted him was the slamming of the front door as Rackford went out. Before long, Rackford arrived at Knight House in his curricle. Though he was still stung by the way his father had brushed him off, he knew that the sight of Jacinda's sweet face would soothe him.

He jumped out of his carriage and left it with the groom, striding up to the entrance. He supposed he probably came here too much, but after all, Jacinda was expecting him. Mr. Walsh promptly let him in. The dignified butler had become a familiar sight through the past weeks.

'My lord,' the stately fellow intoned, opening the door wide for him.

Removing his hat, Rackford greeted him and showed himself up to the drawing room, stopping along the way to greet the duchess and to give little Morley's cheek a fond pinch as the nurse brought the toddler by.

He was only on the fringes of the Knight clan, he realized, but he had never known what it felt like to be a part of a family before. Never before had it been so easy to imagine spending the rest of his life with a woman.

Every day he felt that he knew Jacinda better, that they understood each other a bit more deeply. He loved her capricious sense of humor and her soft, affectionate touches, like when she pulled him aside at a soiree to fix his cravat, or the afternoon she had taken the reins from him in Hyde Park and had driven his curricle, hell-for-leather, around the Ring to show him how it was done, her hip brushing against his as she stood beside him, fighting with the horses.

To be sure, his golden-haired goddess had little idea of how close he was to pulling her down off her pedestal and ravishing her, but still, he was her willing slave, magnetically pulled into her orbit like a hot, molten planet circling a brilliant star.

Jacinda was the only one who refused to see that her 'friend' Rackford was single-mindedly courting her.

'No, darling, stand outside in the hall until he's said your name. Tom, do it again,' Jacinda commanded the footman.

'Yes, my lady,' the long-suffering servant said.

She and Lizzie sat on the couch in the drawing room on a rainy afternoon, teaching Rackford etiquette between bursts of mirth at his scowling.

'I feel like a damned dancing bear,' he muttered, stomping back out into the marble corridor.

The footman assumed his position, as well, withdrawing into the hallway to open the door yet again. He stepped into the room, facing Jacinda, and announced, 'Lord Rackford, my lady.'

Waiting for his cue, Rackford walked with measured paces into the room and bowed to her.

'Not too deeply,' she chided, giving him her hand while her eyes sparkled with mirth. '*Enchantee*, monsieur.'

'Mademoiselle.' He bowed over her hand. 'Wipe that impish grin off your face, or I promise I shall turn you over my knee,' he murmured, just loud enough for her to hear.

'Isn't he charming?' She turned with a bright, arch smile to Lizzie.

'Miss Carlisle.' He repeated his elegant bow to her.

'You're doing splendidly, Lord Rackford.'

'Would you care for refreshments?' Jacinda gestured gracefully to the tea, sandwiches, biscuits, and fruits that had been prepared for their training exercises.

He eyed the carefully laid table with wariness.

Lizzie looked on in fond amusement as Jacinda tested him on the use and designation of each piece of silver that he might encounter on a well-laid table. Through much laughter at Rackford's long-suffering grumbling, he slowly mastered the finer points of etiquette.

In her effort to 'civilize' him, Jacinda further laid out a program of cultural exhibits to which she and Lizzie took their pupil, including the city's array of art galleries and museums, recitals, and concerts of the newly formed London Philharmonic. They attended scientific receptions at Ackermann's, where they heard the latest theories of political economists, botanists, linguists, archeologists who had visited the Pyramids, even naturalists who spoke about the fossils in the rocks. He loved learning, and when Jacinda considered how he had been forced to leave school at an early age, watching him absorb it all warmed her heart.

She soon concluded, however, that no amount of cultural enrichment could change him from the nasty man who had fascinated her from the start, for one day, he sent her a present wrapped in crepe paper with a small note that said, *Saw this in the tobacco shop and thought of you. Enjoy. R.*

When she opened it, alone in her chamber, she found it to be one of those shocking slim blue-books with indecent sketches of lovers in the throes of passion. She cursed him repeatedly under her breath as a scoundrel and a fiend, but eagerly studied every page. Here and there in the margins, he had written naughty comments to her about some of the various positions. Yet no matter how many nights in a row she dreamed feverishly of his tattooed body entwined with hers, she refused to surrender to his velvet enticements.

Her mind, if not her heart, had fixed upon the notion of being one day as free as the glamorous Lady Campion, beating Society at their own game, her private revenge for what they had done to Mama.

She refused to be dissuaded from her plan. Though it was

Billy who made her heart leap and brought a smile – usually an arch, disapproving smile – to her lips, she charged on with her campaign to ensnare Lord Drummond.

Though she found herself spending more and more of her time with Rackford and the group of friends he was gathering about him, she made a point of visiting with Lord Drummond at each of the endless round of balls, routs, soirees, water parties, and lavish at-homes of the ton.

By June, Rackford announced to her and Lizzie that he had purchased the plantation in Australia and had his agent there tracking down each one of his former friends to make sure each would be brought there.

Other old friends found him one afternoon at Hyde Park when Jacinda was driving his curricle at a breakneck pace around the Ring. He sat beside her, enjoying the spectacle of his fair speed-demon. Pink-cheeked with wind and excitement, she pulled the light, elegant vehicle to a halt as two young gentlemen waved excitedly to him.

'Who are they?' she asked, but he was staring in astonishment.

'My God,' was all he murmured, then jumped out of the curricle and greeted them with a huge grin.

One was dark-haired and rather anemic-looking, and the other had carroty red hair. She watched, bemused, as they clapped him in bearlike hugs and made much over him.

'Billy Albright, by God! Look at you, man! We came as soon as we heard you'd come back.'

'We knew you were alive all this time. I tell you, we knew it!'

'Are you truly back with your father?' the dark-haired one asked, marveling.

Rackford nodded grimly, but gave him an odd, silencing look. He turned to her and introduced them as Reg Bentinck and Justin Church.

He explained they had been his friends from his short sojourn at Eton, but there was a troubled look in the depths of his eyes that shadowed his warm smile. She asked him later if something was wrong, but he chased away her question by trying to steal a kiss.

The following day, the agreeable young gentlemen accompanied them on their next cultural outing: Jacinda and Lizzie were taking Rackford to see the Elgin Marbles. Lord Elgin kept them in a pavilion attached to his London home. Their amiable group was on their way out of Knight House under Miss Hood's watchful eye when Daphne's followers, Helena and Amelia, arrived with their governess, all abuzz with some bit of gossip they were anxious to share with Jacinda.

She invited the girls along to view the ancient Greek statues with them, and soon, they had all paid their few shillings and walked into the pavilion. The little old man who served as the docent explained to their awestruck party how Lord Elgin and his team of workers had painstakingly removed the life-sized statues one by one from the frieze of the ancient Parthenon in Athens. At great personal expense, His Lordship had shipped the mighty marbles back to England where they could be properly protected.

Jacinda was more interested in watching Messieurs Church and Bentinck paying court to Lizzie. Both young scholars seemed quite taken with the girl, she mused, then Amelia and Hellie came over and pulled her aside.

'You'll never believe what Daphne did,' Amelia whispered. 'You mustn't tell anyone!'

'I won't. What did she do?' she asked eagerly.

The flighty pair giggled.

'She *threw* herself at Lord Griffith—' Amelia started.

'And he rejected her!' Helena finished.

Jacinda's jaw dropped. 'You're jesting!'

'No, we're not. She did it last night at the theater.' *Oh, poor Ian!*

'We just left her. Lord, she's in a *rage*,' Amelia said in wicked mirth. 'She had had her heart set on announcing the engagement at the ball her family is giving next Saturday night. You received your invitation, I trust?'

Jacinda nodded innocently, smiling to herself to recall Rackford's reaction when he, too, had received his invitation to the Taylor ball. He had smiled at her with a rakish gleam in his eyes.

'You and I are going to steal back your diamonds,' he had promised in a sultry murmur.

'Don't you remember she tried to snare Devonshire last Season? Daphne's determined to marry a marquess at the very least. You'd better tell Lord Rackford to watch out.'

'I will,' she murmured. Glancing over at him, she was suddenly taken aback to see him scowling at the Parthenon statues, his arms folded across his chest. Puzzled, she excused herself from her friends and went over to him. 'Something wrong?'

He tossed his chin toward the docent in a curt nod. Jacinda turned her attention to what the old man was saying.

'The collection will be moved to the British Museum later this summer after the sale is complete.'

She furrowed her brow and turned to him again. 'What did I miss?'

'The government has bought these stupid statues for thirty-five thousand pounds. Thirty-five thousand! This, at a time when half the men of England cannot even feed their families—' His words broke off, as though he were too incensed to continue; then he shook his head. 'Perhaps your beau Lord Drummond can explain it, for this Tory logic is beyond me. Your pardon, my lady.' He gave her a curt bow, pivoted on his heel, and stalked out of the pavilion.

Jacinda peered after him in bemusement, then shook her head. There was no telling what odd thing would make Rackford overreact.

Lizzie followed a moment later, also scowling, her cheeks pink with anger.

'Gracious, where are you all going?' Jacinda exclaimed.

'Come, my lady. Let us leave the site of this crime. Defacing the Parthenon!' Lizzie said bitterly, casting one

212

last look at the broken glory of the statues. 'Lord Elgin is naught but a marauding thief.'

Jacinda was the last one left standing in the pavilion. 'But they're beautiful. Heavens, we're British – we couldn't leave them there to decay, could we?'

The docent bowed to her in agreement, then Miss Hood stuck her head back in the doorway. 'Stop dawdling, my lady. The carriage waits.'

She shrugged off her friends' strange reactions and skipped out after them.

Rackford was glad Jacinda had taken him to see the Elgin Marbles, for he went home that afternoon in a brooding humor, awakened to the awesome realization that his new rank in life had put him in a position of great power with which to fight the same injustices he had battled in the rookery, but in a legal manner and on a grand scale.

Aye, now he could do more than stew over the Tory cabinet's foolish expenditures and heartless policies. Galvanized, he attended his first meeting of the Radical party the very next day. He knew instantly that he had found the place where he belonged, where he could contribute to the world in a real and meaningful way.

Though lofty titles like his went against everything they stood for, the Radical leaders had welcomed him with open arms, realizing the value of having a future marquess as one of their supporters. Most of their members were either merchants, industrialists, and other rich commoners or from the ranks of the lower nobility like Reg and Justin, though they had a handful of high-ranking peers in their midst.

Jacinda turned her nose up at his chosen party when he told her later that he had attended the Radical meeting. She continually implored him to consider joining the forward-thinking but still aristocratic Whig party instead, but in his view, the Whigs did not go far enough in their calls for reform. Her objections did not stop Rackford from pursu-

213

ing his newfound political interests, however, any more than Sir Anthony's pair of Bow Street runners stationed outside his door stopped him from sneaking out of the house quite regularly at night to wreak havoc on the Jackals.

He did not dare tell Jacinda this, either, for she would have surely disapproved. He knew she had assumed that he had simply informed against O'Dell, as he had against so many other of his former criminal colleagues, but that was not the case. No, he wanted the bastard for himself.

His attacks of late had been quite ruthless, for he was determined to see the bloody business through before he made Jacinda his wife. He was eager to close the door once and for all on his dark past in favor of his bright future with her.

She was a stubborn chit, of course, but he had every confidence that she would come around once he had won her full trust. Admittedly, his patience was wearing a bit thin at her continued refusal to acknowledge their desire for each other.

He knew her reasons, of course. The lady meant to be free. She was in dread of letting herself belong to him, but he knew that he was getting to her. When he showed up at Knight House with the odd cuts and bruises from his battles, she turned him utterly inside out with the way she fussed over him as though he were a child and petted and kissed him and demanded he tell her how he had hurt himself. He basked in her attentions – he could not help himself – keeping only a loose rein on his randy thoughts. He resorted to harmless lies about his thankfully slight injuries, for he didn't want to upset her or remind her of what he used to be.

The sooner she forgot about that, the better.

Chapter Thirteen

Jacinda finally met Rackford's parents at the huge banquet and ball given the following Saturday night by Daphne's parents, Lord and Lady Erhard.

The handsome but dissipated-looking marquess and his faraway, frail, meticulously dressed wife had come on one of their rare forays into Society. Faced with her Billy's childhood tormentor, Jacinda had all but cut the marquess outright, knowing how he had treated his son. Seated somewhat across from Rackford's tyrannical father at the richly laid table, she held Lord Truro in several cold, deliberate stares that slowly seemed to unnerve the man. She contradicted his opinions every time he offered one at the table, but it seemed he did not dare rebuke her, at least not in public. He drank faster and finally would not look in her direction at all.

Surely by the end of the meal, she mused, Truro the Terrible had realized that she knew of his crimes. As for the marchioness, Jacinda considered her beneath contempt for doing nothing to save her child from his father's drunken violence.

In the drawing room after dinner, she noticed Daphne making herself agreeable to the marchioness, cooing over her white sequined gown. Ah, well. Amelia and Hellie had warned her of this. Daphne's tactics were obvious enough: She was bent on impressing his parents so they would pressure him in her favor in his choice of brides.

Jacinda stood only half listening to Lord Drummond's detailed account of his recent triumph on the golf links, waiting for Rackford's signal.

'My lowest score ever . . .'

'How nice,' she murmured, gazing across the drawing room at where Daphne stood beaming at Rackford.

His back was to Jacinda, so she could not see his reaction to the haughty redhead's flirtations. Surely, he was not fool enough to be so dazzled by Daphne's beauty that he would fail to notice her spoiled temperament?

She scowled faintly as Daphne coaxed Rackford into dancing with her, vaguely aware of Acer Loring off to the side, scowling at them right along with her, for he had been enamored of Daphne for ages. With pursed lips and an angry flutter of her fan, Jacinda watched Rackford bow and Daphne simper.

If only he didn't have to look so blasted gorgeous tonight . . . just as he did every other night. The candles burning brightly in the wall sconces cast a golden sheen over his sleek sandy hair. Her gaze traveled across the wide breadth of his shoulders in his snugfitting midnight-blue tailcoat, then down his lean waist and compact hips to his long legs, clad in black trousers. It was an irksome trend, how he seemed to get better looking each day, the better she got to know him. She knew what his every twisty smile meant; every subtle shade of green that his eyes turned reflected a different emotion, and she had memorized them all. A pale apple green under his spiky dun lashes meant playfulness; but his eyes turned a blazing emerald hue when he was impassioned over politics or some other matter; the deep gray-green of woodland shadows meant he was brooding and should be given a wide berth.

When the dance ended and he disengaged himself from Daphne, Jacinda could not help but smile with satisfaction as he headed back at once toward her. As he made his way through the milling crowd of guests, he sent her a seductive look with a mischievous little flare of his eyebrows. He always kept his distance when Lord Drummond was near, not trusting himself to be civil; tonight, however, they had a special mission together, and he joined her in spite of the old wigsby's presence.

'My lady,' Lord Rackford greeted her with a very correct bow.

Though her feminine senses tingled with pleasure as he came over by her side, she gave him a rather cool nod and turned to her aged companion. 'Lord Drummond, I don't believe you've met my friend, Lord Rackford. He is the son of the marquess of Truro. Lord Rackford, this is the earl of Drummond.'

Rackford bowed to him warily. 'Sir.'

The gruff old statesman lifted his chin and scrutinized him, his spectacles glinting. 'So, this is the budding Radical who has all of London abuzz.'

Rackford glanced uneasily at Jacinda. 'Yes, my lord, I have been quite impressed by Lord Brougham's ideas.'

'Wrongheaded, m'boy. That one is a troublemaker. I mistrust brilliance. Watch out for him. If Brougham had his way, we'd all be called 'Mister.' '

'With all due respect, sir, I prefer to judge a man's value by his actions, not by his birth.'

'Was it India where you learned such demmed exotic ideas, m'boy?' Drummond asked in annoyance.

'Sir, I will thank you not to use such language in front of the young lady,' Rackford said with shocking aplomb, lifting his chin.

Jacinda's eyes widened. After the countless ungentlemanly things 'Billy Blade' had done in front of her, she nearly laughed aloud, but it would not do for either man to make a scene. Apparently, her training was working better than she had foreseen.

'I say!' Lord Drummond huffed.

'Forgive me for interrupting,' Rackford said smoothly to

Jacinda, 'but I wondered if I might trouble you, my lady, for a moment of your time.'

'If you will excuse me, Lord Drummond?'

Before the old man could even utter a reply, Rackford grasped her wrist in a possessive hold and stalked out to a deserted corner of the sprawling, moonlit veranda. The muggy warmth of the June night made her gown cling to her skin, hot and damp, heightening the discomfort of her unfulfilled longing.

'You didn't have to be rude to him, Rackford.'

'Rude? He's lucky I didn't knock him flat.' Maybe it was the weather making both of them testy with frustration, for he seemed to be feeling it, too. 'I can't believe you're still angling after that old Tory hangman. I daresay I am beginning to take it personally,' he muttered, taking a quick swallow from his wineglass. 'If Lord Drummond were interested, don't you think he would have responded by now to your throwing yourself at him all Season?'

'I beg your pardon, I have never thrown myself at any man,' she whispered in haughty indignation. 'The only woman throwing herself at anyone here tonight is Daphne, throwing herself at you!'

'What's this?' A provoking smirk curved his handsome mouth. 'Jealous, my sweet?'

'Are you ready to steal back my diamonds or not?'

He grinned, chucking her under the chin. 'That's my girl. You're a game one, Lady J. Remember everything I told you?'

She nodded.

'Good. Then, go.' With a sly wink, he nodded toward the ballroom and the grand staircase beyond it.

'Right.' Squaring her shoulders, she snapped open her fan and assumed an expression of fashionable ennui.

Pursing her lips to keep from laughing, she went back into the ballroom and made her way through it toward the staircase, greeting acquaintances here and there, bidding them a good evening as she moved on. Waving her fan idly and trying to look nonchalant, she sauntered out of the ballroom into the entrance hall, where she mingled a bit more. Carefully, she ascended the wide double staircase. One of the private salons upstairs had been set aside as a retreat for the ladies; she pretended that she was headed there. Her heart pounded, but she lifted her white-gloved hand and smoothed her hair as she moved slowly, elegantly, up the stairs.

Really, having to steal one's own diamonds!

Halfway up the steps, she saw her coconspirator strolling across the hall below, right on cue. Rackford was gallantly clearing the way for her brother, Alec, who followed on his crutches. He helped her brother into the salon, from which he had told her, a small white door led to a servant staircase. He knew the layout of the house from the night of his robbery here. By slipping into the service corridors, he would meet her on the third floor.

The upper floors were quiet except for the occasional maid or footman gliding past on some task and the occasional bursts of feminine laughter that emanated from the designated ladies' lounge. Moving calmly down the hallway, Jacinda waited for her opportunity, looked left and right, then picked up her skirts and dashed silently across the intersecting hallway and around the corner. Her eyes began to shine with the excitement of her little adventure. She crept up the next set of stairs to the third floor, wincing when one of the boards creaked beneath her slippered feet. The muffled sounds of the ball faded as she hurried the rest of the way up the stairs, sneaking into the central hallway of the family's private residential wing. Holding her skirts up, she went tiptoeing in search of the master's bedroom.

I can't believe he used to do this for a living. She was terrified someone was going to see her, but the excitement and the thought of getting away with it had her cheeks flushed, her heart pounding.

She nearly jumped out of her skin when she edged up to

the corner ever so carefully and Rackford stepped out of the shadows.

She stifled a shriek. He grasped her forearm and yanked her around the corner.

'Shh!' he scolded as she stumbled against his big, hard body.

She had to cover her mouth with her hand to stop herself from letting out a peal of laughter. He bent his head down to her eye level and laid his finger over his lips, but his green eyes danced with wicked merriment.

'I can't believe we're doing this!'

'They're your diamonds. It's not as if we're stealing.'

'It's *fun*,' she whispered.

He shot her a wry look. 'Hurry up.'

She stage tiptoed behind him as he prowled down the corridor, not making a sound.

'What is the penalty for stealing your own diamonds?'

'Do try to take this just a bit more seriously, would you?' he drawled, then nodded toward the elegantly appointed corridor to the left. 'We want the west corner suite. Come on.' The hallway was dimly lit by candles placed on console tables at long, regular intervals. He pointed toward a pair of white double doors far off at the end of the corridor. 'There it is – the room where I lost my freedom.'

She glanced at him, then froze, hearing something down the next hallway. 'Someone's coming!'

'Run.' He grabbed her hand with a sharp light in his green eyes as the footfalls grew louder.

Hand in hand they raced toward the white double doors. Holding her long skirts up around her shins, she glanced frantically over her shoulder. A tea cart appeared around the corner a moment before the servant pushing it did. Rackford had just enough time to open the door and fling into the room, pulling her with him. He closed it silently behind her.

'What can they be—'

220

'Shh!'

Huddled by the door, neither of them dared move for fear of being heard. Wide-eyed, Jacinda held her breath as they listened to the servant pushing the cart nearer. As her vision adjusted to the gloomy darkness of His Lordship's chamber, the creaking sound passed on the other side of the door and moved on.

Jacinda pressed her hand to her heart and sagged against the door, gaping comically at her partner in mischief.

He shook his head, his white, wolfish smile a brief gleam in the darkness. 'That was close.'

'Lord, you are such a bad influence on me.'

He grinned. She followed him as he strode over to the mahogany pedestal near the window. Atop it sat an impressive Chinese vase. Rackford took the vase off the stand and upended it with one hand, catching her diamond necklace neatly in the other. 'Eureka,' he murmured. 'Let's get out of here.'

She hurried after him as he retraced his steps, going back toward the door. 'Give me my necklace, you rogue.' Stifling a giggle, she reached into his coat pocket, but he captured her hand, whirling her around gently so that she found herself backed up against the closed door. She narrowed her eyes at him, fighting a smile. 'What are you up to?'

Lean and tall, his body packed with compact muscle beneath his formal black and white evening clothes, he braced one hand on the door by her head and leaned toward her, dangling the necklace before her eyes. 'Want it? Come and get it.'

She tried to snatch it out of his grasp, but he lifted it higher with a taunting smile. The diamonds winked and flashed with their bright fire in the darkness.

'Billy!'

'Don't you want this fine bit o' sparkle?'

'Aye,' she answered, borrowing his idiom with a defiant toss of her chin.

221

He bent his head closer, the moonlight beyond the window casting a silvery glow along his finely chiseled profile and the narrow plane of his cheek. 'Give me a kiss, and it's yours.'

She pulled back and met his aggressive stare with what she hoped was a stern look, but her gaze dipped to his tempting lips, rather spoiling the effect. 'It already *is* mine.'

'No, no, my lady, you gave it to me.' His emerald eyes gleamed as he slung the diamond strand around his fingers and swung it before her face, mesmerizing her. 'But if you kiss me, I will give it back to you again.'

She gave him a blushing pout. 'But, Lord Rackford, we have agreed that we are only friends.'

'A friendly kiss,' he whispered, moving closer, tilting his head slightly.

She felt herself weakening under the potency of his charm. 'Perhaps ... one.'

His lips skimmed hers, back and forth, in a slow, tantalizing caress that made her quiver. But when he deepened his kiss with leisurely expertise, stroking her neck so seductively, she gave a faint moan and let her body melt back against the door. Her eyes drifted closed. Her head swam with the intoxicating male taste of him. The single-minded passion in his kiss robbed her senses. She was grateful for the solid door behind her, steadying her weak-kneed response.

Rackford trailed his fingertip down her throat to the center of her gown's neckline. Her chest heaved under his deft, sporting touch. His warm, clever hand slipped down inside the front of her bodice, cupping her breast. She gasped with delight against his luscious mouth as his thumb teased her nipple.

For one sinful moment, she longed for him to tear her clothes off her and take her – simply, roughly claim what she could not bring herself to give of her own free will. He confused her so! It had been so easy to surrender that night in the rookery when she had thought she would never see him again – when there had been no consequences – but now, to indulge in this dangerous desire was to risk placing her entire future in his hands. If their absence were noted in the ballroom below – if someone should come looking for them, find them together in this darkened bedchamber – she would be forced to marry him or face utter ruin. Her crazed heart pounded, torn between yearning and a stubborn refusal of that fate.

She was still determined to be the mistress of her own destiny, but pride had also come into the equation, further complicating matters. That night at the Devonshire ball, she had sworn he would never have control of her. A married couple became one person in the eyes of the law and God – and the man was that person. Mama had railed against it in several of her essays. As Rackford's friend, she remained his equal. Yet even now she felt her control slipping away with the intoxicating manner in which he was peeling her long white gloves off her, stroking her hands.

He might not even want her anymore once he had possessed her, she worried as her control leaked away under his seduction. What if it was only the thrill of the chase that attracted him – and in any case, why should she compromise?

If she was smart, she could have her cake and eat it, too, said a pragmatic, if rather depraved voice in her head. Once she had fulfilled her duty to old Drummond and was an independent widow, she could simply take the magnificent Lord Rackford as her lover. But that could be years away. . . .

Her body quivered eagerly as his hand crept in a slow caress down her belly. 'Shall I pleasure you again?' he murmured softly, ever so willing to give.

She hadn't the strength to protest, but kissed him with consuming heat as he gently cupped her mound. His searching fingers pressed the gauzy muslin of her skirts between her legs. She breathed a whisper-soft moan against his lips that was all the acquiescence he required. God, she had wanted this for so long.

He sank slowly to his knees, following the curves of her body with his hands. He drew his possessive touch down her hips and thighs and all the way down to her ankles, then slipped his hands beneath her skirts. Leaning her head back against the door, hazy-eyed with desire, she raked her now bare hands through his dark gold hair as he kissed her belly through her gown, his clever hands slowly lifting her skirts.

Her heart hammered as he tilted his head back and gazed hotly into her eyes. She caressed his hard, aquiline face; then he lowered his lashes and bent his head, drawing nearer. What he did then – *ah, what he did*. She had never known such shocked delight as the sensations that exploded within her as he kissed her virginal mound, paying homage to her very femininity. She had seen this love-act in the wicked little blue-book with its wanton sketches, but she could never have imagined such pleasure. She could do naught but give in to her arousal, lustily enjoying his self-less loving as his tongue caressed her exquisitely sensitized pleasure center. His fingers were inside her, stroking her with assiduous care.

Oh, how deliciously wicked he was, she thought, panting, clinging to the doorknob to keep from falling down.

She did not know how much time passed, but it was not long before he brought her to a powerful, soul-deep climax. She let out a series of soft, wild groans *'Billy, Billy – oh, God, Billy.'* She clung to him in surrender, fevered, ravished, and raw. All worry, all fear, and all control spiraled away in the whirlwind of joyous sensation.

He stood, taking her gently into his arms. They leaned against the door, holding each other until she finally recovered her wits. He kissed her hair, then lightly grasped her shoulders and turned her around, putting her diamond necklace on her. She stood trembling at his nearness as his fingertips danced at her nape, fastening the clasp. She had never felt so close to anyone, so electrified by another's presence.

With a yearning deeper than her air of playful mischief revealed, she let her hand graze the hard, throbbing pike of his manhood that nudged her backside as he stood behind her, fretting over the clasp of her necklace. He gasped sharply at her light touch. She glanced up at him over her shoulder in fascination.

Not taking her hand off him, she turned around, exploring him through his trousers.

'What do you think you're doing?' he asked huskily, staring at her like he would devour her.

She didn't answer, absorbed in discovering more. She could feel his body changing with her every caress, swelling to even larger proportions, but he stopped her, capturing her hands. She marveled at how large and strong his hands were compared to her small, dainty ones as he laced his fingers through hers, lowered his head, and kissed her for another long, lingering moment.

When he spoke again, his lips brushing hers, his voice was a velvet whisper. 'Do you know I would do anything for you?'

'Billy,' she breathed, wrapping her arms around his lean waist. She laid her head on his chest, entranced by the tingling joy of his embrace, but she did not know how to answer.

He held her close and kissed her hair, pausing for a moment. 'I've never felt this way before about anyone, Jacinda.' His voice was very soft, cautious. 'I just – wanted you to know that.'

She pulled back a small space and tilted her head back in trembling wonder to gaze into his eyes. His stare was earnest yet guarded as he awaited her reaction. Slowly, she lifted her hand and caressed his clean-shaved cheek. He closed his eyes, leaning into her gentle touch. She studied him as though discovering him for the first time, unbidden amazement unfurling within her as she realized he was the first, the only man who had ever treated her as an equal. Indeed, next to Lizzie, she considered him her closest friend. But if she was honest with herself, he was more than just a friend.

Much more.

He suddenly turned his head and kissed her hand with a sardonic smile. 'Enough torture,' he murmured. 'Let's get the hell out of here.'

At a loss for words, she merely nodded and followed him as he opened the door, glanced to the right and left, then beckoned her out into the hallway. Together they went hurrying back through the silent corridors.

Somewhat belatedly, she began to worry about whether or not anyone had noticed their absence. Surely Lord Drummond must be wondering where she and Rackford had stolen off to.

They split up a few moments later, Jacinda returning the way she had come, Rackford once more taking the service corridors. He stole a quick, parting kiss before he opened the servants' door through which he had come.

'Hey, beautiful,' he called softly as she paused to glance at her reflection in one of the mirrors hung above the console tables in the hallway.

With a blushing smile, she turned around as he poked his head out of the servants' door one more time.

'Yes?'

'Sweeter than candy,' he murmured wickedly, blowing her a kiss.

She let out a virginal gasp, but before she could reply, he vanished into the shadows. She heard only the faint rhythm of his footfalls fading down the concealed servant staircase. With a slight, blushing smile, she turned back to the candlelit mirror and gazed in private, secretive pleasure at her diamond necklace resting against her glowing, pink skin. She shook her head at her reflection, sighing to see that that rookery scoundrel had left her looking as rumpled and pink-cheeked and as thoroughly well-kissed as she felt.

Quickly smoothing her hair and righting her gown, she flitted back to the ballroom, her slippered feet scarcely touching the ground.

She's mine. Oh, yes. Whether she wanted to admit it or not, his errant, feisty, curly-headed darling was finally starting to feel the same attachment he had suffered now for weeks. He was sure of it. Smiling to himself in the darkness, he cheerfully sprang up the front stairs of his father's house in Lincoln's Inn Fields.

By now, the hour was late. He had just arrived home from the Taylor ball. As usual, Gerald the night butler answered the door before he could knock. Rackford flicked the ashes off his cheroot before going in the house. His mother called his smoking 'a disgusting habit,' but a man had to have his vices.

God, how he wished he could remove to some fashionable bachelor lodgings, preferably on the other side of the city, he thought, but Sir Anthony and the Bow Street officers who were handling his case wanted him here where it was easier for them to keep an eye on him – not just for their convenience, but for his protection, now that he had sent so many villains to Newgate. Those luxurious bachelor hotels, they said, had too many people always coming and going.

As he crossed the entrance hall and strode up the staircase to the main floor, his thoughts raced back, as they often did, to the exasperating, irresistible Lady Jacinda.

Tonight had been a bold risk, but one he was vastly glad he had taken. That was the problem with all these Society rules, he thought. It was practically a labor of Hercules stealing a moment alone with a girl. In the rookery, the lasses were largely free to spend their time with whomever they chose, and if they liked a chap, they were not stingy with their favors. He was not used to all these obstacles that a man had to scale like the battlements of a citadel: chaperons, her governess, her formidable brothers, the eagle-eyed Society matrons. But he trusted that tonight he had given Jacinda a proper dose of persuading. She must see now how good it would be between them.

Aye, and not a moment too soon. God knew he needed relief. He had stopped her from touching him because he knew he couldn't be satisfied with anything less than her maidenhead, and no future wife of his was going to be deflowered in another man's bed. Still, he had to have her soon, or he was going to lose his mind with sheer frustration. Lately he spent far too much time fantasizing about undressing her, untying each dainty ribbon, slowly removing her light, delicate clothing, piece by piece –

'William!' a harsh voice broke rudely into his pleasant thoughts.

He turned around, jarred out of his wayward imaginings to find his father walking toward him down the corridor, his neckcloth hanging untied around his shoulders, his face red with drink. He nearly smiled in irreverent humor at the sight of the man, remembering how Jacinda had scowled at Truro the Terrible over dinner.

Noticing the aggressive light that shone in his father's glassy emerald eyes, however, Rackford's smile faded and his whole mood darkened at once. He knew that look, though he had not seen it in years.

Instantly on his guard, he watched his father coming toward him, staggering slightly.

'Put that thing out, you insolent bastard,' the marquess slurred. 'You know full well your mother said no smoking in the house. When you're under my roof, by God, you'll follow my rules!'

Rackford stared at him for a moment. Apparently his father did not realize that he now had a few inches of height and two stone of weight on him in pure muscle, not to mention fifteen years of fighting for his life.

Perhaps Jacinda's attempts to civilize him were working, he thought, for although every muscle in his body tensed, he managed to respond like a gentleman. There was a small potted lemon tree in the hallway. Rackford quietly walked over to it and crushed out his cheroot in the loose soil. He straightened up again slowly.

'Forgive me. I didn't think it would bother anyone.'

'Well, it dashed well bothers me!'

What a churl you are, he thought, gazing at the man.

'An' I'll tell you something else that bothers me, if you're askin',' the drunken marquess went on, his feverish eyes burning ever more brightly. 'That little Hawkscliffe harlot you're always sniffin' after.'

Wrath flashed in Rackford's eyes as his stare locked on his father's face. 'My lord,' he warned, 'I will not hear that lady abused in my presence.'

'Lady?' he scoffed. 'Forget about 'er. You gave me your word you'd marry at once, and it's been nearly two months. Now, you've had your time to sow your oats, boy. I've spoken with Lord Erhard about his daughter, the redhead with the big tits, and we've decided you and she should be wed—'

'Daphne Taylor?' he exclaimed in contempt.

'Yes, that's the one. Daphne,' he said with a goatish leer.

'Father, that girl is a harpy. I'll be marrying Lady Jacinda.' *If she ever comes to her senses.*

'The hell you will.'

Every authority-flouting bone in his body bristled at the order. 'Why not? Lady Jacinda comes from an excellent family.' Just like buying a milch cow, he reminded himself cynically. 'She's beautiful, healthy, and she's got a dowry of a hundred thousand pounds.' That ought to please the man.

'I don't care how many damned thousands she comes with,' Truro slurred. 'She's a haughty little bitch an' I don't like her.'

She doesn't like you much, either. Rackford struggled to hold his growing fury in check. 'Well, I do.'

229

'Don't you know what kind of little whore she is, you stupid sod? Just like her mother! No son of mine is going to end up wedded to a little round-heeled slut—'

'*Enough*!' he roared in his father's face, losing his temper.

With a grunt, Truro took a swing at him; Rackford caught the man's fist squarely in his right hand. His defensive reaction was smooth and automatic, flipping him over his shoulder, a move honed in countless street fights. His father sailed through the air and landed flat on his back in the marble corridor, the wind knocked out of him.

Rackford loomed over him with murder in his eyes and planted his foot on his father's throat. A thousand memories of his suffering rushed through his mind and coursed like poison through his bloodstream.

'Do you know how easily I could kill you?' he whispered through gritted teeth as his heart hammered.

His father stared up at him with stark fear in his eyes. It filled Rackford with savage but fleeting satisfaction.

'Why – ' Rackford started, but his voice turned to ashes in his throat. His pride refused to let him ask the aching questions that still bled in the core of his heart after all the years. *Why do you hate me so much? What did I ever do to deserve the treatment I received at your hands? How did I fail to live up?*

The moment of weakness veered past.

'Say what you want about me, but if I ever hear you speak another disparaging word about my future wife, I swear I will give you a beating you will never forget.' He removed his foot from atop his sire's windpipe, squared his shoulders, and forced himself to walk away.

His father climbed to his feet and bellowed all manner of abuses after him down the corridor, reminding him, lest he forget, that he was a waste of life, bad, stupid, weak, worthless for every purpose but doing the work of the devil. 'I should've let you rot in Newgate. Better the line should die than leave a sorry excuse like you to fill my shoes!'

Rackford laughed at the sheer, mad cruelty of his father's words, but by the time he reached his room, he was shaking, and the happiness he'd felt driving home from the ball had fled.

He looked around hollowly at his dark, silent room and did not know what he was doing here. Closing the door behind him, he did not light a candle, but walked wearily to his bed; the sheer heaviness of the past seemed to press him down as he lay across it. For a long time, he stared up at the ceiling. He closed his eyes as the old, half-forgotten pain of his unworthiness rose up and enveloped him, and from it there was no escape; the failure, the flaw, was inside him. *Isn't anyone ever going to love me?*

In the darkness, his heart scrabbled toward the one light he had found, the light that was Jacinda, but at the thought of her the pain doubled, trebled. It was so very easy to fear that everything his father said was true – and how could she ever love someone like him? Who was he fooling?

He could give her pleasure, but at core, he was still not worth a damn and certainly not deserving of her love. Anguish convulsed inside of him so sharply that hot, angry tears stung the backs of his eyes. He swiftly sat up, scowling them into oblivion. Rising sharply to his feet, he raked his hand through his hair and drove the demons back with a vengeance, willing himself to remember her many kindnesses to him, her caring questions – and the way she looked at him. She never looked at anyone else like that.

And then, of course, there was the matter of her diamonds. She had left them for him all those weeks ago, a gift freely given, aye, because she had seen something good in him.

She was mistaken, said the insidious voice in his mind. *You're worthless. You're nothing.*

He didn't know which side of himself to believe. With a low, angry growl, he got up, tugging restlessly at his cravat. He paced across his room in the darkness and went to the window. Moving the draperies aside, he glanced

231

down to where his guards were stationed in the street. His eyes flickered with brooding violence.

He let the curtain fall and went to change his clothes.

A few minutes later, a vengeful hiss of metal sounded faintly in the darkness as he took out his favorite knife from the hidden compartment in the drawer. He looked toward the black city skyline beyond the window.

It was time to go hunting Jackals.

Chapter Fourteen

Before long, Rackford was stealing through the shadows of
the rookery. He left his churning anger over his father's
scorn behind as he prowled through a narrow passage
between buildings, making his way toward the entrance of
the abandoned carriage factory that he had been using as his
portal into his former gang headquarters.

The moon shone down like a watchful eye. The rookery
was quiet.

Too quiet.

Maybe more of O'Dell's men had deserted, he thought,
for he knew he had them on the run.

It had started with Bloody Fred, spreading hysteria with
all his ranting about having seen the ghost of Billy Blade.
Rackford had heard that O'Dell had finally taken Fred back
to Bedlam, where he was now kept safely in a cage, but the
damage had already been done.

Chaos reigned in the rookery. Just as Rackford had
planned, the Jackals gang was imploding, O'Dell's control
over his men slowly slipping away.

Baumer and Flash had killed each other in an argument
over the pocket watch. With the scourge of his nocturnal
visits, three other members of the Jackals had been found
dead either in their rooms or in the surrounding dark alleys.
All were those who had participated in the rape of
Murphy's daughter. Numerous others had deserted, for

now all of St. Giles knew that the Jackals were being stalked, picked off one by one, by the ghost of Billy Blade. Wild rumors flew, fueled by the gothic imaginations of the illiterate Cockney ruffians and dirt-poor superstitious Irish stuffed into the surrounding tenement houses.

They had whipped themselves into a frenzy. Half the denizens of the rookery claimed to have seen his shade in numerous different places at the same time. Blade had come back from the grave, they said, to carry out his vow to avenge the honor of the innocent young girl. He was said to be a ruthless phantom, capable of cutting a man's throat – but only the wicked need fear him. He could appear in different quarters of the neighborhood within seconds, they claimed, and would vanish without a sound. The only solid trace he left behind when he killed was the scattered petals of a red carnation.

Aye, he thought darkly, even if O'Dell did not believe in ghosts, his men were spooked, and that made it all the easier to defeat them.

Creeping up alongside the abandoned factory, Rackford glanced around to make sure no one saw him, then laid hold of the barnlike door.

Without a sound, he pulled it open just wide enough for him to slip through. The second he stepped over the threshold into the pitch darkness, pain exploded in Rackford's skull as someone dealt him a crushing blow to the back of his head.

He let out a bellow and staggered down on one knee, stunned and half blinded with pain. Three men jumped on him, wrestling him to the ground. He fought to keep his balance, his head throbbing. He couldn't see straight in the darkness. A fist socked him in the stomach, doubling him over. He fought blindly as they went for his weapons.

Someone tripped him, and the next thing he knew, his face was in the moldy sawdust. He could feel a man's boot on the back of his head. Rackford spewed curses, but the boot heel only pressed his bleeding head down harder, mashing his cheek against the filthy floor. They jerked his arms up tight behind him.

'Well, I'll be damned. He's a live one, all right.'

'Pick him up.'

'O'Dell was right – Blade is alive!'

'Not for long.'

Someone spat very near him; then rough hands on each side of him grasped him by the arms and heaved him to his feet. With blood trickling from the corner of his mouth, Rackford lifted his chin and found himself eye to eye with Tyburn Tim, O'Dell's right-hand man.

'Hullo, Blade. You look diff'rent. Aw, ye cut yer pretty hair. O'Dell's gonna cut your throat.'

His only answer was an icy stare.

A cruel smile spread slowly across Tim's face. 'Cocky as ever. Well, we knew we'd get you one o' these nights.' Tim punched him in the stomach, knocking the wind out of him. 'That's for Jones, you bastard.'

While he struggled to absorb the blow, the men holding his arms jerked him upright again at Tim's curt nod.

'Bring him.'

He was half dragged, half carried next door into the headquarters, where they threw him into a storage room on the first floor and locked him in. Two stayed behind to guard him while Tyburn Tim left to fetch O'Dell.

His head throbbing, he dragged himself up slowly off of the floor with a silent groan of pain. He moved up onto his hands and knees, then sat back on his haunches while the world wove dizzily. God, what had they hit him with? He could feel the warm ooze of his blood trickling down the back of his neck from the blow to his head. *Guess I got careless. Or merely arrogant.* He hadn't thought O'Dell was clever enough to discover how he had been sneaking in, but one thing was crystal clear despite his dazed wits. If he didn't get out of here, he was dead. Rackford reached for his knife, preparing to defend himself, then realized grimly that they had succeeded in disarming him.

Standing a few feet away, one of his guards held up his lucky knife, taunting him with it. 'Guess you're just plain old Billy now – eh, Blade?'

Rackford cast a baleful look around the storeroom, trying to orient himself. He knew the storage room was situated off of the warehouse, not far from the loading dock and the few back steps where he had brought Jacinda in the night he had found her. As a matter of fact . . .

His gaze snagged upon the floorboards in the center of the room. By barest chance, he recalled that this room, too, held a thief's trapdoor. He remembered because Eddie had once popped up merrily through the floor and interrupted him in the middle of enjoying the favors of a juicy lass whose name at the moment eluded him.

If he could do something about his two guards, he could slip down to the clammy, packed-earth foundations under the building and escape in a trice. The thought of running from Cullen O'Dell filled him with loathing, but he was unarmed and wounded; if he could not fight, he had to flee.

Just then, the door opened. Rackford looked up, but instead of Tyburn Tim returning with O'Dell, young Oliver Strayhorn prowled cautiously into the room. He was a newer member of the Jackals gang, a tall, lean, serious-looking lad with black hair and hazel eyes. Rackford's pair of guards stopped their jeering and sobered at the young man's entrance.

Rackford had heard that Strayhorn was gathering the other men's confidence with his intelligence and natural ability as a leader.

Strayhorn approached him with measured paces. 'So, you're the great Blade. At last we meet.'

He said nothing.

'I have heard a lot about you.'

'None of it good, I'm sure.'

Strayhorn passed an assessing glance over his face. 'Quite the contrary. You ran the largest gang north of the Thames. You created it.'

236

He nodded. The Fire Hawks had been the result of several merged gangs, including his own former organization, the Tomahawks, and the Firedrakes of Clerkenwell.

'Even those closest to O'Dell admit that you knew how to make money,' Strayhorn remarked, studying him.

'Aye, takes time,' he conceded with a nod, trying to focus despite his throbbing head. 'And nerve, and a little ingenuity. That's all. What of you? Aren't you among those closest to O'Dell?'

Strayhorn's wary eyes flickered. He shook his head in a subtle negative to Rackford's question. An old proverb came at once to mind: *The enemy of my enemy is my friend.* Perhaps he and Strayhorn could be of use to each other.

Without further remark, the tall, lanky young man rose again and left the room, casting Rackford a shrewd, parting nod before pulling the door shut behind him. Though he suspected that Strayhorn had gone to see what he could do to help him, Rackford knew all too well that the law of the rookery was to look out for oneself first. He had no intention of trusting his fate to either Strayhorn's scheming or O'Dell's mercy, for the man had none. He had to get out of here now.

Furtively sliding his hand along the seam between the floorboards, he felt one of the boards give slightly. It was thick and weathered, only resting in place, not nailed down. It would prove a handy weapon as well as an escape hatch, he thought, eyeing his guards.

He lured them closer with a faint plea for water. They neared him, grinning.

'You want something to drink, you bloody bastard?' One started unhitching his trousers. 'I'll give you—'

With a sudden heave, Rackford brought the board up and swung it at them, knocking both men's legs out from under them. The image of Jacinda's face bloomed in his mind, filling him with new strength. He hit one a second time with the board to make sure he stayed down, kicked the other in the stomach, then tore back the other three floorboards and jumped down the narrow chute, landing agilely on the old, clammy flagstones. Before his guards recovered, he dashed out from under the building and raced across the street into the labyrinth of the rookery.

In moments, he heard the Jackals coming after him. His head pounded in time with his running footsteps on the cobblestones; his breathing thundered harshly in the night's stillness.

He did not glance back. He heard them chasing him – six, seven pairs of footsteps, hollering voices, but only one he recognized for sure.

O'Dell.

'Find him! Follow him! Find out where he's going! *I'll get you, Blade, you son of a bitch!*'

He careened around a corner and kept on running, but the exertion was making the gash on the back of his head bleed faster. With each step he felt more nauseated and light-headed. Fearful that he was on the verge of blacking out, he grasped the door of an old shed crammed between two of the buildings he passed and stumbled inside, pulling the door shut silently behind him. Rackford crumpled against the wall, trying to silence his loud, ragged breathing as he heard the Jackals running past.

'Check down there! Come on; we'll head this way!'

They split up, two sets of footsteps going off in two separate directions, but Rackford knew they had not gone far. *God, that was close.* They would be back – and he was too weak in that moment even to defend himself. Slowly sliding down the wall, he sat on the hard floor and closed his eyes, the sweat standing out cold on his face. The moment's rest felt blissful at first, but then, it all caught up to him in a wave of sickening pain. His head was positively throbbing. He forced himself to his feet again with a grimace.

After his moment's respite, he eased the door open a couple of inches and saw that the street was empty. Gathering up what remained of his stamina, he slipped out of the shed and alternated between jogging and walking the

238

rest of the way back to his father's house in Lincoln's Inn Fields.

Nate, old friend, he thought as he collapsed on his bed some time later, *I could have used your help tonight.* Without bothering to change out of his bloodied clothes, he closed his eyes and let the darkness claim him.

The next morning, he awoke in the middle of the day feeling as if a herd of elephants had stampeded over him. His body was stiff and sore. He felt achy and bruised all over. His abdomen hurt where they had kicked him repeatedly. Pain throbbed from the large knot on the back of his head, but thankfully, the wound had closed. He would have damned well liked to know what they had hit him with.

He ordered coffee and sandwiches instead of his usual large breakfast and took a long bath, rinsing the matted blood out of his hair. Every atom of his body longed for Jacinda and her soft, caring touch.

In truth, he was more shaken by his failure than he cared to admit, and rather humiliated, to boot. Recalling the fight with his father that had driven him to the rookery last night to vent his ire, he learned from Filbert that Truro had left this morning for Cornwall, taking Mother with him.

Satisfied that at least he had put his bullying father in his place, he drowsed in the nickel-plated bathing tub until the headache powder took effect.

Feeling closer to normal, though still beaten and weary, he got dressed and wasted no more time in going to Jacinda. One smile from her could cure whatever ailed him.

He drove his curricle to Knight House more slowly than usual to avoid the jarring ruts in the road, pondering as he went how he was going to explain his cuts and bruises.

Maybe you ought just to tell her the truth, his conscience offered, but he brushed it off. He'd think of something.

Mr. Walsh let him in, as usual. Rackford took off his hat and greeted the butler, but the moment he stepped over the

239

threshold into the white marble entrance hall, Jacinda's sweet voice called to him from above.

'Rackford! Oh, thank heavens you're here!'

He looked up and saw her peering down at him over the banister at the top of the grand curved staircase. Her face was flushed, her curls disheveled, and he instantly forgot his assorted aches and pains as he realized that something was very wrong.

Tears filled her eyes as she rushed down the steps.

He stalked swiftly toward her. 'What is it?'

She did not answer, but dashed across the entrance hall and flung her arms around his waist with a small sob, holding him tightly.

'Sweeting, what's the matter?' he murmured as his arms went around her protectively.

Mr. Walsh cleared his throat in disapproval, but Jacinda ignored him.

'Oh, Billy, it's finally happened – the most awful thing.'

'What's happened, darling?' he demanded, lifting her chin with his fingertips to look into her eyes. Her apple cheeks were wet with tears.

'It's Lizzie,' she choked out. 'Alec has done the most abominable thing.'

'Good God, tell me what's occurred—'

'Come – I'll explain on the way. We must go to her.' She took his arm, turning toward the grand, sweeping staircase that led up to the mansion's main floor. 'I've never seen her like this before,' she confided anxiously as they walked up the curved stairs. 'She's hysterical, packing her things. She says she's leaving, and I think she means it. Maybe you can calm her down,' she said anxiously. 'You know how fond she is of you.'

'Of course, I will do my best to help.'

She rested her head against his arm. 'You are so good. I am desperate to tell Robert what's happened, but Lizzie has forbidden me to say a word.'

'Darling, what is it?' he asked, trying not to sound impatient.

240

She stopped and turned to him at the top of the stairs, searching his eyes. 'You mustn't tell anyone.'

'Of course not. I only want to help.' He rested his foot on the stair above and leaned against the banister.

'It's Alec. The truth has all come out. He never broke his ankle in the course of some mad wager. The situation was much more serious than that, but Alec didn't want to tell anyone that his losing streak at the tables was worse than he let on. When Robert cut him off to try to curb his gambling, it seems Alec turned to some low, cutthroat moneylender to cover his vowels. But when the time came for him to begin repaying the loan, he was still unable to meet the debt. He asked for an extension, but the money-lender would have none of it and sent his thugs out after him to collect. It was they who broke Alec's ankle, to serve as a warning to him that if he didn't pay up, next time it would cost him his life.'

Cold fury leaped into Rackford's eyes at the injury to his friend and the way these men had upset Jacinda. 'Do not be troubled, my lady. I will see to this matter in a trice. I've dealt with these dishonest Jerusalem chambers before. I know just how to handle these sharks—'

She stopped him with a gentle hand on his arm. 'Wait until you hear the rest of the story.' She pressed her hand to her forehead with a sigh. 'Lord, I could wring Alec's neck for not saying anything to Robert or the twins, but nothing galls him more than having to call on his big brothers to get him out of some scrape. He wasn't even going to tell Lizzie the truth about his circumstances, but then he *had* to, because the night before last, while we were at the theater, she saw these men for herself. She heard them making threats against him. They came again demanding payment from Alec.'

'They came here?' he whispered furiously, blanching at the thought of the danger of that sort of criminal coming in so close to the girls and the duchess and little Morley.

Jacinda nodded. 'Lizzie said they came up to the gates.

241

She and Alec were sitting on the veranda playing whist when these rough-looking fellows approached and began harassing Alec through the bars. After he managed to get rid of them, Lizzie prevailed on him to explain. She was beside herself, for they were threatening his life. Only then did he break down and confide in her about his predicament.'

'I trust Miss Carlisle told His Grace at once?'

'No. Alec swore her to secrecy. Lizzie would never break a promise, especially to Alec. The next day – this was yesterday – she went to Robert and asked him to sign over to her all the money that had been left to her by her father. She told Robert she wanted to start the business she had been interested in for years – of buying old and rare books and restoring them to sell to collectors. She told him she was ready to make her first purchases of some musty old medieval manuscripts – something like that. At any rate, Robert interrogated her on her business plans. When he was satisfied with her responses, he signed over her inheritance to her, even though she is not officially entitled to it until she turns twenty-one in September. It's a modest sum, but – ' Her big, brown eyes filled with fresh tears. 'Lizzie gave it all to Alec to repay his debt – to save his life.'

'He lost it at the tables?' he asked grimly.

'No. It seems, in the end, my brother didn't have the heart to take her gift. At first, though, he did accept it. Lizzie said she gave it to him in the morning at about ten o'clock. He left to go repay his loan, but then he did not appear for twenty-four hours. He was just here, but he's left again. He said, in the end, he couldn't go through with it.'

'I'm not surprised,' Rackford murmured. It would have been the ultimate loss of honor for any man. 'But Alec gave her back her money? Did he find another way to repay the moneylender? Because I can help him—'

'Oh, he found a way, all right.' She paled and looked away.

'Jacinda?'

'Alec's become – that is – ' Her cheeks turned from pale to red.

'What is it, sweeting?'

Slowly, dolefully, she turned her gaze back to his. 'Lady Campion has paid his debts,' she whispered. 'Oh, Rackford, this morning when Alec came to give Lizzie back her money, he told her right to her face that he had spent the night with the baroness and would be doing so for the foreseeable future!'

His eyes widened. 'How did Lizzie take it?'

'She is destroyed,' she whispered.

He put his arms around her and pulled her to him as a small sob escaped her. Holding her for a moment, he caressed her arm, then pressed a gentle kiss to her curly head. 'Come. Let us go and see her.'

Jacinda nodded with a sniffle. As she led him to Lizzie, Rackford mulled it over, wondering what, if anything, was to be done.

At least Alec had told Lizzie face-to-face, instead of trying to conceal it or letting her find out some other way. As cruel as Alec's blow had been, Rackford could easily understand how ashamed Lizzie's gift must have made him feel – tangible evidence that he had indeed hit bottom.

Better to sacrifice what remained of his self-respect by becoming the willing male plaything of the rich, worldly baroness than to abandon all honor by taking advantage of an innocent girl's selfless adoration and dragging her down into the bog with him.

'I suppose you should wait here,' Jacinda said as they came to another, smaller staircase. She tucked her hair behind her ear and turned away, her eyes red-rimmed. 'Our chambers are just up the stairs. I will try to coax her down.'

He nodded and waited while she hurried up the smaller set of stairs. He paced, hearing Jacinda's pleading from above. He could hear Lizzie's brief, impassioned shouts punctuated by heart-wrenching sobs.

243

'Please, Lizzie, come and see Rackford—'

'I can't. I have to pack. Please give him my apologies.'

'Where are you going to go?'

'To visit Mrs. Hastings in York.' There was a brittle, jerky quality in Lizzie's words that made Rackford's heart ache; then her voice exploded into rage. 'I'll start my rare book business! He'll see. I'll show him. And when I'm rich, he-he'll come crawling on his knees to me, that – that male whore, and I'll laugh in his face! Just you wait!' she wrenched out.

'Good God,' Rackford exclaimed under his breath.

Ignoring Jacinda's caution, he took the stairs two at a time and walked into Lizzie's chamber, only dimly registering the realization that Jacinda's bedchamber was directly across the hallway.

'Hey, you,' he said softly to the pale, tearstained bluestocking.

Lizzie turned, saw him, and promptly succumbed to a fresh wave of grief-stricken tears. Rackford said nothing more, but walked over and hugged her, letting her have a good cry on his shoulder.

Jacinda came over to them and comforted her friend, as well.

'I wish I had never seen him! He is too highborn for me; I have known that all along,' she said through her tears. 'He is a d-duke's son, and I am only an estate manager's daughter. I know why he always calls me 'Bits.' Because that's how he sees me, s-small and insignificant. I am nothing to him; I never was. I should never have reached above my station—'

'Oh, Lizzie, come, you know full well Alec's real father was only an actor,' Jacinda scolded tenderly, petting her shoulder.

'Where is Alec now?' Rackford asked gently.

'White's,' Lizzie whispered through her tears.

'I will go and talk to him.'

'There is nothing more to say.'

244

'Let him try, Lizzie,' Jacinda cajoled her. The look in her big, brown eyes as she raised her gaze hopefully to his filled Rackford with resolve. Just once, he longed for the chance to be her hero.

Determined to put all the chivalry the girls had taught him to good use, he led Lizzie over to a nearby chair and bade her sit, then left her in Jacinda's keeping and went out to try to shake some sense into that infernal rakehell.

Since White's Club was just down the street, he arrived shortly. He quickly spied Alec sitting with some other young bucks drinking brandy. He walked over to their table by the bow window. Alec met his hard gaze, and at once, a flicker of guilt passed behind his dark blue eyes.

'Well, if it isn't Lord Rack-and-Ruin.'

'Would you gentlemen kindly excuse us?' he ordered Alec's scoundrelly friends.

They bristled at the request from a presumptuous newcomer, but Alec waved them off with a languid flick of his hand, and they withdrew.

'So,' he drawled as Rackford planted his hands on the shiny oaken table and leaned on it, staring at him in stern warning. 'Baby sister has sicced her wolf-dog on me. Are you going to call me out, Rackford?'

'Why would I do that?'

'Don't know. That's the problem. No one knows what to make of you, how you might react. You are quite the wild card.'

'Coming from a gambler of your reputation, I shall take that as a compliment.'

Alec smirked. 'A gambler of my former reputation, you mean. My luck has left me, Rackford. All I can seem to do these days is lose.'

'Your luck is not all you will have lost unless you go home immediately and make things right with a certain young lady.'

'Make things right? What in God's name do you think I've just done?'

'Broken her heart. She is crying her eyes out.'

He said nothing for a moment. 'Lizzie Carlisle can do a hell of a lot better than me.'

Taking a clean brandy snifter from the tray in the center of the table, Rackford poured himself a draught. 'I may be able to help. If it's a matter of money, I can give you a loan—'

'Thank you, but I've got a new situation. Hadn't you heard?' he cut him off in razor-edged cynicism. 'Pleasant work, if a man can get it.'

'Aye, and if a man can live with himself afterwards.'

'You won't see me complaining.'

'Why do you want to be rid of a girl who genuinely loves you?'

Alec dropped his head back with a vexed groan and stared at the ceiling. 'Bitsy is a first-rate, bona fide, doe-eyed innocent, Rackford. She's all brains and no common sense.'

'That's not true. Miss Carlisle is a very intelligent young woman.'

He snorted. 'Not if she loves me, she ain't. She'll wise up now, I warrant.'

Rackford slowly straightened up, holding Alec's defensive gaze. 'Sober up, man. Don't be a fool. If you let that girl slip through your fingers, you will regret it for the rest of your life.'

The bravado seemed to leave Alec all at once. He slouched down in his chair, stared at nothing, then shook his head with a resigned sigh. 'Tell her I'm sorry, would you?'

'Tell her yourself.' Giving the man a hard look, Rackford turned and walked away.

'You should not be alone right now,' Jacinda insisted even as she and Rackford escorted Lizzie toward the waiting stagecoach the next evening.

'I have to, before I lose my nerve. Who knows what waits for me out there in the world? Besides, I'm only

246

going as far as York,' Lizzie reassured her, just as she had ever since Jacinda had been a wee thing. She hugged her hard, then braved a smile. 'It is time for me to leave the Hawkscliffe nest.'

'Only for a little while,' Jacinda insisted. 'Promise you'll write.'

'Of course.'

'I'm sorry I couldn't change his mind, Miss Carlisle,' Rackford said softly. 'For what it's worth, I think he's mad, and blind, and an addle-pated fool.'

She laughed and winced and hugged him. 'Oh, Lord Rackford, if only all the male species could be like you. You tried, and for that, you are a knight in shining armor, as far as I'm concerned.'

Chastened by her kind words, he kissed her cheek before helping her up into the coach. Jacinda fretted, glancing at the other passengers. The stubborn Lizzie wouldn't even let her hire a proper post chaise for her journey, but was resolved to take the mode of transport suitable, as she had put it, to her station.

'You two take care of each other,' Lizzie ordered them softly, squeezing Jacinda's hand through the open window.

'We will,' Rackford assured her, tugging Jacinda back a few steps from the wheels of the coach as the driver made ready to go.

As Lizzie's coach pulled out of the innyard, the two of them stood together, waving at her. When it was out of sight, Jacinda felt Rackford studying her.

She turned to him with a dismayed attempt at a smile. 'Well. She's off.'

'She'll be all right,' he murmured, taking her gloved hand and lifting it to press a kiss to her knuckles. 'Come.'

He helped her into his curricle and took her to Gunter's for ices to try to cheer her up, but noting her still-distracted mood, at length he drove her away from the hubbub of the city to Primrose Hill. At the base of the slope, he left the carriage with the groom.

247

This was no secret, darkened bedchamber in the middle of a ball – it was broad daylight, and she had no chaperon present, she thought, but with Lizzie gone, propriety seemed like a petty irrelevance. Somehow, all in one day, life had become so much more serious. She had to get her thoughts straightened out. She only knew she was ever so glad of Rackford's calm, strong, steadying presence. Together they walked up through the flowery meadows to the summit.

The sun was setting. Near an old, massive, whispering oak tree they sat side by side in the overgrown grasses and gazed at the prospect of London in the distance, sharing their pensive silence.

A chubby shopkeeper's family was picnicking near the bottom of the hill. They had a blanket laid out upon the grass with countless baskets of food and a trio of children tumbling riotously down the hill. Their screeches of laughter floated to Jacinda and Rackford faintly on the evening air.

Other than that, they had Primrose Hill to themselves.

Jacinda looked over and found Rackford watching her in intimate silence. The ruddy light of sunset illumined his tanned skin, softened the hard planes and angles of his face, and brought out the gold dust in the mysterious green depths of his eyes.

'How are you?' he asked quietly.

'I'm all right. I've still got you, haven't I?' She reached for his hand and gave it a fond squeeze, smiling ruefully at him.

His tawny eyebrows flicked upward in momentary surprise at her words. 'Of course,' he said, but a manly blush crept into his cheeks.

It charmed her. On an impulse she reached over and caressed his cheek. 'My dear Lord Rackford,' she sighed, then paused. 'There is something ... I have been meaning to tell you.'

He lifted his eyebrow in wordless query.

'Thank you,' she said softly.

'For what?'

'Must I say it?' she exclaimed, laughing and blushing a bit self-consciously.

'Ah, you mean for the other night?' He took a bite of the red apple he had been polishing on his coat.

Her blush deepened as she watched him eating it. 'No – though it was sublime.' She paused. 'I wanted to say thank you for stopping me from running away from home.'

He stopped chewing and stared at her. He swallowed in a gulp. 'Pardon?'

She dropped her head, picking a blade of grass as her curls fell forward, veiling her face. 'You were right. It's not easy to admit it, but I owe you that.' She forced herself to look at him, smiling despite her chagrin. 'I didn't realize it at the time, but my running away would have been a disaster.' Her expression sobered. 'You stopped me from doing possibly permanent damage to my relationships with my family, and there's nothing more important to me than that. Oh – I'm sorry!' she exclaimed, catching herself too late. 'Forgive me ...'

'For what?' he asked with a blank look.

'It's thoughtless of me to go on about how much I love my family after what yours has done to you.'

'Truro and his wife?' He shrugged it off with a frank snort, leaning back on his elbow in the grass. 'We may share the same blood, but they're not my family.' He looked at her for a long moment. 'You are.'

Staring at her, he took another matter-of-fact bite of his apple. It made a loud, juicy crunch.

His words had made her catch her breath slightly. She held his gaze, not sure how to react, but she was, all of a sudden, intensely aware that without Lizzie or a chaperon or a roomful of eagle-eyed guests in some ballroom below, no one stood between the two of them and their suppressed desire.

Watching the play of emotions on her face, Rackford

249

held out his apple, offering her a bite. Her heart beat faster as she leaned forward and opened her mouth, tasting the sweet, wet fruit.

He stared at her mouth as she chewed it. She had barely swallowed it when he leaned closer and claimed her mouth in a deep, luscious kiss. He tasted of the apple's sweetness and of warm, masculine need. All thought reeled away, flying out of her grasp as his lips urgently coaxed hers apart. She laid her hand on his shoulder to steady herself against the whirling sensation, like the first time they had danced the waltz.

Her arms slid around his neck as she returned his kiss in ardent longing; then he eased her back into the deep, soft grasses, laying her upon a bed of daisies, primroses, and tiny buttercups.

They moved together in the long grasses, every sinuous stroke of his body lighting fires in her blood. She curled her hands passionately around his shoulders, then raked her white-gloved fingers down his back. His low groan of pleasure at her touch emboldened her. She kissed him more urgently, caressing his muscled chest, savoring his strength and power.

Did she really want to be like Lady Campion? Living only for herself, for her selfish pleasures, without a care for who she hurt along the way?

Just like Mama.

She was running her fingers through his hair when he suddenly winced and whispered, 'Ow.'

She stopped at once. 'What is it?' she panted.

'Nothing. Kiss me.' He reached for her again, but she stopped him, drawn back regretfully to her senses.

'Darling, we really shouldn't.'

'Yes, we should.'

She smiled. 'What if someone sees?'

He scowled. 'Oh, very well.'

'Did you hurt your head or something?' she asked as they sat up again.

'It's nothing. Absurd, really.' He fingered the back of his head with a look of boyish chagrin.

'Oh, Rackford, what have you gone and done to yourself now? Let me see.'

He muttered something under his breath that it was of no consequence, but when she riffled through his dark gold hair and found the newly healing gash on the back of his head, she gasped aloud.

'Billy! Oh, my darling!' She wrapped her arms around him protectively. 'Tell me this instant what happened to your poor head!'

'It's nothing,' he protested, stealing a soft kiss from her lips.

'William.'

'It's embarrassing.'

'William Spencer—'

'I backed into a ... nail.'

'A nail?'

He nodded innocently. 'In the stable. My horse nudged me and knocked me off balance. There's the post with a big nail sticking out where the groom hangs the bridle. I fell into it. I told you it was stupid.'

She stared at him very hard for a second. 'Did your father do that to you?'

'*What*?'

'Your father.'

'No! Nothing like that.'

'Do you promise?'

'My father had nothing to do with it.'

'Oh, you silly boy.' She cuddled him; then he laid his head in her lap with a sigh of contentment. 'You must mind those mean old nails in future.' Gazing down at him, she trailed her fingertip down the lordly slope of his slightly crooked nose, then leaned down and kissed the scraggly star above his eyebrow.

He closed his long-lashed eyes, smiling faintly.

As he lay in her arms, she thought of that night in the

251

alley and could only marvel at how much he had lowered his defenses toward her, like a wild stallion gentled to her touch only. It was no small honor, for she knew how the rough school of experience had hardened him, yet he had opened himself to her. Even now, she could feel his vulnerability and it made her tremble inside to see how much he trusted her when she wasn't even sure if she could trust herself. As much as she desired Rackford, she did not take his needs lightly, knowing, especially, how he had suffered. Though her feelings for him were changing, her fear and uncertainty remained. Who was she to try to love such a man? So much responsibility. What did a silly, rather spoiled debutante like her know about emotional sacrifice? Most insidiously, her fears whispered, what if she turned out to be like Mama? What if she hurt him, just like Mama had hurt Father? – hurt her darling Billy, knowing his need for love, knowing how rare and fragile his trust?

But when she looked anxiously at him, her fears eased, and all she felt was tenderness. In the nearby tree, a nightingale warbled, but all she heard was her heart's promise assuring her she never could, never would, hurt this man. How could she ever stray, when he himself was all that she desired?

She chased her confused thoughts away and twined her arms more closely around him, resting her chin on his shoulder.

Together they watched the sunset's glow fading where its swirling colors reflected on the lazy river.

As night fell, London disappeared amid the stars. The crickets sang around them in the field.

'Jas?'

She smiled softly to herself at the sound of his soft, deep voice speaking her nickname. 'What is it, Billy-boy?' she murmured, glancing down at him and stroking his head more gently, careful of his injury.

'I—' He stopped himself, searching her face.

She smoothed back his golden forelock. 'Hmm?'

'I think we'd better get you home,' he muttered, quickly sitting up. 'It's getting late.'

She knitted her eyebrows together, for it seemed as though he was going to say something else, but he remained silent. She took his hand when he stood and offered it to help her up. She caught a glimpse of soulful longing in his eyes before he looked away almost shyly. With a most touching degree of reverent solicitude, he walked her back down the long hill.

I daresay I've made a gentleman of him, after all, she mused in fond, wry humor as he handed her up into his curricle. He got in, took the reins, and clucked to the horses, driving her home.

Pity, she thought in amusement, her gaze trailing over him, from his smart top hat to his flawless cravat and elegant tan-colored tailcoat. *I rather liked him as a heathen.*

Chapter Fifteen

The lie he had told her gnawed at him, but nothing could have convinced Rackford that last night on Primrose Hill had been the time or place to tell Jacinda about his forays into the rookery. She had been upset enough by Lizzie's farewell; he was determined to treat her with extra care and gentle consideration. What she needed right now was all the solid strength that he could give her, not the shocking revelation that he was breaking Sir Anthony's rules and still fighting by night like a savage. And she certainly did not need to know that he had fled capture with his tail between his legs.

Though he was hungry to even the score, he waited to let his injuries heal a bit before returning to the rookery. In truth, now that he had Jacinda to himself, he was in no great hurry to go, for there was always the chance that he might not come back.

Over the next couple of days, they were almost constantly in each other's company, brought closer together by Lizzie's departure. He knew she was in a tumult over her plan to marry Lord Drummond and was questioning her deepening feelings for him, as well.

Rackford was fully aware that Jacinda, in her innocence, had idolized the glamorous, widowed baroness, but Lady Campion's taking Alec as her lover and the unintentional hurt this had caused Lizzie had obviously stricken her with doubts about her scheme – though she tried to hide them behind her usual blithe self-confidence.

And well she should doubt, he thought, trying to keep his impatience under control even as his own need for her deepened, it seemed, every hour. He'd be damned if he'd let her turn into a slut like Eva Campion, who had propositioned him twice since his arrival in the ton – a fact he wisely opted not to tell Jacinda. There was no predicting how she might react. She was too mule-headed to be influenced by anyone and would have to come to the truth on her own.

For his part, he had troubles enough with Daphne Taylor.

He was fortunate that Jacinda had tutored him so carefully on the rules of the ton, or he'd have been forced to marry Miss Taylor weeks ago. The redhead had attempted on several occasions to get caught alone with him. She wanted his title, he supposed, and a lusty spanking – neither of which he intended to give her. She had even tried to lure him into a kiss, but he had smoothly dodged her enticements, repeatedly foisting her off on Acer Loring.

The insufferable dandy was the only one who ever had any success in placating the spoiled beauty; equally arrogant, they would have made a splendid pair. Alas, Mr. Loring did not have the requisite rank and title, so even if Daphne secretly fancied him, she turned her nose up at him, strictly on principle.

It was no wonder, then, that Daphne's chasing after Rackford was driving Acer half mad.

That night at Almack's, having been granted his voucher at last, Daphne wheedled Rackford into dancing with her. He relented, since propriety only permitted him two dances per night with Jacinda. The first he had greedily gobbled up early in the evening; the other, he was saving for last. It was quarter-past eleven when the orchestra struck up the mazy waltz. Daphne was, admittedly, a lithe and graceful dancer.

She gazed up at him with a rapt expression – probably artificial. He was attempting to make idle conversation when suddenly, as they turned about the ballroom, he glimpsed Jacinda talking once more with Lord Drummond. Dark anger surged through him, unbidden, upon seeing her with the old Tory hangman yet again. The vehemence of his emotional response took him off guard. Daphne squealed slightly.

'Lord Rackford, you are squeezing me like a very python!'

He instantly loosened his grip, not realizing he had tightened it. 'Sorry.'

She dimpled at him. 'You may hold me closer if you like, but gracious, not in the middle of Almack's, with the whole world looking on.'

His lips curved drily, but the smile did not reach his eyes. His stare swept back to Jacinda. Knowing how lost she was without her motherly best friend, he had behaved like a perfect gentleman ever since Lizzie had gone – no mean feat for him. He had taken pains to be unselfish, ignoring his own increasingly desperate need for her in his refusal to pressure her. But, by God, there she was, flirting with her old wigsby again, determined as ever, it appeared, to become another Eva Campion.

'Lord Rackford?'

He dragged his narrow stare away from Jacinda and looked down at Daphne.

'Is everything all right?' she asked.

Gazing at the reigning beauty of the Season in his arms, his for the taking, he suddenly wondered if he had made all of this much too easy on his golden, errant, curly-headed darling.

Jacinda had shown a glimmer of jealousy before. Perhaps a bit more of it might jar her out of her complacency. It damned well better, he thought grimly, because until this moment he had not realized how close he was to the end of what he could take.

'Mmm,' Daphne purred as he slid his hand a bit more tightly around her slim waist, his hand resting in the small of her back.

He smiled at her, then laughed aloud at some inane thing she said as they went waltzing past the place where Jacinda stood with her old wigsby. The sound of his laughter caught Jacinda's attention, he noted from the corner of his eye, but he kept his gaze fixed on Daphne.

'When are you going to call on me, Lord Rackford? I am desolate over how you have neglected me,' she said with a pout.

'Why, I have tried, Miss Taylor, but I could never fight my way through the throng of suitors outside your door.'

'No, you've never tried. I'm sure of that.' She paused delicately. 'You are always lurking about Knight House instead. You are fishing in dangerous waters there, you know.'

'Hm?'

'Surely you've heard about the previous duchess of Hawkscliffe and how infamously wanton she was.'

'I have heard something to that effect, yes.'

'If it wasn't for my mama and her friends, that horrid woman might still be here, tainting good Society with her indecency,' she said with a haughty sniff. 'It's bad enough we have to tolerate her daughter among us.' She eyed him in challenge, but he did not rise to the bait.

He knew women well enough to realize that defending Jacinda would only sharpen Daphne's malice. Alas, the girl was not content with his diplomatic silence.

'Everyone says her daughter will turn out to be just like her, you know. Only a fool would seek a wife like that.'

'Oftentimes, *ma chérie*, 'everyone' is wrong.'

'Poor Lord Rackford, surely you have not been taken in by her charms! Beauty, you know, can often hide a wicked heart.'

'Very true,' he agreed sardonically, though Daphne failed to realize he might possibly be referring to her. He

257

stole a furtive glance across the ballroom and smugly noted that he had his lady's full attention.

What he did not realize until the music ended was that he also had gained Acer Loring's attention.

The leading dandy had arrived a short while ago from his club – drunk, brooding, and in defiance of his own punctilious standards, rather disheveled. As the closing bars of the elegant waltz filled the ballroom, Acer shoved his way drunkenly through the dancers, marching toward Rackford and Daphne. The black look on his imperious face plainly said that he'd had enough of watching Daphne throw herself at the barbaric interloper.

When Rackford saw the man stalking toward him, scowling in contempt and glassy-eyed with drink, he experienced a rush of the same internal, knee-jerk hatred as though it were his father coming toward him; for, God knew, Truro had approached him in a similar fashion just a few nights ago and so many times before in the long-buried past. Confused by the momentary overlap of past and present, Rackford didn't react at first when Acer pushed him.

'Why don't you stay away from her?'

'Acer!' Daphne cried, a glow of pleasure rushing into her cheeks at the prospect of two men fighting over her.

Rackford was dimly aware of gasps and murmurs as the people around them cleared back a few feet.

'Did you hear me?' Acer pursued. 'I don't give a damn about your title. You're an ignorant barbarian, and you will stay away from her.' When Acer pushed him again, Rackford's pent-up wrath exploded.

He punched Acer in the mouth with a blow that sent the dandy crashing backward into the duke of Wellington, who happened to be standing nearby.

Daphne shrieked and whirled to him, aghast. 'You punched Acer!'

'He's lucky I don't kill him after the way he's insulted me all Season.'

'Go on!' Acer wrenched out, steadying himself, a small trickle of blood at the corner of his mouth. His drunk, wretched gaze swung to Daphne. 'I'd rather die than watch you marry someone else, especially this blackguard.'

'Fine with me,' Rackford growled, too enraged to care that the victor of Waterloo and half a dozen other men were shouting at him to stop.

He charged at Acer, flattening him with a mighty dive. All around them, men let out gasps and ladies shrieked as they scuffled in the elite ballroom. On top of the snide bastard who had taken every opportunity to make a fool of him, Rackford drew back to hit him again when soft hands grabbed his forearm.

'*Billy, don't!*'

Instinctively reacting to shove away the light hold, he turned and, through the haze of violence, saw Jacinda staring at him in angry command. His raging pulse roared too loudly in his ears for him to absorb her words, but the sight of her blazing brown eyes arrested him, and the firm tones of her voice steadied him, held him back from leaping off the inward precipice of his destructive streak.

'Rackford. Stop it. Listen to me. He's not worth it. He's just jealous—'

'Jealous?' he yelled at her, angrily sweeping to his feet and yanking his arm free of her grasp. He loomed over her, his frustration spilling over. He was unable to stop the words that tumbled from his lips. 'Aye, he's jealous, but I'm not allowed to be, am I? I am so bloody tired of this game!'

'What game?' she asked faintly, paling.

'The game of keeping Rackford on his knees!' he said angrily. 'You flaunt yourself in front of me, knowing I adore you – but I will not wait forever, by God, I won't!' he warned her in a dire tone, even though, deep down, he knew he probably would.

Her posture stiffened. 'Lord Rackford, you forget yourself.'

Her crisp tone alerted him anew to his surroundings. His chest heaving, he cast a baleful look around him and felt his heart begin to sink.

No, this wasn't Cornwall, and it certainly wasn't the rookery.

As Daphne rushed over to the dazed and bleeding Acer, Rackford's gaze swept the glittering ballroom and all the appalled, haughty people staring at him as though he were a rabid dog.

Slowly, quietly, he let out a bitter laugh of disgust. He felt exposed. 'Well, there goes my voucher, eh? Sorry, my lady.' He forced himself to meet Jacinda's bewildered gaze. 'You did your best, God knows, but some beasts can never quite leave the jungle behind. This is all I am and all I'll ever be. Forgive me.' He swept her a bow full of insolent bravado, then walked out, his chin high, his face taut with anger.

Hellfire in his eyes, he scowled at the people in his path toward the door; they quickly removed themselves.

And so it ends, he thought, shamed to the core. He had courted her, pleasured her, loved her with all the pieces of his long-shattered heart, and in one moment's impulse, it all had come to naught. He had lost his temper just like his father.

Tonight, he thought even before he reached the coolness of the night outdoors. Waiting restlessly on the pavement for his carriage, he lit a cheroot, his hands shaking slightly with the aftermath of rage and the chant of his failings whispering in his head.

Bad, stupid, worthless, weak.

How could he lose control of himself that way? Almack's, for God's sake.

She was never going to want him now. Hell, she was never going to forgive him for the scene he had just caused. She had told him that first night that, whatever happened, she would never give the ton the satisfaction they wanted, of seeing her fall into scandal. He was on his own.

He thrust her out of his mind, holding his anger close and tight. Tonight, by God, he would either kill O'Dell or die trying. It scarcely mattered which.

He exhaled a stream of smoke and took the reins when his groom brought up the curricle.

Jacinda was left staring after him in the middle of the ballroom with an expression of dazed dismay. She wasn't sure how many people had heard the anguished tongue-lashing he had just given her; she wasn't sure, either, who all had heard her call him 'Billy,' betraying the forbidden level of familiarity between them. That in itself was enough to cause a scandal, but at the moment, she could only stand there in shock at his appalling words. *Flaunting myself in front of him? This 'game' of keeping Rackford on his knees?*

Was this how he had interpreted her hesitation?

Feeling rather bewildered, she looked across the ball-room at where a very pale, shaken Daphne sat with Acer Loring. Acer was talking earnestly to her while Daphne gazed at him in wonder. Tentatively, the redhead lifted her hand and dabbed at the corner of Acer's bloodied lip with her handkerchief.

The sight of them together filled Jacinda with the strangest rush of grief. *Oh, what am I doing?* she thought in despair. Rackford had just stormed out and she knew that the moment of truth was upon her ... And the truth was, simply, that Rackford needed her.

Truly needed her. No one had ever needed her before.

She suddenly felt a hand on her arm, then a caustic voice reached her, breaking into her thoughts. 'Trouble in paradise?'

Startled, she turned to find Lord Drummond holding her back.

'Might have expected something like this from your young hothead,' he remarked, snorting over his glass of port.

261

She bristled. 'Mr. Loring insulted Lord Rackford to his face.'

'Still a hothead, that Radical. I don't trust him and neither should you.'

She knitted her brows angrily, for once and for all casting off her unworthy plan to snare the old wigsby. In her mind's eye, she saw Lady Campion racing her phaeton through Hyde Park with her mustachioed dragoon by her side, but the figment vanished, driving off gaily into the mists of oblivion. That was not the life she wanted. That was not the person she was.

Her feelings for Rackford would no longer be denied – even if it meant accepting his authority as her husband and trusting herself to be his true, devoted wife. The truth was, she needed him, too. Indeed, perhaps his love had already saved her from the fate of becoming a perfect copy of her mother; Georgiana had never surrendered herself to any man. It had been her glory, and her downfall.

'Really,' Lord Drummond was grumbling, 'I marvel that your brother, Hawkscliffe, high stickler that he is, would let a suitor near you who refuses to give a proper account of where he's been these past fifteen years. I'm telling you, that lad is trouble—'

'My dear Lord Drummond,' she interrupted grandly, drawing herself up to her full height, 'I will thank you to watch what you say about my future husband.' With that, she yanked her arm free of his hold and pivoted toward the exit again, her skirts swirling around her.

'I say, what's this? Such impertinence! Husband? Wrong headed in the extreme! Lady Jacinda! Where are you going?'

Ignoring his indignant sputtering, she pressed on, her bridges burning behind her. Joy and dread pounded in her temples as she hastened through the milling assemblage of Almack's elite subscribers; she felt giddy and indescribably free. She prayed she would find Rackford still standing outside waiting for his curricle to be brought round, for she had to tell him how she felt.

262

She scarcely dared wonder how he would react. Obviously, he had lost patience with her, but she was sure she would win her way back into his good graces when she told him that she loved him and that she was ready at last to commit herself to him. She only hoped he would forgive her for thinking too much of her own fears and too little of his need for her tender care.

As she strode toward the door on legs that shook beneath her, all her awareness focused on catching up to him, she was suddenly accosted by his old friends, Reg Bentinck and Justin Church.

'Lady Jacinda!'

'Mr. Bentinck, Mr. Church,' she greeted them in a fluttery voice, trying to hide her impatience as they blocked her path. 'H-how are you this evening?'

'Never mind that. We have to talk to you!'

'I'm in a bit of a hurry—'

'This will only take a moment.' Reg ducked his head nearer to hers. 'We heard what Rackford said to you about 'the jungle.' So that's where he's been all this time! The jungles of India. Right? Was he with the army? I knew it!'

'Oh, Mr. Bentinck—'

'Tell us! Come, we are his friends. If Rack won't confide in us, then you must. It was India, wasn't it?' Justin implored her. 'We're not going to tell anyone.'

'Gentlemen, I cannot say.'

'Would you reconsider if we told you something about our mutual friend in return?' Reg murmured.

Arrested by his sly tone, she gazed into his eyes. 'Like what?'

The two exchanged a grim look; then Justin spoke, lowering his voice. 'We were there the night he ran away from home.'

'*What*?' she whispered, turning to him in shock.

'You tell us where he's been all these years, and we'll tell you what we saw that ... horrible night at Torcarrow,' Reg murmured.

She gazed at him, riveted, her heart thumping. 'You were there? Truly?'

They nodded.

No wonder Rackford always seemed to be keeping his two childhood friends away from her, making sure she never chatted with Reg and Justin without him present.

She burned to hear what they had seen that night, but she shook her head slowly. 'I can't. I am sworn to secrecy. Besides, I think I'd rather wait for Rackford to tell me in his own time.'

They protested, but she held her ground. Though severely tempted, she knew that in order to learn their story, she would have to reveal his criminal past in exchange, and that was out of the question. No matter how loyal Reg and Justin were, she dared not breathe a word to them about Billy Blade. She would do nothing to compromise his hard-won trust.

'Please excuse me, gentlemen. I must go.' Hurrying past them, she rushed outside into the cool moonlit night, but her heart sank to discover that Rackford had already gone.

Going back inside, she sought out Robert and pled a headache, procuring his permission to go home. The minute she reached Knight House, she asked if any message had come for her, in the hopes that Rackford had regretted his outburst and had sent his apologies, but Mr. Walsh answered that none had.

Rather dejected and unsure of what to do next, she went up to her rooms, where her maid, Ann, helped her out of her elaborate ball gown. Jacinda slipped into her silk dressing gown and dismissed the woman with a nod. She sat down for a moment at her vanity and stared hard into the mirror for a second, plagued by the question of what Reg and Justin had seen that night at Torcarrow and why the devil Rackford had never shared it with her. She thought he had told her everything. Too restless to sit still, she rose again and prowled over to her bedroom window. Pushing the curtain aside, she gazed out at the city for a moment, then determination filled her face. This could not wait till morning. She had to see him, had to be with him.

Tonight.

She let the curtain fall and went to change her clothes.

Remembering all he had taught her that night in the rookery, she removed the rest of her jewelry and dressed in her most ordinary-looking frock, a simple round gown of sprigged cotton. She put a bit of money in her pocket to pay the hackney; then went to the bottom drawer of her dresser and took out a velvet-lined, teakwood box. She opened it and withdrew the elegant lady's pistol that her brother Damien had sent her from Spain.

She held it up for a moment, admiring it in the moon-light. The gun was more a work of art than a weapon, made from gleaming Toledo silver. The butt, engraved with her initials, was inlaid with mother-of-pearl.

Knowing her enthusiasm for target practice, Damien had sent it as a gift for her debut, which he had been unable to attend, away at the war. The note he'd sent had humorously explained that since he could not be in London personally to protect her from the swarms of suitors she was sure to attract, she was now well armed to keep her admirers at bay. It had a rifled barrel three inches longer than Alec's dueling pistols, which gave it greater accuracy at longer ranges. A little panel in the butt opened over a compartment that could store up to six powder cartridges.

Tucking the elegant, deadly weapon into her half boot, she donned a shapeless, hooded cloak over her gown. Rackford would be so pleased that she had followed all of his injunctions on how to move about safely after dark, she thought with growing excitement for her adventure.

Pulling the hood of her cloak up to shadow her face, she sneaked out of the house by the veranda door and stole away through the garden, just like the night she had tried to run away from home. This time, her heart was light, knowing she was going to her lover.

She could not wait to see his face when she told him that she loved him.

Waving down the first hackney coach that passed her on St. James's Street, she took it to Lincoln's Inn Fields, her pulse racing with nervous anticipation. When the coach stopped in front of Lord and Lady Truro's house, she saw the pair of Bow Street runners who had been assigned to watch Rackford around the clock. She chewed her lip and cast about quickly for an explanation for her arrival that would not lead them to realize she was a young lady of Quality dabbling in scandal.

But just then, as she started to get out of the coach, she spied a flicker of motion in the shadows alongside the house, some twenty yards away. An agile, muscular silhouette vaulted up onto the garden wall and disappeared silently over it. She furrowed her brow.

Rackford?

He was already gone, vanishing like ... a thief in the night. The thought filled her with instant apprehension. What the devil was he up to, sneaking out of his own house?

'You got some business 'ere, miss?' one of the Bow Street runners asked, sauntering over toward her where she stood half in, half out of the carriage.

She glanced at the man in distraction. 'No,' she said abruptly, then turned to the coachman. 'Drive on. That way.' She pointed, then nodded to the Runner. 'Good evening.'

The officer tipped his hat to her with a suspicious look. As the hackney rolled into motion, continuing on down the street, she searched the surrounding darkness for Rackford with inexplicably mounting dread.

'O'Dell!'

Rackford's deep, thunderous roar filled the rookery, bounding off the brick buildings and dark cobbled streets.

At last, he stalked into the open before his former headquarters.

266

He was empty-handed, though his weapons waited at his waist. His body bristled as he stood out in front of the building, his feet planted wide.

He was done with sneak attacks. Certain that Jacinda's rejection was inevitable after the way he had embarrassed her at bloody Almack's, nothing else mattered. It was time to finish this once and for all.

'O'Dell!' he bellowed again. 'Come out and face me, you coward!'

Hearing his shouts, the Jackals began prowling out of the gin-shop, edging toward him warily, as though they suspected he had gone mad. He could feel the muzzles of at least ten guns trained on him, but none of the men fired, taken off guard, a bit confused by his slow advance, perhaps even a little intrigued by his audacious approach. Likely they half suspected a trick. Rackford turned his attention to O'Dell's followers and bodyguards, well aware that their leader's control over them had been slipping for some time now. He was determined to shame his enemy out into the open.

'You there! Are you going to keep letting O'Dell hide behind you?' he challenged them.

They shifted uneasily.

'Where is he? Too scared to show his face?'

No answer.

'You call this man your leader?' he pressed on in a tone that rang with command. 'Well, I ask you, are you better off because of him, or worse? I already know the answer to that. Aye, Cullen O'Dell has given you nothing but trouble and grief. He's not a leader. He's a thug. And a coward.'

'There's no cowards 'ere, Blade!' Tyburn Tim yelled in defiance.

The others roughly agreed, bristling.

'No? Then why don't one of you go tell him to come out here and finish this like a man? Just him and me.'

'Well, if it ain't the great Billy Blade!' O'Dell swaggered

267

out of the gin shop, his narrow face etched with bitter scorn, but there was fear in his eyes. 'Look at you back from the dead to teach me how to be a big man, eh?'

Rackford's mouth thinned in a sly, hostile smile.

O'Dell looked at his men. 'Kill him.'

Nobody moved.

Tyburn Tim was the only one who cocked his gun and took aim at Rackford, but Oliver Strayhorn pushed the muzzle of Tim's musket back down to the ground.

'Kill him yourself, O'Dell.' The tall young man coolly issued the challenge. 'Looks to me as though this is between you and Blade. Unless you're afraid, like he said?'

'You scurvy bastard, Strayhorn,' O'Dell hissed. 'I ain't afraid of any man, not you, and especially not 'im!'

'Good. Then let it be a fair fight.' When Strayhorn jerked a curt nod at the others, they retreated a few steps, lowering their weapons.

Rackford sent Strayhorn an appreciative glance; then his stare homed in on O'Dell. The Jackals' leader clearly seemed to realize as he glanced around at his men that he had a serious problem on his hands.

If he fought Rackford, he might very well die; if he refused to fight, he would lose face completely and forfeit his place as their captain.

'Bugger yourselves, the lot o' you,' O'Dell muttered at his men with a look of grim resolve. He tossed his musket to Tyburn Tim, then unsheathed his knife with a cold hiss of metal and stalked toward Rackford.

He flicked his fingers over the hilt of his weapon, adjusting his grip. A surge of savage energy pounded in Rackford's veins as he moved into fighting stance. He and O'Dell circled slowly, sizing each other up.

O'Dell slashed at him in a swift arc that cut the air. Rackford curved deftly, then lunged, striking back. O'Dell evaded the thrust, his rookery instincts as finely well honed as Rackford's.

The world spun faster; the faces of the men looking on

became a dizzying blur. Rackford's heart hammered in his ears.

'Where've you been, Blade? You've lost your touch,' O'Dell taunted him.

He snarled and they clashed, tumbling onto the ground with the force of Rackford's charge. They rolled; he dove for O'Dell's knife. As he struggled to pin O'Dell's wrist to the cobblestones, the man fought like a hellion. Their muscles strained as each strove to overpower the other.

Sweat dripped from Rackford's brow, the salt of it stinging as it ran into his eyes.

The tip of O'Dell's blade nicked Rackford's jaw. He cursed, slamming O'Dell's hand to the ground, but O'Dell suddenly planted his feet in Rackford's stomach and flung him back. Thrown back several feet, Rackford caught his balance, once more at the ready.

O'Dell climbed to his feet and wiped the greasy sweat off his brow with his forearm, then flashed him an unpleasant grin. 'Come on, Billy. This time when you die, it'll be for good. Think I'll cut off your head and keep it on my wall for a trophy. What do ye say to that?'

O'Dell's mad laughter bounded off the flat brick faces of the surrounding buildings. Gazing at him in contempt so sharp he could almost taste it, Rackford shrugged off his enemy's stupid vaunting, but the grotesque threat reminded him of how O'Dell had terrorized little Eddie the Knuckler.

He could still see the boy's round, grubby face as vividly as though that afternoon in Newgate were only yesterday, could still hear his high-pitched voice. *He said if I didn't help him, he'd make me into a wallet*!

Rackford's eyes narrowed with deepening wrath. O'Dell was in better form than he had expected, but as he remembered that bruised, scared, unloved kid, he felt new force seeping into his veins from he knew not where. With pounding intensity, all of his awareness narrowed down to the moment at hand.

He attacked, his every step sure and strong as he

269

advanced relentlessly, driving O'Dell back. He was heedless of the stabbing, slicing blows with which O'Dell tried
to ward him off, dodging each with lightning speed.
Rackford's blade connected twice in rapid succession,
cutting O'Dell's shoulder, then biting into his side with
swift precision.

Cursing, O'Dell lashed out with a roundhouse kick to
thrust him back, but Rackford grabbed his leg and twisted
it. O'Dell crashed to the ground with a furious shout, his
knife clattering out of his grasp as he reached to break his
fall.

At once, Rackford kicked the weapon out of range.

'God damn you, Blade!' Tyburn Tim exploded, but
Strayhorn and his followers held him back.

Rackford slowly circled the man before he deigned to
move in for the kill.

Sitting on the ground, O'Dell stared up at him, his chest
heaving. 'One of you, do something!' he ordered his men,
but Strayhorn stayed them.

'It was a fair fight, O'Dell. You lost. Truth is, we're
bloody sick of you around here.'

'I'll kill you,' he wrenched out at the young man.

'You're not killin' anybody, mate,' Rackford murmured.

O'Dell shrieked as Blade grabbed him by the hair and
yanked his head back, bringing his knife up to his throat.

'Wait!' he gasped. 'Jesus, don't do it, Blade. I – I never
did you any harm.'

He jerked O'Dell's head back farther, and O'Dell let out
another small scream, wild-eyed with fear. In the street
around them, the Jackals exchanged uneasy looks as their
bullying leader was indeed revealed as a coward.

'You invaded my turf. You had my men arrested. You
were my friend and you betrayed me. You and your
mongrel dogs committed atrocities against the people under
my protection. What of the Murphy girl?'

'She wanted it!'

He pricked O'Dell's neck for that. The wound wasn't

deep, but it bled enough to scare the man into blathering shamelessly for his life. 'You can't kill me, Blade. You and Nate would have never survived on your own all those years ago. I took you in, taught you everything I knew. That night – it's all because of that night – it's not my fault. It was Yellow Cane,' he whispered, beginning to sob.

Rackford wavered, struggling with the memory of the terrified boy O'Dell had been on that awful night and the pity it roused in his breast. He was not quite sure why, ever since then, he had felt vaguely responsible for O'Dell's actions.

He held O'Dell's chin up for the coup de grace, but his hands were shaking, and he could feel his resolve crumbling. 'Damn you, why didn't you just stay with us? Nate, the others. We would have looked out for you!'

'Don't kill me, Blade. For the love of God. You saved my life once.'

Slowly, he released his grip on O'Dell's hair, his shoulders rising and falling as he panted with tumultuous emotion, wrath and pity and grief all rolled into a jumble of pain. He could not simply cut the poor bastard's throat in cold blood as he sat there. He was not capable of it. Not anymore. O'Dell was beaten, broken, disgraced before his men, and unarmed – and they had once been friends. At bottom, he had never really hated O'Dell, but had been more angry at himself for not being able to turn him around.

'Strayhorn!' Rackford called in a dark tone.

The tall young man walked over and looked at him in question.

'There is a large bounty on O'Dell's head. Tyburn Tim's, as well. Turn them over to Bow Street and the gold is yours.'

Strayhorn answered Rackford's hard stare with a shrewd nod. 'I will. You have my word on it.'

'Then it seems my business here is done,' he said softly. He passed one last, farewell glance over his former home,

271

then sheathed his knife and turned around, weary behind his bravado as he began walking away.

His back turned, he was unaware of O'Dell reaching for the pistol hidden beneath his coat. Before Strayhorn could stop him, O'Dell, still sitting on the ground, stretched out his arm, taking aim at Rackford's back.

A shot rang out.

Rackford whirled around as O'Dell slumped to the ground, shot in the head.

Some of the men were shouting; all looked around in confusion. Rackford saw the pistol in O'Dell's hand and thought for a second the man had shot himself.

'Up there!' someone yelled.

Rackford lifted his gaze and saw the slim figure on the rooftop of the opposite building, where he had often posted his sentries in the past. Dark against the starry sky, the sniper was wrapped in a large cloak that billowed slightly on the night breeze. As he watched, the figure pushed back the cloak's hood. His eyes widened as moonlight kissed the outline of her long, billowing curls.

Jacinda.

'What the hell?' said a voice in unchecked fury nearby. In the blink of an eye, Tyburn Tim grabbed the musket back that one of Strayhorn's followers had taken away from him and aimed the muzzle straight at her.

Rackford did not think. He swept his knife out of its sheath and hurled it at the man. The shot flew wide as the blade plunged in between Tyburn Tim's ribs. The man screamed at the same moment the bullet slammed into the brick facade just below her position.

Somehow he knew she hadn't even flinched.

'Get out of there now, Blade!' she yelled down to him in regal fury, a lioness watching over him. 'I've got your back.'

Strayhorn turned to him with a twinkle of amused understanding dawning in his eyes. 'If I were you, I'd do as she says.'

An astonished smile spread slowly over Rackford's face as he lifted his gaze once more to his lady's victorious silhouette. With her pale hair gleaming in the moonlight, she was, he thought, the mightiest, fairest, most dazzling star in the firmament.

She had come after him.

The chit had just saved his life.

Chapter Sixteen

Feeling her way through the darkness of the old, abandoned building, Jacinda ran down the several flights of stairs, careened around the cobwebby newel post, and fled outside just as Rackford approached the entrance.

She rushed out the doorway and flung herself at once into his arms, holding him tightly in fierce protectiveness. As his arms wrapped around her, she stood on tiptoe and pulled him down to her, capturing his mouth in a fevered kiss.

His response was full of aggressive ardor, his mouth claiming hers in unbridled need. She squeezed her eyes shut against the tears of jumbled emotion rising behind her eyelids, torn between ire at the man for putting himself in such danger and exultation that he was safe.

She parted her lips wider for his possessive kiss, running her hands all over his muscled body as she reassured herself that he was indeed – miraculously – unharmed. Her mind still reeled with the knowledge that she, Jacinda Knight, had just killed the treacherous Cullen O'Dell. Having seen him raise his weapon to shoot Rackford in the back, she felt nary a pang of remorse for his enemy's death.

Rackford ended the kiss, tearing his lips away from hers, then cupped her face between his hands, searching her eyes in the moonlight. 'What the hell are you doing here?'

'Come, I'll explain in the hackney.' Taking his hand, she led him hurriedly around the corner, where the hackney coach she had hired earlier still waited.

She could hear the coachman making conversation with his horses, bravely trying to calm his own nerves in this dangerous quarter of the city. 'Easy, Thunder. Now don't you mind that, it's just an alley cat—'

'Coachman!' Jacinda called as she and Rackford strode toward him.

The little man looked over, his shoulders sagging in relief. 'Lud, m'um, thank heavens you're back safe!'

She tossed him her small bag of coins as his reward. 'Take us back to Lincoln's Inn Fields!'

'Yes, Ma'am!'

Rackford opened the door for her. She sprang up into the coach's dark interior. He followed her in, pulling the door closed as the driver urged his team into motion.

'You're bleeding,' she said anxiously, noting the scratch on his jaw as he slid into the seat beside her.

'It's nothing,' he muttered, blotting the small nick on his jaw with the edge of his sleeve.

She took his face between her hands and inspected it. 'Oh, my poor Billy.' Shaking her head with a prayer of thanks that this was the worst of his injuries, she kissed his cheek.

Without warning, he pulled her onto his lap. 'How did you do that? You never told me you were such a fine markswoman, Jacinda! You must have been twenty yards away from the target, and there was scarcely any light. Egads, girl, you got the blackguard right between the eyes!'

She winced, though his praise filled her with modest pleasure. 'Oh, it was a lucky shot, that's all. My brothers always used to challenge me to try out my target practice while wearing a blindfold, but never mind that. You, my dear, you were magnificent! Such daring, such strength,' she said with relish, leaning her face nearer to his. 'Such prowess,' she added, running her hand down his chest.

275

'Prowess?' he echoed.

'Most definitely.' With a naughty smile and a small tug, she unfastened the top button of his shirt.

'Jacinda?'

'Yes, Rackford?' she murmured, opening the second button.

'What the hell is going on?'

With a philosophical sigh, she shifted her position and hiked up her skirts to sit astride his lap. She wound her arms around his neck and stared for a moment into his eyes. 'Oh, Billy, what happened tonight at Almack's brought me to my senses.' She lowered her head. 'I left there shortly after you did—'

'I'm sorry I stormed out,' he interrupted in chagrin. 'I lost my temper. I shouldn't have let Acer Loring get to me. I owe you an apology for what I said to you, as well—'

She laid her finger gently over his lips, silencing him. 'He deserved it, and so did I. Hang Almack's, anyway, and hang the Patronesses, too. If they won't let you in, then I don't want to be there, either. I prefer the rookery, or the rooftops, or the surface of the moon – as long as it's where you are. I love you, Billy,' she said softly. 'I had to come and tell you. And if, by chance, your offer still stands – ' she hesitated, chastened but hopeful as she peered into his eyes, 'I would be most honored to become your wife.'

He stared at her, thunderstruck. 'You – love me?'

She gave a fervent nod, a blush stealing into her cheeks.

'You'll marry me? Truly, Jacinda?' He gripped her shoulders. 'You're sure?'

'I've never been more sure of anything my whole life.'

With a shout of amazed laughter, he tumbled her onto her back on the cushioned squab and eased down atop her with a playful growl. 'So, you'll wed me at last, will you, you little sharpshooter?'

'I will.'

'To honor?'

'Completely.'

276

'Cherish?'

'Forever.'

'Obey?' he asked skeptically.

She narrowed her eyes with an arch smile. 'Let's not get ahead of ourselves.'

He laughed softly, but his stare turned wistful. He wound a length of her hair around his finger. 'Are you real? Is this happening? Because if it is a dream, I don't want to wake up.'

'It's real.' She stroked his cheek, searching his eyes. 'I love you, Billy. Nothing will ever change that and wherever you go, I will be there, looking after you, whether you like it or not.'

He took her hand and pressed her palm to his chest, staring soulfully at her. 'My lady,' he whispered, 'you have my heart.'

'I will take good care of it.' She closed her eyes and kissed his brow, right on his scraggly star-shaped scar. When she moved back, his eyes were dark as pine forests, solemn. She laid her hand tenderly on his cheek. 'What is it, my darling?' she asked gently.

'It's just – you could have anyone. I can't think what you see in me.'

'I see my dear friend Rackford; my heathen Blade – the man I adore. The man I desire. Kiss me,' she whispered.

He did, gathering her gently in his arms. She parted his shirt as she savored the warm, masculine taste of him.

'Your father's gone to Cornwall?' she murmured between kisses.

'Aye.'

'Your mother, too?'

'Mm-hmm,' he purred, languidly kissing her throat. His hands wandered down over her body. 'I've got the house ... all to myself.'

She wrapped her arms around his broad shoulders. 'Let me stay with you tonight.'

He shivered with desire at her whisper, but captured her

face gently between his hands and searched her eyes. 'Are you sure about this?'

She nodded slowly, her longing for him betrayed by her blushing gaze and racing pulse.

His green eyes smoldered at her silent answer. 'Well, then, my lady,' he whispered. 'Consider it an invitation.'

By the time they reached his father's house, they were hot and trembling with impatience. His lips were swollen from her kisses, his hair tousled from her caresses. The moment the hackney rolled to a halt, Rackford jumped out into the moonlit darkness and turned back to lift her off the metal step. He carried her toward the house in his arms, kissing her all the while.

'The gate,' he whispered raggedly between kisses as the coachman drove off down the avenue. His horses' clip-clopping hoofbeats resounded in the stillness of the street. Jacinda fumbled with the wrought-iron latch. She had only just gotten it undone when the Bow Street runners posted outside his house approached.

'Lord Rackford?'

'Sir? We were not aware you had gone out.'

'I went out the back,' he said readily. 'A man's got to find himself a bit o' muslin every now and then, don't he?'

The officers exchanged an amused glance. Jacinda huffed as she realized he was attempting to pass her off as a prostitute.

'Now, now,' the shorter of the two men chided harmlessly, 'Your Lordship's not to be leavin' for any reason without lettin' us know about it. Those are Sir Anthony's rules.'

'Come, fellows. I'm a twenty-eight-year-old man, not a saint.'

They laughed. 'Very well. Fine choice, my lord.'

'How much does she charge?' the other jested.

'Trust me, you can't afford her,' he replied with a chuckle, laughing harder when Jacinda flicked him indignantly in the side of the head.

He soothed her with a kiss that grew more urgent by the

278

second. Neither she nor Rackford spared a glance for anyone else whom they passed on their way to his bedchamber, neither the butler who opened the front door, nor the scandalized housekeeper who gaped as His Lordship carried her up the wide, sweeping staircase.

In moments, they were in his room. By the dim glow of the light-box shining atop the parquetry table next to the door, her brief glance swept the opulent suite, taking in the lustrous silk-hung panels, the heavy blue velvet draperies, and the rich Persian carpet underfoot. Smart, spare, parcel-gilt furniture in the latest Roman style was grouped in the sitting room, but she forgot all that as he led her into the adjoining bedchamber.

She paused at the moonlit threshold, staring at his massive four-poster beyond. The bed, she thought, glancing from it to him and back again with an anticipatory shiver, where she would lose her virginity.

It was a bed fit for an emperor, the towering canopy draped with cascades of blue velvet that matched the curtains. Intricate roundels depicting Roman gods adorned the dark rosewood headboard. He lit a candle; she took off her cloak.

He turned to her and smiled fondly at her somber, wide-eyed stare. He touched her cheek in soft reassurance; then his gaze traveled down over her body. She followed his stare, glancing down at herself, simply clad in her sprigged cotton round gown. Smoothing her skirts, she looked at him again in rather hapless uncertainty. It was surely the simplest frock she had ever worn in his presence. If she had known she was truly going to be deflowered tonight, she thought in nervous irony, she would have worn her finest. White silk and jewels—

Rackford gave her chin a gentle tweak. 'You look beautiful,' he soothed, reading her thoughts, as he was wont to do.

She smiled ruefully at him.

'In fact ... I like you even better like this. You intim-

279

idate a man when you're dressed like a goddess.'

'Do I?' she asked, pleased.

He tossed her a lazy grin and turned away, taking off his jacket. 'Don't let it go to your head.'

Scoffing, she kicked off her half boots as he went to the washstand in the corner. He poured some water into the basin, then tugged his shirt off over his head.

Biting her lip as she gazed at him, Jacinda had no intention of resisting the temptation of his fascinating body tonight, so big and hard and lean, tanned and tattooed.

She joined him as he leaned over the basin of water, quickly splashing his face and washing up after his violent fight. Standing beside him, she ran her hand down the sinuous curve of his back, then traced the outline of the phoenix tattoo outspread between his shoulders. His skin was warm and smooth; she could sense his pleasure at her simple touch.

Making herself useful, she picked up the washcloth that lay atop the stand and wetted it in the basin. The water was cool in the heat of the summer night. She squeezed out the excess water as he straightened up and turned to her. Leaning his hips back against the dressing table behind him, he watched her as she slowly wiped his chest, neck, and chiseled abdomen with the wet washcloth, bathing his skin. She trailed it over his muscled shoulders and down his powerful arms. A leonine glow kindled, gathering power in the depths of his green eyes.

She could feel his stare burning into her as she turned away to freshen the washcloth, but before she could return, he was behind her, closing the distance between them. He buried his face in her hair, capturing her around her waist. When his other hand curled around her neck, she laid her head back weakly on his shoulder and tilted her head to receive his urgent kiss.

He swept her long hair forward over her shoulder; then his deft, thief's fingers unfastened her gown, making short work of the row of copper hooks and eyes down her back.

'God, I've wanted you for so long,' he whispered as he slipped her bodice down off her shoulders, kissing the crook of her neck.

Her heart pounded as her gown dropped to the floor. She stepped out of it and backed slowly toward his bed, luring him to her, taking off her thin white chemise. His eyes smoldered fiercely as he unfastened his dark trousers.

Wearing nothing but her ribbon garters and white silk stockings, she sat down on his bed, staring with an eager blush as he freed his rigid member, showing it to her. Thrilled and awed by his primal, barbaric beauty, she lifted her hand and touched him, caressing the smooth, steely length of him with her fingertips.

He flinched with pleasure, his chest rising and falling more rapidly. He backed away just a few inches to finish undressing. Easing down onto her side on his bed, she propped her cheek on her hand and watched his every movement as he pulled off his boots, then peeled off his drill trousers. Magnificent in his nudity, he joined her in his bed, gently easing atop her. The first contact of their naked bodies stole her breath, skin to skin, his hard chest pressed to her bare breasts. She could feel his heart thundering within him.

From the moment his lips descended upon hers, there was no turning back even if she had wanted to. His kiss overwhelmed her with its drugging depth; his hands beguiled her, caressing her hair and running in sure, smooth warmth all over her body. Dear heaven, this was what she had longed for, dreamed of – this wild and sweet abandon in his arms.

He moved back and stared at her breasts as he played with them, kneading them. She smiled languidly as he bent his head and kissed them. Petting his hair, she watched him hungrily sucking her nipple; then his kisses moved lower, and his hand ventured between her thighs.

Shivering with pleasure, she reached for him as well, and commenced experimenting with light and firmer touches as she stroked him. With a groan, he stopped her, pressing her down onto the mattress on her back.

'Are you ready for me, sweeting?'

Her eyes flickered with wild desire as he covered her body with his own. She wrapped her arms around his neck. 'I love you, Rackford,' she panted.

'And I you, my lady.'

She could feel his erection pulsating against her as he lay between her legs. His lips hovered inches from her own.

'Jacinda,' he whispered slowly, as though her name could work magic. 'I love you, angel. I love you more than you'll ever know.'

As he guided his hard, smooth flesh to stroke the outer folds of her virgin passage, she arched her body in hot impatience, trembling for him in frantic yearning. She had never needed anything more desperately than this man inside of her *now*. He wrapped his arms more firmly around her. Cradling her body to him, he pressed a fevered kiss to her brow and took her, thrusting in deep to the core of her body; she cried out softly, throwing her head back against his pillow as he shattered her maidenhead. At last, they were one, and it hurt, and she felt a belated surge of fear, wondering if this was wise – if she had made a mistake, if he indeed loved her as much as she hoped – but in moments, he soothed her fears away.

His anxiously whispered apologies for the momentary pain filled up the compass of her dazed awareness. He petted her hair, murmuring love words. 'I will always cherish you, Jacinda. You know that, surely, don't you? I'll never leave you, never abandon you.' His breathing was ragged; every word seemed dragged from his most secret soul. 'You're the only one I trust. You've helped me. You've cared for me. You could have thrown me to the wolves, but you saved me, didn't you? My angel, my golden goddess. I need you so much, Jacinda. I love you. Never leave me. I love you.'

His words wound around her like silken threads binding

her to him, bringing tears to her eyes as he told her of her beauty and played with her hair, waiting for her body to accept him. He whispered to her of how good she tasted, and how he loved the smell of her skin, and her walk, and her laugh, and her eyes that were sweeter and darker, he said, than pure chocolate.

Gradually, his skilled seduction eased the discomfort. She turned to him in silence, met his gaze, then brushed his lips with her own, a hesitant invitation. He returned her kiss with light leisurely slowness and took her hand, linking his fingers through hers. Cautiously, with her other hand, she touched him, running her right palm slowly up and down his side, exploring the lean, muscled curve of his hip and buttock.

As his kiss ended, she looked up into his eyes, ready, restless, and wanting. She knew so little of yielding, but he kissed her again more deeply, gently schooling her in how she should open to him. Tentatively, she obeyed, parting her lips widely, letting him thrust his tongue into her mouth until she could barely breathe with the overwhelming pleasure of being filled. Never had she imagined there was such intoxicating pleasure to be had from surrendering utterly, letting her man have his way with her.

He grasped her thighs, guiding her to wrap her legs around him. His low groan of pleasure sent a thrill racing through her body. She clasped her hands behind his neck and watched him in fascination as he rose up on his hands over her and began making love to her in earnest.

His dark gold hair was tousled; stormy passion lit the bright chips in the shadowy depths of his eyes, so that they glowed. His sculpted body shimmered with a light sheen of sweat. The candle-lit room was filled with the sound of their panting and low moans and the creaking of the unfamiliar bed. He reached down between their bodies, rubbing his middle fingertip in circles over her pleasure center even as he made love to her. His efforts transported her to new heights. When she dragged her eyes open and looked up at him again, his beautiful face was rapt with bliss, his eyes closed with exquisite pleasure. She let her gaze drift down to the sight of his stomach, every muscle perfectly carved and gleaming with the exertion of each thrust into her body, hungrily joining them.

His hard male beauty took her breath away. She pulled him down in trembling urgency to kiss her as she felt the galloping approach of her release.

'Billy,' she gasped against his mouth as it overwhelmed her in drowning pleasure. 'Oh, God, darling, don't stop.'

He didn't, riding deep between her thighs. He gave and gave with determined vigor as her spirit hurtled through a dark heaven of sensations that exploded through her, one brilliant star-burst after another. He moaned loudly and gasped her name; then he went rigid above her, every sinewy inch of him straining and throbbing with release. She felt each pulsation of his hardness, swollen to an even greater size within her as his climax seized him, wringing and wrenching each spurt of his seed into her womb.

She was already sore by the time he collapsed on her, panting with a look of astonishment.

'I love you,' he whispered, then kissed her cheek with boyish sweetness and laid his head on her chest, spent, sweaty, and trembling.

She held him in her arms, a dreaming Adonis in all his pagan splendor. His heavy head cradled on her bosom, she stared up at the ceiling in lingering amazement at the glory of their joining. She had never experienced anything like the tangible bond their lovemaking had wrought, so warm and strong between them. Had there been a life before this? Before him? In giving herself to him she felt reborn.

His hand caressed her everywhere, as though to reassert his possessive entitlement to every inch of the woman he had so thoroughly ravished.

She felt so ... claimed. And much to her surprise, it felt wonderful.

Chapter Seventeen

Rackford awoke the next morning' in a state of luxurious bliss. His body felt heavy and sated, wonderfully rested. For several minutes, he was too comfortable to move. Between the linen sheets, he was warm, but the air drifted coolly over his bare shoulders and arms.

A soft rain was falling. His eyes still closed, he listened to the music of its gentle drizzling patter. The fresh, clean smell of the raindrops falling on the broad green across the street floated in through the slightly open window not far from his bed, along with the silvery, tumbling arias of the birds' morning song. He purred and stretched slightly, nestling against his pillow. He was in love, and all was well with the world.

He reached across the rumpled bed to see if Jacinda was really here or if it had all been a voluptuous dream. He stared. Wonder of wonders, she was there, dozing beside him, her nymphlike body as bare as the day she was born, her resplendent golden corkscrew curls spilling across his pillow. Her dark, thick lashes fanned across her sweet apple-cheeks as she slept. He stole a long moment of simply admiring her dainty profile and the delicate rose shade of her lips.

A burst of crazed joy exploded inside him as he remembered anew that she had told him last night that she loved him. Had agreed to marry him, by Jove!

He moved closer to her with reverent tenderness. Jacinda sighed as he gathered her up in his arms and held her.

As he inhaled the strawberry-jasmine scent of her golden curls, he knew that the peace of that moment would never leave him; it ran deep like a subterranean spring – as if all the tears he had never shed had been transformed into life-giving water, crystalline, fresh, bubbling up from the core of his spirit, all purified and new.

He felt Jacinda respond, shifting subtly under his stroking hand. He kissed her ear, caressing the elegant curve of her hip. She arched her back slightly; the soft roundness of her derriere brushed his stirring member. He could not seem to help himself.

'Oh, Rackford,' she scolded with a seductive laugh, though her eyes were still closed.

'Good morning,' he murmured in a wicked singsong. 'What would you like for breakfast, my lady?'

'What are you offering me? Sausage?'

He laughed aloud at her bawdy jest. 'God, I love this woman.'

'Who, me?' she asked innocently as she rolled onto her back.

'Yes, you.' He lowered his head and kissed the tip of her nose.

She smiled, twining a length of her hair around her finger, as he withdrew a small space. With unmistakable intent, he walked his fingers slowly, deliberately down her body.

She scowled faintly, but made no effort to stop him. 'Really, Rackford, I just woke up. I must look a perfect horror.'

'You could not look a 'horror' if you wanted to, my lass.'

'Flatterer.' She rubbed her eyes and yawned. 'In any case, I'm sure no decent people do *that* in the morning.'

'You'd be surprised.'

Then she noticed his state of supreme readiness and came

286

up onto her elbows, gazing at his hard cock for a long moment. She lifted her eyebrow at him and shook her head. 'What a heathen you are.'

'Aye, and you love me for it.' With a playful growl, he tackled her onto her back once more, teasing and tickling her into submission with an attack of nuzzling kisses all over her lithe body.

Soon her girlish laughter turned to groans of want. The sheets wound around his hips as they rolled across his bed. Jacinda landed atop him – and instantly seemed to fancy it there.

With a feline smile, she urged him to sit up against the headboard. His heart slammed in his chest, but he fought to restrain himself as she straddled him on her knees, staring hotly into his eyes. She lowered herself slowly until she was sitting firmly astride his lap, his rigid flesh buried deep inside her steamy heat. He grasped her hips, kneading them. She put her arms around him and drew him to her. He kissed her throat as she began to move against him.

Her body sang vibrantly in his arms. Her swollen nipples pressed eagerly against his shoulders and his chest as she writhed slightly against him, arching her back. He adored them, sucking each one in turn as he ran his hand down her flat stomach and dipped his thumb lightly into the silken curls that veiled her womanhood. She responded with a needy shudder as he grazed her pleasure center.

'God, woman, I love you,' he whispered roughly.

She closed her eyes with a gentle moan of climbing ecstasy.

The rain fell faster, thick and lush. He held her hips, letting her take her pleasure of him, letting her rule his every movement. She tipped her head back as she rode him with a slow, deep, languorous rhythm, every stroke wrenching his very soul with the blinding pleasure of it. No woman had ever made him feel such things, such fierce, single-minded devotion. He would have killed for her, died for her.

She grew demanding, moving faster, pushing him back flat onto the bed. He kneaded her tender buttocks in his hands, pulling her down deeper on his shaft. The perfection of her tight passage intoxicated him. Her luxuriant curls ran wild, tumbling over her shoulders and swinging silkily in his face as she quickened the rhythm, her firm young breasts bouncing. He gritted his teeth, struggling to hold back until she fairly screamed with release. His control slipped away at the sound of her gasping his name in an agony of passion. Her orgasm rushed over him like a warm, wet sea, drowning him. He surrendered completely, lost to everything but the feel and smell and taste of this woman, his mate, his bride.

When the storm of love had passed, they lay in each other's arms like two survivors of some shipwreck washed onto the shore. His fingers were tangled up gently in her hair; her arms were wound loosely around his neck.

'Jacinda,' he whispered after what seemed like hours of floating peacefully in heaven.

'Billy-boy,' she purred.

'I love your name. Have I ever told you that? It's like a church bell's chimes floating on a spring breeze.'

She lifted her head from his chest and smiled slowly, wryly at him. Instead of answering in words, however, she kissed his crooked nose. As an afterthought, she moved higher and kissed the scraggly scar above his eyebrow.

Her loving choice of targets made his smile fade pensively. As she moved back down to reclaim her spot, resting her head on his chest, he felt her long lashes brush against him. Something quivered inside of him, something newborn and hopeful and small. Something that made him feel like singing and crying at the same time. He did neither, of course, but wrapped his arms more tightly around her, remembering anew that this delicate creature, mighty as the fairy queen, had saved his life last night. In truth, she had saved far more than his life, and he suspected she knew it. Aye, she had saved his very soul.

'What time do you suppose it is, love?' she murmured.

'I doubt it's seven yet.' When he raised himself up onto his elbow and craned his neck to see the mantel clock, his eyes suddenly widened with horror. 'Ten.'

She jolted upright in alarm. 'Ten o'clock? Good God! I've got to get home! My maid comes to wake me every morning at ten-thirty!'

Immediately, they were both out of bed, scrambling to dress to get her home before the duke and the rest of the household discovered she was missing.

'Gracious,' she muttered, ducking behind the Oriental screen to wipe away the virgin blood that had dried between her thighs.

Rackford dressed in three minutes flat. Jacinda emerged from behind the screen with her gown on, but she raced to him to fasten the hooks and eyes that he had so swiftly undone last night. Then she turned and tied his cravat for him. She only knew one fashionable knot – called the mail-coach – but with five brothers, neckcloth-tying was a handy skill to have. The trembling of her hands at the prospect of being discovered slowed her progress, but soon his ensemble was complete without having to involve his unpleasant little valet.

Within minutes, they were in his curricle, careening through the streets toward St. James's and Green Park. The rain had stopped, but the skies were still gray. He drove with the black leather top drawn up over the curricle in case the drizzle started again.

'Now, here's what you must do. Pretend you got up early and went walking in the park,' he instructed. 'I'll drive up and create a distraction to keep Hawkscliffe busy.'

'What distraction?'

'Why, I'll ask him for your hand in marriage, of course.'

'Oh!' She sighed, a smile breaking across her face like a sunbeam emerging from behind the clouds.

They exchanged one last, hasty kiss before she jumped

out of his carriage in Green Park behind the cover of some trees. He drove off toward her house while she did her best to look nonchalant, strolling through the park.

The minute she was alone, however, she looked around, stifling laughter born of pure joy, and twirled around once in a circle beneath the whispering boughs, her arms flung wide. Oh, love! What a miracle it was! She couldn't wait to tell Lizzie she and Rackford were getting married.

Meanwhile, he drove up to Knight House as though to pay one of his usual frequent calls there. Mr. Walsh greeted him at the door, like he did every other day. But this time, as Rackford swept off his hat, he turned to the butler and asked if His Grace was at home. In short order, his heart pounding, he was shown into Robert's study.

The serious, dark-eyed duke shook his hand. 'What can I do for you today, Rackford?'

He cleared his throat, hoping he had given her enough time. 'Your Grace, I have come to ask again for Lady Jacinda's hand in marriage. I have reason to believe that my suit will be favorably received at this time.'

Now, that was an understatement, he thought, vastly satisfied with himself and the satin memory of his recent performance, but he managed to swallow his cocky smile.

'I see.' Hawkscliffe lifted his chin, his piercing dark eyes boring into him. 'You believe she will be receptive even after your brawl last night at Almack's? It was quite a shocking display, sir.'

He bowed his head contritely. 'I apologize for that, Your Grace, but Mr. Loring did insult my honor.'

'Why did you not simply call him out, then?'

'He wouldn't have had a chance,' he blurted out.

Slowly, wryly, the duke smiled. 'Do you love my sister, Rackford?'

The frank question startled him. He did not know how to answer without an unmanly display of emotion. It was bad enough to feel a telltale blush creeping into his cheeks. Hawkscliffe arched his eyebrow.

290

'I do, sir,' Rackford admitted. 'More than I knew it was possible to love.'

He dropped his gaze awkwardly after he had said it. He could feel Hawkscliffe studying him, sizing him up one last time. He forced himself to lift his chin and meet the man's gaze evenly.

The duke gave a satisfied nod, then rang for the butler. 'Summon Lady Jacinda,' he ordered. He glanced at Rackford again after Mr. Walsh withdrew. 'I hope you know what you're doing. She is quite a handful when you're the one responsible for her.'

When several minutes passed and she still did not arrive, Rackford, standing at attention as he awaited her entrance, began to worry if she had gotten caught trying to sneak back into the house.

'What can be keeping her?' the duke muttered.

'I suppose it's still rather early for callers,' he offered gingerly. 'Perhaps I should come back later.'

'Of course not. I am not totally insensitive to the apprehensions of a young man undertaking a call such as this, Lord Rackford. You got your nerve up. The least she can do is get herself out of bed for it.' He rang the bell again in lordly impatience just as Jacinda came rushing in, self-conscious and charmingly disheveled.

'Yes, Robert? Oh, Lord Rackford! What a surprise!' she exclaimed rather shrilly. Her cheeks bloomed bright red when she saw him.

What a miserable actress she was. Rackford shot her a communicative scowl, trying to warn her to act natural or she was going to give them away.

Her esteemed brother gazed fondly at her for a second, then lowered his gaze with a private smile. He clasped his hands behind his back. 'Now, then, Sister. I have asked you to join us because this morning I have received a most generous offer from this excellent young man, who wishes to be joined with you in holy matrimony.'

Her little gasp was somehow genuine.

Rackford slid her a besotted glance. Her face was radiant with delight. He could scarcely believe it was all due to him.

'Ahem,' said Hawkscliffe, glancing shrewdly from one to the other. 'Lord Rackford gives me reason to hope that his proposal may find favor with you?'

'Oh, *yes*,' she vowed a bit too ardently. 'That is – it does. He does. I mean, that would be perfectly agreeable with me.' Wide-eyed, she nodded so vigorously that her curls bounced all the way down her back.

Hawkscliffe lifted his eyebrows at the sophisticated Lady Jacinda's uncharacteristic lack of cool composure. 'Forgive me if I seem too frank, but am I to understand, my dear, that you are ... in love with this man?'

Tears rushed into her eyes as she nodded again at her brother. 'I am.' Her voice came out in a teary squeak.

The duke stared at her for a long moment. The aura of power and patriarchal control cracked for a moment in his smile. His dark brown eyes, so like Jacinda's, misted. 'Well, then, my dear,' he murmured, 'it seems you finally found him. Marry, then, and love each other with my blessing.'

With a small sob of joy, Jacinda bounded out of her chair and ran over to hug her brother. Hawkscliffe embraced her in fatherly pride and kissed her head, then clasped Rackford in a warm and hearty handshake.

'We have to tell the others,' she said a moment later with a sniffle, gathering herself. 'Oh, I need Lizzie here right away! Bel will help us plan our wedding, and Miranda – but Alice, of course! We must consult her, above all. This sort of thing is exactly her forte! How soon can we marry, do you think? What shall I wear? Can we live near Regent's Park, Rackford, in one of those new villas? They're all the rage. Perhaps we should give a dinner party here tonight to announce our betrothal?'

'Jacinda,' Hawkscliffe called, putting his head down over some inconsequential bit of correspondence on his vast baronial desk, as though he required a moment to compose himself over the realization that he must give away his baby sister. 'One moment, please, before you go running off in a thousand directions.'

'Yes?' Beaming, she turned to him in question.

'Ahem. How shall I say?' The duke looked up blandly. 'Your dress is inside out.' He shot Rackford a stern, knowing glance, then dismissed them with a small flick of his hand.

Three weeks later, Jacinda and Rackford were married at home in a private, late-morning ceremony at Knight House. The white-painted partitioning doors between the salons were opened up to accommodate their fifty or so guests. Robert walked her down the makeshift 'aisle' in the flower-bedecked drawing room and handed her over to her fiancé with a bit of a tear in his eye.

Lizzie, her sole bridesmaid, gave a sentimental sniffle beside her as Rackford spoke out his confident 'I do,' holding Jacinda's hand a bit more firmly in the crook of his arm.

From the corner of her eye, Jacinda noticed her beautiful sisters-in-law exchanging softhearted looks. Rackford had enchanted them with his shy, almost boyish eagerness to be accepted by his new family. The ladies felt especially sorry for him because of his parents' hurtful decision to embarrass him for his defiance by refusing to come to the wedding. The marchioness of Truro had offered some excuse, but the snub was unmistakable.

The minister turned gravely to her. 'And do you, Lady Jacinda Knight, take this man as your lawful wedded husband, to love, honor, and obey . . .'

The two of them exchanged a dubious glance that brimmed with laughter.

'For richer or poorer, in sickness and in health, for as long as you both shall live?'

Jacinda considered for such a long pause that Rackford

293

slid her a sudden look of panic. She slipped him an arch smile. 'I *suppose*. Yes.'

The minister looked nonplussed at her reply, but Lucien coughed, swallowing a short laugh. He stood at the altar with them, for Rackford had asked him to serve as his groomsman.

The ceremony ended in the usual way, the minister beaming, the bride blushing, the groom all outward steady pride, inwardly a quivering mass of besotted emotion.

'I now pronounce you man and wife. You may kiss the bride,' the reverend added.

Rackford turned to her with a wicked glow in his eyes, but behaved himself with admirable restraint, bending to press a simple, heartfelt kiss to her lips. Family and friends applauded as they signed the register; then everyone crowded around them. Lizzie hugged her tightly. Rackford accepted his new clan's congratulations with a manly blush.

After the ceremony, Bel served them a splendid luncheon followed by a magnificent bride cake. Rackford held Jacinda's hand often at the table, making her acutely aware of the gold band on her finger that bound her to him forevermore.

'I can't believe you're going to the Continent for three whole months,' Lizzie exclaimed, shaking her head with an envious sigh.

'Indeed!' Reg and Justin agreed.

'I suppose it seems extravagant, but that is how long the builders told us they would need before our new house in Regent's Park will be ready,' Jacinda answered gaily.

Rackford's friends sat at the corner of the table with them. She was all the more glad of their attentions to Lizzie, for Alec was sitting way over on the other end of the room with Lord Griffith, Damien, and Miranda. The cad had whiled away the past few weeks at Lady Campion's country villa, presumably 'working' off his debts. Alec had congratulated her and Rackford, but Jacinda had received his embrace coolly. His ankle was healed, and he looked as fit and handsome as ever, but there was a lost, bleak look in his blue eyes and an ironic bitterness in his smile that she thought the bounder quite deserved.

Lizzie was careful not even to glance in his direction. 'How exciting,' she murmured with a carefully arranged smile. 'Where all will you be going?'

'Everywhere! A full-blown Grand Tour, isn't that right, darling? Rackford's never been abroad.' She smiled at him, giving his hand a squeeze. 'Paris, Rome, Florence—'

'Maybe you'll run across Acer and Daphne in Calais,' Reg drawled.

'I think they went northward,' Justin corrected him.

'Gretna,' Jacinda agreed. 'Everyone says so.'

The scandal of the Season had been the leading dandy and the reigning beauty's elopement after his bout of fisticuffs at Almack's. Helena and Amelia had told Jacinda that it had been Lady Erhard pushing Daphne to snare a title all along. Jacinda was happy for them. If ever a pair had deserved each other—

'Venice is the place I most want to see,' Rackford was telling the others. 'Just like Canaletto's paintings.' He winked slyly at her and took a bite of chicken.

'Venice, of course. We shall have to buy some marvelous art for our new home.'

'Buy it?' he asked quizzically.

'Darling.' She shot him a playful scowl, took a dainty sip of wine, and turned back to her best friend. 'Eventually, we'll arrive in Vienna and, if we're inspired, we may even travel on to St. Petersburg.'

'How wonderful.'

'You should join us at some point, Lizzie, honestly. You know you're always welcome—'

'I will not intrude on your honeymoon,' she scoffed. 'Besides, I have a bit of a mystery waiting for me later this week.'

'Is that so?'

She and old Professor Alfred Hamilton, Bel's father and a former Fellow of Oxford, exchanged a fond glance. The old scholar shared Lizzie's passion for books, especially old books. 'Indubitably, my dear Miss Carlisle. Excellent young lady, what?'

'Why, Miss Carlisle, you cannot keep us in suspense,' Justin protested amiably.

'Yes, do tell!' Reg demanded.

Lizzie smiled. 'Before I return to Yorkshire, Dr. Hamilton is going to be introducing me to the representative of a publisher based in Leipzig who needs someone to translate German manuscripts for English publication.'

'This publisher is willing to hire a lady?' Jacinda asked, raising her eyebrows. 'How very forward-thinking.'

Lizzie smiled wryly. 'My efforts would be anonymous, of course, but, you see ...' She leaned closer. 'Dr. Hamilton gives me to understand that this German publisher has acquired a manuscript which is being handled with great secrecy. We are beside ourselves with curiosity to find out what all the fuss is about, aren't we, Alfred?'

'In good time, my dear, all shall come to light.' Bel's white-haired father smiled, his unlit cob pipe clamped between his teeth.

Just then, Lucien's wife, Alice, strode to the front of the room. 'Ladies and gentlemen, may I have your attention?'

'Hear, hear!' Lucien chimed in, quieting everyone for her announcement.

With a smile, Alice turned toward the bridal table and gave a small curtsy. 'Lord and Lady Rackford, in honor of your nuptials, we will now present the entertainment. Aunt Miranda,' she added, 'we'll need your voice.'

The tall, raven-haired beauty got up out of her chair and strode lightly across the room to Alice's side. The twins' wives waited amid much cheering and applause from the rowdy Knight brothers.

'Quiet, you ruffians,' Alice scolded. 'You are going to scare our performers.' She nodded to the footman, who opened the door.

296

In came the nursery maids, escorting their charges: Alice's nephew and ward, little Harry, Baron Glenwood, who was nearly five. Harry held hands with Bel and Robert's two-year-old, the earl of Morley, known to his mama as Bobby. The two diminutive lordlings advanced shyly into the center of the room. Their hair was neatly combed, and they were dressed in tiny tailcoats, trousers, and cravats.

At Alice's cue, Harry bowed; Morley followed suit, nearly toppling headlong. One of the uniformed nursery maids placed Alice and Lucien's one-year-old daughter, Pippa, on the floor in front of her cousins. Then, with Miranda's help, the children sang them a bon voyage song, wishing them off safely, though Pippa did little more than lean her bald head against Miranda's bent knee and wave her arms in excitement.

Lucien, visibly smitten and laughing, shook his head, watching his daughter. Harry was struck with stage fright midway through the song. He popped his finger in his mouth and glanced uncertainly at his old nurse, Peg. Morley, a serious little fellow like his papa, gave his best effort, staring at Miranda and faintly echoing her words.

'Bravo!' Jacinda applauded when their song came to an end. The rest of the family did likewise.

Pippa beamed at everyone, though, in truth, she was applauded for every tiny thing she ever did; Harry rushed off to pounce on his favorite uncle, Alec; while Morley came over to Jacinda. He stood there regarding her thoughtfully until she picked him up and set him on her lap.

'That was a wonderful song, Morley! How handsome you look today. Do you know who this gentleman is?' Jacinda asked the tot, turning to her husband.

It was then that Jacinda noticed the wary, mystified way Rackford was watching her brothers playing with their children. If high society had been a strange world to him, his first experience of being a part of a loving, close-knit family appeared even more so. Her gaze softened at the impact it seemed to be having on him, of seeing the tender kindness of these young fathers to their little ones. Lucien had taught Pippa how to rub noses with her papa, a game that filled the baby with endless delight – and all the world knew she was the apple of her father's eye. Miranda had given the nursemaids permission to bring down her lusty, squalling twins so that Jacinda could bid Edward and Andrew farewell before leaving on her journey. Lizzie asked if she might hold Andrew, while Damien came over to them and put his arm around Miranda, boasting proudly about how strong Edward's tiny grip was on his finger.

When Rackford turned to Jacinda with a hundred questions in his eyes, her heart clenched to think of the dearth of love and affection he had known in his early life. She leaned toward him, pressing a gentle kiss to his cheek.

As the afternoon shadows grew long, it soon came time to leave Knight House. They would set out at once for Dover, where they would take the packet across the Channel with their entourage of three carriages – one for themselves, one for the servants, and one for the mountain of luggage they would require for so long an absence. Jacinda fully intended to show Rackford the pleasures of traveling in style.

Good-byes were always a long, drawn-out affair at holidays and other celebratory occasions, and this was no exception. It took them half an hour to get as far as the entrance hall. As Jacinda waited for Rackford to leave off joking around with Lucien and Alec, her nephews, Harry and Morley, came racing over to her.

'Auntie Jacinda! Auntie Jacinda!'

'Yes, darlings?' she asked, bending down to gather them near her.

'We found a note!' Morley shouted.

'You dropped it under your chair.' Harry handed her a piece of paper with an air of great self-importance.

'Thank you, boys.' Noticing the Truro seal embedded in the wax, she realized the letter must have fallen out of Rackford's pocket.

298

'What does it say?' Harry asked solemnly.

'Well, it appears to be Lord Rackford's. We wouldn't want to pry ...' On the other hand, he still had not confided in her about the night at Torcarrow, even though Reg and Justin knew about it. Besides, the children had already unfolded the letter.

She stole only a brief glance at the large, exquisitely formed handwriting that flowed urgently across the page, but upon reading the first line, she knew instantly that something was very wrong. Devil take his privacy, she thought; then she read the rest.

Dearest William,

Did you not receive my earlier letter? I have not had an answer from you yet. Please come. I know that you are angry, but if you have any pity for your mother, you must know I need you at this difficult time.

The physicians say your father will not live long. The apoplexy has taken the use of the left half of his body, and they fear a second attack is imminent. They are bleeding him and giving him all the best care, but he worsens by the day. Surely you can find it in your heart to come to us. Anxiously awaiting your arrival.

With all my love,
Your Mother

Jacinda read it again, barely able to believe her eyes. Lord Truro was dying? What on earth had happened? she wondered. Then she turned her gaze slowly to her husband, who stood, laughing and talking, with her brothers. She couldn't believe he had not seen fit to mention to her that his father was on his deathbed.

Quickly folding the letter, she grasped his hand, bid her guests and family a final, rather terse adieu, and led her husband to the waiting coach.

'Coachman, to Dover!' Rackford called merrily, waving one last time to everyone as he handed Jacinda into the festooned, beribboned carriage.

She suspected he was slightly foxed. She paused on the carriage step. 'Belay that order. One moment, please. Husband, may I have a word with you?' She tugged him into the coach.

'Growing impatient, my love?' He sprang up into the coach and dropped into the opposite squab with a jaunty grin.

She pursed her lips and handed him the letter. 'You dropped this. Care to tell me what the deuce is going on?'

Instantly, his smile faded. He took the letter from her and cast it aside, then gave her an insolent look. 'Not really.'

'What happened?'

He rolled his eyes and looked away. 'The old bastard collapsed in a fit of apoplexy. Something like that.'

'Rackford! When?'

'A week ago.' He gave a disgusted sigh. 'My mother said Truro was in a foul temper for days after I wrote, informing him of our betrothal. Then one of the servants sparked his wrath with some insignificant mistake and he flew into a rage – drunk, of course. Mother said he was screaming at the footman when his fury brought on the apoplexy. He fell to the ground, convulsing, and lost consciousness for twenty-four hours. When he came to, the left half of his body was paralyzed.'

She stared wonderingly at him. 'I can't believe you weren't going to tell me this. Rackford.'

'Yes, Jacinda?' he asked in a bored tone.

She searched his eyes. 'We must go to them.'

'Absolutely not. We are going to the Continent, my dear. I promised you we would. I'm not going to let that bastard ruin our honeymoon. Everything is arranged.'

'It can wait. This is more important, Rackford. We must go to Cornwall.'

'No, it isn't. People die every day. So what?'

'But this is your father.'

'All the more reason.'

'Darling, I know you are deeply, deeply angry at the man. You have every reason to be, but think of your mother. We cannot leave her to face this on her own.'

'Why not? Many a time that woman left me to face that blackguard alone. I survived. So will she.'

'Rackford!'

'Jacinda, I am not going to Cornwall. Ever. They don't deserve a visit from us. They insulted you. If he could have found it within him to be happy for us and come to the wedding, instead of working himself into a fit of rage over my choice of brides, this would not have happened to him. He did it to himself. The blackguard can go to the devil for all I care. Come, let us leave now for France.' He started to rap on the inside of the coach to signal the driver to go, but she stopped him.

'Be practical! If he is going to die, that means you are about to come into your inheritance. Don't you think it might be wise to speak with him and make sure everything is in order? There may be items of business related to the marquisate of which you may need to be informed before it comes down to you.'

'Our solicitors will advise me of anything I need to know.'

'Weren't you even going to answer your mother's letter? The woman is frantic.'

'She is always frantic, Jacinda. She exaggerates every-thing to try to gain my pity. Every other day is a calamity.'

'This time, I daresay, it's real. Rackford, this may be your last chance to make peace with your father.'

'He's the one who needs to make peace with me,' he said bitterly.

'Yes,' she whispered. 'That's exactly my point.'

'I vowed never to return to Cornwall.'

'Things are different now, sweeting. I don't see how you can avoid it. When your father dies, you will be the marquess of Truro and St. Austell and the master of Torcarrow, as will your son after you. Your rank puts you in a position of responsibility that I *know* the man I love would never shirk.'

He closed his eyes and turned away. 'You don't know what you are asking of me.'

'Yes, I do.' She reached over and caressed his shoulder, pausing as she weighed her words. 'Rackford, when are you going to confide in me? I know now that Reg and Justin were there the night you ran away.'

He turned back to her, paling slightly, his angular face etched with slowly deepening shock. 'You know?'

She nodded. 'Do you want to talk about it?'

'God, no.'

She closed her eyes briefly, striving for patience. 'I didn't think so. Rackford, everything in me is certain that you must do this – if not for your father's good, then for your own, and for the good of our children in the future. This poisonous hatred must end.'

They stared at each other for a long moment. She watched him warring with himself. His green eyes churned with bitter resentment, and his square jaw was taut.

'You won't have to face it alone, darling,' she said softly, taking his hand. 'I will be there with you every step of the way. Then we'll go to Europe. I promise it will still be there.'

He searched her eyes in stormy defiance, but when she gave him an encouraging nod, he climbed out of the coach and gave the driver his new instructions – not east to Dover, but west.

To Cornwall.

With frequent changes of horses at the posting inns along the way, they made the journey in four grueling days, traveling each night until the summer light failed at around ten, taking to the road again at dawn. It was Rackford who set this booming pace, not from any eagerness to arrive, but

302

merely because he wanted to get the whole ordeal over with. He was distant and moody for most of the journey, grumbling about the miserable food at the coaching inns, the heat, the dust, the incessant creaking of the coach springs, and his boredom with sitting in the carriage for so many hours on end.

'This is not,' he grumbled every few hours, 'how I envisioned spending my honeymoon!'

Jacinda was careful to treat him gently, aware that few things could have been more difficult for him than revisiting the setting where he had long ago fled such heartless cruelty. He seemed slightly happier when he rode on top of the coach, lying idly across the secured luggage with his coat off and the sun on his face. She knew he was mentally gathering himself to confront not merely his father, but the painful memories of his distant past. For her part, she wondered what sort of reception she would receive from her in-laws.

The weather remained cooperative, and the major coaching roads were smooth and fast as far as Exeter; but their progress slowed considerably when they ventured westward on smaller, regional byways. Through the rugged Dartmoor terrain they labored, at last crossing the River Tamar into Cornwall. The landscape's reprieve was brief, for soon Bodmin Moor swallowed them up, in turn – a bleak, sweeping expanse of pensive beauty. Jacinda rode atop the coach with Rackford, watching the cloud shadows sculpt the broad valleys and windswept hills.

As they traveled down the center of the ever-narrowing peninsula, Rackford told her that St. Austell, one of the towns from which his father's title had been taken, lay about ten miles east. It was famous, he said, for the excellence of its fine hard-paste clay, which was regularly shipped to the famous Midlands potteries to be used in the making of England's most distinctive porcelain and fine china. Truro, the larger town with its grand, flamboyant cathedral, was situated about fifteen miles farther south.

At half-past seven in the evening of the fourth day, they neared the little fishing village of Perranporth and climbed the dramatic hillside until they could see the ominous, weather-beaten castle overlooking the crashing waves of the Atlantic.

She glanced at Rackford. He was staring at Torcarrow in brooding defiance, the wind rippling through his sandy hair.

Chapter Eighteen

Jacinda's presence beside him helped him stand firm against the hissing devils in his head that whispered, *You're worthless*. He stared at Torcarrow in the distance with his fists clenched in long-nursed anger and a shocking degree of childlike fear. He did his best to hide the churning whirlpool of emotion that this homecoming had wrought in him. As their caravan of three carriages rolled up the long drive, she seemed to sense the rising tide of sadness in him.

She took his hand between her own, giving him her silent, sturdy comfort as he struggled to take the grief in stride. He did not wish anyone, not even her, to see the tears that he refused to shed for all that he had lost in this place.

Instead, he clung to bittersweet memories of the happy moments, pointing out the stand of trees where he and his brother had once had a long rope swing, the overgrown garden folly where they had found a nest of baby owls. He could feel the change in the air as they neared the ocean – the steady wind, the abrasive cleansing salt, the scent of which unfurled countless memories that he had deemed forever lost.

As they drove closer, he did not have the heart to point out the family crypt to Jacinda. The small building was modeled on a Grecian temple and sat amid a serene grove of oaks near the ornamental pond. Percy had been laid to

305

rest there among their ancestors; Father, also, would be buried there if the old blighter indeed saw fit to pop off.

Rackford still doubted it, despite his mother's vows that Truro the Terrible was dying. The man had always seemed to him a force of nature. How could a mighty, evil djinni die?

When they pulled up to the entrance, Jacinda glanced nervously at him. 'They're going to hate me, aren't they?'

He kissed her hand. 'It's not you they hate, Jas. What they hate is the fact that they cannot control me. Don't let them get to you.'

He realized that, despite his earlier refusal to come, his mother must have told the servants to expect him at any moment, for six footmen marched out at once and formed a waiting corridor to receive them, while a butler and a heavyset older woman in an apron rushed out of the entrance.

'Oh, it's Master Billy! Master Billy's come home!' she called to the rest of the staff. More servants came hurrying out to the front of the house.

Rackford stared incredulously. 'Why, it's Mrs. Landry, our old cook! And Mr. Becket, the butler! I can't believe they're still here!' He bounded out of the coach into their midst.

Jacinda fondly watched his exuberant reunion with the kindly old servants who had been with the family since before he was born.

'Dear old Cooky. You are the best part of coming home.' He hugged the plump old woman for a long moment, whispering his gratitude in her ear for the bag of coins she had secretly stowed away in his satchel for him the night he had run away. Her blue eyes twinkled with adoration as she patted his cheek.

'Now, then, Master Billy, I've made a special treat for your return to us.'

'Not clotted cream?' he exclaimed in anticipation.

'With black treacle,' she answered knowingly. 'Your favorite.'

With a short bark of laughter, he whirled around. 'Jacinda! Come here, darling. Meet our cook, Mrs. Landry. You have not *lived* until you've had a proper Cornish cream, and Mrs. Landry's treacle is the envy of the county.'

'Oh, hush. What a charmer you always were even as a boy, Master Billy,' she scolded with a blush of pleasure. 'I can't believe how big you've grown!'

He laughed and introduced each of the other servants to his beautiful young bride. They all seemed awed at first by Jacinda's golden beauty and London-bred sophistication, but her warmth and the laughter in her merry brown eyes quickly put them at ease – and they seemed to have a similar effect on her.

Before long, Mr. Becket bustled them along into the house. 'Your rooms have been made ready, Lord and Lady Rackford. This way. The marchioness awaits you.'

They tarried in their rooms just long enough to freshen up and steal a kiss; then they braced themselves and obediently went to pay their respects to Lady Truro.

Alerted of their arrival by a footman, she joined them in the hallway outside his father's sickroom.

'Mother.' Checking his habitual irritation with the woman, he bent and gave her a dutiful kiss on the cheek. 'How are you faring?'

'I am tired,' she admitted with a sigh full of martyrdom, 'but, oh, it is just so good of you to come, William. I was not sure if you would.'

'You have my wife to thank for it,' he said meaningfully.

Lady Truro turned warily to Jacinda.

Jacinda curtseyed, lowering her head. 'Madam.'

'How do you do,' his mother said coolly.

'I am so sorry for the sufferings that have been visited upon Lord Truro. It must be a very difficult time for you.'

Her compassionate words took both Rackford and Lady Truro off guard. Why, the girl could be as diplomatic as Lucien when she wanted to, he thought.

'Thank you, my dear,' the marchioness answered cautiously, nodding to her. 'I hope you will enjoy your stay. The gardens are in bloom if you care to walk in them, and the beach is very pleasant this time of year – only mind you bring a parasol. The sun is very strong. 'Twill ruin your lovely complexion.'

'Thank you, ma'am. I shall be mindful.' Rackford was impressed. Lady Truro eyed the eighteen-year-old Jacinda's milky skin in envy, but said nothing.

It was not lost on Rackford that his mother had still not congratulated them on their marriage nor extended toward Jacinda even a token 'welcome to the family.' He pushed the vexing thought aside. 'How is he?'

'Weak,' Lady Truro replied, then paused. 'And frightened, as well. The paralysis has affected his speech. You mustn't anger him, William—'

'I never *try* to anger him, Mother.'

'The surgeon, Mr. Plimpton, is with him now. He says His Lordship must be kept calm. Another bout of anger is all that is needed to trigger a second fit of the apoplexy. If that happens, your father will die.'

Rackford considered for a long moment. 'Perhaps I shouldn't go in. He could fly into a rage merely seeing me.'

'Oh, I'm sure he will be glad you've come. You must go in. You've traveled all this way.'

'Aye, on my honeymoon,' he reminded her, resting his hands on his waist.

'Indeed.' The marchioness looked away.

There was an awkward silence.

Rackford exchanged a bolstering look with Jacinda. She gave him a subtle nod.

'Right,' he muttered. 'Let's get this over with. You don't have to go in there with me. It is bound to be unpleasant.'

'I am going with you,' she said firmly, slipping her hand in his.

She followed a step behind him as he opened the door, but Rackford released her hand as he ventured into his

308

father's chamber. The sight of the man stopped him in his tracks. *My God.*

The surgeon was wrapping the marquess's arm from the incision where he had just treated his patient with another bloodletting. His father was ghastly pale. The once mighty and terrifying Lord Truro appeared dwarfed in the vast state bed, a ruined god. He seemed to have aged twenty years instead of a mere few weeks since the last time Rackford had seen him. The ruddy tone of his skin had faded to a waxen pallor. The rest of his dark hair had turned gray at his ordeal. His cheeks were hollow, his eyes were sunken, and the left side of his mouth sagged in a permanent snarl. When his gaze swung to them, however, his eyes blazed with a wild emerald brightness, as hell-bent as ever.

'So, the vultures have begun circling already,' he drawled, slurring only a little more pronouncedly than when he was foxed.

Jacinda's eyes widened at his taunting remark, but Rackford's nostrils flared as he inhaled slowly, determined to keep his cool.

'Try to contain your delight, my lord. I am here for Mother's sake, not yours.' He sauntered into the chamber with a careless air of insolence.

Mr. Plimpton glanced at him in alarm. 'With all due respect, sir, His Lordship is not to be agitated.'

Truro snorted. 'Little bastard's been agitating me since the day he was born.'

'Am I a bastard, Father? Is that why you hate me so?' Rackford asked in a pleasant tone, leaning against the satin-wood highboy.

'What do you think?' Truro grumbled.

Jacinda looked from father to son, clearly uncomfortable.

'Don't worry, wife. I am quite legitimate. Can't you see the resemblance?' he asked bitterly.

'Rackford,' she warned him softly.

He scowled at her, then folded his arms across his chest and lowered his gaze, stewing. Why had he come here? Simply to give his father one last chance to hurt and humiliate him, this time in front of his bride? He knew that Truro's hackles were up because his almighty pride could not bear for anyone to see him this way, enfeebled and struck down seemingly by the hand of God as a punishment for his brutality. But Rackford, too, felt himself moving into an equally harsh mood. He could not countenance his father's insults when he had come all this way just to take the enormous risk of showing one more time that some daft, small part of him ... cared.

Jacinda glanced worriedly at him, then broke the stormy silence. 'We are very sorry for your suffering, my lord. We have come to do whatever we can to help you recover as speedily as possible.'

'Prettily spoken, child. But I am not a fool.' He dragged his piercing stare away from Rackford and inspected her.

Instantly, Rackford felt his protective instincts rising.

'You've merely come to butter me up to make sure I leave you my fortune as well as the properties.'

Perhaps it was so many weeks of managing the famous curmudgeon Lord Drummond that enabled her to smile at Truro's baiting rudeness. 'Don't be absurd, my lord. I've a dowry of a hundred thousand pounds and an estate of my own in Hertfordshire. It was left in trust to me as a wedding gift from my papa, the eighth duke of Hawkscliffe,' she said, her tone sharpening ever so slightly as she reminded him of her rank, 'who – if we are speaking vulgarly – was as rich as Croesus. Rackford and I shan't starve.'

'Well, you are a cheeky thing, ain't you?'

'I give as good as I get, my lord. That is all.'

'Damn your impudence, girl—'

'Father,' Rackford warned between gritted teeth, 'you are speaking to my wife.'

'Perhaps Lord and Lady Rackford should withdraw,' Mr. Plimpton said anxiously.

'Ach, let them stay,' Truro grumbled. 'They're not upsetting me.'

310

'No, Father. You must listen to your doctor,' Rackford said coldly. 'Come along, Jacinda.'

But she did not follow. Standing by Truro's bedside, she folded her arms across her chest and studied him.

'What's this, you want to climb into bed with me?'

'Father!' Rackford said, aghast, but Jacinda merely rolled her eyes.

'You don't frighten me, you know, nor do I shock easily.'

'No wonder, considering who your mother was.'

'That will do, sir!' Rackford feared he would have a fit of apoplexy himself if his father said one more indecent word to his bride.

'It's all right, Rackford,' Jacinda said drily, noting his appalled expression. 'His comments don't bother me. At least he says them to my face. To be sure, he is an ogre, but I actually think ... this may be his way of being friendly.'

The fixed snarl on Truro's lips widened in what might have been a piratelike, lopsided sort of grin. 'Bugger off, ye cheeky wench!'

'Humph,' she answered skeptically. 'Get your rest, you ogre. With any luck, it may improve your disposition.'

Rackford put his arm around her and escorted her bodily out of the sickroom. In the corridor, she waved off his flurry of mortified apologies with a little laugh.

'We'll leave immediately—'

'Nonsense. Do you want to give him the satisfaction of knowing he successfully chased us off within ten minutes? Come, show me to the kitchens! I want to try this fabled Cornish cream.'

He gazed thoughtfully at her for a second, then shrugged, sighed, and shook his head. She smiled and tucked her dainty hand through the crook of his arm; he escorted her to Cook's domain in the back of the house.

Soon, they were sitting at the scuffed wooden worktable in the kitchens. The windows were open, admitting the evening breeze. Cook bustled about, humming and laughing and telling them stories of the local people, who had married whom during his absence. Pleasant as it was, Rackford could feel the memories swirling around him like unseen sharks beneath the surface of the present. He could feel them circling closer; he kept his smile pasted on by sheer dint of will.

Proud and beaming, Mrs. Landry placed two bowls of cream in front of them, then poured on the warm, dark treacle. 'There you are, Master Billy. Just the way you like it, only fifteen years late in coming,' she added softly. 'You never did get to eat it.'

He turned to her with a fractured look. *Fifteen years.*

'Oh, it's heavenly, Mrs. Landry!' Tasting it, Jacinda raved in ecstasy, but Rackford, suddenly, could only sit there, rigidly immobile, stricken, staring down into his bowl with tears blurring his vision.

Every detail of that horrible night filled his mind with vivid, excruciating clarity. He did not realize he was shaking until he saw his hand trembling; he held his spoon in a white-knuckled grip, as though it were a weapon.

He was staring at the melting mush of treacle and cream, but his mind was a million miles away.

'Billy?' Jacinda's tone had instantly sobered. She touched his arm gently. 'Darling?'

'Excuse me. I'm sorry. I can't – excuse me.' He pushed up abruptly from the table and walked out, blinded by tears and gritting his teeth against the sheer anguish of the sob he felt building in the back of his throat. He refused to give in to it.

'Billy!'

He heard the door creak as Jacinda ran out after him, but he pulled his arm away when she came and touched him. He refused to meet her gaze, pushing his hand roughly through his hair.

'Leave me for a while. I need to walk.'

'I'll come with you—'

'No. Just – I'll be fine, all right?'

She searched his face. 'Are you sure?'

He stole a brief, sideward glance at her and gave a curt nod. Sliding his hands into his trouser pockets, he trudged off through the fading twilight toward the beach.

Jacinda gazed in distress at his broad, retreating back as Rackford walked away.

Oh, what a mess this family was, she thought. She had seen the fractured look in his eyes; she had no intention of leaving him alone for more than a few minutes. Taking note of which direction he had walked, she turned around and went back inside.

She exchanged a worried look with Mrs. Landry, thanked the woman for her kindness, then ventured back up to Truro's sickroom. When she knocked quietly, the surgeon answered. The marquess was still awake. Promising Mr. Plimpton that she would be brief, she was admitted to see him.

'Back for more, are you? What do you want this time?' he demanded hoarsely in his slurred voice as she sat down on the chair beside his bed.

'You and your son,' she said, 'remind me of the old saying about a rock and a hard place.'

'Humph. Demmed bullheaded, that one. Always was.'

She smiled wryly at him for a moment before her expression sobered. 'My lord, you must know you hurt William very deeply. He is a good man, and I suspect you are secretly proud of him.' She ignored his snort of denial. 'I am begging you to tell him so. Mr. Plimpton has surely explained the seriousness of your condition. There may not be another chance. It was not easy for Rackford to come here, but I insisted he give you the chance to apologize.'

'Apologize!' he demanded in a shaky tone. 'Why, you impertinent little baggage!' He started to sit up from the bed, but lay back again with a wince of pain. He glared banefully at her. 'Do you know what my father taught me, Lady Rackford? Never apologize to anyone! What good does it do,

313

when it is too late and the damage is already done?'

'You still have time to undo some of that damage, my lord. I don't know if you deserve to be forgiven, but what I do know is that your son is here. All he wants from you is one kind word.'

'I saved his life, didn't I? I got him out of Newgate.'

'In William's view, that was merely for your own interests, not because you care about him.'

'Care about him?' he retorted. 'Didn't you see the curricle I bought him? The horses? Did he tell you I gave him an allowance of a hundred-fifty pounds a week?'

'Is it honestly beyond your power to admit that you love him? To say you are glad to have found him alive? He cannot see it, but you don't fool me. I see how you look at him. I know you are proud of him and that in your own flawed way, you do love him. But how is he to know if you don't say it? Surely you have the courage to speak a few simple words that could change everything for him. Is that too much to give to save your soul?'

'You are cruel.' He looked away, pressing his head against his pillow. 'Leave me,' he whispered after a moment. 'Mr. Plimpton, show my daughter out.'

Jacinda was so taken aback by his acknowledgment of her as his kin that she paused and squeezed his hand – his right hand, for the left he kept curled lamely against him since the apoplexy. It was the same hand that had bloodied Billy's face so often as a boy. She let go of it quickly, tears shining in her eyes before she quickly blinked them away.

'May God have mercy on you, Lord Truro. I will keep you in my prayers.' She left the sickroom, her skirts whispering over the hardwood floors. Returning downstairs, she went outside in search of Rackford.

At once, the sea breeze ran riot through her hair and rippled gracefully through her skirts. She exited past the clouds of moths that fluttered about the brass lamps fixed on either side of the back door. Beneath the dark sky full of stars, bats swooped overhead. She followed the path

314

through the moonlit rose garden out to the rickety wooden steps leading down to the beach.

Far off the shore, there was an islet with a lighthouse whose search-beam swept the black waves in a slow, continual rhythm, but its solitary ray was not strong enough to penetrate the darkness of the sandy cove below.

She felt her way carefully down the stairs, steadying herself on the rough handrail. She heard – indeed, felt in her chest – the vigorous power of wave after lulling wave beating the rocks. As her eyes gradually adjusted to the deeper darkness away from the illumination of the house, she made out the white plumes of sea spray where the waves broke.

By the time she reached the bottom of the precarious wooden stairs, the dim glow of the stars showed her the dark wonderland of bizarre rock formations that rose up amid the sand – stone arches and somber, gnarled pillars roughly coated in green velvet lichen. Around them, the bed of sand was soft and pale. It muffled all sound like a blanket, so she did not bother calling out to him when she spied her husband standing upon a cluster of large, black rocks over the crashing waves.

The lighthouse beam revealed him in its fleeting glow. He was staring out to sea, his profile bleak and wistful. The wind riffled through the longer front section of his dark gold hair and billowed through his loose white shirtsleeves.

Jacinda paused to take off her shoes and stockings, then walked toward him through the cool, deep sand. She noticed he had taken off his cravat. He was barefooted, as well, his black trousers rolled up around his shins. Having left his coat draped over his chair in Mrs. Landry's kitchen, he had unbuttoned his waistcoat, as well. He was throwing rocks into the ocean, but he stopped when he saw her approaching.

He was tall, lean, magnetically handsome – a man in his prime. But when he turned to her, his face looked haunted, and his eyes were those of a lonely little boy.

She wasn't sure what to say. He leaned down, stretching out his hand toward her. She lifted her skirts around her ankles, ventured through the little moat of seawater that ringed the boulders, and accepted his warm grasp. He pulled her up onto the rocks. At once, she gasped, feeling the sea foam fleck her face.

Rackford leaned down and kissed her cheek, tasting the salt on her skin. Instead of pulling back, however, he leaned his forehead against hers and closed his eyes. She captured his face between her hands and held him like that, gently.

'Are you all right?' she whispered.

'I don't know.' Starlight limned the hard planes and angles of his face as he drew back, staring into her eyes. 'Perhaps you can explain one thing to me.'

'What's that, darling? I will try.' Gazing earnestly into his eyes, she stroked his hair. 'I so want to help.'

'Why do you love me?' he asked barely audibly.

His question took her aback, but her heart welled with devotion. She caressed his face slowly. 'So many reasons. You're intelligent, brave, loyal, strong, caring, gentle, honorable, chivalrous, charming, kind, forgiving, patient, wise.' He turned to her with a look of surprise, but she wasn't through. 'You always keep your word; you make me laugh; you listen to what I have to say; you have interesting views on things; you're incredibly handsome; a magnificent lover – I could go on.'

His lips twisting in a rueful smile, he looked away, slightly abashed.

'I consider you not merely a wonderful husband and a beloved friend, but a great man, destined to make the world a better place – especially for those who have no voice. That's why I married you – aside from your tattoos, of course.'

'Do you really mean all that?' he asked, staring at the sea.

'With all my heart,' she whispered slowly, emphatically,

sliding her arms around him. 'You are one of the most genuinely good people I've ever met.'

'You think I'm a good person?' he asked, turning to her in surprise.

'Of course. Don't you think so?'

He shrugged, then leaned his head on her shoulder without answering.

Brushing her blowing curls behind her ears, she studied her toes curled against the jagged rock, then looked at him cautiously. 'Why do you ask me these questions, Rackford?'

He did not answer for a moment, watching the lighthouse beam sweep over the onyx waters.

'I'm just ... trying to make sense of it all.' Disengaging himself from her embrace, he stood, bracing his left foot upon a higher rock. He slipped his hands into his pockets while his brooding, restless gaze swept the horizon. 'I have been standing here remembering how bad it all was and trying ... to convince myself like a reasonable adult that I didn't deserve it somehow.'

'Oh, Billy, of course you didn't deserve it, sweeting. You were only a child.'

'I didn't feel like one.'

'But you were.'

'How could someone do that? How could he do that to me?' He glanced bitterly at Torcarrow, then looked at her in lonely, urgent anger. His jaw was taut, and though there was an edge of insolence in his stare, she knew he hung upon her answer, desperate for reassurance.

'Humanity, my dear, is a blind, mad parade of sorry fools,' she said softly. 'People are flawed, and sometimes they make terrible mistakes. You must never let yourself be deceived into thinking that your father's hideous mistakes were somehow your fault. They were not.'

His eyes flickered as he registered her words, but still, he turned away again, shaking his head. 'You tell me that, and I know you're right, but as much as I want to believe

317

you, somehow I cannot be rid of the sense that I must have done something wrong.'

'I can understand why you might think that, because what we learn as small children stays with us throughout our lives; but surely, my darling, in some remote corner of your heart, you must know better than that by now.'

'But I must have done something to deserve it. He never treated Percy that way, only me.'

'You were innocent,' she insisted. 'By telling you that you deserved your beatings, Lord Truro could avoid his own damning guilt. By putting the blame on you, he did not have to face the horror of having done violence to his own child.'

'It isn't fair,' he whispered abruptly. 'He beat the hell out of me. Right in front of Reg and Justin. They had come home with me on holiday from school.' Distantly, he shook his head. 'All I did was borrow his stupid spyglass.'

With tears in her eyes, she held out her arms to him. 'Come to me. Let me hold you.'

He sharply turned away, making no move to come closer.

'What's wrong?'

'Don't look at me like that.'

'Like what?'

'Like I'm some pathetic little boy you want to save. I already have one mother, for all the good it did me.'

She fell silent and lowered her arms. 'Don't push me away, Rackford.'

'I hate it that you know all this!' he cried. 'It's humiliating. I hate that you saw me that night in the alley – that first night. I'm not good enough for you—'

'Stop it. I love you, Rackford. I'm not going to hurt you.'

He turned to her, silent for a long moment. The lighthouse beam showed her the stark, unsettling war of emotion in his face before they were plunged in darkness again.

'You love me?' he challenged her in a dark tone. Moving closer, he loomed over her.

318

'You know I do.' She tilted her head back bravely to continue to hold his gaze.

Seething, tempestuous need gleamed in his eyes. 'Prove it.' He touched her hair, gently at first, then grasping a handful of her curls. His eyes flickered with heat. 'Show me,' he ordered in a whisper.

She went very still. 'Right now? Here?'

'Yes. Now.'

She hesitated. His fierceness frightened her, but when she looked up into his burning eyes, she didn't dare say no, aware of the complexity behind his brash request. He was a proud warrior of a man, but that pride had been wounded deeply. Somehow she understood his need to reassert his power after the vulnerability of having been revealed to her as a powerless battered child; perhaps he was even trying to drive her away, scare her off, so that his self-fulfilling prophecy that no one could ever love him would come true. She was not going to let that happen, no matter the cost.

Looking deeply into his angry green eyes, she knew she had to tread carefully, ever so carefully.

'Very well,' she whispered, lifting her hand to caress his thigh as he stood over her. 'How do you want me?'

He held her stare, windblown, dark, and dangerous. He looked almost suspicious at her willingness. 'On your back.' He took her hand and pulled her off the rock.

She moved down onto the sand, slowly lying back. He turned, as well, kneeling between her legs. He eased down atop her, taking her mouth in raw, starved hunger while he placed her hand on his manhood, demanding her caress.

Jacinda was overwhelmed by his raw, angry neediness. She could feel his hands sliding up deftly under her skirts, lifting them. He kissed her like he would consume her, but the familiar taste of him and the feel of him in her arms stirred her passion in seconds. Ending the kiss, he pushed up to kneel over her again. The shape of his tousled hair, his square jaw, and broad shoulders were silhouetted against the fading sky.

'What an obliging wife you are,' he murmured as he unbuttoned his trousers.

She flinched with fleeting, confused pain at his mocking tone, but refused to back down before his demons. If this was what he needed to test the limits of her love, she would not fail him. Obediently, she reached for his manhood as he freed it, stroking him. He caressed her hand as she guided him to her.

'You love this, don't you, my little wanton?' he asked, closing her hand around his rigid shaft in a taunting squeeze.

'I love *you*,' she corrected.

'I'm not a good man, Jacinda. Don't believe it. I'm a killer and a thief. I'll only disappoint you.'

'I'll take my chances,' she answered in defiance.

His dun lashes veiled his eyes as he lowered his gaze. He spread her legs as he knelt over her, but when he touched her core, he wrung a soft groan from her with his probing fingers. He watched her moving with his hand for several moments before he mounted her. She wrapped her arms around him in warm sensual welcome, gasping softly with pleasure as he pressed inside of her. He paused, buried to the hilt within her body. They lingered like that, savoring their joining in throbbing stillness.

'You could never disappoint me, Billy. I have always believed in you,' she whispered as she stroked his hair. 'That's why I left you my diamonds.'

He paused but said nothing, drawing her thighs up around his lean sides, his arms draped over her bent knees. His large, warm hands encircled her ankles gently; he toyed lovingly with her feet. She lifted her hips, growing impatient for him.

'Make love to me, Billy. I need you.'

He reached down and caressed her, rousing her to new heights; then she pulled him down into her arms and held him as he loved her, baring all the old wounds and loneliness in his soul, bringing each hurt forward for her to kiss,

320

shyly at first, then more desperately. She could feel him coming undone.

His strokes followed more forcefully, unleashing a rhythm in time with the sea's tempestuous crashing against the rocks. He whispered her name over and over while the stars dotted the sky behind him like a shower of diamonds, each one a glistening jewel. She kissed his beloved, oft-bruised face, unsure if the salt she tasted was his tears or her own, or merely flecks of sea foam. She only knew that by the time they were both on the edge of release, she was hazy-eyed with need, drowning in her love for him; he was shaking with fierce, stormy emotion.

'I'm sorry, Jacinda. I'm so sorry.'

'No, Billy. You are good enough. I love you, sweeting.'

He groaned with anguish, his needy embrace tightening with viselike intensity. 'Never leave me, girl. You're the only person on this whole goddamned earth who's ever cared about me.'

'I love you, Billy. I always will. I'll never let anyone hurt you again.'

He ordered her in a raw, panting voice to come for him, and she could do naught but obey, writhing under him in wanton, helpless longing. He followed her into the dark, sweet, mindless bliss of release a few seconds later, sheathed deeply inside of her.

The lighthouse beam swept over him, illuminating the harsh rapture on his face. His deep, soulful moans entranced her; then he lay in her arms, spent and still.

She nestled her cheek against his golden hair and petted him, kissing his head in bonded intimacy. His embrace was warm in the cool of the night. At length, he rolled onto his side next to her. He propped his head on his elbow and smiled at her with a rueful sigh.

'What is it?' she murmured.

He shook his head slightly. 'I'm not sure.' He cupped her breast lovingly. 'You make me wonder if I ever fooled you for an instant or how I ever won you, if you saw through me.'

She smiled. 'When I first saw you in the alley that night, I thought you were Conrad come to life. That's the moment I started falling in love with you.'

'Who the hell is Conrad?'

'From *The Corsair*. You know – Lord Byron's book.'

'Your silly pirate book?'

'It isn't silly,' she retorted. 'Conrad may be a pirate, but he's a good pirate, not a bad one.'

'How very dashing. Would you like to know the first moment that I fell in love with you?'

'Do tell,' she giggled, snuggling against him.

He captured her hand and curled it gently into a fist, kissing her knuckles. 'The moment you smashed Flaherty a facer.'

'In the alley?' she exclaimed.

He nodded, laughing with her, watching her. 'There you were, the queen of Sheba, tucked into the garbage heap. 'I am perfectly comfortable,' you said. I'll never forget your face. Then you darkened Flaherty's daylights for him—'

'He deserved it.'

'And I thought to myself, 'Careful, mate. This one's dangerous.' '

'Dangerous, eh? I think I like that.' With a cat-like stretch and a contented sigh, she curled her body against him.

He gathered her closer, gazing at the ocean. 'Maybe we should spend the night out here beneath the stars, the moon—'

'I don't think we'd get much sleep, you insatiable beast.'

'Must be this fresh sea air,' he growled playfully. 'Brings out the pirate in me.'

She pouted at his teasing. Laughing softly, he tackled her onto her back in the sand, kissing her.

'Mmm.' She closed her eyes and returned his kiss with tender passion, when suddenly, a voice floated down to them from the promontory above.

'Lord Rackford! Lord and Lady Rackford! Are you down there? Hullo?'

'Gracious!' Jacinda gasped, hastily making sure her skirts were pushed all the way back down to her ankles.

'Don't worry; they can't see us in the darkness,' Rackford murmured. 'That sounds like the butler. Down here, Mr. Becket!' he yelled loudly over the rhythm of the waves. 'What is it?'

'Lord Truro is asking for you, sir. Please come quickly! He has suffered a second attack of the apoplexy!'

They exchanged a worried glance. Without further ado, they climbed to their feet and hurriedly put their clothes in order, then grabbed their cast-off shoes and ran back up to the house.

'Oh, Master Billy, this time it has struck him blind!' Mr. Becket was wringing his bony hands in distress when Rackford and she arrived at the top of the rickety wooden steps leading up from the beach.

'Good God,' Rackford murmured.

'Mr. Plimpton fears His Lordship will not last till morning. He asks for you, sir.'

Jacinda passed a hard, questioning glance over Rackford's face.

'I'll let him speak his piece,' he said cautiously.

They strode inside and went up to the north wing, where the marquess's room was situated. As they crossed the hallway, the marchioness slipped out of her husband's chamber, weeping quietly. When she saw them coming, she rushed down the hallway and flung herself into her son's arms, crying harder.

'Oh, William! Is he really dying? I fear his time has come.'

'Calm down, Mother,' Rackford said firmly. 'Jacinda, would you show Her Ladyship to the sitting room and pour her a glass of wine for her nerves? Mother, take a moment to collect yourself. I'll go to Father and see how he is faring.'

'There, there, Lady Truro. Come along.' Jacinda put her

arm around the woman's frail shoulders and walked her into the drawing room.

He braced himself and went into the sickroom.

'William, is that you?' his father asked hoarsely.

'It is I, Father.'

'Come near me.' The order was slurred, raspy.

Rackford swallowed hard and obeyed. He was shaken by his father's wraithlike appearance. He exchanged a grim look with the surgeon, then saw that Mr. Plimpton had his instruments out, preparing to bleed Truro again.

'Leave off, man,' he ordered, waving the doctor away. His father already had the pallor of death in his face. Rackford had seen it far too many times in the rookery to mistake it.

The marquess stared blindly at nothing, his emerald eyes intense and resolute as ever. 'I wish to speak privately with my son.'

'Yes, my lord.' The surgeon exited quietly.

'Is he gone?' Truro asked.

'Yes.' Rackford sat on the chair beside his father's bed.

Truro's breathing was labored. 'I am – dying, William.'

Rackford did not know what to say. 'Yes, sir,' he admitted rather lamely.

'Take – take care of your mother.'

'I will.'

'Don't let the tenants cheat you. God knows they will try everything.'

It was well that his father could not see his slight, wry, irreverent smile. He lowered his head. 'Yes, Father.'

'Now, then. I have something to say to you, sir.'

Rackford stiffened at his frank tone.

'I know you feel that you have received unduly harsh treatment from me.' The marquess spoke slowly, as though every word cost him a great effort of concentration.

'Yes, sir,' he said succinctly.

'But I would have you know that it was – no different than the way my father treated me.'

Rackford's stare homed in more closely on him. 'Sir?'

Truro slowly took the glass of water off the tray that rested beside him and took a careful sip, wetting his pale lips. 'You heard me. You think I pity you? I had it just as bad as you did. It didn't do me any harm, and obviously, you've turned out well enough in spite of it.'

He searched his father's haggard face in shock.

'Are you listening? Because I'm only going to say this once.'

'Yes, Father.'

Truro hesitated. 'A part of me was glad – glad for both of us – when you ran away. I wanted to when I was a boy, but I never dared. Though I sent men to track you, a part of me was glad they did not find you – the part of me that was capable of – of loving you. The part that was a good-enough father to know that if I had you back, I would only destroy you, and turn you into ... what I myself became.'

Rackford stared soberly at him.

His father's chest heaved with his labored, shallow breathing. 'Instead, you made yourself something finer, better than I ever could have made you. I admit it. By the time I was your age, all I knew how to do was destroy, but you went into the very rookery and instead of destroying, you built.' He paused, his speech pained and difficult. 'You could have made those people walk in dread of you, but instead, they loved you. You could have fed off of them, grown rich off of them, but instead, you gave them food, you gave them riches, shelter. I did not think it was p-possible for a man to be as proud of a son as I am – of you, William.'

Rackford got up out of his chair, bent down, and gathered his father's wasted, bony frame in a fierce embrace.

'Forgive me, Son,' Truro cried, breaking down in his arms. 'Every time I looked at you, I saw myself, the very self my father had taught me to hate.'

'I forgive you, Papa,' he whispered, kissing his father's temple.

*

325

He sat with his father throughout the night. Mother retired with a splitting headache, unable to face it, but Jacinda joined them, bringing Truro a taste of Mrs. Landry's treacle and cream. As the hour grew later, she fell asleep in her chair.

Rackford woke her gently and told her to go to bed. Barely able to keep her eyes open, she agreed to nap in the sitting room down the hallway. From that point, Rackford kept his vigil over his father alone. He felt so strange, made whole somehow, acknowledged at last by the man who had been both Satan and God Almighty to him.

Toward dawn, a peace seemed to come over the marquess, and he spoke of happy memories of his mother and his school days. Rackford silently committed every detail to memory. He felt closer to his father through those last hours than he ever had before at any point in his life. He entertained Truro with tales of some of his adventures in the rookery, in turn, rousing a chuckle from the dying man at his account of how he had won the Gypsy girl, Carlotta, in a card game.

'You'd have liked her, Father.'

'Not as well as I like your little blonde. Spitfire, that one. How did you meet her?'

Rackford smiled and soon had Truro laughing again at his description of finding the queen of Sheba in a garbage heap.

Jacinda smiled slightly to herself, hearing soft masculine laughter on the other side of the door, though she could not make out the topic of their conversation. Newly roused from her light nap, she had come to check on them, but she had no wish to intrude now that father and son seemed to be getting on.

Maybe Lord Truro might even pull through. Wrapping her arms around herself with a yawn, she decided to walk outside for some fresh air.

The filmy gray half-light before dawn rang with birdsong. The air was moist and cool. She could taste the salt on the languid breeze. The sea drew her.

She began walking with no particular destination in mind, but it was not long before she stood once more on the promontory overlooking the sea. Behind her in the east, the sun had edged up over the horizon. Its pink light turned the cliff-top turf a soft golden green, the water a celestial shade of pale turquoise. The sea was calm.

The gentle surf laved the gleaming rocks, casting nets of sea foam over them. Even the gulls were subdued, hovering lazily on the currents of air, some floating in the waves. The wind was stronger here on the edge of the sea, but it did not scare her; rushing up the cliff face, it blew her long hair over her shoulders and stirred her skirts, but she closed her eyes, standing on the very western edge of England, and enjoyed its mildly bracing caress. Perhaps it was the discovery of a whole new depth to her life, or the close look she had just had at death – perhaps it was merely the lack of sleep – but she had never felt so gloriously alive.

Drawing a deep breath of the bracing salt air, she turned to go down the rickety wooden steps to the beach when she saw Rackford walking toward her across the green. She waited for him, her gaze softening as she took in his expression of haggard exhaustion. His strides were long but weary. His hair was tousled, his clothes a rumpled mess. The serene sadness in his eyes as he approached told her without a word that his father had died.

She put her arms around him as he joined her near the edge. They held each other for a long time, saying nothing.

'He's gone?' she whispered, just to be sure.

He nodded.

'I'm so sorry, darling.' She caressed his hair and cradled his head on her shoulder, offering up a mental prayer for her father-in-law.

After several moments, he drew a long, shaky breath and straightened up to his full height, his gaze cast pensively far out to sea. She turned, as well, to stare again at the ocean.

327

He stood behind her, holding her around her waist. She stroked his hands where they rested on her belly.

After a while, he lowered his lips to her ear. 'Thank you, Jacinda.' His whisper paused. 'That never would have happened if not for you. He wouldn't have budged, and I would have left yesterday evening. Hell, I never would have come in the first place if it weren't for you. You have given me . . . an extraordinary gift.'

'You are an extraordinary man.' She smiled and laid her head back against his warm, strong chest. 'Most people would not have been able to forgive him.'

'Well,' he said slowly, as though carefully choosing each word, 'I know now why everything happened as it did. I was bitter for many years, but now I can see the good that came of it – my running away. Our family 'curse,' as he put it, has been broken. As for me, I saw a side of life in the rookery that most men in my position never see, and now I have a chance to do something about it. But in the meantime, I just wanted you to know that I couldn't have gotten through that without you.' Gently, he turned her to face him.

She looked up lovingly into his sea-green eyes. His tender words had inspired her all of a sudden. 'Might we stay here for a while, Rackford? Cornwall is such a beautiful place.'

He grazed his knuckle along the curve of her cheek. 'I don't see why not, if you wish. After all, this is your home now. Our home,' he added softly, nodding toward Torcarrow standing proudly in the distance.

The morning mist softened its dove-gray ramparts. The sea shimmered beneath it, reflecting the breathtaking sunrise in glorious swirls of teal and gold and pink.

She glanced at the castle, then at him, startled by the reminder that he was the marquess of Truro and St. Austell now; she had just become the marchioness, rightful lady of the manor. But in the next moment, she noticed the dark circles under his eyes and cupped his cheek fondly.

'Come now, to bed with you before you fall asleep on your feet.'

'Always taking care of me,' he remarked in wry amusement as they started back to the house, their arms twined around each other.

'Oh, I know you don't really need it,' she assured him with a wifely twinkle in her eyes, 'but it makes me happy, looking after you.'

'Don't I?' he countered softly.

She looked up at him in surprise, for his stubborn refusal of all aid was strongly etched on her mind. He gave her a knowing, rueful smile and an affectionate squeeze around her shoulders, leaning on her just a little as they walked back to the house.

Author's Note

Dear Reader,

Those familiar with the real-life history of the Countess of Oxford will no doubt recognize this grande dame of the Regency era as the model for my scandalous Duchess of Hawkscliffe and her variously-sired brood. Most of the ton knew that Lady Oxford's numerous children had been sired by her many lovers; however, her husband, the Earl of Oxford (famous for his contributions to the Bodleian Library) acknowledged them all as his own. When I came across their story in my research, I was electrified by the notion of modeling a family series after them. I have always adored both reading and writing books in family series, but giving the grown siblings different fathers from widely different backgrounds has given this sprawling project a deliciously unique twist for me as a writer, and, I hope, for you, as well. Not only does it provide me with greater variety in the types of characters I get to write about in each tale, but also, as you've probably noticed if you've been following the series so far, Georgiana's amorous adventuring has left each of her grown children a bit wary and cynical when it comes to love. The greatest joy for me is bringing each of them together with a strong, worthy 'opponent' who will challenge that cynicism, overcome their wariness, and awaken their guarded ability to love.

Once that happens, each of the Knight brothers (and their sister!) are one-hundred percent devoted and tenaciously determined to make it last forever.

If this is your first taste of the Knight Miscellany and you wish to read the other siblings' books which have so far been completed, they are:

The Duke (Robert and Bel)
Lord of Fire (Lucien and Alice)
Lord of Ice (Damien and Miranda)

Happily, I am only halfway through the series at this point. There are still two brothers left to torture (Jack and Alec) and possibly the impeccably polite lost soul whom Jacinda terms her 'extra' brother, Ian Prescott, the Marquess of Griffith.

Next, however, I am going to be writing about Lizzie Carlisle, Jacinda's 'bluestocking' companion. Having grown up with the family, I consider Lizzie a nominal Knight sibling. Look for her story sometime near the end of '02 or in early '03. If you wish to receive a reminder about my new releases, please visit my Web site at www.gaelenfoley.com and sign up for my e-mail newsletter.

I hope you enjoyed *Lady of Desire* ... and thanks again for reading.

With warmest wishes
Gaelen